Canary Girls

Canary Girls

A Novel

Jennifer Chiaverini

HARPER LARGE PRINT
An Imprint of HarperCollinsPublishers

HarperCollins books may be purchased for educational, business, or sales promotional use. For information, please e-mail the Special Markets Department at SPsales@harpercollins.com.

FIRST HARPER LARGE PRINT EDITION

ISBN: 978-0-06-332274-5

Library of Congress Cataloging-in-Publication Data is available upon request.

23 24 25 26 27 LBC 6 5 4 3 2

To Marty, Nick, and Michael,
with all my love

Canary Girls

1
August–December 1914

Lucy

Lucy rested the heavy sack of vegetables and paper-wrapped meat on her hip, reluctant to set it down at her feet beside her suitcase despite the ache in her arms. She didn't really fear that some hungry villain would dart across the train platform and snatch away her hard-won provisions the moment she relaxed her guard, but with two sons and a footballer husband to feed, she dared not take that chance. London had been in a state of anxious turmoil when she and the boys had departed for Surrey four days ago, and, glancing about Paddington station as they waited to change trains, Lucy could not tell whether things had settled in their absence or had grown more desperate.

Less than a fortnight before, Germany had ignored

the British government's midnight ultimatum to withdraw its troops from Belgium, plunging Great Britain and Germany into a state of war. Excited, boisterous crowds had filled the streets of London, shouting and cheering and waving their hats in the air, and at Trafalgar Square, two rival demonstrations had broken out on either side of Nelson's Pillar, one for the war and one against. A vast throng had assembled outside Buckingham Palace, singing "God Save the King" with tremendous sincerity and fervor. The song had dissolved into roars of approval when King George, wearing the uniform of an Admiral of the Fleet, had appeared on the balcony overlooking the forecourt, where the Queen, the Prince of Wales, and Princess Mary had soon joined him.

Lucy and her husband had been at their tan brick, ivy-covered home in Clapham Common at the time, but they had heard frequent shouts of "War! War!" outside their windows, and learned the rest from the papers and neighbors who had ventured out. Lucy had hardly known what to think. In school, she had been taught that another major war in Europe would be highly improbable in the future because modern weapons were so dreadful that they served as a deterrent rather than a threat. But highly improbable was not impossible, and now Great Britain was at war.

The next morning, it seemed that nearly every housewife in England had been seized by an irresistible impulse to fill her cupboards for an imminent siege. Unaware of the rising panic, Lucy had gone out to do her marketing as usual and had been startled to discover other women bustling about, empty baskets dangling from their elbows, strain evident in their pinched mouths and furrowed brows. Long queues had formed at the doors of several of her favorite shops, and hand-lettered signs had appeared in some front windows announcing that the store had sold out and closed early. After waiting in a queue for two hours and finally gaining admittance only to discover little more than a few bits and bobs left over, Lucy made her meager purchases and set off for home, uneasy. She could manage tea and supper that day, but what about tomorrow and the day after that?

"I hear delivery vans are being ransacked on the streets," Lucy's neighbor Gloria told her later that afternoon as their children played together in the private, enclosed garden all the homes on their block shared. "My sister in Bayswater says her neighbor was on her way home from the shops, arms full up with parcels, when three women, complete strangers, accosted her and accused her of hoarding."

"Hoarding?"

"Exactly! How can it be hoarding if she can carry it all in her own two arms? Anyway, these so-called ladies, bold as brass, helped themselves to my sister's neighbor's groceries. The shops may be empty, they declared, but their families wouldn't starve for others' greed. Then they scurried off and left her to carry the scraps home. Didn't give her a penny for what they took, either."

"That's robbery," said Lucy, aghast. "Where were the police?"

Gloria shrugged. "Guarding the shops or keeping watch for German spies, I should think."

Lucy could only shake her head, speechless. Such madness in their own city. And it was only the first full day of the war.

Unsettled, she returned her gaze to her sons, who laughed and shouted as they passed a football back and forth with the other children. Jamie, the eldest, was slim, black-haired, and fair-skinned like herself, while Simon was ruddy and sturdily built, his square jaw and thick, sandy hair so like his father's. How guiltily grateful she felt knowing that at eight and six years of age, her sons were too young to go to war. At thirty-two, Daniel, though strong and fit and brave, was just old enough that he would not be expected to volunteer. Though her husband loved King and Country as much as any Englishman, Lucy trusted that he would not be tempted to enlist. How could he abandon his thriving architecture firm with his career on the rise? And how could he leave Tottenham Hotspur without their star center forward, so close to the start of the season and with his inevitable retirement drawing ever nearer? Only a few days before, as Lucy had massaged the aches from his hamstrings after a grueling practice, he had confided that he knew his best days on the pitch were behind him. As beloved as he was by fans and teammates alike, eventually he would be replaced by a younger, stronger, swifter man.

But only on the pitch. No one could ever take Daniel's place in their family or her heart.

Lucy had known Daniel all her life, or at least, she could not remember a time before knowing him. In Brookfield, the village in rural southwest Surrey where they both had been born and raised, Daniel had been Lucy's elder brother's friend first. Both boys were three years older than herself, three years wiser and infinitely bolder, although Daniel had always been kinder and more patient than Edwin. It was Daniel who had taught Lucy how to swim in the shallows of the deep, rushing brook that had given their village its name, while Edwin had splashed and shouted with the other boys, ignoring her or perhaps having truly forgotten she was there. Daniel never teased her the way Edwin did, mocking her shyness, jeering when she blushed, tugging her braid sharply whenever she forgot to keep a respectful distance. Daniel was her defender. After one mild rebuke from him, Edwin would roll his eyes and let her be.

Eventually, as the years went by, Edwin outgrew his bullying ways—a fortunate thing indeed, since after university he would become headmaster of the village school. Meanwhile, the other girls discovered what Lucy had known all along: Daniel was the handsomest, cleverest, and most wonderful boy in Brookfield, perhaps in all of Surrey. What silent torment Lucy suffered when her friends sighed over his warm brown eyes and swooned at his smile! She had no choice but to feign indifference rather than reveal how much and how hopelessly she adored him. In this pretense her customary shyness served her well, and her friends— and Daniel himself—had been none the wiser.

In those days, she could not have imagined that Daniel might one day return her affection. He had always been kind to her, but he was kind to everyone. Sometimes he walked Lucy home from school, carrying her books, but he would have done the same for anyone younger and smaller, and her house was on his way home. When Daniel danced with her on festival days, that, obviously, was because she was an excellent dancer; even boys who equated shyness with dullness enjoyed dancing with Lucy. But none of those other partners lingered very long after the music faded. Invariably, their attention would drift from her bashful, nearly inaudible conversation to light upon another girl, one who could charm and flirt with aplomb. Sometimes, though, when Daniel held her gaze and smiled, Lucy could almost believe she was as charming as those bright-eyed, laughing girls. At a dance or after church or wherever their paths happened to cross, Daniel's face would light up when he spotted her, and they would fall effortlessly into conversation like the nearly lifelong friends they were, sharing observations and confidences and private jokes, with no need to impress each other or anyone who might be watching.

One day in her sixteenth autumn, Lucy was posting a letter to Daniel at university when she was struck by the dismaying notion that perhaps the fondness between them existed only because Daniel thought of her as a younger sister—nothing less, but nothing more. How lamentable if it were true! Even as a child, Lucy had never thought of Daniel as a brother. She already had two: Edwin, of course, and George, the eldest, who was studying medicine in Edinburgh, preparing to join their father's practice.

Lucy loved her brothers dearly, but two sufficed.

Many months later, near the end of the spring term, Lucy was walking in the village with friends when the conversation turned to the absent young men who, they hoped, would soon return to Brookfield for the summer. Naturally Daniel's name came up, and as several of her companions sighed longingly and others began scheming how best to catch his eye, Lucy felt warmth rising in her cheeks. Her friends were all such pretty, laughing, good-hearted girls. Surely one of them would win Daniel's heart before the autumn—

"Oh, would you stop, all of you?" exclaimed Nettie, Lucy's best friend. "Can't you see you're making Lucy absolutely miserable?"

"Nettie, no," Lucy murmured, but it was too late. All eyes were on her, some sympathetic and understanding, others astonished.

"Lucy and Daniel?" said Kathleen in wonder, pitch rising with each word. "Are you in love?"

"Of course not," Lucy replied, shaking her head, forcing a laugh. "Don't be silly."

"You've adored him for ages," countered Nettie, amused. "Deny it if you like. Go on, tell me I'm a liar, if I am."

"A person can be *wrong*," Lucy said carefully,

wishing, as ever, that she did not so easily blush, "without being a liar."

Nettie laughed. "Well, I'm neither, at least not now and not about this."

"The rest of us never stood a chance," another girl lamented, smiling. "Lucy has always been Daniel's favorite."

"No, I haven't," said Lucy, startled. "Have I? What do you mean?"

A ripple of laughter rose from the circle of friends. "Oh, Lucy," said Nettie fondly. "How could you not know?"

"Lucy and Daniel," mused Kathleen, nodding. "Well, of course. It's obvious once someone says it aloud."

Lucy begged them not to make a habit of *that*, for Brookfield was a rather small village and gossip spread swiftly. Oh, but how wonderful the phrase sounded, even when her friends teased: Lucy and Daniel.

Whether her friends ignored her pleas and echoed the phrase until it eventually made its way around to Daniel, or whether he came up with the idea entirely on his own, by late summer, he and Lucy had shared their first kiss. Three years later, they were married. Lucy followed Daniel to London, where he was playing for Chelsea and working as a junior architect. In the nine years that had passed since then, he had become a partner in his own architecture firm, the captain of

Tottenham Hotspur, an Olympic champion who led England to two gold medals, and a devoted father to the two most wonderful boys in England.

And now that war had come, Lucy would not give up her beloved husband, not even for King and Country.

When Daniel returned home from the office later that afternoon, Lucy raced to the door and flung her arms around him, pressing her cheek against his chest, overcome by a wave of terrible gratitude that she would be spared the grief and loss that would inevitably afflict so many other wives.

The fierceness of her embrace surprised her husband. "What's all this?" Daniel asked, kissing the top of her head. "I'm only a few minutes late. Surely dinner isn't spoiled."

"You know that's not why I'm upset," said Lucy, her voice muffled against his lapel. "Still, it's kind of you to pretend to misunderstand, so *I* may pretend I'm not a coward."

"You're no coward," said Daniel, cupping her chin and lifting her face toward his. "England is at war with a formidable enemy. Concern and, yes, even fear, are perfectly reasonable responses."

He might feel differently when he learned how their fellow Londoners' fear and concern had affected his dinner. Collecting herself, Lucy took his hand and led him to the dining room. "Prepare to be underwhelmed," she warned him as Jamie and Simon darted in, hands and faces freshly scrubbed. The family settled around the table and Lucy served thin slices of pork in onion gravy, with roasted turnips and bread and butter. At first all Jamie and Simon wanted to talk about was the war—the recruiting posters they had seen plastered up and down the street, the older lads in the neighborhood who had rushed off to enlist, and the tragic unfairness that boys their age weren't allowed.

Lucy knew most of the lads her sons had mentioned, if only through her acquaintance with their mothers. "Seems rather rash to enlist so soon," she said, keeping her voice even as she spooned the last of the turnips onto the boys' plates and the pork onto Daniel's. "It's early days yet. One could not possibly know what one is getting oneself into."

"Billy Warren says it'll be over by Christmas," said Jamie. "He says he's got to win valor on the battlefields of France before then or it'll be too late."

"If he don't go now, he'll miss the war," Simon chimed in.

"If he *doesn't* go now," Lucy corrected. "Which sounds like a splendid idea. If it'll be over so quickly, it hardly seems worth the trouble."

"But Mum," said Jamie, brow furrowing, "'Your King and Country Need You.'"

"Not *her*," said Simon. "She's a mum."

"I'm only saying what's on the posters."

Noting Lucy's deepening frown, Daniel quickly changed the subject. Soon the boys were caught up in an eager discussion of football, the team's pre-season training, and the traditional cricket match between Tottenham Hotspur and Chelsea coming up on Saturday. When Lucy thanked Daniel with a smile, his warm brown eyes shone with affection.

Only after the boys were asleep and they were preparing for bed themselves did Lucy tell Daniel about her misfortune at the market and the frightening robbery of Gloria's sister's neighbor. "I'm terribly afraid I'll find nothing but bare shelves when I assail the shops again tomorrow," she said, trying to make a joke of it. "I know everyone says the war will be over by Christmas, but we can't go hungry until then."

"Not everyone says it'll be over by Christmas," Daniel warned, deftly removing one of her hairpins, and then another, until her dark locks tumbled free from their upswept coil. Facing her, he ran his hands through her hair, spreading it like a silken cloak upon her shoulders.

His touch sent a delicious, warm frisson of pleasure

down Lucy's spine, but, with an effort, she kept her focus on the immediate crisis. "Whether it's over by Christmas or Easter or Sunday next, between now and then, we have to eat. What am I to do?"

"What indeed?" Daniel took her hand, sat down on the edge of the bed, and pulled her onto his lap. "There's always Brookfield."

She rested her hands lightly on his shoulders. "Go all the way to Surrey for groceries?"

"Why not? Our families would be delighted to see Jamie and Simon, and what could be better for the boys than a week in the country? As for groceries, I can't imagine they had a run on the shops in Brookfield."

"No, I suppose not." Surely their sensible friends and former neighbors, reassured by the abundance of local farms and their own kitchen gardens, would have stubbornly refused to panic despite the chilling declaration of war.

"You might not even need to visit the shops," Daniel continued, smiling as he kissed her cheek. "My mother would gladly fill your basket with as much veg and cheese and sausages from her own cellar as you could carry."

"I'd need a second basket for my mother's jams," said Lucy, warming to the idea. "And I could stop by Brandt's bakery for a loaf of rye and some of your favorite raisin buns."

"You're an angel," Daniel declared, kissing her. Then his smile faded. "I only hope . . ."

"What?"

"Well, Dieter Brandt—he's German, you know. I hope no one gives him any trouble on that account."

Lucy was so surprised she laughed. "Why should they? He and Mrs. Brandt have lived in Brookfield for ages, since long before you and I were born. Their own children were born there, too, and their grandchildren. Surely by now the Brandts are as English as we are."

"I agree with you, darling, but not everyone will. With war fever sweeping the country . . ." Daniel shook his head.

When he left the thought unfinished, Lucy ventured, "Shall we go tomorrow, then?"

"You and the boys shall." Daniel touched her gently on the nose. "Sadly, I can't get away."

"Of course." Lucy nodded briskly to conceal her disappointment. "The cricket."

"And the Henderson offices," he reminded her. "I'm meeting with the foreman and the owner on Tuesday. If all goes well, we'll break ground next week."

"Very well, then." Lucy sat up straight and squared her shoulders, as best she could, seated on his lap. "The boys and I shall undertake this mission ourselves."

"That's my girl." Daniel cupped her chin in his hand and kissed her.

The next morning after Daniel left for the office, Lucy packed a bag for herself and another for the boys, locked up the house, and set out for the train station. The boys trailed along at her heels, fairly bounding with excitement as they planned their week's adventures. By early afternoon they had arrived in Guildford, where Daniel's father met them and carried them the last few miles to Brookfield in the horse-drawn wagon he used for his carpentry business.

Lucy's mother met them at the front gate of the Evans family home, a two-story brick-and-timber Edwardian residence just off the town square. The medical practice—once their father's, then his and George's both, and now George's alone—took up the front half of the ground floor, with the kitchen in the back. Mum shared the spacious living quarters above with George, his wife, Eleanor, and their two daughters.

It was a lovely homecoming, and the days flew past in a whirlwind of outings in the countryside with the boys and joyful reunions with friends and family, occasionally interrupted by grave discussions of the country's preparations for war. Recruiting posters sprung up like crocuses in the spring on signposts and fences throughout the village, and every day brought news of more local men who had enlisted.

One night at dinner, George confessed that he had considered joining the Royal Navy as a medical officer, but had reluctantly decided against it. "Even if the war *is* over by Christmas, four months is simply too long to leave Brookfield without its doctor. Unless, of course, I found a substitute—"

"We discussed this," protested Eleanor. "We agreed you should not go. If this hypothetical substitute has no practice of his own, let *him* enlist and go to France."

"I never expected to go to France, dear," said George mildly, peering at her over his glasses as he took her hand. "I supposed I might serve in a hospital for wounded soldiers here in England."

"We're going to need more hospitals than what we've got," said Edwin, frowning as he ran a hand through his hair, as dark as Lucy's, without a thread of the silver-gray that had begun to color their eldest brother's head and beard. "I hope the government has a scheme to build more. Say, Lucy, that sounds like ideal war work for your Dan. Building hospitals. He'd be a very busy fellow, I should think."

Lucy sipped water to clear the lump forming in her throat. "If Daniel's only alternative is the infantry," she said, setting down her glass, "I'll be sure to suggest building hospitals, but I should prefer he not enlist at all."

"Goodness," her mother exclaimed. "Daniel in the infantry. George in the navy. What nonsense! You three are married men, and you're not as young as you once were."

"No need to be unkind, Mother," said Edwin, feigning injury. "I'm only thirty-two."

"Precisely. Lord Kitchener called for one hundred thousand volunteers aged nineteen to thirty. That means young, vigorous lads, not men approaching middle age."

Edwin's wife laughed. "Edwin, George, and Daniel—especially Daniel—aren't as decrepit as you suggest. They're in the prime of life."

"Quite so, Alice," said George. "In my particular case, I daresay my experience as a physician—"

"No, dear," said Eleanor firmly. "You'll find another way to serve, one that doesn't require you to abandon your responsibilities here."

George offered Edwin a helpless shrug. "What can I say? She loves me too much to let me go."

"Yes, I see." Edwin turned to Alice. "Darling, *you* aren't trying very hard to persuade *me* not to enlist."

"Why should I?" said Alice. "Someone has to go. Someone has to defend poor Belgium."

"But why me? Aside from my belief that Britain is honor-bound to stand by her allies, and the fact that I'm loath to ask another man to fight in my place while I cower fearfully at home."

"Because you love your country, of course, and you want to defend England from a German invasion. As a teacher you're a natural leader of men, and—" Alice smiled dreamily. "You would look absolutely splendid in an officer's uniform."

As the others laughed, Lucy managed a smile. She knew that Alice teased Edwin only because he surely had no intention of enlisting. As for George, it was all too true that the army would soon need skilled physicians most desperately. And despite Edwin's remarks, she could not imagine the army recruiting droves of architects, and how thankful indeed she was for that.

Glancing to the far end of the table, she was relieved to find her sons conversing in hushed, eager tones with their cousins, cheerfully ignoring their elders. Good. There was no reason for them to fear, even for a moment, that their father or uncles might suddenly march off to war.

On the last day of their visit, Lucy packed up the provisions her mother and mother-in-law had shared from their own pantries and a few other staples purchased at the shops. In the afternoon she stopped by

Brandt's bakery for the treats she had promised Daniel, and was taken aback by subtle changes to the storefront. A large Union Jack flew above the entrance, and in the display window, a large sign announcing "Good British Breads & Buns" had replaced the trays of pumpernickel, *Brötchen*, and *Stollen*, and a platter of *Hörnchen* was labeled "Croissants." Inside, Lucy found one of the Brandt daughters arranging loaves, rolls, and sweets in one of the glass cases while another swept the floor, both of them wearing identical lace-trimmed white aprons over their muslin summer shirtwaists and long skirts. The young women glanced up from their work and cheerfully greeted Lucy by name, although their smiles faded slightly when the only other customer left without purchasing anything.

At that moment, Mr. Brandt emerged from the kitchen carrying a tray of fragrant, perfectly browned loaves of rye bread in his thickly muscled arms, his face flushed from the heat of the oven, his thinning blond curls damp with perspiration beneath his white toque. "Ah! Miss Evans," he exclaimed in his rich, accented baritone, setting the tray down on the counter. "Welcome, welcome."

"It's 'Mrs. Dempsey,' Papa," chided the elder daughter, throwing Lucy an apologetic smile.

"Of course, of course." Mr. Brandt chuckled and

waved a hand as if to shoo away his mistake. "What would you like today, my dear? This good Suffolk rye bread is fresh from the oven. I know it's one of Mr. Dempsey's favorites."

"And mine too," said Lucy, bemused. She had never heard the baker refer to the bread as Suffolk rye before, and as far as she knew, rye from Suffolk wasn't inherently superior to grain grown and milled elsewhere. Why mention it at all, except to distinguish it from German rye?

She selected a loaf of rye and a half dozen raisin buns, resisting the temptation to ask what had become of the German baked goods that had always been so popular there. As Mr. Brandt boxed up her selections, he inquired after Daniel and the boys, and she asked about his family in turn. "Our Herman and Otto have enlisted in the East Surrey Regiment," Mr. Brandt said, his smile both proud and strained. "They were among the first boys from Brookfield to volunteer."

"How very brave of them," said Lucy, hiding her dismay. Of course the Brandt boys would hasten to prove their loyalty, for their family's sake as much as their own. Only a few days before, the government had announced that all "enemy aliens," including longtime residents like Mr. and Mrs. Brandt, were required to register at their nearest police station. Alice thought the new measure was a necessary precaution to foil German spies, while Edwin predicted that it would burden good, law-abiding immigrants with suspicion and restrictions. "You and Mrs. Brandt must be very proud."

"*Ja*, we must be, but we miss our sons very much already." Mr. Brandt mopped his brow with a handkerchief and shrugged. "But everyone says the war will be over by Christmas, so they will not be away such a very long time."

"Surely not," Lucy agreed, wishing she believed it.

A day later, Lucy and her sons were back in London, the tasty bread and buns neatly tucked into Jamie's knapsack on top of several jars of jam and a peck of apples the boys had harvested that morning from their grandmother's orchard. Simon carried a somewhat lighter load in his pack, and the remaining supplies filled Lucy's bags. Along with their luggage, it was quite a lot to carry through Paddington station, but Daniel would meet them at their last stop and help them the rest of the way home.

As they made their way through the concourse, Lucy was surprised to see so many men in uniform already, less surprised by the recruiting posters that had multiplied on walls and posts since she had last passed through. They reached their departure platform with time to spare, and Lucy reminded the boys to keep close to her and stay away from the edge while they waited. Keeping one eye on the clock and another on her sons, Lucy allowed her thoughts to wander, from parting conversations with her mother and brothers, to her eager longing to reunite with Daniel at home, the Brandts' plight, and what she might make for dinner that evening.

"Mum, look!" Simon shouted. "That's not allowed!"

Startled from her reverie, Lucy turned and glimpsed Simon's wide eyes and outstretched arm and Jamie beside him gazing in disbelief. Once assured that her sons were safe and sound, she followed the line of Simon's pointing finger and discovered nearly four dozen men descending the platform to the rails below. Lucy's first thought as she watched them pick their way across both sets of tracks was that they were railroad workers, but they wore no uniforms, just ordinary suits and hats. Upon reaching the other side, the men climbed onto the opposite platform, which had been virtually empty until then, a curious thing for that time of day. There sat a special train bound for Falmouth, according to the sign, but the blinds were drawn and the men made no attempt to board. Instead they assembled on the platform near the parlor car, removed their hats, and began to sing, deeply and with intense passion:

"*Deutschland, Deutschland über alles, über alles in der Welt.*"

Stunned, for a moment Lucy could only stare in disbelief as the German national anthem echoed off the stone walls.

The British passengers exchanged looks of astonishment and wild indignation. "What infernal cheek!" a gray-haired woman to Lucy's right scolded, wagging a finger at the Germans.

"Well, I'm blowed," a young man in a straw hat exclaimed, hands clenching into fists as he approached the edge of the platform. "'Germany over All' sung in London—and with a war on!"

Somewhere behind Lucy, a rich baritone voice sang, "God save our gracious King, long live our noble King, God save the King!"

All around, other voices took up the song. "Send him victorious, happy and glorious—"

At the sound of her sons' treble voices, Lucy also quickly joined in. "Long to reign over us, God save the King!"

The two groups sang and shouted their anthems across the tracks at each other, louder and more fiercely with each verse. Then, as suddenly as they appeared, the German men replaced their hats and swiftly dispersed, some disappearing down one corridor, others up one staircase or another. None dared cross the tracks to confront the Britons glaring at them—but perhaps that was because a shrill whistle had announced the arrival of the train.

Lucy's hands trembled as she beckoned to her boys and ushered them aboard. "I can't believe it," Jamie fumed as they settled into their seats. "How dare they sing their national song here! We're at war, and they're in our country!"

"Very disrespectful of them, and imprudent as well," said Lucy, stowing their bags, glancing about to make sure they had all of their belongings. "They could have been set upon by an angry mob of patriotic Englishmen."

Jamie's face lit up. "Do you really think so?"

"No, of course not," Lucy quickly amended. "Not in the middle of Paddington station."

Simon's brow furrowed in serious contemplation. "Mum, do you s'pose they were German spies?"

When Jamie guffawed, Lucy silenced him with a look. "Germans, yes. Spies, no," she said. "Spies would have to be terribly bad at their jobs to reveal themselves so dramatically, don't you think?"

Simon nodded thoughtfully. Lucy smiled and straightened his cap, but the scene had unsettled her. She supposed she understood why a German abroad in wartime might be moved to burst spontaneously into his national anthem, but this incident must have been coordinated ahead of time. Why enemy aliens would so imprudently declare their loyalties to Germany was one question. Another puzzle was why they had chosen Paddington station for their defiant serenade. Why not Waterloo station? Why not Trafalgar Square?

She pondered the questions as the train carried them on the last leg of their journey, but she was no wiser by the time they reached Clapham Junction. Lucy and her boys quickly disembarked and reunited at last with Daniel on the platform. As they walked home, the boys described the strange event, talking over each other in their eagerness to astound their father.

"I believe I know what that was all about," said Daniel as he unlocked their front door and the boys raced inside ahead of them. "The Austrian and German ambassadors were expelled from Great Britain. Count Mensdorff was expected to leave London by train today for Portsmouth, and then sail to Genoa."

Lucy and Daniel followed the boys inside, carried the bags into the kitchen, and set them on the table. "I'm surprised there was no military guard to keep anyone from getting near his train." Shuddering, Lucy removed her hat and hung it on the back of a chair. "It was such a strange thing to witness. It made the war feel so close. I dread to think how much closer it will come before it's all over."

Daniel embraced her from behind and kissed the back of her neck. "Don't worry about that now, darling," he murmured, his voice low and comforting. "We're all together again, safe and sound."

Sighing softly, she leaned back against his strong chest and relaxed into his arms. She wanted him to promise her that the war would never cross their threshold, but Daniel never made promises he could not keep, nor would she find any comfort in empty reassurances.

In the days that followed, Lucy was relieved to discover that order had been restored to London's markets and food was reassuringly plentiful. Jamie and Simon prepared for the new school term, or rather, Lucy prepared them for it. After a worrisome few days during which Daniel's client considered postponing construction until after the war, the crew broke ground for the Henderson offices. To Lucy's relief, Daniel completed pre-season training with no serious injuries—more aches and pains and fatigue than he cared to admit, but nothing that would keep him off the pitch.

Yet ordinary life unfolded amid a rising war fever and its inescapable consequences. Several football clubs found their training regimens disrupted when their pitches were commandeered by the War Office for military training. Territorial battalions marched and drilled on Everton's pitch at Goodison Park. Manchester City's grounds were turned into a stable for more than three hundred cavalry horses.

"It could be worse," said Daniel, as Lucy rubbed liniment on his lower back after a particularly grueling practice. "Politicians and others are questioning whether it's appropriate to carry on with football at all in these circumstances. Some teams have had so many players enlist that they've scratched their fixtures for the season."

Lucy felt her breath catch in her throat. "Not Tottenham, surely."

"No, not Tottenham," he replied, frowning slightly. "Not yet."

But evidently not enough men were enlisting, for throughout London, recruiting posters seemed to increase daily in number and variety. Particularly disquieting for Lucy were the specific appeals for sportsmen to enlist, and for women to urge their sons and husbands to answer the call to arms. The press enthusiastically described training exercises and dignitaries' reviews of the troops at military encampments, often focusing on certain Pals battalions—groups of men from particular towns, schools, or professions who had enlisted together with the understanding, backed by the promise of Secretary of State for War Lord Kitchener, that they would serve together. By the end of September, Kitchener's scheme had produced the Stockbrokers' Battalion from the City of London, the Grimsby Chums comprised of former students of Wintringham Secondary School, and more than fifty battalions from towns and cities throughout Britain.

To Lucy that seemed like a great many soldiers indeed, but the call to arms persisted, with heightened urgency. Rumors that conscription might be on the way compelled many young men to enlist while they could still choose a favorite Pals battalion. The women of Britain found their own way to contribute to the war effort when Queen Mary and Lord Kitchener called upon them to knit three hundred thousand pairs of socks for the army by November. Dutifully, Lucy purchased skeins of yarn and took up her needles. Working a few hours in the evenings and in spare moments throughout the day, she could produce a new pair of socks every second day. She and her friend Gloria occasionally knitted together in the garden while their children played, quietly discussing the rumors that not all was going well for the British Expeditionary Force in France. Sometimes rumors were all they had. Thanks to overzealous censors, when it came to reports from the Western Front, the newspapers were often too vague or understated to merit reading.

What the press did make clear was that it would take more than warm, dry socks to sustain the troops and the dependents they had left behind. On Saturday, 22 August, several professional football clubs organized a series of matches to benefit the Prince of Wales's National Relief Fund. Tottenham Hotspur would play Arsenal at White Hart Lane, and Lucy had promised to take Jamie and Simon to watch their father play. She hoped the charitable effort would quiet the grumbling from certain quarters about athletes playing games on manicured pitches while braver, more patriotic men bled and died on the muddy battlefields of France and Belgium. But her hopes plummeted when she and the boys arrived for Daniel's match only to discover a small crowd of mostly older gentlemen demonstrating near the entrance, brandishing signs demanding that football be suspended for the duration. Jamie and Simon stared in astonishment as the gentlemen called out to fans as they approached the turnstile, urging them to go home rather than share in the teams' disgrace.

"That's Daniel Dempsey's wife," one of the men suddenly shouted. Lucy jumped as many pairs of eyes turned her way. "Say there, Mrs. Dempsey! Aren't you ashamed of your husband, running around on a pitch while our country is engaged in a life-and-death struggle? Wouldn't you rather see him a hero in uniform?"

Mortified, Lucy lifted her chin, seized her sons' hands, and marched past the protestors without acknowledging them, breathing a sigh of relief only after she and the boys had passed through the gate. Inside, a large and enthusiastic crowd had assembled, mostly working-class men who evidently did not object to sport in wartime. And why should they? It seemed to Lucy that football provided a welcome distraction from the war, an essential release of tension that sustained morale.

"Why do those men hate football?" Simon asked as they made their way to their seats.

"I don't believe they *hate* football," Lucy replied, "but they see it as . . . an extravagance during wartime."

Those men were not alone, she knew, and their numbers were increasing.

Not even the extraordinary sums footballers raised for the National Relief Fund and other charities could shift the tide of public opinion in the teams' favor. One by one, prominent gentlemen from the military, government, and business publicly condemned the playing of games during a national crisis. Lucy dreaded to see Daniel brooding over their denunciations. "This is the worst controversy the sport has faced since the conflict over paying players first arose," he said, studying a particularly irksome pamphlet.

"Surely it's not as bad as that," protested Lucy. Thirty years before, a few disgruntled teams had accused certain rivals of paying their players, giving them an unfair advantage. Although paying players was not prohibited, opponents contended that it would harm the sport, forsaking the ideals of sportsmanship and the true spirit of the game in favor of the false idols of financial incentive and profit. Outrage and hostility had fomented through the years until the Football Association had finally split into two factions, professional and amateur. Although in recent years the sides had warily reconciled, some amateur abhorrence for professionalism lingered, despite three decades of evidence that paying players had not ruined the game. Nor had any footballer become wealthy on his earnings. Most professional players earned only a few pounds a week, hardly enough to support oneself or raise a family. Most players earned a living from another trade or profession, trained and played matches in their off hours, and appreciated the extra measure of comfort and security their football income provided. Only a very few footballers were paid enough to forgo other work if they wished, and Daniel was not one of those.

In September, as the fledgling controversy worsened,

the Football Association issued a statement declaring that the season would go on as scheduled, but any player who wished to enlist would be released from his contract without penalty, and those who did not enlist would engage in military drill and rifle training as a team. Recruitment posters would be displayed prominently at each team's grounds, and dignitaries would be invited to address audiences during the interval to urge all players and spectators who were physically fit and otherwise qualified to join the army at once.

Yet even those efforts did not quell the grumbling. In October, Lucy and her sons encountered more protestors outside St. James' Park when Tottenham played Newcastle United, men in black wool coats and fine top hats holding signs with slogans such as "Your Country Needs You" and "Are You Forgetting There's a War On?" and "Be Ready to Defend Your Home and Women from the German Huns!" As the season progressed, Lucy and the other Tottenham footballers' wives noted White Hart Lane's dwindling crowds, as recruitment drives claimed some spectators and negative publicity drove away others.

"It's not fair that our husbands must endure such unjust criticism while men in other professions—indeed, in other sports—escape scrutiny," said Minnie Bailey, thoroughly vexed, keeping her voice low so the spectators seated nearby would not overhear. She had been Lucy's closest friend among the wives ever since they had traveled to Stockholm together to attend England's final against Denmark in the 1912 Olympic Games. Minnie's then fiancé, Horace, had been England's reserve goalkeeper; although he had not played, he still shared in all the honor and praise and adoration England's fans had bestowed upon the team.

What a difference two years made, Lucy thought ruefully. Britain's footballers, only recently a source of tremendous national pride, had become the objects of scorn and derision.

"Minnie's right," another wife chimed in. "I don't hear any lords or legislators demanding that golfers, cricketers, and polo players cease playing for the duration and trade in their team kit for a soldier's khaki."

"And yet footballers are condemned, when they've enlisted in greater numbers and raised more relief funds than any other sportsmen," said Lucy.

"It's class prejudice, that's what it is," said Elsie May, sighing. "Football is the people's game, the pastime of the working classes rather than the gentry."

Lucy and the others agreed there was nothing for it but to bear the indignity with grace and support their husbands through it. All would be forgotten after the war ended and life returned to normal.

But as the weeks passed and the controversy smoldered, two distressing truths became evident to Lucy: The Football Association was steadily losing its case in the court of public opinion, and the war was very unlikely to be over by Christmas.

In late November, Daniel told Lucy that a group of Heart of Midlothian players had enlisted together in a new battalion of the Royal Scots being raised by Sir George McCrae, a former MP for East Edinburgh. "A few days before, the *Edinburgh Evening News* had suggested that the club should be renamed 'The White Feathers of Midlothian,'" he said, grimacing.

Lucy was aghast. "They ran off to enlist because of some childish name-calling?"

"What better way to silence their critics? The Hearts' entire first and reserve team joined up, along with members of the board and the staff and nearly five hundred fans. Now players from other Scottish teams are racing to join them before McCrae's Battalion is entirely filled." Daniel shook his head and grinned. "What a terrifying sight that would be—hundreds of fierce Scotsman footballers and fans hurling themselves at the unsuspecting enemy. I've faced them on the pitch. I wouldn't want to confront them on the battlefield."

"I could almost pity the Germans," said Lucy. Then

her thoughts darted to the nearly seven hundred civilians slaughtered by the Kaiser's army in the village of Dinant, the countless numbers the Germans had killed elsewhere in Belgium and in France, the young British soldiers who had already lost their lives—and she decided that the Germans deserved every moment of terror, in equal measure to all they had inflicted upon innocents.

"Heart of Midlothian are leading the Scottish League," Daniel said, as if lost in thought, "and yet they're willing to cast aside their shot at the cup in order to enlist. No dodgy reporter can fault their courage now."

Uneasy, Lucy made no reply. Daniel's admiration for the Scottish footballers filled the room with a heavy, haunting presence, and she was afraid to say something that might persuade him to join them.

In early December, Tottenham Hotspur received a letter from the Football Association inviting the club to send delegates to a meeting at the FA offices in Russell Square. "The owner and manager will attend, and I've been asked to represent our players," Daniel told Lucy.

"Sounds like quite an honor," she said, bracing herself, for a certain intensity in his expression warned her that he had more to say.

"Lucy, darling." Daniel took her hand, kissed it, and

pressed it to his heart. "McCrae's Battalion may have been first onto the pitch, but we English footballers play to the whistle. The purpose of the meeting is to discuss whether to form an English Footballers' Battalion for Kitchener's Army."

Lucy's heart plummeted. Daniel was trying to break the news gently, but she knew him too well.

If a Footballers' Battalion was formed, when the whistle blew, Daniel would take the field among them.

2
January–March 1915

April

In her four years at Alderlea, April had never seen Lady Rylance as flustered and indignant as she was that frosty January morning, moments after her husband's startling announcement.

Not even on Boxing Day a fortnight ago had the mistress been this upset. It was meant to have been the merriest day of the festive season for the household staff, but Harrison Rylance, the eldest son and heir, had spoiled their holiday by stealing away to accept a commission with the Derbyshire Yeomanry. Her duties complete, her half day off barely begun, April was in her shared attic bedroom dressing for the traditional Housemaids v. Footmen Boxing Day football match when the mistress had shrieked so horribly that she might have witnessed a murder in the drawing room, or a maid clumsily overturning an ashtray on the best Persian rug.

A moment later, the staff had been summoned to attend to Harrison's distraught parents and bewildered younger siblings as they came to terms with his patriotic disobedience. April had served brandy and tea and biscuits in the drawing room, silently mourning the cancelled football match, which was always great fun, and the lost Boxing Day afternoon off, which was all but sacrosanct. Eventually Lord Rylance had convinced his wife that their son had done a splendid thing by pledging to serve King and Country and to defend England's honor. "I would accept a commission myself, if not for this blasted leg," Lord Rylance had grumbled, slapping his thigh above the knee, which he had injured years before in a fall from a horse. "I might still, if His Majesty commands."

"Heaven forfend," Lady Rylance had exclaimed, laying a long, slim, beringed hand over her heart. She had embraced her eldest, then held him at arm's length, scolding him with one breath and praising him with the next. How thoughtless he was to have deceived them, but how honorable and courageous he was to answer the call to arms! They were exceedingly proud to have an officer in the family, but if Harrison had only told them his intentions, his father could have arranged a more advantageous commission.

"If I had told you," Harrison had protested, laughing, "you would have tried to stop me."

"Could I have done?" his mother replied, her smile wavering. Then she had pressed a handkerchief to her mouth and fled the room.

While the scene unfolded, April had been obliged to keep her eyes down and expression placid, revealing not the slightest flicker of astonishment, even though she had never seen the mistress so upset. Not that she spent much time in Lady Rylance's company. April occasionally served at table, but most of her work—washing, cleaning, fetching, scrubbing—was done out of the family's sight, beginning before dawn while the family slept until long after they had retired for the night.

April's mum had not told her what domestic service would be like, perhaps because she did not herself know. A word of warning wouldn't have changed April's mind anyway. The Tipton family desperately needed their eldest children to earn wages, and the position at Alderlea was simply too great an opportunity to let slip by. It had only come April's way because the housekeeper, Elizabeth Wilson, was April's mum's cousin. They had been good chums when they were girls, and had kept in touch through letters after their lives had taken them in dramatically different directions. Mrs. Wilson had achieved a position of respect and authority in one of the most gracious country houses in Derbyshire, while April's mum had followed a well-trod path into marriage, motherhood, and increasingly reduced circumstances.

"This could be your chance at a better life," April's mum had reminded her as she set off for the station, adjusting April's hat, picking a stray thread off her coat sleeve. "Be pleasant, be quiet, work hard, and do everything Cousin Bitsy tells you to do, and you could make something of yourself. You might even rise to become a cook or a housekeeper yourself someday."

"I will," April had replied solemnly, giving her mum a peck on the cheek. Though she was only fifteen, she was terribly eager to go, not because the work sounded particularly exciting, but because it was either domestic service or the mills, and she didn't want the mills. The only other respectable alternative was to stay home and mind the little ones while her elder sister accepted the housemaid position, her mum took in more piecework, and her dad drank his pay away.

It was a long journey by train to Derbyshire, and after that a jostling ride in a farmer's hay wagon to reach the estate. April was weary and disheveled when she finally knocked on the back door of Alderlea, a glorious three-story Elizabethan mansion of buff sandstone and gray slate set amid vast, rolling lawns at the edge of a pretty wood. The tall, golden-haired housemaid who answered her knock looked only a few years older than herself. "Yes?" she asked, friendly enough. "What d'you need?"

"I'm April Tipton," she said. "I'm here to see Mrs. Elizabeth Wilson, please."

"Oh, you must be the new girl." The housemaid opened the door wider and beckoned her inside. "Congratulations or condolences, as the case may be."

"Erm, congratulations, I hope. I don't have the job yet. And thanks."

"Don't mention it." She tossed April a grin over her shoulder as she led her down the hallway to the housekeeper's room. "Here we are at the dragon's lair," she said in a conspiratorial whisper as they halted outside the door. "Good luck."

With that, the maid swept off, leaving April alone in the passageway amid the clatter of dishes and enticing aromas drifting from a kitchen somewhere nearby. Collecting herself, she took a deep breath, knocked on the door, and entered when commanded to do so. Inside, a woman in her middle forties sat at a desk studying a ledger and receipts through wire-rimmed glasses attached to a fine silver chain around her neck. When she glanced up inquiringly, April bobbed a curtsey. "Good day, ma'am. I'm April Tipton," she said, handing over an envelope with her references and a letter from her mum. "Hannah Tipton's daughter."

"Yes, of course." The housekeeper rose to accept the papers, and April tried not to fidget while she read them. Elizabeth Wilson had her cousin's gray-streaked chestnut hair, apple cheeks, and cleft chin, but otherwise April saw no family resemblance. She wore a navy blue wool suit, a crisp white blouse, and perfectly polished, sensible heeled boots, finer clothes than April had ever seen her mum wear. April's mum often smiled, though sometimes tiredly, and she hunched her shoulders, a habit developed from years bent over her sewing. Studying her mum's cousin while she read, April noticed that her expression was stern, her gaze coolly appraising, her posture straight and imposing. April reminded herself that her mum was very fond of the housekeeper. She must be a good sort, even if the blonde maid had called her a dragon.

The housekeeper invited April to sit, queried her about her schooling and prior work experience, and explained the rules of the household. First and foremost, April was never to call her Cousin Bitsy, not even when they were alone; it was always to be Mrs. Wilson.

As the newest maid, April would rank below everyone in the house except the scullery girl, and she must show all due respect. Her workday would begin at five o'clock sharp, when she would rise, wash, put on her day uniform, and light the kitchen fire. Next she would tend to the rooms on the ground floor, cleaning the grates, dusting, polishing, sweeping the hall and the stairs, washing the front steps, and polishing the brass door fixtures. Then she would light fires in the family's dressing rooms and carry hot water to their bedchambers. After breakfast, she would clear and air the bedchambers, turn the mattresses, and make up the beds, then clean other rooms such as the library and the study, lighting fires where necessary. All this must be accomplished by luncheon, when April must be prepared to wait at table if the footmen were occupied with other duties. In the early afternoon, after changing out of her morning work clothes into her more formal uniform of black dress, white apron, and white cap, she would mend and darn, answer the door and the telephone, and announce callers. As evening approached, she would prepare the dining room for dinner and serve at table if needed; afterward, she would bring tea to the drawing room for the family and any guests, and light fires in the bedchambers. In addition to these daily responsibilities, every week April would assist with the laundry and ironing; clean the carpets, wallpaper, and windows; and wash down the paintwork.

"That sounds like rather a lot," April managed to say.

"You'll have Sunday afternoons off."

"Even so," April said without thinking, quickly adding, "That is, thank you, ma'am."

Mrs. Wilson's expression softened a trifle. "You won't be responsible for everything yourself, my dear. You'll share the work with three other housemaids. You met Mary on your way in. You'll meet the others later." Mrs. Wilson rose. "Pending approval from her ladyship, of course."

April quickly stood and tried to smooth the wrinkles from her dress. "I'm to meet Lady Rylance? Now?"

"Don't panic, child. Of course now. If she doesn't like the look of you, you'll have time to catch the train back to Carlisle this evening." Mrs. Wilson studied April for a moment, then sighed. "Just keep your gaze down modestly, clasp your hands in front like so—" She demonstrated. "And don't say anything unless her ladyship addresses you. You'll be all right. Come along, now."

April swallowed hard and obeyed, wishing she had time to wash the dust of travel from her hands and face and arrange her flaxen hair, stick-straight and butter yellow, into a tidier bun. As she trailed after the housekeeper down corridors and up two flights of back stairs, she tried to tuck stray wisps under her cap, but without a mirror, she might have been making a worse mess of it.

All too soon Mrs. Wilson led her into a splendid sitting room, with a marble fireplace at one end, a gleaming piano at the other, and all sorts of lovely gilded and brocaded furnishings in between, warm wood and fabric in shades of sage green and lavender. It seemed that every level surface boasted a crystal or porcelain vase bursting with fragrant flowers. Tall windows adorned with heavy lavender velvet curtains let in sunlight and breathtaking views of the lush forest and rolling hills.

It occurred to April that this single room was larger and more abundantly furnished than her family's entire home. And Alderlea had many more such rooms. How could even four housemaids clean the entire mansion in a single day?

In the center of the room, three women dressed in elegant frocks sat chatting and sipping tea around a low table laden with a tea service and trays of tiny sandwiches and pastries. One woman perched gracefully in a lavender brocade armchair, the two others on the floral, claw-legged sofa opposite her. The woman in the armchair appeared to be in her late forties, slender and fair-skinned, with glossy black hair and an aquiline nose. Her dark eyebrows arched at the sight of Mrs. Wilson entering with April. "Yes, Wilson?" she inquired. "What is it?"

"If you please, ma'am, we've taken on a new housemaid." With a turn of her wrist, Mrs. Wilson indicated April, who bobbed a curtsey. "I'm well acquainted with her mother, and she brings two characters, one from a former schoolteacher and another from her minister. They both attest that she is a hardworking, reliable girl."

April felt the lady's eyes weighing and measuring her. "Is she an experienced maid? She looks quite young."

"She's fifteen, ma'am, the third eldest of eight. This would be her first position, but she has been helping her mother keep house and mind her siblings since she was quite young."

"Hmm." Sighing, Lady Rylance turned to her elegant companions. "It's so difficult to find good servants these days. One has to bring in novices and train them oneself." The other ladies murmured in commiseration. Turning back to Mrs. Wilson, Lady Rylance asked, "What is she called?"

"April, ma'am. April Tipton."

"April?" Lady Rylance's nose wrinkled in distaste.

"Oh, no. That will never do. April is too frivolous for a maid. We shall call her Mary."

"We already have a Mary, ma'am."

"Do we indeed?" Lady Rylance put her head to one side, thinking. "Oh, yes, the lanky girl, saucy grin. Well, let's call this one Ann. Unless we already have an Ann?"

"No, ma'am."

"Ann it is, then." April's new mistress bathed her in a radiant smile. "Welcome to Alderlea, Ann. Work hard, be punctual, and we'll get along splendidly."

"Yes, ma'am. Thank you, ma'am," April murmured, heart thudding as she curtsied again, but the mistress and her friends had resumed their conversation and took no notice. Ann the housemaid was quickly forgotten.

Mrs. Wilson inclined her head deferentially to the unwitting ladies and silently left the room. A bit stunned, April followed. "You made a good impression," Mrs. Wilson remarked quietly when they were alone in the hallway.

April murmured a reply, bewilderment giving way to annoyance. She *liked* her name. It was fresh and bright and lively like spring itself, like *April* herself. Lady Rylance might not think it suitable for a girl of her station, but no one had any right to change it.

But if April wanted to keep her new job, she supposed she would have to go along with it.

Mrs. Wilson led April back downstairs to the housekeeper's chamber and instructed her regarding her wages and room and board. Afterward, she summoned the same housemaid who had answered April's knock. "Mary will take you to the laundry and give you your uniforms," Mrs. Wilson said. "After that, she'll show you to your bed in the maids' quarters so you can settle in. You can begin work bright and early tomorrow morning."

With that, Mrs. Wilson dismissed them.

"Come on, then, Ann," said Mary, beckoning April to follow her down the passageway. "Let's get you sorted. What did you think of Lady Rylance?"

"She changed my name," said April woefully. "I'm not really Ann."

The other maid shrugged. "That's all right. I'm not really Mary. My name's Marjorie."

"Let me guess." April stuck her nose in the air, and in a plummy voice intoned, "That's too frivolous a name for a maid."

Marjorie laughed, delighted. "You have her exactly! But listen—" She halted for emphasis, and April did too. "Don't ever let Mrs. Wilson or the butler—or anyone but me, really—hear you mocking the family or you'll be sacked without a character. And without a character, you'll never get another job in service, although there are worse fates than that, surely."

"Thanks for the warning," said April. Apparently she had already found her first friend and ally at Alderlea.

"As for your new name, don't let it bother you," Marjorie said, continuing toward the laundry, which, judging by the smell of bleach and starch on the air, could not be far. "Mrs. Wilson and the butler will call you Ann, but you won't see her ladyship very often, and when you do, she likely won't address you at all."

That much, like most of the advice and warnings Marjorie had shared with her in the four years since that awkward first day, had proven true. April almost never saw Lady Rylance or her husband except brief glimpses with the length of a corridor between them. Nor was April seen. Unlike ladies' maids, who dressed their mistresses and arranged their hair and often became companions and confidantes, girls like April and Marjorie were meant to be invisible.

Yet April saw enough of her mistress in four years' time to know that she was often indifferent but never cruel. She had many friends but preferred to go out rather than entertain. She loved horses but merely tolerated dogs. She had very specific opinions regarding what was appropriate, or tasteful, or amusing, or ridiculous, but she never raised her voice in conversation when others disagreed. In fact, she almost never lost her composure, which was why Boxing Day stood out. Yet wouldn't any mother have got a bit teary to hear that her son had enlisted, when from the sound of it, the Western Front was cold, wet, muddy, dangerous, and in every other way awfully bad?

But as upset as Lady Rylance had been then, she was even more so now, staring daggers at her husband over the breakfast table, holding out one slim, pale hand for the letter from the War Office.

"You may read it, my dear, but it won't change a thing," Lord Rylance remarked as he placed the folded page in her hand. "I've already consented to the War Office's request to billet soldiers on the estate."

"How could you, without consulting me?" his wife said in a strangled voice, her cheeks flushed.

"There's a war on," he replied, calmly buttering his toast. "Needs must."

Lady Rylance's hands trembled as she read the letter. "The War Office gives no consideration whatsoever to the great inconvenience to ourselves. Oh! And this. We're expected to feed the soldiers as well."

"The government will pay us two shillings and sixpence per day for each man."

"A pittance that will scarcely cover the expense. Mrs. Wilson says food prices have been soaring! We might as well give the government's largesse to Monsieur Pierre to compensate him for the additional work this billeting business will undoubtedly require of him."

Lord Rylance swallowed a bite of toast and sipped his tea. "Splendid idea, Catherine. I daresay Monsieur Pierre will earn that bonus."

"Nothing about this is splendid," she retorted. "I don't like this at all, Reg, and I should like to know what you intend to do about it!"

Standing side by side against the wall as they awaited the cue to clear, April and Marjorie exchanged the tiniest of startled, sidelong glances. Never, truly never, had either of them heard the mistress raise her voice to her husband.

Lord Rylance regarded his wife for a moment, his thick black eyebrows nearly meeting at the bridge of his nose, his expression becoming ever more serious. "What do I intend to do about it." He dabbed at the corners of his mouth with his napkin. "What do I intend indeed."

His wife creased the letter, set it beside her teacup, folded her hands in her lap, and met his gaze with a silent challenge, lips pressed together, chin trembling.

"The police have allocated eight soldiers to Alderlea for billets," he said, his voice utterly calm. "We could easily accommodate twice as many."

"Yes, we have room. That's not the point."

"No, indeed, it is not. Wartime requires sacrifices of us all, my dear, and our sacrifice apparently will be to host eight soldiers while they train for battle, eight young men like our Harrison. Britain is honor-bound to go to war due to our alliances and treaties, and it is decidedly in our own self-interest to prevent Germany from controlling Western Europe. If, God forbid, Germany conquers Belgium and France, do you understand that the Kaiser's next move, if he continues to hold off Russia, will surely be to attempt an invasion of Great Britain?"

He paused for an answer. His wife gave him the barest of nods.

"You asked what I intend," Lord Rylance continued. "Well, I intend to welcome these eight soldiers as I hope another family would welcome our Harrison, and to make them as comfortable and cheerful as possible before they sail for France. I should be ashamed to do otherwise."

Silence descended.

"Well," the mistress eventually said, "you make me feel quite ashamed for complaining."

Her husband took her hand and kissed it. "My dear, let us hope this is the only sacrifice we are required to make for England in this dreadful, unsought war."

Lady Rylance murmured something April could not quite make out, but she knew the lord and lady were thinking of their young lieutenant.

In the days that followed, Lady Rylance resigned herself to her uninvited guests and worked up a scheme for how best to accommodate them, bringing to bear all the skills she had perfected over decades of planning shooting parties, dinners for twenty, and holiday balls. It was up to Mrs. Wilson and the butler to see that the mistress's instructions were carried out. For nearly a week April and her fellow servants prepared for the soldiers at a frantic pace—cleaning, preparing beds, planning meals and leisure activities—but despite the unexpected addition to her workload, April was looking forward to the soldiers' arrival. The novelty of their presence would add a bit of spice to days that were otherwise all very much the same.

Marjorie was even more delighted than April that Alderlea was preparing to welcome a more interesting bunch than the family's usual guests, and she fervently hoped their soldiers would be enlisted men, lads of their own class rather than officers. "Lads we can talk to, have a bit of fun with," she explained as she and April scrubbed the foyer's slate floor for the second time that day, since the younger Rylance children had tracked in mud.

Amused, April sat back on her heels and wiped her forehead with the back of her hand. "Better not let the mistress or Mrs. Wilson catch you flirting," she advised, dunking her scrub brush into the bucket of soapy water.

"I won't get caught."

"Don't bring any of them up to our room, either."

"I wouldn't," Marjorie protested, pushing a honey-gold curl out of her eyes with one hand while vigorously scrubbing the floor with the other. "The other girls would tell, and I'd find myself out of work without a character. You wouldn't tell, though, would you? Even though Mrs. Wilson is your aunt?"

"She's my mum's cousin," April said, wishing yet again that no one knew they were related, however distantly. She wouldn't want anyone to think she was getting special treatment, for she certainly wasn't. Mrs. Wilson always gave her the most difficult chores at the worst times of the day—except for the scullery girl, of course, who without a doubt had the hardest, grubbiest work of them all and was paid the least for it. If the Rylances instructed Mrs. Wilson to hire a new housemaid, then the new girl would be the lower in rank, April would earn some privileges, and—

But there was no point in hoping for it. From what April had overheard, it was very unlikely that any new servants would be hired at Alderlea, even though billeting the soldiers meant more work for everyone. Lord Rylance could certainly afford more staff, but as Lady Rylance and her friends often lamented, good servants were all but impossible to find these days. Footmen and grooms were quitting domestic service for the adventure and honor of Lord Kitchener's Army, while housemaids and scullery girls were hiring on at businesses and factories to replace men who had enlisted, doing work that women had never been allowed to try before. April and Marjorie marveled at the stories in the Rylances' discarded newspapers about girls not much older than themselves operating streetcars, delivering the Royal Mail, and operating machinery in factories. How interesting their work must be, every day something new and different, with better wages and possibilities for advancement a mere housemaid could only dream of!

"I've thought about stealing away to London and taking one of those jobs," Marjorie had admitted one afternoon as they cleaned the master's study. "Wouldn't it be grand to work at something they never let girls do before, and to be well paid for it?"

April had felt a catch in her throat. How could Marjorie even *say* such a thing, that she might run off and leave April behind? "Why go all the way to London where a German zeppelin could drop a bomb on you?" she asked, determined not to sound forlorn. "I'm sure they have those sort of jobs in Liverpool and Manchester too."

Marjorie had shaken her head. "That would be too close, and in the wrong direction. I have to go *away* from home, not toward it, or my folks might fetch me back. London would be too far for them to travel." She paused to laugh. "Oh, don't look so reproachful! I wouldn't actually do it, not without saying goodbye."

April had felt somewhat better. Her dearest friend would not abandon her anytime soon.

But that was days ago. At the moment, Marjorie was giving her a pointed stare. "Of course I wouldn't be a telltale," April belatedly replied. Marjorie was two years older than she, far more experienced in work and in life. Without her help and advice, April never would have settled in so quickly at Alderlea. How could April not adore and admire her friend, and consider herself lucky to have that friendship?

As Alderlea continued to prepare for their guests,

Lord Rylance received word that two were officers, the rest enlisted men. Bedrooms were made
up for the captain and the lieutenant as befitting
their status, while cots and mattresses, all with thick
blankets and soft pillows, were set up in the library
for the others. The official instructions specifically
noted that billets were required to provide their soldiers with candles, vinegar, salt, the use of the fire,
and utensils for the dressing and eating of meat, so
Mrs. Wilson checked and double-checked to make
sure all that was sorted too.

On the day of the soldiers' arrival, Mrs. Wilson
assigned the housemaids tasks downstairs so they
would not be tempted to gawk and giggle as the men
settled in—but any hopes she may have had to keep
the maids and the enlisted men separated indefinitely
were doomed from the start. Within days they had
all crossed paths and exchanged names, and before a
fortnight had passed, nearly everyone in one group had
chosen a favorite among the other. April liked a dark-
haired private from Pilsley best, but she rarely said
more than a few words to him at a time, so determined
was she to remain in Mrs. Wilson's good graces.

The soldiers spent most of the day drilling and training near Chesterfield, but they usually had breakfast
and dinner at Alderlea, and tea as well if they returned

in time for it. It soon became apparent that Lady Rylance and Monsieur Pierre had badly underestimated how much eight healthy young soldiers would eat. The weekly grocery delivery frequently ran short, obliging Mrs. Wilson to send servants into the village for supplies. A large order required footmen to go with a cart, but if only a few items were wanting, a maid or two could go on foot. Marjorie and April were always quick to volunteer, for the two-mile walk was easy and pretty, even in February, and running errands was infinitely preferable to scrubbing floors. Marjorie enjoyed flirting with the handsome young men who happened to cross their path, although she had become more discerning in recent months, and now smiled only at men in uniform.

As for April, she loved the different shops, all with their particular wares arranged so prettily to entice a customer to buy. She never had enough money of her own to buy any of the things she admired—a box of creamy ivory stationery, a pair of fine tan gloves, an oval brass picture frame etched with roses—but it amused her to make purchases for the estate and pretend she was buying them for herself. Her errands rarely sent her to the milliner, the dressmaker, the newsagent, or the confectioner, but she admired the window displays and sometimes pondered how she might rearrange the wares to make them more appealing. Marjorie admired the dressmaker's front window as much as April did, but on the whole, she preferred to keep her eyes open for handsome fellows.

"I adore having soldiers at Alderlea," Marjorie proclaimed one sunny, frosty February afternoon as they walked to the village, her breath emerging above her scarf in faint white puffs. "I think Bob is in love with me."

"Yesterday you were in love with Joe," remarked April, tightening her grip as her knitted mittens slipped on the handle of her basket.

"I never said I was in love. I still like Joe. Can't I like them both?"

"As long as they don't find out."

Marjorie laughed. "The lieutenant is the most handsome of them all, but I can't get more than a polite smile and a thank-you out of him when I lay his fire or bring him his post."

April shot her a look. "Have you *tried* to get more out of him? The mistress wouldn't like it."

"I'm just being friendly. It's not my fault he's so good-looking." Marjorie elbowed her, grinning. "Don't worry. I'm not going to make a fool of myself. But it's so hard not to admire our Tommies, don't you agree?"

"Of course." How could April not admire them? Officers and enlisted men alike, they all looked so dashing in their uniforms, so brave and strong and proud, each willing to sacrifice his life for King and Country in the defense of good old England. In December, April's elder brother had joined the Lonsdale Pals, the 11th Battalion of the Border Regiment, earning her respect and envy. She wished she too could do her bit, serve her country, make her mum burst with pride. She was less enthusiastic about risking her life, but fortunately, and alas, no one wanted her to. That bit belonged to the lads.

"I think no young man is so admirable as one who bravely answers his country's call to arms," Marjorie declared, stepping gracefully around a puddle of slush between ruts in the frozen mud. "And none is as despicable as a coward who shirks his duty."

"My," said April, surprised by the venom in her friend's voice. "Strong words."

"I mean every one of them. I consider myself a member of the Order of the White Feather."

"The what?"

"The Order of the White Feather. It's from cockfighting—you know, because a cockerel with a white feather in its tail always proves to be a timid fighter. The Order says that whenever a girl comes upon a lad in civvies who ought to be in khaki, she should give him a white feather as a symbol of his cowardice."

"That seems unkind," said April. "She wouldn't know why he isn't in uniform. Maybe he's not fit. Maybe he has bad eyes or a trick knee. Or maybe he's a soldier on leave."

"Or maybe—" Marjorie lowered her voice as they approached the village; in the past, certain curmudgeons had complained about her to Mrs. Wilson, that she laughed and talked too loudly in the streets, unbecoming behavior for any young woman, but especially a maid. "Maybe he's a coward or a shirker. Listen. I have two white goose feathers in my pocket, one for me and one for you. I'll give mine to the first slacker we see so you can learn how it's done. You can do the next."

"I don't want to," said April, a bit plaintively. "And I don't think you should either. If you ask me, the army's better off without lads who don't want to fight. Not everyone is up to it."

"Lord Kitchener doesn't agree." Marjorie smiled brightly at two strapping lads in uniform, who smiled back admiringly as they passed. "He says women can help in the national crisis by influencing our men to enlist. Lord Kitchener says every girl with a sweetheart should tell him that she won't walk out with him again until he has done his part."

"Told you that himself, did he?"

"I read the papers, now and again, and we've all seen the posters." Marjorie gestured up and down the street, where, sure enough, every wall and fence boasted a poster or two. "See there? 'Every able-bodied man is needed.' And right here, the one with the pretty girl: 'If he does not think that you and your country are worth fighting for, do you think he is worthy of you?'"

April wavered, thinking of her brother. Henry had enlisted eagerly, not only to serve his country, but also for the pay and the opportunity to better himself. Now he was training with his regiment at Blackwell Race-course, while three of Marjorie's brothers, the ones old enough, had already sailed for France. They all had willingly volunteered. Who better than their sisters to urge other lads to do their bit too? The Tommies needed all the help they could get to defeat the Hun.

"You make a fair point," April admitted, just as they arrived at Mrs. Wilson's favorite grocer. "Are you going in or shall I?"

"You go," Marjorie said, her eyes fixed on a trio of handsome soldiers entering the pub across the street. "I'll keep watch for German spies."

April laughed and agreed.

She filled her basket with the things on Mrs. Wilson's list, charged the order to the estate account, and hurried back outside. Next they went down the block to the butcher's—who happened to be a German immigrant, though probably not a spy—and there, April waited outside with the groceries while Marjorie shopped. Uncomfortable standing around idle in the middle of the day, April kept out of the way of passersby, took in the scene such as it was, and tried to stay warm, pulling up her coat collar and scarf, tucking her mittened hands into her pockets, and marching in place a bit now and then to keep the blood flowing. The temperature had steadily dropped as a bank of thick gray clouds passed in front of the sun, and the air smelled of snow.

"So sorry, bit of a queue in there," Marjorie said when she finally bustled out of the shop, her basket full of joints and cuts wrapped in paper. "D'you want to go in and warm yourself before we set out?"

"No, I'm fine." April glanced up at the sky, where a few thick flakes drifted and swirled. "I'd rather hurry back to Alderlea before the storm."

"Right, then." Marjorie set off down the pavement, her longer stride forcing April to quicken her pace to keep up. By the last half mile, though, April knew she would pull ahead while Marjorie gradually slowed. The tortoise and the hare, Marjorie sometimes called them, which April didn't really like, since she was no slow, plodding tortoise. Marjorie might beat her in a short footrace, but in a long-distance run—

Marjorie abruptly halted, and April stopped just in time to avoid jostling her. "Look over there," she said quietly, nodding toward the footbridge just ahead, where a lanky young man with a knapsack had paused to tie his bootlace. "Here's our first slacker. He's not in the army, and he's not at work, either. Hold this."

Abruptly she handed her basket to April, who seized it just before it would have overturned. "Leave him be, won't you?" she begged as Marjorie slipped a hand inside her coat and withdrew a white goose feather from her skirt pocket. "Maybe he's on his way to work."

Marjorie laughed shortly. "Not likely." She marched ahead to confront the lad, April trailing along reluctantly after her. He straightened as they approached, his brow furrowing in curiosity. "Hello," Marjorie greeted him, smiling. "What's your name, dearie?"

"My name?" he echoed, his voice leaping an octave between the two words. "It's Peter, miss. Peter Bell."

"Well, Peter Bell—" Eyes narrowing, voice hardening, Marjorie thrust the white feather at him. "Aren't you ashamed not to be called Private Bell?"

He blinked at her for a moment, and then took the feather. "What's this about?"

"Marjorie, let's go," April murmured, aware of the other villagers who had paused to observe the scene.

Marjorie ignored her. "This is a white feather, a symbol of your cowardice," she informed Peter, as haughtily as Lady Rylance explaining the difference between silver and silver plate. "How dare you idle about here while other men fight for King and Country?"

The lad flushed. "I'm only fifteen. I'm still in school." He gestured to his knapsack, which no doubt carried his books and pencils. "I'm not allowed to enlist."

"You're fifteen?" Marjorie studied him. "How're you so tall at fifteen?"

"I'm—that is—" Voice cracking, he drew himself up even taller and glared. "Well, how'd you get so tall for a girl?"

April seized the crook of Marjorie's elbow and tugged. "Let's go. Please."

"Say, you there," a woman's voice bellowed from behind them. "Did you just give my boy a white feather?"

"Be sure to enlist when you're old enough," Marjorie ordered Peter, then clutched her basket close and turned away. "Let's go," she murmured to April, setting off briskly as the woman shouted after them. They hurried away without looking back, pretending not to hear that angry voice, moving as quickly as they could without breaking into a run.

They both agreed not to mention the incident to anyone else at Alderlea, but a few days later, Mrs. Wilson summoned them to her chamber for a scolding. Peter's father was a village councilor, his mother one of the most respected women of the community. It was she who had written, outraged and indignant, to complain about how her boy had been "unduly scolded by a pair of impertinent Alderlea maids."

"She hinted very strongly that she wanted you both sacked," said Mrs. Wilson, her gaze icy as she looked from one chastened maid to the other. "I persuaded her to settle for a formal apology from me, a fruit basket from the estate orangery, and a solemn promise that you will never again display such shameful disrespect in the village."

Eyes downcast, April and Marjorie murmured apologies. "It was me who gave the boy the feather," Marjorie added, her voice clear and steady. "April—I mean, Ann had nothing to do with it. She tried to stop me."

April felt Mrs. Wilson's eyes on her. "It's a pity she didn't try harder. This unpleasantness could have been avoided." She lectured them a bit longer about how Alderlea had always been on excellent terms with the village, and why that longstanding cordiality and mutual respect must endure. Then she turned to their punishment. April and Marjorie would no longer be sent on errands, at least not until they had earned back Mrs. Wilson's trust. If they entered the village on their afternoons off, they must be on their absolute best behavior. If a single letter of complaint attested that they had not, they would be sacked immediately and not provided with a character.

Heart thudding, tears springing into her eyes, April nodded and thanked her, knowing the punishment could have been far worse.

"Let's try to put this unfortunate business behind us," Mrs. Wilson said, sighing. "Mary, you may go. Ann, I need another word."

Marjorie threw April a worried, sympathetic glance as she curtsied to the housekeeper and hurried away. April braced herself as the door closed and Mrs. Wilson studied her over the rims of her glasses. "I realize you and Mary are friends," she said, "but you might wish to reconsider that friendship. You're a good girl on your own, but too often you disregard your better sense and follow Mary into mischief." She held up a hand to forestall any argument, not that April had any intention of interrupting. "I know you weren't the one who gave that boy the white feather, but when guilt by association is the rule, you would do well to keep better company."

April swallowed, hard. "Yes, ma'am."

At last Mrs. Wilson dismissed her. April left the housekeeper's chamber only to find Marjorie waiting for her in the passageway. "What did she say?" Marjorie whispered, glancing at the closed door. "Is she going to tell your mum?"

"I hope not," April replied quietly, ignoring the first question.

They fell in step together as they headed up the servants' staircase to resume their interrupted duties. "I only did what hundreds of girls have been doing all around Britain," Marjorie said, contrite. "Lord Kitchener himself supports the Order."

"He doesn't support enlisting fifteen-year-old schoolboys."

"I didn't know—" Marjorie inhaled deeply. "Please, don't you be angry with me too. He didn't look like a schoolboy."

"No, I suppose he didn't."

Marjorie paused on the staircase and stuck out her hand, her skin as red and chapped as April's own. "Still chums?"

"Always," April replied as she shook her hand.

As the days passed, they endured the embarrass-

ment of knowing that everyone belowstairs was aware
of their disgrace. Whispered conversations halted when
they entered a room, and an occasional joke at their
expense was shared at the servants' dinner table until
the butler put a stop to it. By early March, as the first
signs of spring brightened the estate, April had begun
to hope perhaps that the whole unfortunate business, as
Mrs. Wilson had called it, would indeed eventually be
forgotten.

But soon thereafter, Marjorie was again summoned to the housekeeper's chamber for a scolding.
April first heard about it from the scullery girl rather
than from Marjorie herself. The handsome lieutenant, a married man, had become annoyed with her
"chattiness and familiarity" and had requested that
another maid attend to his room for as long as he remained billeted at Alderlea. He had shared his concerns with his captain, who fortunately had known to
take the matter to the butler. If either of the officers
had complained directly to the lord or lady, Marjorie
would have endured a more serious punishment, but
as it was, she would be reprimanded and assigned to
other duties that would not bring her anywhere near
the lieutenant. Any further violations of the household rules and expectations would result in her immediate dismissal.

April knew that if servants weren't so difficult to replace, Marjorie would have been sacked already.

"I don't know how much longer I can put up with this," Marjorie grumbled later that afternoon as they worked on the household mending. "I wasn't even flirting."

"You were just being friendly," said April wryly, threading her needle.

"That's all it ever was on my part, honestly!" Marjorie jabbed her needle into her pincushion, sank back into her chair, and folded her arms, defiant. "*He* kissed *me.*"

Startled, April set her sewing down on her lap. "He *kissed* you? No one said anything about kissing."

"Well, of course he wouldn't mention *that*. He's married, and he's an officer, and I'm just a nobody housemaid from Warrington. I was making up his bed when he walked in, startling us both. He said it was a lovely surprise to find me there, and I made a joke about how it was always a surprise to find me working. He laughed, and then he just rushed over and kissed me, with my arms full of bedclothes and everything. I'm on thin ice already, as everyone knows, so I pulled away and told him I couldn't."

"What did he do? Did he threaten you?"

"No, not that. He got red in the face and begged my pardon. I told him not to mention it, no harm done, and I left." Marjorie frowned, eyes narrowing. "Obviously, he thought I might squeal on him, so he came up with his own version first, just in case."

"Maybe if you tell Mrs. Wilson what really happened—"

"That wouldn't do any good. She would still blame me for staying to talk to him instead of just bobbing a curtsey and scampering from the room the moment he walked in."

"It's not fair."

"What's ever fair for girls like us?" Marjorie asked scornfully, but April had no answer for her.

The next morning, April woke at half four o'clock, as she did every morning, and went to rouse Marjorie, only to find her bed empty. Her uniforms hung neatly on their pegs, but all of her belongings were gone.

Anxious, April quickly threw on her day uniform only to find a note in her apron pocket.

Marjorie had gone off to London, to find a new job and a fresh start. "Goodbye, chum," she signed off cheerily. "Thanks for making Alderlea more bearable, while it lasted. Think of me doing my bit of war work and be proud of your chum, and try not to miss me too much."

But a sudden pang of loss told April that it was too late. She already missed Marjorie more than she could have imagined only a day before.

Folding the letter, steadying herself with a deep breath, April finished dressing and pinned her hair up beneath her white cap, wondering how in the world she would break the news to Mrs. Wilson.

3
November 1910–June 1915

Helen

Helen would never forget the moment two years before when she realized with heartbreaking certainty that the only way to keep her beloved childhood home was to abandon it forever.

It was the sort of ironic tragedy that would have intrigued her father, the renowned classicist Heinrich Stahl, had he discovered it in one of the ancient Greek texts he studied and taught as a Professor of Literae Humaniores at Oxford. Helen had always adored and revered her father. His snug, paneled study, with its rich mahogany desk laden with manuscripts and floor-to-ceiling shelves packed with books and antiquities, was her very favorite room at Banbury Cottage, the only home she had ever known. The red-brick Edwardian residence on Divinity Road in the historic district was cozy but spacious enough for Helen, her parents, and her two sisters to share in comfort, with rosebushes and a pair of lovely plum trees in front and a larger, walled-in garden in back. Banbury Cottage was only a brisk twelve-minute walk to the Bodleian Library, a few minutes more to the Ashmolean. From childhood Helen had loved to stroll the route with her father, admiring the neighbors' front gardens, noting the alterations of the seasons in the foliage and flowers in the parks they passed, chatting in German, or discussing Greek myths and epic tales. Once ,as Helen ran home from school, a glimpse of her home from the top of a low rise in the curving street brought her to a halt, overcome with joy and affection. She vowed right then and there never to live anywhere else.

For many years, Helen truly believed it was a vow she could keep. At seventeen she began studying at Oxford, although as a woman she could not be admitted as a full student and would not be able to claim a degree. Her happiest hours were spent working as her father's secretary and research assistant, and while her mother often hinted that she and her elder sister, Penelope, would find husbands and homes of their own someday soon, neither had any inclination to begin the hunt.

"I shall never marry," Helen confided to her sister

one late summer afternoon as they walked home from a vigorous tennis match in which Helen had barely eked out a victory. Penelope's best friend's family had a court on the grounds of their estate, and they kindly allowed the Stahl sisters to play anytime they liked. "I cannot imagine I could ever love any home more than Banbury Cottage, or find any occupation I enjoy more than assisting Papa."

"Not marriage and motherhood?" teased Penelope. Her face was lightly dusted with freckles, as was Helen's own, her auburn hair a few shades darker. She was decidedly the most beautiful of the Stahl sisters, although Daphne, the youngest, was a close second. "Not even a leadership role in the Women's Social and Political Union, toiling side by side with the Pankhursts for woman suffrage?"

"The latter would be tempting," Helen admitted. "But not the former. I'd prefer to be an eccentric spinster aunt to your children and Daphne's."

"Daphne's, perhaps, but not mine," said Penelope. "I shall never marry either."

"Do you mean that?" asked Helen, surprised. "You're so lovely, you should have been the one called Helen."

Penelope rolled her eyes. "And you should have been Penelope, the faithful wife and queen?"

"No, that doesn't suit me. Atalanta, perhaps. I'm a swift runner."

"Yes, I've noticed. Without that speed, you never would have beaten me today."

"But Penny, why shouldn't you marry? You have so many admirers. When Papa invites his students home to dine with us, they barely acknowledge the rest of us, they're so busy gazing at you."

"That's not true," Penelope retorted, allowing a smile. "Well, if it is true, their attention is misplaced. None of them could ever be as dear to me as my sisters, or Margaret."

Helen nodded. Penelope and her best friend were so devoted to each other that Helen sometimes felt a bit jealous. "I often think that you would marry Margaret if you could," she teased.

"Perhaps I would," Penelope replied lightly, "but she's already engaged, and the neighbors would gossip. Nor would I be able to provide for her."

Something in her sister's tone gave Helen pause. "Is that why she's marrying Mr. Aylesworth, to be provided for? But her family is one of the wealthiest in Oxfordshire. What of her inheritance?"

"She'll receive a modest income through her mother, but her father's estate is entailed upon her elder brother. Margaret doesn't wish to be a burden to him."

"So she and Mr. Aylesworth—it's not a love match?"

"They are fond of each other," Penelope said, seeming to choose her words carefully. "They're good friends. He needs an heir, and she has always wanted children. Satisfactory matches have been based upon far less."

"I suppose," said Helen, dubious. They had reached the top of the rise, where the front gate and the roof of Banbury Cottage were visible in glimpses as the wind stirred the leafy boughs of the sheltering trees. "Poor Penny," she said sympathetically, "to be abandoned so cruelly."

"I haven't been abandoned entirely." Penelope hesitated, and again she seemed to weigh her words. "After the wedding, when the newlyweds move to Devonshire, I'll be going too, as Margaret's lady's companion."

"What? Penny—"

"Please don't say anything at home. It's all decided, but Mother and Papa don't know yet, and I should be the one to tell them."

"Certainly you should," said Helen, a bit dazed, and not from too much tennis in the bright summer sunshine. "But a lady's companion, Penny? Are you sure that's what you want?"

"It's the next best thing to what I truly want."

"And what is that? Once woman suffrage is won,

which surely can't be too far off, true equality will follow, and then—"

"No, Helen, no." Penelope shook her head and laughed, a bit sadly, or so Helen thought. "Not even Mrs. Pankhurst could help me gain my heart's desire. While this arrangement may seem a bit old-fashioned, it's more likely to assure my future happiness than any other scheme." She fell silent for a long moment. "Of course, things cannot carry on as before. Mr. Aylesworth requires fidelity—"

"Don't all husbands?"

"Well, yes, but our . . . friendship will necessarily change. The . . . closeness Margaret and I have shared—" Penelope inhaled deeply, pressing a hand to her chest as if it pained her. "It cannot be the same."

"Are you unhappy because Margaret will spend less time with you? Are you worried that you'll feel like the odd one out?"

"Yes. No." Penelope closed her eyes and gave her head a quick shake. "That's only part of it."

Helen studied her. "I don't understand. You seem utterly bereft. Are you sure you'll be happy with this arrangement—which, let's be honest, seems rather archaic?"

"It's better than having no place at all in Margaret's life." Penelope managed a reassuring smile.

"Mr. Aylesworth's diplomatic duties will require him to be in London or travel abroad quite often. He himself said that he's grateful I'll be there to keep Margaret company in his absence."

"Well, at least he isn't jealous of your friendship. And Margaret won't be married for another eight months. You have time to reconsider." Inspired, Helen added, "Perhaps one of Papa's students will sweep you off your feet unexpectedly."

"Believe me," said Penelope wryly, "nothing would be more unexpected."

"What about the handsome Mr. Herridge? Or the brilliant Mr. Purcell?"

Helen winced. "Not for me, thank you. They're so old, nearly thirty."

"Practically ancient."

"Also, I think Mr. Purcell prefers you."

"Nonsense. He thinks you're beautiful and I'm annoying. He's always picking apart my arguments, seeking miniscule flaws in my logic."

"That's precisely it," said Penelope, smiling, as they descended the rise and approached their own front gate. "He respects your mind enough to take your arguments seriously. Another man wouldn't want you to join the conversation at all. It's not just because you're his tutor's daughter, either."

"Certainly not. It's because he dislikes me and wants to prove me wrong at every opportunity."

Penelope laughed, a true, full-hearted laugh this time. It made Helen happy to hear it.

The days passed. Summer blazed brilliantly and faded into autumn. All too soon, as Margaret's maid of honor, Penelope became so busy with preparations for the upcoming wedding that Helen felt she hardly saw her anymore.

"Come with me to London for the suffrage demonstration tomorrow," Helen begged one November day. "We're going to march from Caxton Hall to the Houses of Parliament to protest Mr. Asquith's betrayal of his campaign promise to allow limited women's suffrage. We suffragettes supported him, raised funds for him—and how has he repaid us as Prime Minister?"

"Not well, I assume?"

"Not well at all! The suffrage bill passed its first and second readings, but he refused to let it proceed. Now he's called for a general election, Parliament will dissolve at the end of the month, and nothing more will be done on our account." Helen seized her sister's hand. "The greater our numbers, the stronger our message. Please say you'll come."

"I'm sorry." Penelope squeezed her hand before letting go. "I have plans with Margaret."

"Change your plans. Bring her along. We'll all go together."

Penelope shook her head, smiling. "I'm sorry but it's simply not possible. Margaret has a gown fitting."

"Well, bring the dressmaker too," said Helen, laughing at herself, knowing there was nothing for it. Fortunately, she had already arranged to meet some girlfriends at the train station, and together they would ride into London, march to Westminster, and return to Oxford by nightfall.

The demonstration began at noon with a rally at Caxton Hall in Westminster. Clad in a deep purple skirt, white shirtwaist, and dark green wool coat and matching hat, a satin sash bearing the phrase "Women's Will Beats Asquith's Won't" draped from her right shoulder to left hip, Helen cheered and applauded the speakers, her heart thrilling to their brave, inspiring words. Next she and her friends joined their assigned group of twelve and took their place about two-thirds of the way back from the head of the procession, which was led by Mrs. Pankhurst and the other suffrage dignitaries who formed the official delegation. The delegation would attempt to enter the Palace of Westminster at St. Stephen's entrance and demand an audience with the Prime Minister. Meanwhile, the roughly three hundred other marchers would demonstrate peacefully in Parliament Square.

A cold, brisk wind buffeted the marchers as they set off, brandishing their signs and banners with dignified resolve as they made their way to Victoria Street, which they followed to Parliament Square. The event had been widely publicized, and members of the press and curious onlookers lined every block of the route. As her group drew closer to Parliament Square, Helen observed with some trepidation that a large crowd of angry men, spectators as well as policemen, awaited them at the Westminster Abbey entrance.

"What should we do?" one of Helen's friends asked fearfully as up ahead, shouts from the men met with cries of alarm from the women.

"The women in front of us are marching on," Helen replied, more bravely than she felt. "We shall do the same." The police had protected them during previous demonstrations when angry onlookers threatened violence. She trusted they would do the same that day.

The procession had slowed, but still the women moved ever forward—until, suddenly, Helen felt as if they had slammed into a wall. All around them, men shoved the marchers back, shouting furiously, as the women struggled to stay within their groups in formation. Hats were knocked from the women's coiffures;

sashes were torn off and flung into the gutters. Ears blistering from the men's ugly epithets, Helen braced herself and grimly continued on, gasping aloud when she saw one woman take an elbow to the nose, streaming blood, another a fist to the eye. To the left and to the right, her comrades were being slapped, struck, shoved to the ground, seized around the torso and hauled away by men in suits and men in laborers' clothing, their faces twisted in ugly rage.

"Be careful!" a woman cried out somewhere behind her. "They're dragging women off down the alleys!"

A frisson of alarm ran through Helen. Struggling to keep her feet as the crowd surged around her, she looked wildly about for the police, only to spot several officers shouting and jeering at the women they had been assigned to protect, striking one, shoving another, grabbing others by the arms and hauling them out of the procession. Suddenly Helen felt rough hands groping her. She cried out in pain as a man squeezed her breasts and wrenched, tearing buttons from her coat as she stumbled and fell back, shocked and disoriented.

Steadying herself, she rejoined what was left of the march. She had become separated from her friends, but she steeled herself, chest aching and anger rising. She took one step forward, and then another. Hours passed in which it seemed she progressed barely inches, but she did not turn back, even as other women, bruised and bleeding, stumbled out of the lines and headed back toward Caxton Hall. Up ahead, just beyond the gauntlet of raging men, Helen glimpsed battered suffragettes holding up torn sashes and broken signs in Parliament Square, some parading as planned, jaws set and expressions defiant. Others berated the police and begged them to intercede, only to be arrested for their trouble.

Thirsty, sore, and increasingly fatigued, Helen saw a clearing open up a few yards ahead and tried to make her way to it—only to be brought to an abrupt halt as two men seized her, one on each arm. "Steady there, lass," a policeman growled near her ear as he hauled her toward a wagon. "A few weeks in Holloway will settle you down all right."

Helen felt a surge of fear at the dreaded name and tried to wrest herself free, but she was exhausted and the men were stronger. They easily lifted her dragging feet off the pavement and shoved her inside, locking the door behind her.

For two hours or more she and her unfortunate fellow captives sat on hard benches in the back of the dim, increasingly crowded police wagon, sharing information and tending one another's wounds as best they could. Eventually, when the wagon was overfull, the captives were taken not to the dreaded, notorious Holloway prison as they had feared, but to the Bow Street Police Station in Covent Garden. Soon Helen was processed and assigned to a cell, where she and her companions refused to eat and demanded the status of political prisoners. "You'll be treated like the common hooligans you are," the scowling matron retorted.

The suffragettes resigned themselves to an indefinite wait. Night had fallen, and the stone walls of the cell radiated cold, but Helen wrapped herself in the thin, coarse blanket she had been issued and ignored the gnawing hunger pangs in her stomach. The women prayed and sang together until they grew too weary for anything but sleep. Some managed to lie down, two to a bench, while others sat and leaned back against the walls or one another, but restlessness and chagrin kept Helen awake. Other suffragettes were arrested rather regularly, but Helen had never been. She hoped her family knew what had happened and where she was. She could well imagine the worry and embarrassment she had caused them.

She was still brooding over how she could make amends to her parents without renouncing the cause when the matron approached the cell door, a ring of keys jingling in her hand. "Miss Stahl?" she barked.

Helen sat up straighter and raised her hand. "I am Miss Stahl."

"Come with me. You're free to go." The matron swung open the barred cell door. "Leave the blanket."

Helen stood, but then she hesitated. "Why am I free to go? What about my companions?"

"My orders are for you. Everyone else stays."

Helen promptly sat back down. "Then I shall stay too."

Some of the women applauded drowsily, but one of the older women hushed them. "You should leave while you can," she told Helen. "Tell everyone what happened to us out there and how we're being treated."

"Are you coming or not?" Peeved, the matron began easing the door closed but left a gap. "It's up to you. Your father paid your fine and we don't give refunds."

Helen's heart thumped. "My father is here?" She wasn't sure whether to be relieved or mortified. To think that he had come so far on her account, and on a Friday! He must have cancelled his afternoon tutorials and left Oxford the moment he learned of her arrest, and now he was missing formal hall.

"Go on, dearie," the older women urged. "Don't leave him waiting."

"Wish my father would come for me," another woman remarked, to subdued laughter. "I'd go in a heartbeat."

Helen was tempted to stay, not only to show solidarity with her sister suffragettes, but to avoid her father's weary rebukes. Still, she would have to face him eventually, so she might as well get it over with.

Offering her scratchy blanket to the older woman, she left the cell and followed the matron through a maze of grim, poorly lit corridors to an office where a bored-looking clerk shuffled papers and stamped documents with official seals and eventually indicated that she was free to go.

"Worried your father sick, you have," the matron muttered as she escorted Helen to reception, giving her a little shove through the doorway for emphasis. "You should be ashamed of yourself, ungrateful girl. He's been pacing for the better part of an hour."

Helen braced herself for an onslaught of questions and rebukes from her father—but she found herself facing a taller, slimmer, and much younger man who paced away from her, turned, and halted abruptly when he saw her.

Wavy brown hair, piercing green eyes, high, angular cheekbones—Mr. Purcell. She was so astonished, she gasped.

"Miss Stahl," he said, his glance swiftly examining her from head to toe. "Good Lord. Are you all right? Have you been mistreated?" His expression hardened as he turned to the matron, who was hastily closing the door between them. "If Miss Stahl has been in any way abused," he snapped, striding toward her, "I swear you'll sincerely regret it—"

"I'm all right," said Helen, seizing his coat sleeve to restrain him. She must look truly dreadful to have provoked such indignation. "I'm only exhausted—and hungry."

"Right. Of course you are." The matron forgotten, he patted his coat, frowning, then brightened as he took a small red apple from his front pocket. "Will this do until we can find you something more substantial?"

"Yes, thank you." Helen plucked the apple from his hand and took a larger bite than was perhaps polite. It was the sweetest, most delicious apple she had ever tasted, unless that was the influence of her hunger. She swallowed and asked, "Where's my father?"

"In Oxford, of course. He had lectures and tutorials, so I offered to come fetch you in his place."

"But the matron told me—" She broke off, but not quickly enough.

"She told you your father had come." Mr. Purcell appeared wounded. "You certainly do look very young, but I hope I don't seem so terribly old." Before she could decide whether to give reassurances or an apology, he offered her his arm. "Come. Let's get you home. If we hurry, we may catch the late train."

"And if we miss it?" she asked, taking his arm as they headed for the exit.

"Then we'll find a train going in our direction, take it as far as we can, and drive from there."

They hurried outside, where Mr. Purcell quickly hired a cab, promising the driver an ample gratuity if he got them to the train station within a quarter hour. "Done," the driver declared cheerfully, barely waiting for them to seat themselves before he chirruped to the horses and sped off.

In the first, or perhaps second, stroke of good luck Helen had found all day, they arrived with minutes to spare. Before Helen could offer to pay her own fare, Mr. Purcell purchased two tickets, and then they were running to the platform, climbing aboard as the whistle blew, and settling into their seats even as the train chugged out of the station. Immediately Mr. Purcell had a quiet word with the porter, who returned soon thereafter with a cart of tea and sandwiches. "Tuck in," Mr. Purcell instructed, and she almost forgot to thank him before doing exactly that.

By the time the train left the city behind, she was feeling much better—sated, comfortable, and relieved, but also a trifle embarrassed. "Thank you for breaking me out of prison," she said lightly.

"Happy to be of service."

"You must think I'm quite a little fool to end up in such a dreadful place."

"Not at all. I entirely support the suffrage cause—" He paused, wincing. "If not all of Mrs. Pankhurst's methods."

Helen smiled to conceal her annoyance. "Smashing windows as a form of protest is a time-honored British tradition."

"Perhaps, but when such forms of protest regularly lead to broken bones and prison sentences for the protestors, alternative methods might be considered."

"If women's bones are broken in a protest," said Helen, voice trembling, hot tears springing into her eyes as she remembered rough, groping hands, "perhaps the fault lies with the despicable men who inflicted the injuries, and the contemptible police who stood by and allowed it to happen—or worse yet, joined in, abandoning any oaths they may have sworn as peace officers!"

She turned away and stared determinedly out the window, but she felt Mr. Purcell studying her. Then she felt his hand clasp hers, resting on the seat between them. "Were you ill-treated?" he asked quietly, his voice too low for anyone else to overhear.

Still gazing out the window, she nodded. "Others endured far worse than I."

"Do you—would you prefer to go directly to a physician or nurse when we arrive in Oxford? Or perhaps this is a matter for the police?"

"Goodness, no." Shuddering, Helen turned to face him. "I've had enough to do with the police for one day, thank you very much."

"Miss Stahl—" He studied her intently for a moment, then let his gaze fall to their clasped hands. He promptly pulled his away. "I'm concerned about you, but I confess I'm at a loss for what assistance to offer. If you would like to tell me what happened today—"

"I can see that I *must* tell you," she interrupted, "or you will imagine something quite worse." And so she described, as best she could remember, everything that she had witnessed and experienced since setting out with her group of twelve from Caxton Hall.

"I'm terribly worried about my friends, the Oxford girls who attended the march with me," she added when she had finished the harrowing tale, fresh tears springing to her eyes. "None of them were arrested with me, and I don't know what has become of them."

"I can put your fears to rest on that account, if nothing else," Mr. Purcell said. "They're all home, safe and sound. When they saw you being put in the police wagon, they left the demonstration and took the next train back to Oxford. They immediately went to tell your mother, and she telephoned your father. I happened to be with him when he received the call, so I offered to come in his place."

"I'm so grateful that you did," said Helen fervently. "Were my parents very distressed?"

"I haven't seen your mother," he said. "Professor Stahl was concerned about your safety, as any parent would be, but he was not overly anxious."

"That's fortunate," she said, relieved. Her father had been experiencing some shortness of breath and chest discomfort in recent months, and his doctor had advised him to avoid emotional upset.

As the train carried them homeward, the conversation turned to other, more pleasant matters—the Stahl family's annual dinner party in early December to mark the end of Michaelmas term and herald the festive season, to which Mr. Purcell had been invited, along with her father's other students; a book her father had recently published, to significant acclaim; and Mr. Purcell's doctoral research on Philoctetes, archer and hero of Troy, which he hoped would culminate in a book as well.

"Philoctetes is best known from Sophocles's play and Homer's *Iliad*," said Mr. Purcell, quickly adding, "which, of course, you already know. I intend also to draw upon Aeschylus's and Euripides's plays about him, but only fragments remain."

"Perhaps you shall find the rest," remarked Helen, smiling.

"If I did, the discovery would likely make my academic career. At the very least, it might allow me to continue it."

"Why shouldn't you continue? You're in no danger of dismissal from the program. You're one of my father's star pupils."

"Listen at keyholes, do you?"

"Only occasionally, and it wasn't necessary in this case. My father has made no secret of his preference. Don't tell the others, though," she added hastily. "I wouldn't want any hurt feelings."

"Your secret is safe with me. And thank you for your vote of confidence, but your father isn't the obstacle."

When he didn't elaborate, Helen remarked, "As I recall, Philoctetes competed for the hand of my namesake, the princess of Sparta."

"Indeed, and he lost decisively. My focus isn't his thwarted pursuit of the most beautiful woman in the world, though, but his abandonment on the isle of Lemnos by his shipmates. They were so offended by the smell of his festering wound that they essentially left him there to die."

"With friends like those, who needs Trojan enemies?"

"Quite right. My premise is that Philoctetes's sufferings presage his—" Abruptly Mr. Purcell broke off, chagrined. "Festering wounds, agony, abandonment. What fine topics of conversation I choose to discuss with a young lady. My sister scolds me that this is precisely why I remain unmarried."

"At the ripe old age of?" Helen prompted.

"Thirty."

Mr. Purcell wasn't so ancient after all, though still ten years older than herself. "I must respectfully disagree with your sister," said Helen. "I think this is an excellent subject for conversation. There are deep human truths to discover in pain and suffering. And in the fear of abandonment, in the rejection and isolation all too intrinsic to the human experience."

He regarded her for a moment, eyebrows rising. "I'm going to tell my sister you've refuted her theory."

"Ah, but tragically, I haven't," said Helen, feigning regret. "To disagree is not to disprove. Until you marry a young lady with whom you've discussed these grim topics, your sister may yet be proven correct."

The sound of his laughter was drowned out by a deep, resonant blast of the train's whistle as they approached Oxford station. Helen found herself without anything to say as they disembarked and passed through the concourse. Mr. Purcell probably intended to escort her home, although he had not offered to, and she shouldn't presume, since he had done so much for her already. Once outside the station, she prepared to bid him goodnight and walk home alone when he gestured to a parked automobile. "Shall I give you a lift home?"

She looked at him, incredulous, then again at the automobile, a Rolls-Royce Silver Ghost, gleaming in the moonlight. "Certainly," she joked, playing along. "Do you think the owner will object if we take her for a spin, as long as we return her unharmed?"

"He won't mind at all." Mr. Purcell opened the passenger-side door and gestured for her to climb in. When she didn't, he regarded her quizzically and stepped back as if to clear her path. "Come on, then. All aboard. Never fear, I'm an excellent driver."

She didn't budge. "This is your car?"

"Yes, Miss Stahl," he replied, the first hint of exasperation in his voice that she had heard all day, which was really quite remarkable given the circumstances. "Please take a seat and I'll crank 'er up."

Feeling foolish, she did as he asked. In her defense, there was no reason why she should have known he owned such a luxurious automobile, or any automobile at all. He had always come to Banbury Cottage on foot, and he was only a student, after all.

There was more to Mr. Purcell than she had realized, Helen thought as he drove her through the darkened streets toward home. He was certainly not the irritable old curmudgeon she had imagined him to be.

When they arrived at Banbury Cottage, Helen's parents appeared in the doorway to meet them as soon as they passed through the gate. Her father began interrogating her the moment she crossed the threshold, his German accent more pronounced than usual, a sure sign of his perturbation. Her mother fussed over her disheveled appearance and asked her again and again if she was *sure* she was all right. Then Daphne darted into the room, flung her arms around her sister, and began peppering her with more questions, bursting with curiosity and excitement. Helen looked around at her family, unable to reply to one for listening to another, until Mr. Purcell's voice rose above the din. "Miss Stahl is unharmed but terribly fatigued. Perhaps the questions can wait until tomorrow?"

"Yes, yes, of course, tomorrow," her father said, seizing Mr. Purcell's hand and shaking it vigorously. "I cannot thank you enough for bringing her home to us."

Helen would have thanked him again too, but her

mother and Daphne were ushering her upstairs, mandating a hot bath and a good night's rest. She glanced back over her shoulder as they led her away, but Mr. Purcell was engrossed in conversation with her father and did not notice.

The next morning, Helen soberly told her parents what she had witnessed at the demonstration and patiently accepted their rebukes, lovingly meant, that she should not have put herself at such risk. She understood their point of view better after reading the newspapers. Eyewitnesses and victims alike reported utterly brutal treatment at the hands of the mob—marchers groped and beaten, women's skirts lifted over their heads, men seizing women from behind and clutching their breasts, women hauled into alleys and assaulted. Police were observed dragging suffragettes aside, beating them, and throwing them back into the hostile crowds for further abuse, their crimes preserved forever in photographs.

In one of the most shocking incidents, the revered suffragette May Billinghurst, who had been partially paralyzed by polio as a child and was obliged to convey herself in a tricycle chair, had been overturned and dumped onto the street by the police. Two officers had picked her up, twisted her arms behind her back, causing her agonizing pain, and pushed and dragged her down a side street. Other officers followed, trundling her empty chair. They threw her to the ground in front of a gang of young street toughs, removed the valves from the chair's wheels to render them useless, and left her to her fate. The joke was on the police, though, for the rough fellows possessed gallantry the officers did not. Instead of assaulting Miss Billinghurst as the police had expected, they rescued her, repairing her chair and conveying her safely to Caxton Hall.

More than one hundred suffragettes had been arrested, but all had been released by nine o'clock, only two hours later than Helen. Two or three men had also been arrested, none of them police officers.

"Promise me you won't attend any more of these rallies," her mother begged, as Daphne chimed in her own pleas. Helen couldn't bear to do that, but she did promise to be more watchful and cautious in the future—if there ever were more rallies to attend. She suspected the WSPU would shift tactics in the aftermath of what the suffrage press was already calling Black Friday.

Helen hoped to see Mr. Purcell soon, to thank him again for relieving her father of the burden of fetching her home, but he did not call at Banbury Cottage, at least not when she was at home to receive him. Though disappointed, she looked forward to seeing him at her family's party at the end of the term. She had some thoughts about Philoctetes and the fragments of Aeschylus's work she hoped to discuss with him.

But when the long-awaited day came, the party had been underway for hours and still he had not appeared. Puzzled, and a bit annoyed, Helen managed to catch her father alone long enough to ask why he supposed Mr. Purcell refused to be more punctual.

"He's not late, *Liebling*," her father said. "He's not coming."

"Why not?" she protested. "He always attends our—your parties. What could have enticed him away?"

Her father shrugged, regretful. "Perhaps Mr. Purcell found himself unable to celebrate, knowing that he won't be joining us for Hilary term. I organized a farewell dinner for him a few days ago. We all said our goodbyes then."

"Mr. Purcell finished his degree?" asked Helen, bewildered. "I thought he had a year or two left."

"He does, but he has withdrawn from Oxford." Her father sighed. "What a shame. He has a very good mind and would have made an excellent professor."

"But—" Helen shook her head. "I don't understand. Why would he abandon work he loved?"

"Filial duty, *Liebling*. For years Arthur's father indulged his desire for an Oxford education, but the elder Mr. Purcell always intended for Arthur to join the family business eventually. Apparently he considered Arthur's thirtieth birthday in October to be a finish line of sorts. Time to put aside old plays and epic poems and join the working world."

"*My* father isn't the obstacle," Helen murmured, thinking aloud, remembering Mr. Purcell's cryptic remarks on the train. "*His* father is."

"Arthur convinced his father to let him finish the term, hoping his father would change his mind in the meantime, but he only became more resolute."

"Poor Mr. Purcell," said Helen, heartbroken for him. "Do you happen to know what the family business is? Please tell me they deal in antiquities, or run a museum, or plan excursions to Greece, or—"

"Manufacturing." Her father clasped her shoulder in a gesture of comfort, his face full of tender commiseration. "Sewing machines, or perhaps it was parts for industrial sewing machines. Perhaps both. Or was it looms?"

"What's the difference?" asked Helen morosely. Whatever it was, it wasn't studying ancient texts about Philoctetes. It was commerce, and as a profession it was particularly unsuitable for a scholar of the classics.

In the days that followed, Helen wanted to offer Mr. Purcell her most sincere sympathies, but he had left Oxford, and she was reluctant to ask her father for his postal address and prompt uncomfortable questions. She longed to know if working for his family's business had turned out to be unexpectedly rewarding, or at least not the miserable fate he had clearly tried to avoid. She truly hoped so.

Months passed, and then a year. Helen heard nothing of Mr. Purcell, but she thought of him now and then and wished him well, wherever he was.

Then, unexpectedly, tragedy brought him back into her life.

Her father's heart condition had worsened over time, so much so that he began to contemplate the unthinkable: retirement. He had just declared his intention to reduce his tutoring load and prepare to accept emeritus status in five years when, two days after the close of Trinity term, he suffered a heart attack at his campus office while marking exams. He died the next morning.

Helen, her sisters, and her mother were utterly bereft. Shattered by loss, they informed the university, arranged a funeral, and accepted condolences from hundreds of colleagues and friends. Several former students spoke at the memorial service, among them Mr. Purcell, grief-stricken and dignified as he honored his mentor and friend. He approached Helen at the reception afterward, and they chatted briefly, but she was barely holding herself together and she forgot to ask him anything about himself and his new career.

She trusted he would forgive her.

Since Penelope returned to Devonshire a few days after the funeral and her mother was preoccupied with poor, heartbroken young Daphne, the melancholy business of settling her father's estate fell to Helen. Working with his executor, she discovered that her father had left behind only a few miniscule debts, easily settled from the household accounts. Although this came as a tremendous relief, he had made almost no provision for future income. There would be a small pension from the university, and some earnings from his books, while they remained in print. But the latter income would be negligible, as his books were not the sort one would find on the shelves of a typical home alongside Dickens and Austen, but might, in a good year, sell a few copies to scholars and academic libraries.

Helen painstakingly went over the ledgers with her father's trusted executor, and then again with her mother, but each time she reached the same unhappy conclusion: They had scarcely enough money to live on at present, and eventually even that would run out. Their best hope—their only choice, really—was to sell Banbury Cottage, find more affordable lodgings, and live frugally from that day forward. Although it would deeply sadden them to leave their cherished home, they assured one another that it would all work out in the end.

Throughout the summer, as Helen and her mother made inquiries and arrangements, many of her father's former students and colleagues called to pay their respects, to inquire about their needs, and to offer their services. One former student who visited weekly was Arthur Purcell, who never failed to bring a welcome gift for their dinner table or the library. In fair weather, he and Helen frequently walked together through the beautiful Oxford campus with its stunning architecture and familiar gardens, every scene evoking tender memories of her father.

In early September, Mr. Purcell tactfully asked about their future plans. Knowing that he must have guessed their financial straits, Helen saw no point in embellishing the truth for the sake of politeness. She told him frankly that they could not afford to keep Banbury Cottage, and although parting from the home that held so many cherished memories would rend their hearts, they would manage.

"If I could find a position as a tutor, my earnings would help quite a bit," Helen mused aloud as they strolled along the Thames. "But what might be available in Devonshire for an aspiring young female tutor with no teaching experience is another question. I'm sure I'm capable of instructing children in Greek, German, and—"

"Hold on." Abruptly Mr. Purcell halted, placing a hand on her arm to bring her to a stop too. "Why Devonshire? Surely you don't have to go so far to find an affordable home."

"I'm sure I mentioned it," said Helen. Hadn't she? "As you know, Penelope serves as a lady's companion in Devonshire. Her employers have offered us the charming gatehouse on their estate, and for a pittance. They'd let us have it gratis except my mother refuses to accept charity."

"What about your father's collection of antiquities?" Mr. Purcell asked, brow furrowing. "I could help you arrange to sell them. I could put you in touch with an auction house, or with my contacts at various museums, private collectors—"

"Thank you, but except for a few favorite pieces he left to me and my sisters, my father bequeathed his entire collection to the Ashmolean Museum." Smiling through a pang of loss, she resumed walking along the river, and Mr. Purcell promptly fell in step beside her. "You would hardly recognize his study, the shelves and walls are so depleted."

"I'm truly very sorry that it's come to this."

"Please don't think badly of my father. He never meant to leave us in such straits, and we'll be perfectly content. Well, perhaps not *perfectly*—"

"If there is anything I might do to secure your happiness—" Mr. Purcell halted again and took her hand. "Miss Stahl, for more than a year I've longed to ask you, but you've made your love for your home and your abhorrence of marriage abundantly clear—"

"*Abhorrence* is a bit strong. My parents had a wonderful, loving marriage. You imply that I want the custom abolished, but—" Words abruptly failed her. He had longed to ask her . . . what? In context, only a few very particular options made sense.

"My dear Miss Stahl—Helen—" He took her other hand. "I love you. I've adored you ever since you strode out of that prison cell more concerned for your father's inconvenience than your own suffering. And then you devoured that apple as if your only desire was to build up your strength for the next battle."

"I didn't devour it," Helen protested, her cheeks growing warm. "I was very hungry. I hadn't eaten since breakfast. This is a very odd proposal."

"It's my first attempt," he said wryly. "Please, dearest Helen, would you do me the honor of becoming my wife?"

Her heart was pounding, but she tried to keep her

voice steady. "Are you asking me out of a sense of duty to my father, some misplaced obligation to provide for his widow and children?"

"Good God, Helen, no. I wouldn't marry a woman I didn't want to spend the rest of my life with just to keep a roof over her family's head. I would buy her a house."

He tossed that off as if it were eminently reasonable, as if one bought houses for friends every day. But that was not what riveted her attention. "You want to spend the rest of your life with me?"

He squeezed her hands, nodding. "I'll repeat myself in Greek, if it would convince you."

"I wouldn't annoy you beyond reason, always besting you in argument?"

"Even so." He raised her hands to his lips and kissed them. "Now you're deliberately tormenting me. I think you love me and want to say yes, but you want to prolong my suffering a bit longer."

"Top marks for you, Mr. Purcell." Happy tears sprang into her eyes, and she kissed him.

They married in December in Oxford, in her father's favorite chapel. Rather than choose between her sisters, Helen had two maids of honor. Margaret attended as Penelope's guest, as did Margaret's one-year-old daughter, Hestia, upon whom Penelope doted like a proud auntie. As for Helen's mother, after Arthur became her son-in-law and his generosity could not be mistaken for charity, she permitted him to pay off her mortgage. Banbury Cottage was hers, and she need never again fear losing it.

Until Helen accepted Arthur's proposal and accepted invitations to meet his family, she had not understood that his late grandfather was the founder of Purcell Products Company, which manufactured sewing machines for the home and for industry, as well as small motors and parts for other factory machines. In hindsight, it all made sense—the expensive car, the fine suits, his father's insistence that he help run the family business. Of course she had heard of the Purcell empire—she and everyone else in Britain—but it would have been impolite to inquire if he were connected to *those* Purcells.

"I assumed your family business was a small concern," Helen admitted while they honeymooned in Greece. "A wholesale warehouse or a repair shop."

Arthur burst out laughing. "You thought I would throw over my Oxford education to work in a repair shop?"

"Well, why not? The pull of filial duty is very strong, and it's really only a matter of scale."

"You're absolutely right, of course," he said, kissing her.

They kept two houses, a gracious estate in Oxford and a smaller residence in Birmingham, where the Purcell Products Company's largest factory was located, and where Arthur was required to work alongside his father and elder brother four days a week. The other three he worked from his study at their home in Oxford, which they both preferred. Often Helen did not accompany him to Birmingham, where she knew no one and had little to do but read and walk alone and wait restlessly for Arthur to come home from work at the end of the day. As the months passed, she remained in Oxford more often, contenting herself with her family, friends, books, and suffrage business in her husband's absence. She could walk to Banbury Cottage to visit her mother and Daphne anytime she wished, so although she once believed she must abandon her beloved childhood home to save it by marrying Arthur, the cottage had not been lost to her at all.

Helen and Arthur had planned to celebrate their first anniversary in Italy, but after war broke out, they decided a romantic winter holiday in Scotland would be just the thing. By that time, the British Army had added half a million soldiers to the ranks and was urgently calling for more recruits, and each one would need uniforms, weapons, and ammunition.

Industrial sewing machines were essential to the war

effort, but several smaller Purcell Products factories were swiftly converted to other war manufacturing. Helen found the change disconcerting, although she well understood the necessity. Great Britain had not sought this dreadful war, but Britons would not shirk from their duty to stand by their allies and to defend their island. She saw less of Arthur as the military's insatiable need for shells and bullets obliged him to work longer, more strenuous hours. In this he was not alone. The entire munitions industry, longtime arsenals and newly converted facilities alike, could not keep up with demand. The situation collapsed into a political controversy known as the Shell Crisis, which Arthur had no time to follow in the press but Helen did, almost obsessively.

By late spring, the Shell Crisis came to a tipping point. Parliament established the Ministry of Munitions to oversee production and to ensure that the military's needs were met. "I welcome the organization of a formalized chain of command," Arthur told Helen wearily after another very late night at the factory. "However, I'm concerned about potential bureaucratic interference that could decrease efficiency."

For a moment Helen could only stare at him, astonished to hear her scholarly husband sounding so much like a businessman industrialist—but of course, that was what he had become. She often missed the clever fellow who loved to read Greek poetry aloud to her, but she told herself he would return to her after the war. In the meantime, she must support him so he could carry out his important duties. A victory for the Allies depended upon his success.

One evening in June, after a fortnight away, Arthur at last came home to Oxford. Helen hurried to meet him when she heard him enter the foyer, but as she embraced him and took his hat and briefcase, she silently noted the shadows beneath his eyes, the deep groove that worry had carved between his brows. She had held dinner back in anticipation of his homecoming, and while they ate, he told her that his father had asked him to take charge of a long-idle sewing machine and parts factory. Shuttered in the depression that had followed the Panic of 1873, it had been cleared of its antique machinery and fitted out with modern technology for the manufacture of explosive shells.

By then Helen had learned that a request from Arthur's father was actually a command, and Arthur had surely accepted the promotion on the spot. There was nothing left for her to do but praise and encourage. "Congratulations, darling," she said, reaching across the table to take his hand. "Or rather, I should congratulate your father, for having the good sense to give you your own command at last instead of assisting your brother."

"That's not quite fair. I've learned a lot from Phillip," said Arthur. "He was working in industry while I was still whiling away the days scouring Greek tragedies for elusive meaning."

Helen regarded him for a moment, taken aback. He spoke almost as if he regretted his academic pursuits, the studies that had once enriched his life and had brought the two of them together. "My apologies to my absent brother-in-law," she said, sipping her wine, carefully setting the glass down. "So. Where is this new enterprise? Birmingham?"

"Thornshire, on the Thames on the outskirts of London."

"I've never heard of it."

"Most people haven't. Let's hope the Germans never do." He sighed and clasped his other hand over hers. "Darling, I'll have to remain in London throughout the week. No more jaunts to Oxford for long weekends. I wouldn't be able to visit for months at a time."

"But Oxford is so much closer to London than to Birmingham. I would have thought you'd be able to come more often, not less."

He shook his head. "My responsibilities simply won't allow it, certainly not until this blasted Shell

Crisis is resolved. Perhaps for the duration." He sat back in his chair and regarded her bleakly. "We'll keep this house, of course. We're both very fond of it, and you could never leave Oxford forever. I'll let the Birmingham place go. The question is—" He hesitated. "Will you come with me to London, or would you rather stay here?"

She was surprised he had to ask. "Of course I'll come with you, if the alternative is to spend months apart. In case you've forgotten, Mr. Purcell, I love you."

He raised her hand to his lips. "And I love you, Mrs. Purcell."

He smiled, but the relief in his eyes told her he had expected her to refuse. She was too bewildered to ask him why.

4
December 1914–June 1915

Lucy

Lucy's intuition had not misled her. At the 8 December meeting at the FA offices at Russell Square, the club representatives passed an official resolution declaring that they "heartily favoured" organizing a Pals battalion for Lord Kitchener's Army. The Footballers' Battalion, its ranks 1,350 strong, would be made up of professional and amateur players, staff, officials, and club enthusiasts. Since many footballers were small in stature, the usual army height requirements would be waived. While the battalion was undergoing military training in Britain, players would be granted leave to play for their clubs in league and cup matches. The Footballers' Battalion would officially be known as the 17th Service Battalion, Middlesex Regiment, the "Die-Hards."

On 15 December, more than four hundred footballers and enthusiasts showed up for a recruitment meeting at Fulham Town Hall, so many that at the last minute the organizers were obliged to move to a larger room. In rousing speeches greeted by thunderous applause, dignitaries from both football and politics lauded the formation of the Footballers' Battalion as a powerful and irrefutable response to critics who dared question their courage and loyalty. When the patriotic fervor in the room had reached its zenith, the chief recruiting officer for London took the stage and appealed for men to come forward and add their names to the battalion rolls.

"Were you the first to enlist?" Lucy asked Daniel as he described the event afterward.

"No," Daniel replied. "That honor went to Spider Parker."

Lucy nodded. Fred Parker, the enormously popular captain of Clapton Orient, was married with three children. Lucy and his wife were good friends. She took a steadying breath. "And you?"

"I was tenth." He studied her, awaiting her reaction, his expression pensive. "Tenth of thirty-five."

Although she had been expecting it, his announcement struck her like a physical blow. "I see," she said tremulously. "Thirty-five out of four hundred. Perhaps the other players wanted to speak with their wives before signing up." She knew she should tell him how proud of him she was, but the proper words wouldn't come. All she could think of was the bleakness of his inevitable absence.

"Darling, don't be unhappy." Quickly Daniel enfolded her in his embrace. "I don't have to report quite yet, and even after I begin my training, you and the boys can see me at my matches."

Blinking away tears, she drew back so she could meet his gaze. "That's true," she said, forcing steadiness and courage into her voice. "Your leaving will be more bearable that way. Most soldiers' wives aren't so fortunate."

She refrained from noting that thirty-five recruits fell far short of the battalion goal. Was it unpatriotic to hope that the ranks of the 17th Middlesex filled but slowly, delaying her husband's departure? She could only hope that the war would end before he had to leave England.

There were practical matters to discuss before Daniel reported for duty. Ideally, Lucy thought, they should have discussed them before he enlisted. First and foremost were their finances. Daniel expected to receive a final payment for his work on the Henderson offices soon, but while he was in the service, he would be unable to take on any new projects and his dividends from the partnership would be reduced. He would receive his soldier's pay, and the government provided a separation allowance for families of married recruits, but Daniel's military income would not make up the difference in his lost earnings as an architect and footballer.

"I'll have to draw from our savings," Lucy fretted. "That, or impose some sort of household austerity scheme."

"All will be well," Daniel assured her, and went over the accounts with her again. Lucy acknowledged that she could manage, but only if the war didn't drag on for a year or more, and only if they avoided calamitous household expenses such as replacing the roof or the furnace. Still, every soldier's wife had to confront the same problem of household economics, and Lucy was more fortunate than most. She would manage, because she must.

The cold December days passed and the festive season approached. Lucy did her best to make the holidays merry and bright for the family, but to her, the candles seemed dimmer, the hearth cooler, the carols dissonant. On the morning of Christmas Eve, she and

Daniel discovered shocking news in the early papers: On 23 December, a German aeroplane had crossed the Channel and had bombed Dover, the first time Great Britain had sustained an aerial attack. Heavy fog had obscured the view of the skies, so only a few observers had caught even a glimpse of the enemy plane. There had been no warning. A single bomb had exploded in a garden, breaking some windows in nearby homes and frightening everyone, but thankfully no one had been injured. Then, on 26 December, the newspapers reported that on Christmas Day, a German plane had flown up the Thames, presumably headed for London, but had been driven off by anti-aircraft guns near Erith.

Lucy and Daniel mentioned nothing of the thwarted attack to the children. It was unsettling to think that a malevolent German had fixed their city in his sights and might have killed them, and on the day sacred to peace and goodwill. Yet the Germans had already slaughtered countless thousands of Belgian and French civilians; Britons must be prepared to suffer the same. The English Channel afforded them some natural protection from bombardment and invasion, but centuries of history proved that the British Isles were hardly impenetrable. These two German aerial attacks showed beyond any doubt that another assault could and surely would come again, with little or no warning.

The festive season passed, and a New Year began. As recruiting efforts persisted and intensified, the ranks of the 17th Middlesex steadily grew. On 11 January, the first 250 recruits assembled outside West Africa House, Kingsway, under the watchful gaze of their commander, Colonel Charles Grantham, and other officers. Mr. Joynson-Hicks inspected the battalion, and then, as a massive crowd of onlookers roared approval, the 17th Middlesex marched through the streets of London six miles west to White City, where they would encamp at Machinery Hall.

Lucy, Jamie, and Simon were among the spectators on the pavement cheering and waving as the men marched past in a swinging stride, looking more like sportsmen than soldiers in their suits, caps, and topcoats, some with their hands in their pockets, others grinning and nodding to the crowd in appreciation for the hearty sendoff.

"There's Dad!" Jamie suddenly exclaimed, jumping up and down and waving frantically.

Craning his neck, Simon rose up on tiptoe, trying in vain to see over the taller people blocking his view. "Shall I pick you up?" Lucy offered, but Simon regarded her in horror and shook his head. She smothered a laugh. Of course he was much too old for that sort of thing, even if it meant missing one last glimpse of his father.

Not one *last* glimpse, she quickly corrected herself. They would see him in five days at White Hart Lane when Tottenham Hotspur played Bradford City. Daniel had already warned Lucy that he was ordered to return to White City immediately after the match, but he hoped to spend a few minutes with them before he was ushered away.

Lucy watched Daniel march off with his teammates until she could see him no longer. As the crowd began to disperse, she and her sons walked home, the boys talking excitedly about the parade and the war, Lucy murmuring responses when required, her thoughts elsewhere.

When they were nearly home they passed a schoolyard with a small seven-on-seven pitch. "May we play, Mum?" Jamie begged, pointing to a ball abandoned by one of the goals. "All of us, please? Just for a minute?"

"Please, Mum?" Simon quickly chimed in, tugging on her coat.

Suddenly memories flooded Lucy, impressions of the many meetings of the Dempsey Four, as Daniel called them, impromptu matches in the garden or any level field wherever they happened to be when the mood to play struck. They usually divided themselves into pairs, with Daniel and Simon versus herself and Jamie, and with Daniel playing at about ten percent and Lucy working as hard as she could, the teams were almost equally matched. The boys usually preferred to play sons versus parents, probably because they invariably won. Daniel played just well enough to challenge the boys and help them improve their skills, and Lucy couldn't bear to steal the ball away from her children or block any of their shots on goal.

Knowing her sons both wanted to play forward like their father, Lucy volunteered to play keeper. They exchanged a knowing look. "That'll be fine, Mum," said Jamie, "as long as you play properly."

"Truly try to block our shots," Simon added, for clarification. "We insist."

Lucy laughed. "Very well, I shall do my best. You may regret insisting."

The ball was slightly deflated, and the pitch was wet from melted snow, but they had good fun all the same. Lucy was quite overmatched, competing in her heeled boots and long skirt against two energetic, athletic boys in proper trousers and shoes, but she did not mind. How wonderful it felt to run until she was breathless, as the vigorous exercise and the thrill of competition drove her loneliness and worry to the back of her mind.

Or so it was until Simon stole the ball from her, made an astonishing feint around Jamie, and took a shot on the goal—only to watch the ball bounce off the cross-bar and soar out of bounds.

"Bad luck, Simon," Jamie called as his younger brother trudged off to collect the ball. "Brilliant run, though."

Simon did not acknowledge the praise or comically lament the missed goal, as he would have almost any other time. Lucy and Jamie exchanged a puzzled glance as, instead of kicking the ball in, Simon picked it up and carried it slowly back to them. Only after he drew nearer did Lucy realize that his eyes were red and he was breathless from the effort of holding back sobs. "It's not as much fun without Dad," he gulped, a tremor in his voice.

Lucy felt a pang of grief. "No, it isn't, is it, darling?"

Jamie jogged over and put an arm around his brother's shoulders. "It's all right, Simon. You still have me, and Dad will be back as soon as he wins the war."

Simon shrugged, eyes downcast.

"You know what we should do?" said Jamie, inspired. "We should train every day while Dad's in the army, and get really, really, really good. When he comes home and the Dempsey Four take the pitch again, he won't believe how much better we are!"

"If we play sons against parents, we'll catch him by surprise," said Simon, warming to the idea. "We could finally beat him for real! Unless—" Simon turned to Lucy. "You won't tell him about our secret plan, will you, Mum?"

"Well, I don't know," said Lucy. "After all, Dad and I would be on the same side. It seems like I ought to warn him."

"Don't warn him, please?"

Lucy pretended to consider it. "Very well. I'll keep your secret, but only because—" Suddenly she ran toward them and pretended to tickle their tummies. They darted away, yelping with laughter and surprise even though she didn't get close enough even to brush their coats with her fingertips. "Because secret plan or no, Dad and I will win because we're better!"

They headed home, pleasantly fatigued and ready for tea. Simon's spirits had improved tremendously, and he chattered happily as they walked along. Jamie caught Lucy's eye and nodded, as if to say that as the elder brother, he understood his responsibility to keep Simon's spirits up while their father was away. Her heart welled up with love, laced with gratitude and regret. A few weeks ago, Jamie's greatest concerns were football, school, and whether his parents would ever let him get a dog. At his age he should not have to bear heavier burdens, but how thankful she was that he was willing.

Lucy counted the days until Daniel's next match. There were only five, but she was as impatient to get through them as if there were five hundred. When she and the boys arrived at White Hart Lane, they passed the usual protestors with their signs and slogans, still determined to shut down the sport despite the existence of the Footballers' Battalion, not to mention the hundreds of players who had joined other regiments and were already in the fight. The protestors could not be unaware of the Footballers' Battalion either, as numerous posters within their line of sight announced its formation and encouraged spectators to join.

Simon paused to read one poster aloud. "Play the Greater Game!" his voice rang out as his eyes followed the bold black type over an illustration of three grinning Tommies kicking a German *Pickelhaube* like a football across a grassy field. "Sharpen up, 'Spurs. Come forward now to help to reach the goal of victory. Shoot! Shoot!! Shoot!!! And stop this Foul Play! Join the Football Battalion of the DIEHARDS (17th Middlesex)!"

Lucy assumed Simon was reading aloud for her benefit and Jamie's, but then he directed a steely glare over his shoulder toward the protestors. "Maybe you should make a Grousers' Regiment," he called, but they didn't hear him over their own voices.

"That'll do, Simon," said Lucy, taking his hand and briskly leading the boys inside.

They took their seats among the other spectators. More continued to arrive up until the moment the match began, but it seemed to Lucy that attendance, though still approaching twelve thousand, was down slightly despite the clear and sunny weather, as perfect a day for football as one could hope for in January. Daniel started at center forward, but although he did not make any errors, his pace lagged. In the first forty-five minutes of play he had two shots on goal, one of which went wide, the other deftly blocked by the Bradford City keeper.

"Dad seems tired," said Simon, frowning, as the whistle shrilled to mark the end of the first half.

"No doubt he is," said Lucy, her gaze fixed on Daniel as the players cleared the pitch. "Remember he has army training every day now, too, all that marching and drilling, while most of these other players have only football."

As she spoke, two gentlemen in fine topcoats and tall black top hats approached a platform that had been erected between the pitch and the spectators' seats on the home side. The audience had been buzzing with hundreds of conversations, but the din subsided as the gentlemen took center stage. The younger introduced the elder as William Joynson-Hicks, MP, the founder of the Footballers' Battalion. Thunderous applause greeted him, perhaps less to welcome the MP than to express appreciation for the troops. Mr. Joynson-Hicks certainly did his best to add to the battalion's numbers in his rousing speech, urging all fit and loyal men to follow the example of the players they admired as well as other enthusiasts like themselves and join the 17th Middlesex.

"I tell you, whether the censor likes it or not, that we are holding our own in Flanders and no more," Mr. Joynson-Hicks warned the audience, the rapt and the skeptical alike. "Unless we are able to send enormous numbers of reinforcements by April and May, we shall do no more than hold our own. Germany has Belgium and the North of France in a vise, and she will not give up until she is forced, step by step, by the lives of Englishmen and Frenchmen."

Lucy felt a stir of unease as the audience broke out in applause punctuated by low rumbles of concern. She hoped Jamie and Simon would not follow the thread of logic and realize that one of those lives sacrificed might be their father's.

"I am inviting you to no picnic," Mr. Joynson-Hicks

continued, his gaze stern and unflinching as it traveled over the audience. "It is no easy game against a second-rate team. It is a game of games against one of the finest teams in the world. It is a team worthy of Great Britain to fight!"

A louder cheer erupted on both sides of the field, and Lucy too, though silent, joined in the applause. Lastly Mr. Joynson-Hicks announced that would-be Die-Hards could enlist either there at White Hart Lane or later at West Africa House, then he bowed and left the platform.

The second half soon began, and after another hard-fought forty-five minutes, the match ended in a scoreless draw. The spectators began filing out of the stadium, and when Lucy saw Daniel breaking away from the other departing players to approach the stands, she urged the boys along and hurried to meet him at the edge of the pitch. Heedless of the amused onlookers, she flung herself into Daniel's embrace, holding him even tighter when he laughed and warned her that his sweaty, soiled jersey might offend. The boys cared even less about a bit of perspiration, if they even noticed; they flung their arms around their father, exclaiming about how happy they were to see him, how much they had enjoyed the game, how they wished he could come home with them but understood it was against the rules.

When Lucy felt Daniel pull away, she remembered that he had only minutes to spare, and she reluctantly released him. "How are your accommodations?" she asked, taking his hand and falling in step beside him as he headed toward the players' exit, glancing over her shoulder to make sure the boys were following after. "Comfortable, I hope."

"Tolerable, but only just. Machinery Hall is cavernous—vast, dim, cold, and damp. Already men are reporting sick with colds and coughs. Don't worry," he quickly added, no doubt spotting the concern in her eyes. "We're supposed to move to another building soon. How are things at home?"

"Oh, we're fine, everything's fine," she said, forcing cheer into her voice.

"I'm keeping an eye on things, Dad," Jamie interjected, jogging to catch up.

"Me too," Simon chimed in eagerly, beaming up at his father.

Lucy had to smile as Daniel laughed and tousled the boys' hair. She only wished he wasn't walking so briskly, so they could prolong their time together. "I've reunited with some old teammates," he said, turning his smile back to Lucy, warming her all over. "Vivian Woodward and Walter Tull have joined the Footballers' Battalion."

"Have they?" Vivian Woodward, an icon of British football, had represented England on the same Olympic gold medal teams as Daniel. He had played many years for Tottenham Hotspur, and had retired in 1909 only to sign with Chelsea a few months later. Walter Tull, the son of an immigrant from Barbados and an English girl from Folkestone, was one of the few Black players in the league. He had joined Tottenham the same year Woodward left it, but after two difficult seasons in which he had endured racist derision from opponents' crowds, he moved to Northampton Town, where he switched to halfback and was enjoying some of the best performances of his career, and, Lucy hoped, much kinder treatment from audiences. "It must feel good to be playing for the same side again."

"Indeed it is." Daniel squeezed her hand as they reached the players' exit. "Darling—"

"I know. You have to go." She lifted her face to his and kissed him, but the kiss lasted only a moment as the boys interposed, flinging their arms around their father again and chorusing their goodbyes. He kissed them each on the top of the head and bade them all farewell, his smile broad, his voice hearty, although

Lucy sensed the effort behind it. Then he turned and hurried off to join the other players who were due back at White City within the hour, soldiers once more. The boys called out goodbyes after him, and he paused once to wave back. Then he turned a corner and was gone.

Lucy tried to ignore the hollow loneliness in her chest, the lingering ache for Daniel that their brief reunion had only intensified. "Come along, boys," she said briskly, rearranging her soft woolen scarf around her neck. "Tea and homework await us—well, only tea for me."

"Lucky," Jamie grumbled cheerfully, and she had to smile. He complained about school as boys his age were expected to do, but he was clever and earned top marks.

On the way home, Jamie and Simon reminisced about the match, so engrossed in conversation that they were oblivious to her quiet sadness, and even to the changes that the war had wrought on their city. Perhaps they had already become accustomed to the ubiquitous recruiting posters on nearly every building and shop window, on the sides of passing omnibuses and tramcars, and to the young men who had answered their summons. Soldiers clad in khaki were everywhere, while middle-aged men too old for Lord Kitchener's Army patrolled the streets in the uniforms of Special Constables. Uniformed guards were posted at railway stations, and sentries at all public buildings—excluding Parliament, where ancient law decreed the military should not be present. The bells of clock towers no longer chimed the passing of the hours, and at night their faces were not illuminated, lest the sound and light act as beacons for German aircraft. Only a few months ago, Jamie and Simon would have stopped short at any one of these unexpected sights, astonished and curious, but by now all had faded into the background noise and clutter of the city.

Not so for Lucy. As they walked along, her gaze fell upon a poster that made her breath catch in her throat. "Women of England!" the bold headline thundered. "When the War is over and your husband or your son is asked 'What did *you* do in the Great War?' Is he to hang his head because you would not let him go? Women of England, do your duty! Send your men *to-day* to join our Glorious Army."

She felt no satisfaction in knowing that the poster's admonition did not apply to her. Would Daniel have resented her someday, she wondered, if she had not willingly let him go? Not that she'd had any say in the matter. Daniel had not included her in his decision, although it profoundly affected them both. If he were killed, God forbid, would she regret not entreating him to stay? She would far more willingly bear his resentment than his death—a possibility simply too horrible to contemplate.

By mid-February, the ranks of the 17th Middlesex had grown to 850 men, still insufficient for a complete battalion. Lucy learned from another football wife that Mr. Joynson-Hicks and Lord Kinnaird, president of the Football Association, had written to every professional player in England who had not yet enlisted to encourage them to do so. "A large number of some of the finest players in the Kingdom have already joined the Battalion, but we do not see your name amongst them," the gentlemen noted. "We do urge you as a patriot and a footballer to come to the help of the country in its hour of need."

No letter had come to the Dempsey household, but Lucy's chagrined friend had shown her the copy her husband had received. "You're lucky," her friend grumbled, folding the letter and shoving it into her pocket as if she would rather burn it. "*You* can hold your head high."

"I don't feel particularly lucky," Lucy admitted, but her friend brushed that aside and declared that she wished their places were reversed.

A few days later, Lucy and the boys again traveled to White Hart Lane to see Tottenham Hotspur play

Notts County, a 2–0 victory in which Daniel made a brilliant assist and several daring shots on goal which, though blocked, turned the momentum in the team's favor and electrified the crowd. When the family briefly reunited afterward, Lucy was relieved to see that Daniel seemed to be in good health and excellent spirits. He was getting used to the military training, he said, and their new quarters, while still cold and drafty, were drier and more comfortable than Machinery Hall. "We often march from White City to the West End," he said, already edging backward toward the exit, nearly late for the return journey. "We halt at Hyde Park near Marble Arch and rest for a quarter hour before marching back. It would be grand to see you all there by chance."

"Never mind chance. If you could tell us when, we would arrange it," Lucy called after him, but he had broken into a jog and was already out of earshot.

A fortnight later, Lucy was astonished by an unexpected visitor on their doorstep carrying a vegetable crate—her brother Edwin, clad in the khaki tunic, jodhpurs, service cap, and high leather boots of the Royal Flying Corps. "Edwin," Lucy exclaimed, frozen in the doorway, her hand on the latch. "What on earth—"

"Special delivery," he said, inclining his head to the crate. "Are you going to let me in?"

"Of course." She opened the door wide and moved out of the way.

He threw her a grin as he crossed the threshold, and she trailed after him to the kitchen. "Gifts from Mother's garden," he said, setting the crate on the table with a soft thud. Drawing closer, she glimpsed bundles of rhubarb, parsnips, and brussels sprouts tucked alongside jars of preserves and a paper sack from Brandt's bakery. "The bread is from me. I know how much you love their rye."

"Thank you," she replied automatically, still astounded that he was standing there, dressed as he was. "What are you doing in that uniform?"

"Showing off, obviously," he replied. "What? You didn't think I was going to let Daniel seize all the glory, did you?"

"What does Mother think?"

He shrugged. "She was a bit weepy at first, as one might expect. Alice, however, is exceedingly proud." He glanced around. "Where are my nephews?"

"At school, as you should have guessed, being a schoolmaster yourself."

"Of course." He removed his hat and tapped it lightly against his leg, peering around as if he hoped to spot the boys in a corner regardless. "Bad luck. I must be off in a moment. Looks like I'll miss them."

A trifle exasperated, Lucy gestured, taking in his uniform from boots to cap. "Are you planning to fly aeroplanes, then? Do you even know how to drive an automobile?"

"I'd make a fine pilot with the proper training, thank you very much," he replied archly. "But no, I've been assigned to an observation balloon squadron—aerial spotting, photography, and so on, or so I'm told."

"That sounds . . . ridiculously dangerous." Lucy took a steadying breath. "If you're here, who's running the village school?"

"Alice, naturally. She was a teacher before she married me."

"But she's never run a school before, surely."

"True, but many women are taking on duties they've never done before, or that no Englishwoman has ever done, for that matter." Suddenly he strode forward, clasped her by the shoulder, and kissed her on the cheek. "I must be going. This errand cost me a few favors to be named later, and I don't want to push my luck."

She held on to his tunic and pulled him into a fierce hug. "You could have volunteered to be a mechanic and stayed safe on the ground," she admonished him, as if she were the elder sibling. "Be careful. If you upset Mother, you'll answer to me."

"I'm duly forewarned."

Then he was off, his visit so brief and his departure so sudden that she could almost believe she had imagined it, except for the crate of vegetables he had left behind. So Edwin had decided to do his bit. She should have guessed he was considering it, given the way he had lightly mocked the idea the last time they had all gathered around their mother's table back home in Brookfield. Daniel had enlisted. Her brother George was caring for wounded veterans who had returned to Surrey. Alice was running a school, of all things, truly impressive. And what had Lucy contributed to the war effort? A few pairs of knitted socks each month, a trifle.

Jamie and Simon were in school most of the day, no longer requiring her constant attention. Surely she could do more for the war effort.

She had heard that as more men quit their jobs to enlist, replacement workers were urgently needed. Earlier that month, the government had established a Register of Women for War Service, a unified list of women throughout Great Britain who were willing to work in industry and agriculture for the duration. After much careful thought, and without seeking Daniel's permission, she submitted her name to the register.

Then she waited, hoping to be called in for an interview, but weeks passed and no one from the bureau contacted her. Feeling slighted, the next time the women of the neighborhood gathered to knit for the soldiers, she mentioned the register in an offhand manner, too embarrassed to admit that apparently she had been deemed unqualified and unworthy of a response.

Her friends' responses surprised her. "The Register of Women for War Service indeed," said Gloria scornfully. "That's useless. I don't know of a single person who's found work through that list. It's a shambles, poorly planned and even more poorly executed."

Before Lucy could ask her how she knew this, other friends chimed in assent. "For war work, all anyone needs to do is put their name down on the ordinary register at a Labour Exchange," one noted, shrugging. "My brother-in-law is a manager at Brunner Mond in Silvertown, and he says they get most of their new workers from the Labour Exchange. Some applicants just show up at the factory gate and ask around until someone directs them to the proper office."

"That's what I've heard too," another knitter replied, to a murmur of assent.

Lucy muffled a sigh, glad that she had mentioned it. She regretted that she had wasted her time with the new register, but at least she knew their silence was nothing personal.

She and the boys saw Daniel play at White Hart Lane several more times in April, but the season drew to a close with the Cup Final on 24 April when Sheffield United beat Chelsea 3–0. Daniel said it was generally understood that, having completed a full season despite heated controversy and the loss of players and spectators to the military, professional football would now be suspended for the duration. An official announcement was expected soon.

That same day, the 17th Middlesex received orders transferring them to Hombury St. Mary, near Dorking in Surrey, where they would continue their training in camp on Joynson-Hicks's country estate. The battalion now totaled fourteen hundred men, two hundred short of what the War Office now required. Although Daniel was moving farther away, it was comforting to know that he would be near Brookfield, in familiar country where she could imagine him clearly.

Again Lucy and the boys turned out to watch the 17th Middlesex march through London on the day of their departure, this time from White City to Waterloo station. Lucy searched the ranks in vain for a glimpse of her husband, but it was impossible to spot him in the lines of uniformed men marching in stoic unison, unrecognizable as the casual, smiling recruits who had paraded from West Africa House to Machinery Hall in January.

The next day while the boys were in school, Lucy went to the local Labour Exchange and hesitantly asked the clerk how she might register for war work. "You came to the right place," the white-haired man replied, smiling kindly at her shyness. "What sort of work would you like to do?"

On her way to the exchange, Lucy had passed a recruiting poster she had never seen before, an illustration of a young woman clad in a factory worker's tunic and trousers, smiling demurely as she pulled a cap over her dark hair. In the background, more sparingly sketched to suggest a great distance, a soldier loaded shells into an enormous gun. "On Her Their Lives Depend," the caption above the images declared. At the bottom left, in smaller letters, appeared the phrase "Women Munition Workers," and at bottom right, "Enroll At Once."

"Munitions work, please," she told the clerk. If soldiers' lives—Daniel's life—depended on women making shells and bombs, then that was what she needed to do.

"You want to be a munitionette, eh?" The clerk's smile broadened. "Ever done any sort of factory work before, love?"

"No, sir," she said, heart sinking. "I helped with the

paperwork and books for my father's medical practice before I married, but now I keep house."

"A doctor's daughter? Why not go for a nurse?"

"No, thank you," she said emphatically. Growing up, she had seen enough to know that nursing wasn't for her.

The clerk eyed her for a moment, thoughtful. "You seem like a good lass. Clever too. If you don't mind me asking, is your need for wages urgent or can you stand to wait a bit?"

"I wouldn't say the need is urgent, but I will need to earn a wage eventually."

"Then may I suggest you enroll in a training course first? You'll make but a fraction of what you could earn if you go straight to work, but you'll learn essential skills and earn a higher wage later, when you do take a job. It's a sound investment of one's time, for those who can afford it. You'll qualify for better jobs too— cleaner, less dangerous, you know."

Lucy did *not* know, not really, but she kept that to herself. "And I'll be paid during the training?"

"Yes, love, but as I said, not as much."

A small wage was better than none, something to help make up for Daniel's lost income, and to compensate for the steadily increasing prices for everything from bread to clothing to matches.

"I'd like to enroll in the training program, please," she said. The clerk beamed and gave her the proper forms.

She felt a surge of pride as she signed her name, and yet not without a nervous fluttering in her stomach. Never in her life had she ever imagined herself working in a factory, much less as a "munitionette," surely a new addition to the English language, a word for daring girls who made bombs and shells and she could hardly imagine what else.

She would be mad to think she fully understood what she was getting herself into. She could only hope that the war would end in victory for the Allies before she finished her training course.

5

July 1915

April

Eight weeks passed without any word from Marjorie. In the aftermath of her sudden departure, Mrs. Wilson had wrung April dry of information, asking where Marjorie had gone, how long she had been planning to quit, whether April had known, if she had tried to persuade Marjorie to stay, if not why not, if April understood what a dreadful thing it was to throw a household's smooth operation into chaos by quitting without properly giving notice—

"Don't scold *me*, ma'am," April finally exclaimed when she couldn't endure the interrogation any longer. "I've done nothing wrong. I'm still here!"

Mrs. Wilson fixed her with a hard, level stare. "Indeed

you are, Ann, and until I can hire a replacement for Mary, the duties of four will be divided among three."

With that, April was dismissed. Setting her jaw so she wouldn't talk back, she bobbed a stiff curtsey and got back to work. It wasn't fair that *she* had to suffer the resentment of the entire household because she was Marjorie's best friend and Marjorie herself was out of reach. Wasn't it punishment enough that April would now have one-third of Marjorie's work added to her usual duties, without an equal increase in pay? Perhaps she too ought to be furious with her absent friend, but she couldn't be, not when everyone's surly behavior proved that Marjorie had been quite right to go. Not sneaking off in the middle of the night like a prisoner fleeing a cell—that was badly done—but taking another job if she wished. Why shouldn't she, especially if she contributed to the war effort? It was impossible to miss the newer posters in the village scattered among those urging men to enlist, the ones practically begging girls to take jobs in industry and agriculture. "On Her Their Lives Depend," one declared, calling on women to become munitions workers. "Be the Girl Behind the Man Behind the Gun," another entreated. Which was more important: ridding the floors of Alderlea of every last speck of dust, or building the weapons the Tommies needed to fight the Germans?

April hoped the answer was obvious. Even if the Rylances considered only their own son's safety, they should support any measure that kept Great Britain's military forces amply supplied.

April was aware of the urgent and growing need for war workers only because Mrs. Wilson had permitted her to run errands to the village again, not because the incident with young Peter Bell was forgiven, but out of necessity. No other servants could be spared. Soon after Marjorie quit, two footmen and a groom had resigned in order to enlist, further reducing the staff even as billeting the soldiers increased everyone's workload. At that rate, by December, neither the housemaids nor the footmen would be able to put together a side for the Boxing Day football match. Perhaps that was just as well. Marjorie had been the housemaids' goalkeeper, and they didn't stand much of a chance without her.

April thought of her fellow Alderlea servants every time she spotted a particular poster near the village hall. Titled "Five Questions to Those Employing Male Servants" and unadorned by pictures, it offered a list asking whether chauffeurs, gardeners, and other staff shouldn't be putting their skills to use in service to their country rather than a single estate or household. "A great responsibility rests on you," a caption at the bottom admonished employers. "Will you sacrifice your personal convenience for your Country's need?"

April could well imagine Lady Rylance haughtily replying, "No, indeed we shall not." Yet as far as April knew, their consent wasn't required. Likely the new recruits from Alderlea had seen the poster and realized for themselves that Britain needed them more than the Rylances did. Or maybe, like Marjorie, they had glimpsed opportunity and adventure elsewhere and had decided to pursue them.

Whatever it was that had inspired them, April marveled at their daring. In comparison, she was dutiful, safe—and as dull as dirt. Her mum and elder siblings would have reminded her that she had a guaranteed wage and a roof over her head, which was more than some people could say, so she ought not to complain. But it was hard to stay stuck when friends were setting off on adventures and she never ventured any farther than the nearest village.

Often when April was sent there on errands, she collected the post. On one such day in late May, she spotted a letter in the bundle, postmarked from London and addressed to her using her true name in unfamiliar handwriting. She longed to pause at the footbridge and tear open the letter on the spot, but Mrs. Wilson and the cook were impatiently awaiting her return, so she tucked her letter into her pocket, hastened through the errands, and hurried back to Alderlea as fast as she could with the heavy market basket weighing down her arm.

Later, after luncheon, when she was meant to be mending a soldier's torn trouser cuff and replacing a lost button on the master's favorite riding coat, she waited until the other servants had left the room. Then she draped the pile of mending on her lap, concealed the letter within the folds of fabric, and eagerly read.

The letter was, as she had hoped and expected, from Marjorie. "I hope this letter finds you well, dear friend," her friend wrote cheerfully. "I hope it finds you *full stop*, and that Mrs. W doesn't throw it on the fire on sight, the bitter old crone! Sorry, I should scratch that bit out. I forgot she's your auntie."

"My mum's cousin," April murmured out of habit, glancing up from the page to make sure no one had overheard. Marjorie wrote exactly the way she spoke, airily with a bit of cheek. April could almost hear her voice as she read on.

Marjorie was doing wonderfully well, she wrote. Leaving Alderlea had already proven to be the best decision she'd ever made. She had found work at Woolwich Arsenal, a vast factory complex on the south bank of the Thames in southeast London. She had started out in custodial, sweeping up metal filings that fell around the machines that made shell casings, but after proving herself to be prompt, tireless, and reliable, she had recently been promoted to making fuse caps. "It's a bit dull and repetitive," she admitted, "but you pick up speed once you get used to it, and it's easier on the knees than scrubbing floors. I only make caps, not a whole shell. No one makes an entire shell alone. Everyone makes their own small part and someone farther down the line puts them all together. So I never see the shell-cases being made or a finished shell with my little perfectly made cap firmly in place, but I know it's there, and that's enough for me!"

She worked six days a week, from seven in the morning until seven at night, with one hour off for lunch and a half hour for tea. Other munitionettes worked the exact opposite hours, on the night shift. The various departments staggered their shifts so that not all of the thousands of workers were arriving and departing at the same time. "Some of the girls grouse about the twelve-hour shifts," Marjorie wrote, and April imagined her rolling her eyes. "Isn't that comic? With the breaks, we work only ten and a half. It's clear *some people* have never had to rise at half four, and work fourteen hours or more, and then drag themselves up three flights of narrow stairs and collapse into a cot in the attic, too tired even to dream."

Neither did Marjorie, anymore. Now she shared a cozy room with another girl in a hostel reserved for Woolwich munitionettes. She had a bed to herself—a proper bed, not a cot—and a small bureau of her own and the entire left half of the wardrobe. "I don't have enough clothes to fill it properly yet," she noted, "but I soon may, the wages are so good."

How good? April wondered, feeling the tiniest prick of envy.

The hostel was too far from the arsenal to walk without adding hours to the trip, but it was impossible to find affordable rooms any nearer. Houses had been built for munitions workers on the Well Hall Estate in Eltham, but those had filled up long ago, and newer workers had to find lodgings farther and farther out. "Our landlady wakes us at five o'clock," explained Marjorie, "and we snatch a hasty breakfast before dashing out the door at half five to catch the tram. It's not so bad, really."

Not so bad? What a luxury it would be, April thought wistfully, to have an extra half hour of sleep every morning!

It was a long, tiring journey to and from the arsenal on the overcrowded trams, but Marjorie traveled with her new friends and they made a merry time of it, gossiping and laughing together as they rode, smiling and chatting with the Tommies if any happened to be on board, so handsome and dashing in their uniforms. Sometimes the soldiers asked the girls to write to them, and sometimes the munitionettes agreed. Marjorie already had two pen pals and her roommate had three.

"Now you understand why I've been too busy to write to you," Marjorie concluded. "Please ignore my poor example of friendship and write back to me as soon as you can."

April did as her friend asked, but the Alderlea gossip she shared was embarrassingly dull compared to Marjorie's adventures. April's letter contained mostly questions. How had Marjorie managed to get hired without a character from her previous employer? How much better *were* her new wages, exactly? Was there anything about Alderlea she missed—the lovely countryside, the cook's delicious meals, anything?

"Only you, dear chum," Marjorie responded a fortnight later. She then proceeded to describe all the larks she was having with her new coworkers, from songs around the canteen piano at tea to the impromptu football games after lunch and bicycle rides through the park on their days off. Twice she and her roommate had given white feathers to lads in civvies on the tram, embarrassing the hapless shirkers so thoroughly that they had each disembarked at the next stop, red-faced and eyes downcast. Marjorie's half of the wardrobe no longer looked quite so bare thanks to the lovely cotton summer frock she had just purchased, and she had treated her mum to a gorgeous silk shawl for her birth-day. "She adored it, of course," Marjorie remarked. "She's quite forgiven me for leaving Alderlea now."

As for her wages, depending upon the number of hours she worked and whether she took on any over-time, she typically earned around three pounds a week.

April gasped. Three pounds! That was nearly thirty times what April earned as a housemaid, not including room and board and whatever came to her on Boxing Day. No wonder Marjorie could afford larks and finery and gifts for her mum.

But the wages were only part of it, Marjorie ex-plained, turning uncharacteristically earnest. At Wool-wich she felt appreciated, and she needed only to hear news from the front to understand just how essential she was to the war effort. She was "The Girl Behind the Man Behind the Gun," doing her bit for King and Country, respected and admired and independent. No one at Woolwich would dream of calling her anything but Marjorie, her own proper name, except to call her

"Miss" or "Dearie" or some other fond nickname, which she rather liked. And while it was true that munitions work was by its very nature dangerous, the risks she took were far less than those her brothers and all the other Tommies faced in France and Belgium.

"There's always room for one more here at Woolwich, you know," Marjorie wrote in closing. "Your auntie will forgive you eventually, just as my mum forgave me. (The gift of a shawl may be required.) Say you'll come soon, or you may receive a white feather from me in the next post!"

"You wouldn't dare," April murmured, aghast. Quickly she folded the letter, slipped it into her apron pocket, and carried on with the mending. It wasn't fear that kept her from flitting off to London and joining Marjorie in the arsenal—well, fear of her mum and Mrs. Wilson, maybe, but not fear of the job itself. From the sound of it, munitions work was easier than domestic service, the pay was much better, and the girls were treated with respect. Why shouldn't she go? When she told her mum how much more she could earn as a munitionette, surely she would not object. Mrs. Wilson had hired a girl from the village to replace Marjorie; likely she could find someone to take April's spot, especially if April gave her two weeks' notice.

Or maybe one week would be enough. Now that

April had made up her mind to go, she was eager to get on with it. She would tell Mrs. Wilson the next morning, after breakfast, and soon thereafter, her own adventure would begin.

She slept poorly, dreading an unpleasant confrontation in the housekeeper's chamber, but to her relief, Mrs. Wilson accepted the news with calm resignation. "At least you did the proper thing by giving notice rather than stealing away in the middle of the night," she said, sighing. "For that reason, I shall provide you with a character. I trust it will help you secure another position, both now and after the war, God speed the day."

"Yes, ma'am. Thank you, ma'am."

Mrs. Wilson sat back in her chair and studied April over the top of her glasses. "A word of caution, Ann. You're usually a sensible girl, but you're too easily influenced by those you admire and hope to impress. Think twice before you stumble blindly after Mary, or she may lead you into trouble."

"Yes, ma'am." April hesitated, cheeks burning. "Are you going to tell my mum I've resigned?"

Mrs. Wilson's eyebrows rose. "Certainly not. That responsibility belongs to you alone. Good luck."

April managed a weak smile as she bobbed a curtsey and hurried off to work. One week more, she reminded herself as she turned the mattresses and made up the beds. Four more days, she thought as she hauled the heavy baskets of soldiers' damp, freshly laundered clothing outside and hung it on the line to dry. She waited until the day before her departure to write to her mum, determined to be settled in London with a new job by the time her family got the news.

The same day she posted her letter, she received another from Marjorie. "If you're coming, don't look for me at Woolwich," she had hastily scrawled. "It wasn't easy to persuade the foreman to give me a leaving certificate, but now he has done, so I've hired on at Thornshire Arsenal. It's a newer factory, not the building but everything inside, and the canteen is loads better. (The food at Woolwich was dreadful. I didn't mention it before because I didn't want to put you off.) I'm in one of the Danger Buildings now, which means better pay. Grand!"

April felt her stomach drop as she read the letter over again. What was a leaving certificate—as in school?— and why did Marjorie need one? Did April need one to work? Where was Thornshire Arsenal? Was Marjorie even still in London? What was a Danger Building, and was there a place for April in it, if she could find Thornshire, and if the ominous name didn't scare her away? All of her plans seemed suddenly thrown into shambles, mere hours before she meant to depart. Maybe she should ask Mrs. Wilson if she could stay after all. That would be the safest thing, the surest thing.

Then she remembered the better wages, her brother Henry training with the Lonsdale Pals in Yorkshire, and the soldiers' desperate need for munitions. She imagined opening a letter from Marjorie only to find a white feather tucked inside, and she knew she must go through with her plans.

The next morning, she rose at the usual hour, but she put on her nicest summer dress instead of her uniform. She packed her few other belongings into the same pasteboard suitcase she had brought with her to Alderlea nearly five years before and had not used since. After one last breakfast at the servants' table, where everyone genuinely wished her well, she collected her final wages and her letter of reference, thanked Mrs. Wilson for everything, and left the estate for what was surely the last time.

The nearest train station was at the next largest town four miles away, but just outside the village, a passing farmer gave her a lift in his wagon. In another stroke of good luck, when she told the farmer her plans, he replied that he had a cousin in Thornshire. It wasn't far from Woolwich, he assured her. If she took the train into London, a ticket agent at St. Pancras could direct her to her connection.

"Ever been to London?" he asked, and when she told him she had not, he grinned and shook his grizzled head. "It's nowt like Derbyshire. A young lass like yourself could get lost. I trust you have friends there to meet you?"

"One friend," she replied, although Marjorie didn't know she was coming, and April didn't know where to meet her. If Marjorie had been obliged to leave the hostel when she quit Woolwich, the return address on her letters was no good anymore.

April had hours to consider her options on the train as it rumbled southeast through rolling countryside bright with summer greens and golds. Her carriage was packed with soldiers in khaki, a few silver-haired couples in tweeds, and several young women near her own age, perhaps aspiring war workers like herself. None of them looked as anxious as she felt, so she took a steadying breath and gazed out the window and pretended to be as nonchalant as the other girls. By the time the verdant countryside gave way to the outskirts of the city, she had decided to make her way to Thornshire Arsenal, wait outside the main gate, and search the crowd at each shift change until she spotted her friend. Marjorie would tell her what to do next.

At last the train halted at St. Pancras station, a bustling marvel of Victorian architecture with striking red brickwork and a soaring roof of iron arched trusses and glass. A lady ticket agent kindly told April which ticket to purchase to continue on to Thornshire and directed her to the correct platform, just as the farmer had promised. April had not thought to ask which direction she would be heading and how far, but, watching through the window as the train lurched forward and pulled out of the station, she figured they were traveling mostly east but also south. The train kept north of the Thames, a ribbon of brown that rippled in and out of view as spaces between the tall buildings allowed brief glimpses.

At last she reached her final stop. Suitcase in hand, she disembarked, smoothed loose strands of flaxen hair back into the roll at the nape of her neck, and appealed to the nearest ticket agent for directions to the arsenal. "Haven't a clue, love," he said. "Maybe it's near the old sewing machine factory. You might ask there." He beckoned the next customer in line, so she stepped aside before she could explain that she didn't know where the sewing machine factory was either.

Weary and stiff from sitting so long and increasingly hungry, she paused to gather her thoughts. Glancing around the small stationhouse in hope that another stroke of luck would find her, she spotted another lady ticket agent crossing the platform. April quickly hurried after her before she could disappear into the crowd, and, catching her just as she was about to enter a private office, she repeated her question.

"You're not far, dearie," the lady agent assured her, pointing her toward the correct exit and describing the route. "Now, I can't say whether you'll see signs for Thornshire Arsenal when you get there. It's newly converted, so it might have the old name still. If you see Purcell Products or anything to do with sewing machines, you've likely found it."

Sewing machines—so the first agent had been nearly correct. April thanked the lady agent and hurried on her way.

Ten minutes later, she spotted the Purcell Products sign on a smokestack from a block away, but as she approached and discovered high stone walls encircling a vast complex that must have covered scores of acres, her footsteps slowed. Scores of men and women streamed through an imposing entrance beneath a sign marked "Gate No. 3," while police stood guard and sentries checked identification badges. Rooftops and chimneys covered in soot were visible over the wall, but she could not tell what was making the awful metallic grinding and clattering and screeching on the other side. She hesitated on the opposite side of the street from the gate, intimidated, something acrid in the air stinging her nostrils. Clutching the handle of her suitcase in both fists, she took in the scene, swallowed hard, and suddenly remembered that she ought to be watching the departing workers for Marjorie. She was afraid to go any closer out of fear that the guards would chase her away, so she rose up on tiptoe and craned her neck, hoping desperately that her friend would appear.

Suddenly, a woman who looked to be around her mum's age noticed April searching the crowd and paused to peer back at her, curious. April quickly looked away, but when she stole a glance back, she felt a frisson of alarm—the woman was crossing the street and striding directly toward her, with several younger women dutifully following after. April tried to look perfectly innocent, as if she had a right to be stranding there, because of course she was and she did, but her heart leapt into her throat when the woman—broad-shouldered and several inches taller than herself—halted not two feet in front of her and folded her burly arms over her chest.

"Mind yourself, dearie," she said, amused, as the younger women looked on, curious and grinning. They all had gingery hair and a faint yellow tinge to their skin, as if they spent too much time in the sun, or not enough. "Stand there gawking long enough and the police will think you're a spy. You're not one, are you?"

April gulped. "No, ma'am, I'm not."

The woman laughed, and the other girls smiled. "A lass who shows proper respect. I like that. Are you looking for a job?"

April nodded. "My friend works here already, and she said there's room for one more." Too late, she remembered Marjorie had said that about Woolwich, not Thornshire. Had April come all this way for nothing?

The younger women smiled and exchanged amused glances. "They need loads more than one," remarked the tallest, a pretty girl whose braided hair was reddish along the length of the strands but darkened to light brown closer to the root.

"Your friend might've told you that you need to apply at the Labour Exchange first," said the burly woman. She glanced over her shoulder and nodded to the tall younger one. "Peggy, you can take her."

"But I'll miss tea," Peggy protested.

"No you won't, not if you just show her the way and hurry back. That's a good girl." The woman turned back to April. "What's your name, dearie?"

"April. April Tipton." On impulse she added, "My friend is Marjorie Tate."

"Oh, yes, we know her," the eldest said. "She works in the same Danger Building as we do."

"She's probably in the canteen," another girl piped up. "She won't pass through the gates until shift change at seven o'clock."

April nodded, heart sinking. It was only four o'clock, hours to go yet.

"Mum, I only got twenty minutes left," Peggy told the eldest in an urgent undertone.

"Well, off with you, then." Her mother waved her along and threw April a reassuring grin. "Tell the clerk you want to work at Thornshire Arsenal and he'll send you right back."

April nodded. "Thank you, ma'am."

She laughed. "I can tell you were in service. It's Mabel, not ma'am. See you soon."

"Come on, then," said Peggy, not unkindly, already heading down the block. April hastened to catch up to her, wondering if she ought to apologize for making Peggy late for her tea, her own stomach growling at the thought of it. She decided to keep quiet rather than say the wrong thing.

They turned the corner, heading away from the arsenal rather than around it, and walked another two blocks before Peggy abruptly halted and pointed to an office building clearly marked with a sign. "That's the

Labour Exchange. If you want to work right away, best to take whatever job they offer. Think you can find your own way back?"

"Yes, thank you."

"Good luck." Peggy offered a brief smile and hurried on her way.

Alone again, April approached the building, took a steadying breath, and opened the door, only to find that she couldn't open it all the way or it would have struck the woman standing inside at the end of a rather long queue. Slipping in through the narrow opening, she eased the door shut, took her place in the queue, and set her suitcase down at her feet. She found herself in a narrow foyer, separated from the rest of the single large room by waist-high partitions, more to keep the applicants in a corral than to create privacy. On the other side of the low walls, a dozen clerks, as many women as men, worked at identical desks sorting papers, answering phones, or chatting with applicants.

The queue led to a single, taller desk in the middle of the office, where April quickly deduced the applicants were sorted, either directed to one of the other desks or dismissed outright. As the queue inched forward, two women, one scowling, one nearly in tears, passed April on their way out, evidently rejected. An anxious shiver prickled the back of her neck. From what the posters said and Marjorie too, she assumed that the need for workers was so great that no one would be turned away. She had no factory experience, only domestic service and Mrs. Wilson's letter to recommend her. Would that be enough?

She felt lightheaded from hunger and worry by the time she reached the front of the queue. As closing time approached, the clerk had begun sending applicants to the smaller desks in groups of two or three to get through them faster. He asked April only a few cursory questions before directing her to join two other applicants at a desk near the front window, where an interview had already begun. Hurrying over, April gave her name when asked, presented Mrs. Wilson's character, and explained that she wanted to work at the Thornshire Arsenal. The other applicants' quick, appraising looks told her that they were after the same.

The agent questioned each of them briefly. The first girl, small and wiry, claimed three years' experience as a housemaid, but she looked younger than April had when she had first gone into service. The other, who looked to be perhaps ten years older, was currently employed in a hat shop, but her husband was in the navy and she wanted to do her bit too, for his sake. Neither had traveled as far as April, which gave the agent a moment's pause. Then he scanned Mrs. Wilson's letter, shrugged, and returned it, apparently dismissing whatever objection he might have momentarily entertained.

"The only positions currently open at Thornshire are in the Danger Buildings," he said, giving each of them an appraising look. "It's not hard work—no heavy lifting, I mean—but precision and a steady hand is essential."

"Is there nothing else?" the sailor's wife asked. "I have a young child. I can't take a dangerous job."

"Then perhaps munitions isn't for you, miss," said the agent sympathetically. "However, I can keep your papers on file in case something else comes in."

"I'll do it," said April quickly. "In fact, I'd prefer the Danger Building."

"I'll do anything," the wiry girl said, shrugging. "It don't bother me what, so long as the pay is good and the work is steady."

"You'll have plenty of work, no worries there." The agent studied the two of them a moment longer. "Very well. Are you willing to sign on for three years or the duration?" When they agreed, he passed them some paperwork and indicated where they should sign. Next he took two small yellow cards from a stack on his desk, filled in a few blanks, marked each in red ink with a rubber stamp, and gave one to April and one to the wiry girl along with some of the papers they had signed. "This will get you through the front gate. The rest is up to you. Good luck."

With that, all three were dismissed. The sailor's wife quickly departed, frowning, but the wiry girl lingered close to April as they left the office. "Where d'you suppose the front gate is?" the girl asked, nose wrinkling as she studied her card.

"I found Gate Three earlier," April mused. "I suppose the front gate is Gate One. We could walk around the outer wall until we come to it. Want to go together?"

The girl agreed, and they set off with April leading the way, retracing the route Peggy had shown her. The streets all around the complex were choked with traffic, automobiles and wagons and the tram, and the pavements were crowded with pedestrians, most of them workers, April guessed. Walking counterclockwise, they found Gate One, grand and imposing opposite a small park with gravel paths, flower beds, and shade trees, a bit of countryside in the city.

They showed their papers and yellow cards to one of the sentries, who waved them through the gate, which led into a covered entrance with a high ceiling. On the other side, two policemen halted them, examined their papers and passes, and directed them to the medical shed, a long, low building a few yards from the entrance. April was relieved it was so close, for the factory complex was almost a village unto itself, with industrial buildings of all sizes arranged in a grid connected by roads, where lorries and wagons vied for space. Workers in coveralls and caps bustled about, some pushing carts loaded with mysterious crates, others striding purposefully from one building to another, and more strolling and chatting with friends, evidently on break or at the end of a shift.

April and the wiry girl entered the medical shed together through double doors at the nearest end, but they quickly became separated amid the crush of other women, dozens of them, all looking as uncertain and wary as April felt. Word quickly spread from the front of the throng to those nearer the door that they must pass a medical exam before they could be hired. Sure enough, a stern woman in a nurse's dress and cap called to the new arrivals above the din, instructing them to remove all their clothing except for their shoes and coats, to leave their belongings in one of the cubicles along the walls, and to proceed to the other end of the room in groups of three.

Reluctantly, April obeyed, quickly shedding her clothing and pulling on her coat again. It was such a fine day that many of the girls had not worn an outer garment, but tried to cover their nakedness with a blouse or a sweater instead. April had worn hers only because it would not fit in her suitcase, which she stowed in a cubicle, hating to let it out of her sight.

The other end of the shed was divided into small cubicles for modesty, such as it was, and each trio was directed to wait in one, shivering and embarrassed, until two lady doctors arrived. They examined each of the girls thoroughly in turn, even checking their hair for lice. April had never been so poked and prodded before, and as she felt heat rising in her face, she knew her cheeks must be bright red and she could not bear to make eye contact with anyone. But at last it ended. One of the doctors made a few notes on April's yellow card, praised her for being so healthy and fit, and handed her a small blue book embossed with "Thornshire Arsenal" in gold on the front. "This is your rule book," the doctor told her as she hastily pulled on her coat. "Your registration number is printed on the inside cover. Memorize your number and learn all the rules before you report for work Monday morning at seven o'clock sharp."

"Thank you," April murmured, clutching the rule book in one hand and holding her coat closed with the other. Hurrying back to her cubicle, she threw on her clothes, tucked the small blue book into her suitcase, and left the medical shed as soon as the doorway cleared enough for her to squeeze through it. She had never been more mortified, but at least she had the job. Gripping her suitcase tightly, she looked around to get her bearings, found the gate, and headed toward it.

"April!" a voice called out behind her. "April!"

She halted, turned, and sighed with relief at the sight of Marjorie running toward her, waving and beaming with delight. April set down the suitcase and held out her arms just in time for Marjorie to embrace her. "You came!" Marjorie exclaimed. "I never doubted it!"

April was so glad to see her friend that tears sprang into her eyes. "If you'd warned me about that medical exam, I might have stayed at Alderlea. I've never been so embarrassed!"

"That's why I didn't tell you! Did you get the job? Did you ask for the Danger Building?"

"Yes and yes," said April, picking up her suitcase. "I start Monday morning, seven o'clock."

"Wonderful!" Marjorie linked her arm through April's and steered her toward the gate. "We'll be working together again!"

"Just like old times," said April, smiling so broadly her cheeks ached. How swiftly the day had turned from mortification to joy, all because she had found her friend.

"You'll stay with me, of course," said Marjorie as they passed through the gate. She waved to one of the sentries, who grinned and tugged on the brim of his cap. "Our landlady can find a spare bed in another room for Edith."

"Your roommate? No, she shouldn't have to move. I'll take the other room." April would be grateful to have any bed at all. She had prepared herself to sleep on a blanket on Marjorie's floor until she could find lodgings of her own.

"Don't be silly! You're my best friend, and I just met Edith. She'll understand. I bet she'll volunteer to move before I need to ask."

"If you're sure—"

"Of course I'm sure." Marjorie squeezed April's arm. "Are you hungry?"

"Starving, rather."

"Not to worry. Our landlady always has a bite to eat ready for us when we get home. But first I'll teach you something every munitionette must know."

April felt a thrill of excitement. Yes, she was a munitionette now. How astonishing, and how wonderful! "What's that?"

"How to catch a tram home when hundreds of your fellow workers are trying to do the same. Come on." Marjorie released her arm and took her hand. "Hold on tight to that suitcase, soldier. Let's march!"

April laughed as Marjorie broke into a jog, pulling her along after her.

6
July–September 1915

Helen

By midsummer, Arthur had taken a lovely Georgian house in Marylebone at No. 14 Great Cumberland Place near Marble Arch, beautifully furnished and boasting every modern convenience Helen could have desired. Hyde Park was only steps away, and she enjoyed a brisk walk there every morning, admiring the flowers, savoring the fresh air and birdsong, tolerating the occasional rain or fog, smiling at the nannies and mums pushing prams or strolling hand in hand with their toddling children. She and Arthur had chosen No. 14 in part because of its charming nursery, which they both hoped would not remain unoccupied much longer. Helen saw less of her husband than she liked, and much less than she had expected, considering that the whole point of moving to London was so that they would be together. Arthur kept long hours and often collapsed into bed shortly after a late dinner, too exhausted to do anything but sleep, but when he was fully rested, he relished making love to her as much as he ever had.

"You must be very eager to be a father," she teased him breathlessly one July evening as she lay in his arms, a faint sheen of perspiration on them both. The blackout curtains were tightly drawn, a single candle illuminated the room, and they had left the door open to encourage a breeze from the hallway, but the air was warm and so still that the candle barely flickered.

"Very eager," he murmured sleepily, and then he truly was asleep. Sighing fondly, she rolled over to blow out the candle, then returned to his embrace, carefully so she did not wake him.

The truth was, though she wouldn't dream of complaining, she missed him during the long, lonely hours between his departure for Thornshire Arsenal soon after breakfast and his return, usually after twilight, often even later. Arthur frequently took a Saturday or a Sunday off, but never both, and sometimes neither. She understood that until the Shell Crisis was resolved, bringing Thornshire Arsenal up to full production capacity must be Arthur's priority. She worried to see him exhausting himself, day after day, and yet she was grateful for the essential war work that kept him in London, far from the carnage that had made widows of too many other women on both sides of the conflict.

Not that she dared express sympathy for her father's homeland. Outrage against Germany, kindled by the declaration of war and stoked by German atrocities in Belgium and the deaths of young British soldiers in the trenches, had burned searing hot ever since the devastating attack earlier that spring on the RMS *Lusitania*, a Cunard ocean liner en route from New York City to Liverpool. Nearly twelve hundred men, women, and children, including some of the world's most prominent industrialists, socialites, and entertainers, had perished in the cold waters off the southern coast of Ireland after a German U-boat fired a torpedo on the ship, sinking it in eighteen minutes. In response to international outrage, Germany had insisted that they'd had every right to treat the unarmed ship as a military vessel, since in addition to the great many civilian passengers aboard, she had also carried American-made munitions, in defiance of the German blockade.

Helen was not surprised that the British people refused to accept that justification, but she never expected the shocking riots that followed. The tumult first erupted in Liverpool, the *Lusitania*'s home port and the hometown of many of its crew, and rumor had it that friends and families of the lost sailors struck the first blows. Angry men attacked a German grocery in the North End, smashing windows and throwing food onto the pavement. Two more groceries were ransacked before police arrived on the scene, but the officers failed to contain the surging violence. Butchers' shops and shoemakers were looted, their goods stolen, their shutters and awnings torn down and broken. The homes of German immigrants were broken into, their furniture and belongings hurled from upper windows to smash on the streets below.

The furor spread swiftly through Liverpool and leapt to other cities across the country, wherever a significant German population had thrived before the war. Any business owned or believed to be owned by Germans became a potential target, although in their fury the rioters also destroyed buildings owned by Scandinavians, Russians, and their fellow Britons. When calm was finally restored days later, it was said that the windows in virtually every German-owned business in Great Britain had been smashed, nearly two thousand in London alone.

Nor was the compulsion to avenge the sinking of the *Lusitania* by punishing Germans in England confined to the working class. In London, two thousand indignant stockbrokers clad in their finest suits and top hats marched from the Stock Exchange to the Houses of Parliament to demand that the Prime Minister intern for the duration of the war thousands of Germans living or working in London. Thus far the outraged public had targeted their neighborhood butchers, bakers, and barbers, but the businessmen insisted that the real danger came from men in positions of greater influence. Naturalized Germans and enemy aliens alike must be removed from the city and confined behind high walls and barbed wire to prevent them from attacking Great Britain from within.

Suffragettes who attempted to storm Parliament had always found the doors barred to them, but the stockbrokers were permitted to march directly into the Central Hall. Prime Minister Asquith was absent, but two sympathetic MPs met with the businessmen and listened respectfully as they aired their grievances. Eventually the stockbrokers were persuaded to leave after the two MPs assured them that Cabinet was considering many of the preventative measures they demanded. "Who knows how many of these thousands of Germans, naturalized and unnaturalized, intend to assume strategic positions to assist the enemy in the event of another Zeppelin attack on London?" one of

the MPs said to the press afterward. The second offered an ominous warning: "If ever Zeppelins drop incendiary bombs on London, many Germans among us
would set fire to the city in twenty or thirty different
places."

It was utterly preposterous, but thoroughly harrowing, and Helen waited anxiously for the government's
response. Two days after the stockbrokers' protest,
Prime Minister Asquith revealed new policies for the
management of Germans in Britain for the duration.
Naturalized subjects of enemy origin were to be left at
liberty, unless there was sufficient reason for internment in individual cases, and all must register with the
police and would be subject to observation. Male enemy
aliens of military age, seventeen to fifty-five, were to
be interned at camps on the Isle of Man and elsewhere
in the United Kingdom. Men over fifty-five, women,
and children were to be repatriated whenever possible.

Yet despite pressure from the opposition and even
members of his own party, Asquith refused to treat
naturalized citizens as enemies and spies. Most of them
were surely loyal British subjects and decent, honest
people, he declared. It would be disgraceful to initi-
ate a campaign of persecution against them, not only
from an ethical standpoint, but in the best interests of
the country. These naturalized citizens contributed to

British society, the economy, and even the national defense, for many of them, or their children, had enlisted in the military.

As heartening as it was to know that the Prime Minister refused to condemn nationalized Germans, Helen followed reports of public outrage and suspicion with increasing alarm, deeply afraid for her sisters, half German like herself, and for her mother, who bore their German surname. "Don't worry about us," her mother assured her, preternaturally calm, when Helen finally got her on the telephone. "We're Englishwomen through and through, and your father was beloved in Oxford, God rest him. No one will trouble us here."

Helen hoped her mother's trust was not misplaced. "Even so, would you warn Daphne not to speak German outside of the house?"

"She doesn't even speak it *inside* the house anymore, what with you and Penny and your father all gone." Her tone suggested that Helen's father too had only moved to another city. "You know I don't speak enough German to carry on more than a rudimentary conversation, although I do manage a few carols at Christmas."

"Would you please warn her all the same?"

"I suppose soon you'll be asking us to change our

name from Stahl to Steel. Did you know the Sauers on Bankside call themselves Sawyer now? That's not what Sauer means, even I know that."

"They could hardly call themselves the Sour family, though, could they? They're confectioners." Helen closed her eyes and muffled a sigh. "Promise me you'll be careful."

"I will. You too, *Liebling*."

"Mother, honestly—"

"Got to run," she said cheerily. "Bye, now. Love you." And with that, her mother disconnected.

To Helen's relief, her family suffered no anti-German retribution, but even as her concerns for their safety subsided, she missed them all the more. In Arthur's absence, she longed for the company of her mother and sisters, for a tennis partner, for her old days full of purpose and useful work. None of the Stahl daughters had been brought up to be ladies of leisure, and Helen found the role an uncomfortable fit that constrained and chafed. Idleness made her restless, and she could walk around Hyde Park only so many hours of the day before the neighbors declared her an eccentric. Even managing their home took up little of her time. Although other ladies she had befriended in Marylebone lamented the "Servant Problem," as the alleged perpetual lack of good help was known, the Purcells' staff ran their household so expertly that Helen hardly had to do anything except approve their suggestions and make sure their wages and the bills were paid on time.

Even her service to the suffrage movement, once her greatest passion, had diminished. When Helen had first joined the Women's Social and Political Union, the organization's call for politicians to deliver "Deeds Not Words" had resonated with her, as had its commitment to nonviolence. In the aftermath of Black Friday, however, a few militant factions had adopted more dangerous, destructive tactics, including arson and mail bombs. On one occasion a suffragette had thrown a hatchet at Prime Minister Asquith, and on another, a bomb had been discovered beneath the Coronation Chair in Westminster Abbey. Horrified, Helen had withdrawn from the WSPU entirely. She wanted the vote as badly as ever, but she could not condone violence. She was willing to suffer for her convictions, but never to kill for them.

Then, unexpectedly, Emmeline and Christabel Pankhurst abruptly halted all militant campaigning from the WSPU. The crisis required suffragettes to put their country's needs before their own, Mrs. Pankhurst declared. What good would it do British women to win the vote if Germany conquered Britain and civil rights for Englishmen and Englishwomen alike were suddenly swept aside? To avoid that terrible fate, brave English-women must devote all their strength and courage to the fight to keep Britain free.

Helen welcomed the call to serve, and she had no desire to sit at home, safe in idleness, while other women responded. In recent speeches, Mrs. Pankhurst had argued that if women were unwilling to work in a time of national peril, they did not deserve the vote. Helen was inclined to agree, but what part could she play?

After considering the possibilities, she chose a Monday morning to broach the subject with Arthur, knowing he would be well-rested and in good spirits after a relaxing Sunday off. "Darling," she ventured as he sipped his coffee and scanned the newspaper headlines, "I'm determined to do my bit, and I don't mean knitting socks or distributing white feathers."

His eyebrows rose. "Is that so?" He folded the newspaper and set it aside. "What did you have in mind?"

"I thought I could put my German fluency to good use—as a translator for military intelligence, perhaps, or as a language instructor."

Arthur's brow furrowed. "No, darling," he said, shaking his head. "That would never do."

"Why ever not?" she asked, astonished. He hadn't even spared ten seconds to consider the idea. "I've grown up with the language. I speak, read, and write as a native would. I'm Oxford educated, although of course I was denied a formal degree. Is it because I'm a woman?"

"Of course not—"

"You might have noticed that all the men are preoccupied at the moment."

"It's not because you're a woman, and I'm not questioning your qualifications." Arthur sighed and rubbed his jaw, his green eyes shadowed and wary. "I believe we shouldn't call attention to your German heritage for the duration—not only to spare you abuse from the unruly and the ignorant, but so you can avoid the restrictions being imposed on German nationals. I won't have you interned on the Isle of Man or deported to Germany."

Helen was so astonished that she laughed. "For goodness sakes, I'm not an enemy alien. I'm an Englishwoman by every definition. I was born in Oxford to an Englishwoman, and I'm married to an Englishman. None of those restrictions apply to me."

"Your mother was born an Englishwoman, but according to law, if a British woman marries a foreigner, she takes on her husband's nationality." Arthur reached across the table for her hand, and she let him take it. "I doubt anyone will trouble the English-born widow of a revered Oxford professor who happened to be German. Nevertheless, perception matters. Your loyalties, which I know are above reproach, must never be doubted."

She studied him. "You mean *your* loyalties must never be doubted, because of your position. You can't have anyone thinking that Thornshire Arsenal's head man is married to a German, complete with horns and a forked tail."

"Mock me if you wish, but you can't deny that I have good reason to be concerned. The Lusitania Riots are evidence enough of that. I don't want to see my workers harassed, the factory ransacked, the equipment destroyed. Production would grind to a halt, and you can well imagine what that would mean for our soldiers."

"I thought you said Thornshire is protected by armed guards."

"Yes, to fend off German saboteurs. I don't want them firing upon misguided Englishmen in East London. Do you?"

"Of course not." After a moment, she added, "Darling, I love you, but you're being ridiculous."

He frowned and drank his coffee, his eyes never leaving hers. "One of us is, at any rate."

She felt a faint heat rise in her cheeks. "Very well. Have it your way. No translating, no instruction, no

German at all. But I must contribute somehow." Then inspiration struck. "I'll come to work for you."

Her words were ill-timed; he had taken another sip and now spluttered into his napkin as he returned his cup to its saucer. "Work for me? At Thornshire Arsenal?"

"Where else? Why not?" She sat back in her chair and folded her arms. "I promise to speak only English."

"No offense, darling, but I'm not sure you've got what it takes to be a munitionette. Most of our girls have worked in factories or in service for years. You're better educated, fair enough, but as far as this work is concerned, they're qualified and you're not."

"I'll be your secretary, then, or a clerk. I worked as my father's assistant for years, handling his correspondence, attending to paperwork, minding the books, doing the occasional bit of research. I could do the same for you."

"I'm sure you'd be a marvel of efficiency and order, but I already have a secretary, and he has a family to support. How would it look if I sacked Tom to hire my wife?"

"It would be very bad form, I suppose," she replied, somewhat grudgingly.

"Yes, I should think so. I'll tell you what. If Tom resigns to enlist, I'll put your application on the top of the pile."

"I'd have to apply?"

"Of course. You and everyone else. It's only fair that the most qualified applicant should get the job."

"What if I refuse to accept a salary?" she countered. "How would that affect my chances?"

"It would improve them considerably. Yet, darling—" He sighed and reached for her hand again, and she gave it to him, along with a wry pout. "Thornshire Arsenal isn't your father's study. It isn't the Bodleian or the Ashmolean. You might not find it suitable as a workplace."

"I understand the difference between a factory and a library or a museum." Helen put her head to one side and studied him, curious. "I can tolerate mess and noise. If I didn't, I wouldn't want children. Is there some other reason you wouldn't want me about?"

He lifted her hand to his lips and kissed it, his breath warm on her skin.

"You're stalling," she said. "Stop being charming and answer the question."

He clasped her hand in both of his and brought them to rest on the table. "Helen, munitions work is inherently dangerous."

Her heart dipped. "How dangerous?"

"Very dangerous, of course. What do you want me to say? We're working with explosive materials, creating weapons to destroy and to kill. Everyone is trained to be scrupulously careful, but accidents happen."

"In that case," she said, keeping her voice even, "if it's too dangerous for me, it's too dangerous for you. Perhaps you should resign."

He fixed her with a look of fond disbelief. "You know I can't do that. Someone has to make shells, and my father accepted the responsibility on behalf of our family and his entire company. Running Thornshire Arsenal is my war service, and it shall be for the duration. Best get used to it."

Lowering her eyes, she nodded to show him she understood. "I don't like it, Arthur."

"A moment ago you wanted to be my secretary, and now you don't want either of us anywhere near the place." He leaned forward, rested his elbows on the table, and squeezed her hand. "Here's a thought. What are your plans for the day?"

"I don't have any, not really."

"Why don't I take you on a tour of the arsenal? You'll see for yourself the many precautions we take and how safe—how *relatively* safe—it is."

She barely let him finish speaking before she accepted.

Determined to make a good impression, Helen hurried upstairs to change into one of her most becoming walking suits—a sapphire blue silk moiré jacket with a pointed rear hem, rouleaux frogging fasteners, and ivory lace at the collar and cuffs, with a matching hobble skirt, discreetly pleated to allow for a more comfortable stride. She knew that while she was inspecting her husband's workplace, his workers would be inspecting her. When she descended the stairs and saw her husband gazing up at her with unmasked admiration, she knew she had chosen well.

Helen had assumed they would take the tram or the underground to East London, but Arthur wanted to drive the Silver Ghost, to give the engine a good run while they could still get the petrol. On the ride over, she queried him about the various armaments his factory produced, and he answered, patiently and amiably, with clear descriptions that avoided bewildering jargon. She couldn't help thinking that he would have made an excellent professor.

They were still a few blocks away when she glimpsed a Purcell Products sign on a tall smokestack in the distance. "Is that it?" she asked. "Why doesn't it say Thornshire Arsenal? Wait, don't tell me. Why announce to the Germans what you're doing here?"

"Might as well paint a bull's-eye on it for the zeppelins," he replied. "They might not waste a bomb on us if they think we still make only sewing machines and bobbins."

Helen fought to suppress a shudder at the thought of a bomb falling on her husband's workplace while he sat at his desk, making telephone calls or perusing contracts.

As they drew closer, she was surprised and a bit awed to discover that the factory was a complex the breadth of several city blocks, all encircled by a massive stone wall topped with barbed wire. The streets were packed with vehicles, the pavements with arriving and departing workers on foot, but the crowd parted before the gleaming Rolls-Royce as it slowly approached an imposing gate. Helen observed several of the men tugging their hats and women bobbing curtseys to her husband as they passed, and he acknowledged each gesture with a courteous nod. She was glad to see that he was apparently well-regarded by his workers. It was almost as if they knew they had the kindest and most generous of the Purcell gentlemen as their boss.

After Arthur showed his identification badge to a sentry, they were waved through the gate and drove into the complex proper, a seemingly haphazard collection of industrial buildings of all kinds and sizes, some gleaming with metallic newness, others stone and soot-covered. They drove for a few minutes down a paved road and turned onto cobblestones before halting behind a low, tan brick structure that looked more like a barracks than a manufacturer's. As she soon discovered, the building housed Arthur's offices and those of his subordinates, many of whom he introduced to her as he led her around inside. She met his much-lauded secretary, Tom, who turned out to be in his mid-fifties, a bit rotund, with spectacles and very little hair. She liked him, and given his age, she ruefully abandoned any hope that he might enlist, leaving a vacancy on the staff that she could fill. Even if he did, Tom had an assistant of his own, a young veteran who had lost a hand in the early months of the war. Surely he would be at the head of the queue, and Helen would be ashamed to snatch the promotion out from under him.

After showing her his office building—which, Arthur emphatically noted, contained nothing more explosive than tempers—he took her around to see one of the factory canteens, a clean, comfortable, spacious hall where workers enjoyed nutritious meals for a small fraction of the cost of bringing lunch from home or running out to a pub. Next they toured the infirmary, where minor injuries such as sprains, burns, and cuts were tended by a staff of dedicated nurses, who were trained to stabilize more serious cases before transport to a nearby hospital. They then viewed the loading dock, where large crates containing finished munitions were loaded onto trains with utmost care.

As they strolled from one site to the next, Helen was especially intrigued by the many munitionettes on the grounds, most clad in identical tan heavy cotton trousers and three-quarter-length jackets, their hair tucked neatly into tan broadcloth caps. She started at the sight of two women with oddly yellowish skin, laughing and chatting as they passed between buildings. "Those women seemed quite—sallow," she said in an undertone, not quite sure if that was the right word for it. "Is it a trick of the light, perhaps?"

"Your eyes aren't deceiving you," Arthur said, also quietly. "The yellow tint of their skin is a consequence of working with trinitrotoluene, a chemical component of the explosives. It seems to happen eventually to all of the girls who work in the Danger Buildings."

"That seems quite serious," said Helen, watching as the pair disappeared through the doorway of another building.

"It isn't permanent," Arthur assured her, smiling. "I hear there are creams that can prevent it—you would understand better than I—something about preventing the color from settling in the pores. But with or without such cosmetics, the color fades with time, if the workers transfer to another department or take an extended leave. The hue has earned the Danger Building munitionettes a particular nickname—canary girls."

"That's rather unkind."

He shrugged. "It's never spoken unkindly, but rather as an endearment, or as a proud boast by the canary girls themselves. They're among our most valuable employees, having taken on some of the most dangerous work, and they know it. It's said that blue-eyed canaries are especially adept at calibration work."

"I hope your canary girls are well compensated for the risks they take."

"Indeed they are, which is why positions in the Danger Buildings are so coveted." He gestured to a factory building directly in front of them, a tall stone structure next to the one the canary girls had entered. "Would you like to see some munitionettes at work?"

She most certainly did, so Arthur escorted her into a fuse factory, where dozens of women sat around long tables gauging metal rings, which other munitionettes collected and carried off to be placed into the machining part of the fuse cap. The room rang with the thudding and clanging of various machines and equipment at the far end of the vast space; though it was not deafening, Helen couldn't imagine enduring it for a twelve-hour shift, six days a week. It was somewhat quieter where the munitionettes sat. Helen was impressed by the speed and surety of their deft movements, and also by the sense of camaraderie, evident in the conversations they managed to have despite the din, occasionally bursting into friendly laughter. None of them, Helen observed as a few girls glanced up to smile or nod as she and Arthur passed, presented with the yellow skin of the so-called canary girls.

"May I see one of the Danger Buildings next?" she asked as Arthur led her to the exit.

"I'm sorry, darling. That's forbidden."

"I thought you were in charge here," she protested, smiling. "Can't you make an exception?"

"Not even once, not even for you." He regarded her with mock severity. "We operate under strict military regulations. Even if I were willing to allow a civilian such as yourself into the Danger Buildings, it would greatly inconvenience our overseers. Are you wearing any silk or nylon?"

"Silk," she replied, waving a hand gracefully to indicate her pretty ensemble.

"Well, that would have to come off."

"What? Here? Goodness, darling. You astonish me."

"In one of the shifting houses," he said emphatically, inclining his head toward a low white wooden structure centrally located amid the factories. "Friction from silk and nylon could cause a spark that would set off a con-flagration. Same with metal." He looked her up and down, examining her attire. "I spy metal clasps, hooks, and eyes on those boots you're wearing. The workers swap their shoes for wooden clogs. You'd also need a cap instead of that charming hat, which, if I'm not mis-taken, boasts a silk ribbon and a metal buckle. But your jewelry and every hairpin in that lovely coiffure would have to go, as would your brassiere, because I happen to know yours has metal fasteners."

"Well, safety first," she replied. "I wouldn't want to sacrifice the entire arsenal to fashion. Do you have a spare uniform, clogs, and cap I could borrow?"

"I'm afraid not. You'd have to take them from an-other girl's cubby, which means she'll find herself without a uniform when she arrives for her shift, which means I'm down one worker and she won't earn any wages."

She studied him through narrowed eyes. "I think you're just trying to discourage me, Mr. Purcell."

He smiled. "I might be. I'm also telling you the ab-solute truth."

She let out a loud, exasperated sigh and took his arm.

"Has it eased your worries at all, seeing the place?" Arthur asked as he led her back to the Silver Ghost.

"A bit," she admitted. "I'm glad to know that your office isn't in the same building as the explosives."

"Did you imagine my desk was a plank balanced on two kegs of gunpowder?"

"Something like that." Arthur opened the passenger door for her, but she hesitated before climbing in. "I do wonder about your canary girls, though. Anything that turns the skin that lurid shade of yellow cannot possibly be good for them."

"As I said, it's not permanent. It fades with time, after they're no longer exposed to it daily." He took her hands. "Weren't your fingertips always stained with ink when you worked for your father?"

"Not constantly, no, but ink isn't tri-ni-whatever-you-call-it——"

"Trinitrotoluene. Just call it TNT. Everyone does."

"Ink isn't TNT, and ink doesn't explode. Do your canary girls carry that yellow powder on their skin and clothing home to their families, to their children?"

"No, darling, they don't." His voice was gentle, patient. "When workers arrive, they change into their uniforms in the shifting houses and stow their own clothing and other belongings in their cubbies. At the end of the shift, the Danger Building workers leave their soiled uniforms in the shifting houses, have a good wash-up, and wear their own clothes home, or to their hostels, as the case may be. The soiled uniforms are laundered on-site, and when the workers arrive for their next shift, they find a clean kit waiting for them in their cubby."

Helen mulled it over. "I suppose you can't be any more careful than that."

"Remember, too, that no one is required to work in a Danger Building. Any worker who feels unsafe can request a transfer to another department." He held her gaze, his green eyes intent. "Munitions work is hazardous, Helen. Our girls know that. I do what I can to minimize the danger."

"I'm sure you do."

"You don't sound convinced." He gestured to the passenger seat. "Climb in. I'll show you something that may make you feel better."

She raised her eyebrows at him, skeptical, but did as he asked. Soon they were driving slowly through the complex, until they halted at a small courtyard that opened onto a grassy field, still within the stone walls. There, a dozen or so women in munitionettes' attire kicked a football back and forth, running the length of the makeshift pitch, laughing and calling out to one another. Even from a distance, Helen could see that nearly half of them were canary girls.

"Very well, darling. I see the point you're trying to

make," she said. "These girls are clearly vigorous and healthy."

"They're thriving," he said emphatically. "All of our girls are. Do you know, most of our workers are eating better now in our canteens than they ever have in their lives?"

"I'm not surprised," she replied. "I'm glad you provide for them." The lack of plentiful, nutritious food in working-class households was a terrible societal ill. Suffragettes wanted the vote in large part to gain the influence necessary to remedy such problems. She regarded Arthur fondly. "I know you would never intentionally let any harm come to your workers. I'm sure you're doing everything you can to keep them safe."

The relief in his eyes surprised her. "Thank you, darling," he said, a catch in his voice. He cleared his throat and smiled. "Shall I take you home? I'll have to come right back, of course."

"I could stay and help you around the office, save you the trip."

He threw her a wry look, adjusted the throttle, and drove on.

A week passed. Helen troubled Arthur no more about coming to work for him at Thornshire Arsenal, but the tour had another consequence that he had perhaps not expected. After seeing the munitionettes hard at work, even risking their lives, she had become even more determined to do her bit.

Then, sometime around eleven o'clock on the evening of 9 September, as she sat up in bed reading one more chapter while Arthur slept beside her, the stillness of the night was suddenly shattered by the thunderous roar of bombs and gunfire.

Arthur immediately woke and bolted out of bed to the window; heart pounding, Helen quickly doused the light just as he pulled back the blackout curtain. Hastening to his side, she stood beside him and watched, horrified, as distant searchlights illuminated a long, silvery object drifting over the city.

She flinched as another explosion boomed; Arthur put his arm around her. "It appears to be over the City, near St. Paul's Cathedral," he said, his gaze following the gleaming object until it disappeared behind a cloudbank or a building—in the darkness, at that distance, she couldn't be sure. Police and ambulance sirens wailed; the searchlights swept the skies. "It's not coming this way. Go back to bed. I'll wake you if there's any danger."

"But darling—"

"Please, Helen."

There was a strange undercurrent to his voice she had never heard before, one that would allow no argument. She nodded and returned to bed, but she could not sleep until the sirens faded and silence returned, and Arthur lay beside her once more.

The next morning, the papers, bound to obey the censors, reported only that "a London district" had been "visited" by a zeppelin, which had dropped incendiary and explosive bombs. Arthur left for work early in case the streets were impassible, so she had to wait impatiently for him to return that evening for any real news.

The reports he had managed to gather were grim. Wood Street and Silver Street behind Cheapside and near Guildhall had been struck in the raid; warehouses and other structures were gutted and smoldering ruins, and large craters marred the roads nearby. Another bomb had destroyed an omnibus on the way to Liverpool Street station, killing all twenty people on board and a housekeeper standing outside on the steps of her workplace. The zeppelin's bombs also struck Bartholomew Close, smashing the windows of Bart's Hospital, but sparing the ancient church of St. Bartholomew the Great. Later Arthur learned from his father's well-placed sources that thirty-eight people had been killed in the raid, including two policemen, and 124 had been wounded. As ever, the papers were required to be vague lest reports of deaths hearten the enemy.

Afterward, Helen and Arthur said little about that harrowing night, except to note that they had never been in any real danger. Nor were they likely to be, Arthur said, as there was nothing of military interest in Marylebone.

"What of Buckingham Palace?" Helen ventured. "It's only a mile and a half away."

"Let's trust that our ground defenses will prevent an attack there," Arthur said. "We might expect more interruptions of our sleep in the weeks to come, but likely nothing worse than that."

So he said, and so she pretended to agree, but Helen didn't think Arthur believed it any more than she did.

7
September–November 1915

Lucy

Jamie and Simon thought it terribly exciting that a zeppelin had struck at the very heart of London, only about five miles from their home. Sorely disappointed to have slept through the attack, they begged Lucy to take them to see the ruins, but she firmly declined. "You have school, and I have my training course," she reminded them, and received a chorus of groans in reply. Without thinking, she snapped, "Show some respect. Thirty-eight people died."

"Sorry, Mum," Jamie said contritely, and Simon nodded. Ashamed, Lucy swept them into a hug and apologized for losing her temper. She caught herself before pointing out that they would likely have far too many opportunities to observe the wreckage of German bombs before it was all over.

"Be thankful your boys weren't terrified," Gloria advised as they stood outside on the pavement watching their children head off to school together. "My Katie was inconsolable. I couldn't get her back to sleep for hours."

"Which means you hardly slept either," said Lucy sympathetically.

"No, but I wouldn't have regardless. I was as frightened as Katie. I just couldn't show it."

Lucy put her arm around her friend's shoulders as they watched their children disappear around the corner. She couldn't bring herself to admit that she had been desperately afraid during the raid too, that her heart had pounded and her hands trembled and tears filled her eyes. She had wanted Daniel there with an intensity that felt very close to anger. Ever since they were children together, Daniel had looked out for her, helping her with her schoolwork, fending off her teasing elder brother, encouraging her to conquer her fears, whether it was swimming or climbing trees or riding a horse. But last night, when she had felt so helpless and imperiled, he had been miles away, and she had been denied even the comfort of his voice on the telephone.

She longed for those afternoons at White Hart Lane when she and the boys had briefly reunited with Daniel on the sidelines after a match. They had not seen him since late May, when most of the 17th Middlesex had been granted a few days' leave to recuperate from a series of essential vaccines. They stayed at the Evans family home in Brookfield with her mother, George, and Eleanor as always, and other friends and relations turned up for tea and dinners. Everyone had news to share. Edwin was training in aerial reconnaissance with the Royal Flying Corps, and he expected to be sent to France any day. Alice was running the village school marvelously, although she admitted concern for the older boys' classes, which were steadily diminishing as one student after another ran off to enlist as soon as they came of age. Dieter Brandt had been interned at the Lofthouse Camp near Wakefield, and his wife and eldest daughters were struggling to keep the bakery open without him. Nearly everyone in the village had signed a formal petition attesting to Mr. Brandt's loyalty and excellent character and requesting his immediate release, but so far they had received no reply except for a perfunctory letter acknowledging that the petition had been duly filed.

As for Lucy, she wouldn't have mentioned her own small contribution to the war effort, but Daniel proudly boasted about her munitions training course at dinner their first night back in Brookfield. Her sisters-in-law were so delighted by the news that they actually applauded. George, ever the physician, furrowed his brow and asked what tasks Lucy was preparing for, because reports were circulating in the medical community about peculiar symptoms and troubling illnesses possibly linked to munitions work.

"I've been trained to run a lathe and a hydraulic press," Lucy said, "and to use various sorts of gauges and calipers. Next week, we're going to begin on the milling machine."

"But no chemical work?" her brother queried. "Just machinery?"

"Yes," said Lucy, "at least, so far. Why? Is something wrong?"

"No, sorry, don't mean to alarm you." Some of the tension left George's expression. "If you're working with tools and equipment, you should be fine, as long as you're properly trained to use them."

"I should think chemicals would be safer than those enormous, clanging metal machines," Alice remarked. "The potential for injury—well, it just seems terribly dangerous."

"I'm sure our Lucy is up to it," said her mother.

"What I wonder is who is minding my grandsons while you're at your course?"

"We can mind ourselves," Simon piped up from the other end of the table.

"Oh, I'm certain you can," said Daniel wryly as the other adults smiled indulgently.

"My neighbor Gloria looks after them," Lucy explained. "It's only a half day."

"Yes, but what about when you take an actual job?" A slight frown appeared on her mother's soft, dear face. "I've heard that munitionettes work twelve-hour shifts. That's a lot of childminding to ask of even the most generous neighbor."

"I haven't quite worked that out yet, but I will."

"It sounds to me like you may need a granny on the premises."

"What's this?" asked Eleanor, suddenly wary. "We need a granny on *these* premises."

"Your children are older than Lucy's, dear," Lucy's mother replied kindly, "and you have George around to help you."

"Let's not fight over Mother," Lucy pleaded, to head off any hurt feelings. "It may not be necessary. I might not even be able to find work."

"Well, keep me apprised, dear. I'll be ready to answer

the call, should you need me." Her mother turned to Daniel. "None of this would be necessary if you hadn't run off to enlist with all your footballer friends. And at your age! I've known you since you were a lad, and I thought you had better sense."

"Mother," Lucy chided, but not too severely. She couldn't fault her mother for saying aloud what she herself had often thought.

The visit, even with its awkward moments, had passed all too swiftly. In the first week of July, the 17th Middlesex transferred to Clipstone Camp near Mansfield, and moved again a few weeks later to a large encampment at Perham Down on Salisbury Plain. Though he was now only eighty miles west of home, Lucy knew better than to hope to see him, for the 17th Middlesex had begun the final stages of their military training. For the first time, Daniel wrote, the men of the battalion fired rifles on long ranges, and all three of the division's brigades engaged in joint live fire exercises. Yet their commanders still made time for football, arranging matches between a side from the 17th Middlesex and several teams from the league and other army battalions—no doubt with the expectation that the spectacle would increase recruits. Lucy hoped that a match would bring Daniel to London, but by early September the battalion team had played no games any closer than Reading.

Daniel was still in Perham Down in late September when Lucy finished her training program. On the last day, she and the other graduates were issued certificates and a yellow card with the name and address of a munitions factory that had requested trained workers, and where they would almost certainly be hired, pending an interview. Lucy's assignment was at Thornshire Arsenal. When she searched for its pin on the large map posted on the common room wall, she was dismayed to learn that it was all the way in Barking in East London, northeast and across the Thames from the better-known Royal Arsenal in Woolwich. Taking a steadying breath, she returned to the instructor who had given her the card. "Excuse me, but isn't there anything closer?" she asked. "This must be fifteen miles from my home. It would take me ninety minutes each way."

"More like two hours, I should think," the instructor replied. "This is all we have at the moment for your training and experience. You could decline this job and try your luck applying elsewhere, but there's no guarantee they'd have anything for you. If they did, you'd likely have to start at the bottom, with a lower wage."

"I see," said Lucy, heart sinking.

"If you can't bear the commute, many girls stay in hostels closer to work. The superintendent at Thornshire could help you find a place."

"I'm afraid that's not possible. I have two children at home."

"Oh, that *is* a problem." The instructor frowned, sympathetic. "Do you want me to ring the arsenal and cancel the interview? Shame to waste your training."

"No, thank you. I'd better keep it." Lucy needed the wages, and if she could do anything to hasten the end of the war by making munitions, she had to try. "I'm sure it'll work out somehow."

She repeated that to herself the following morning as she dressed with care, saw the boys off to school, and raced to catch the train, which was overcrowded and slow. Despite her best efforts, she arrived fifteen minutes late, breathless after the sprint from the station. Guards at the main gate inspected her papers and directed her through to a small, square building resembling an oversized shed not far from the entrance. A queue stretched out from the front door, and she hurried to join it, breathing a sigh of relief when she overheard that the girls in front of her had appointments at eleven o'clock too. The superintendent was evidently running behind, and would be none the wiser that Lucy had arrived late.

The queue moved steadily forward, and before long Lucy crossed the threshold and entered a hallway with one large rectangular room to the right and several small offices along the left. In the room to the right, which was separated from the entry by a waist-high partition, a large central table faced a bench along the wall. Shelves lined the walls between the windows, packed with file boxes, stacks of forms, and boxes of stationery and other supplies. A middle-aged woman in a dark brown suit sat at the table, and the younger woman who had opened the door quickly ushered Lucy and seven other applicants to the bench and invited them to sit. They just managed to squeeze onto it without anyone tumbling off the ends. At the far end of the room, four clerks worked at two smaller desks, one seated on either side, typing reports and sorting blue forms and yellow cards, apparently too engrossed in their tasks to notice the interviews happening nearby.

The woman at the center desk introduced herself as Superintendent Carmichael and beckoned the two girls on the right end of the bench forward. She examined the papers they had brought along and looked over both applicants appraisingly. "How old are you?" she queried the first.

"Twenty-three, miss."

The superintendent turned to the other. "And you?"

"Twenty-one, miss."

"Given your qualifications, I have no vacancies for you except in the Danger Buildings. Are you willing to work with mercury?"

"Yes, miss," the two applicants said in unison.

"Very well." From the neat piles of different-colored forms on the table, she plucked two blue pages and handed one to each woman. "Take these to the office across the hall, and you'll be shown how to fill it in." She beckoned to the next two girls on line on the bench. "Come forward, if you would."

The first two girls left, and the next two quickly took their places before the table. Again the superintendent scanned their papers and looked them over. "How old are you?" she asked the first, tall and sturdy.

"Twenty-eight, miss."

"And you?"

"Nineteen, miss," the younger replied meekly.

To the elder, the superintendent said, "Are you willing to work in yellow powder?"

"What's that?"

"Trotyl. TNT. You'd be filling shells."

"Well, miss . . ." The woman hesitated. "My husband's at the front, and I have my children to look after. I don't feel I ought to run the risk."

"That's all right," the superintendent said briskly. "You look strong. Would you have no objection to heavy work? You might undertake trucking, moving trolleys of shells or parts from one site to another."

"Yes, miss, I could do that." She indicated the younger woman with a tilt of her head. "May my friend work with me?"

The superintendent took in the younger woman's slight frame and narrow shoulders. "No, I shan't put her to that task, but there's a place for her in the fuse factory, and you'll be able to take your meals together in the same canteen."

The pair agreed, and they carried off their blue papers, smiling.

The next two applicants to approach the desk were a gray-haired woman with stooped shoulders and a perky blonde about half her age. The superintendent examined their papers, studied the elder for a moment, and asked, "How old are you?"

The woman shrugged and said nothing.

The superintendent's eyebrows rose. "How old are you?" she asked, slightly louder.

"A lady don't like to give her age," the older woman

protested. The young blonde snickered, and the older woman shot her a withering look.

The superintendent sighed. "What is your age?" she asked again, enunciating each word precisely. "We cannot proceed without that information. There are rules and regulations, you see."

"Forty-nine," the woman replied grudgingly.

"There, now, was that so difficult? What were you doing for employment before you came to us?"

"I take in a bit o' washin' now and then."

"Indeed? It just so happens we have a laundry on-site, for washing the workers' uniforms and such. Would you have any interest in that?"

"The wages any good?"

"Better than you'd earn taking in washing at home. They can tell you more across the hall."

"All right," the woman said, nodding thoughtfully. "Won't hurt to hear more about it."

"I'm eighteen," the blonde spoke up, without waiting to be asked. "I was a girl-of-all-work at a hotel in May-fair. I want a job in a Danger Building, please. I hear that's got the best wages for a girl just starting out."

"You've heard correctly." The superintendent studied the girl's documents. "I see your current employer has provided you with a character. I wonder why they should be so eager to see you go?"

"They weren't eager, miss," the blonde quickly replied. "But hotels don't require leaving certificates, so they couldn't keep me if I had a mind to go."

"I'm pleased you understand the rules," the superintendent remarked, handing her and the laundress their blue cards. "I'll put you to work filling shells, then."

The pair stepped away, but the blonde suddenly turned back. "One more question, miss. Must I wear a cap?"

"A cap," the superintendent echoed, eyebrows rising. "Are you referring to the regulation cap which is a required part of every worker's uniform?"

"Yes, miss. I don't much like caps."

"The wearing of a cap assures your safety and that of your fellow workers," the superintendent said, a touch of frost in her voice. "If you'd ever worked in a mill, and had seen a woman after her hair got caught in the machinery, you wouldn't question the necessity."

"But I won't be working near machinery, will I? Caps aren't comfortable. They make my head itch."

"It's just a bit of fabric, dearie," the laundress said, incredulous. "Hardly worth such a fuss. Wear a cap or go work somewhere else."

The superintendent held up a hand. "That will be all, thank you." The laundress shrugged and muttered under her breath as the superintendent turned back to the blonde. "Caps are required. This is where duty comes into war work—not only performing your assigned tasks, but willingly submitting to discipline. We are His Majesty's servants, and like the men at the front, we must be obedient to regulations."

"Yes, miss," the blonde replied, resigned. Eyes lowered, she followed the laundress into the office across the hall.

Sighing wearily, the superintendent beckoned Lucy and the last applicant forward. When she examined Lucy's credentials, she nodded approval. "I see you've been through the training course, and you've finished school." Her eyebrows rose as her gaze lit upon another detail. "Your previous work experience was helping at your father's medical practice?"

"Yes, miss."

"A doctor's daughter, and yet you're not going into nursing?"

Lucy's heart dipped. Must everyone ask her that? "No, miss. It's not for me."

"How unfortunate. Nurses are desperately needed." The superintendent glanced up and smiled faintly. "But so are munition workers. What is your age, Mrs. Dempsey?"

"I'm thirty, miss."

"Mature, educated, with practical office experience. I'd quite like to hire you to work here, in administration, but we don't have anything open at the moment." The superintendent frowned thoughtfully. "With your machinery training, you could work in the Finishing Shop. How would you feel about a job in the Danger Building? It does mean better pay, as befitting more skilled work."

Lucy remembered George's warning. "I'd be operating machines, not working with chemicals?"

"You'd be using machines to finish the shells, but the shells do contain explosive chemicals. It's the girls in the Filling Shop who pack the explosive powder into the shells before they come to you." She waved a hand dismissively, ready to move on. "It will make sense when the foreman demonstrates. Never fear; you won't be left to finish shells alone until he's certain you're properly trained."

Lucy wanted to think it over, but the next eight girls were squeezing onto the bench behind her, and she knew that if she didn't take the better-paying, more skilled job, someone else would snatch it up and she might be dispatched to the laundry. "I'll take it," she said. "Thank you, miss."

The superintendent nodded, handed her a blue form, and turned to the last girl in the group. "What is your age?" she asked, taking her papers.

"I'm twenty-two," the girl said, flashing a cheerful

grin. "I want to work in the Danger Building too if that's where the higher wages are. I'll work hard at any task given me, I don't complain, and I rather like caps."

"That's the spirit," the superintendent said, smiling as she handed her a blue form. "Very well, you two. Off you go. Welcome to Thornshire Arsenal."

They stopped at the office across the hall, where they were officially registered and directed to the medical shed next door for a health exam. The examination wasn't painful, merely unexpected, and all the more embarrassing for that. Afterward Lucy was declared to be in excellent health and was provided with a small blue rule book she intended to learn by heart before she reported for work in two days' time.

The first thing she did upon returning home was to ring her mother. "I got the job," she told her, feeling a surge of pride at her accomplishment. "I start Thursday."

"Congratulations, dear," her mother said warmly. "I'll pack straightaway, and I'll see you and my grandsons tomorrow."

Lucy had a day and a half to prepare herself, and the boys, for her first day as a munitionette. She went over the boys' schedule with her mother and studied the slim rule book, which contained lists of administrative policies, safety guidelines, and military regulations. She slept restlessly Wednesday night, and woke, more apprehensive than excited, to find her mother already in the kitchen preparing a strong pot of tea and raisin buns from Brandt's bakery, which she must have smuggled into the house in her suitcase or knitting basket, a lovely surprise.

"I'm so grateful you're here," Lucy said in the foyer as she threw on her coat and carefully tugged a hat over her long dark hair, which she had neatly braided and coiled with nary a hairpin. "I couldn't do this without you."

"The pleasure is all mine," her mother said, smiling as Lucy kissed her cheek. "Now I'll get to see more of Jamie and Simon as well as my only daughter. I should be thanking you."

"We'll see how you feel in a week," Lucy teased, giving her mother a little wave as she headed out the door.

It was not yet dawn. The streetlamps were doused for the blackout, but there was enough rosy morning light to see by, with the help of luminescent paint marking curbs and other obstacles. Small blue lightbulbs faintly illuminated the building and platforms of Clapham Junction station, already quite busy despite the early hour. Lucy's train reached Thornshire station at half six o'clock, and it was a ten-minute walk to the arsenal, so she passed through Gate Four twenty minutes before her shift began, just as the rule book recommended. It was not enough to be on the arsenal grounds at seven o'clock when her shift began; workers were required to change into uniform, pass through inspection, and be at their stations at the appointed hour or they were considered late.

Unfortunately, Lucy lost a bit of her head start by going to the wrong shifting house, and by the time a helpful passerby redirected her, she had lost a good measure of her nerve too. The warning bell by the main gate tolled just as she hurried into the shifting house. There she found dozens of other women changing from their street clothes into their trousers and jackets, chatting and joking. Some yawned and looked as if they had risen only moments before, while others were bright-eyed and eager, laughing with friends. Heart thudding as the minutes ticked away, Lucy searched the rows of cubbies until at last she spotted one marked with her own name. As she hurried toward it, shrugging out of her coat on the way, she accidentally struck another worker with her coat sleeve, knocking her cap off her honey-gold curls.

"Oh, I do beg your pardon," Lucy exclaimed, stooping to pick up the cap.

The younger woman snatched it from her. "Watch what you're doing," she snapped, then paused to look

Lucy up and down. "Oh, look, it's Lady Prim, all dressed up for her first day of work. Watch out, girls. This one's clumsy."

A smattering of laughter broke out, and Lucy felt heat rise in her cheeks. "I *am* sorry," she murmured, continuing on to her cubby. In what way had she over-dressed? Her long gray wool skirt, white blouse, and black-and-gray cardigan appeared to be finer quality and better tailored than the light blue chambray dress the other girl had removed, but it was hardly Savile Row. As Lucy changed into her uniform and tucked her coiled braids beneath her tan broadcloth cap, she managed a friendly nod for the girls to her left and right, but only one returned a cheerful grin. The others ignored her.

Her heart sank. She had signed on for the duration. Had she ruined her chances to make friends among the other girls all because of one careless misstep?

"Don't mind Marjorie," a voice spoke quietly behind her. Lucy turned around to find a young flaxen-haired girl regarding her with sympathy. "She doesn't mean any harm, but she always says exactly what she thinks."

"Oh, it's fine," Lucy said, smiling and forcing good cheer into her voice. "It's all in good fun."

"But maybe it's not the nicest way to welcome you on your first day." The girl stuck out her hand. "I'm

April Tipton. I've been here only a few weeks myself. I can help you along until you find your feet."

"Thank you. That's very kind." She shook April's hand. "I'm Lucy Dempsey." She glanced toward the opposite end of the room, where the other workers were lining up at an exit. "I assume that's the way to inspection, and then on through to the Danger Building?"

"It is, but you might want to put that away first." April pointed to Lucy's left hand. "Rules are rules."

Lucy gasped as her gaze went to her wedding ring. "Oh, goodness. Metal is forbidden, of course." Tugging it off her finger, she thought for a moment, reached into her cubby, and tucked the precious ring into the toe of her boot. "Tomorrow I'll leave it at home. I'm so used to wearing it, I didn't think."

April nodded understandingly as they headed to the inspection line. "Been married long, have you?"

"Ten years." Lucy smiled, thinking of Daniel. "We have two sons. My mother's looking after them while I work," she added, lest April think she was neglecting her children.

"What does your husband think about you taking on munitions work?"

"Oh, I think he's proud of me for doing my bit," she

said, stepping carefully as they joined the end of the queue. Those wooden clogs would take some getting used to. "He's in the army."

"So's my older brother, Henry. He's in the Lonsdale Pals, the Eleventh Battalion of the Border Regiment."

"My husband is in a Pals regiment too. The Seventeenth Middlesex. They're still training in Surrey."

"Henry's still training too, though he expects to go to France soon." April paused, thinking. "The Seventeenth Middlesex? Isn't that the Footballers' Battalion?"

"Yes, that's right." They had almost reached inspection, and Lucy watched carefully as the girls ahead of her split into two queues on either side of a table, each with an overseer. As each girl reached the front, the overseer asked her if she had anything to declare, giving them one last chance to rid themselves of anything they were forbidden to carry into the Danger Building. According to the rule book, men were not given the option to declare, but were patted down by their overseers, their pockets scrupulously searched for matches and tobacco.

"Dempsey." April threw her an appraising glance over her shoulder as she moved up the line. "Is your husband Daniel Dempsey, of Tottenham Hotspur?"

"Yes," Lucy said, lowering her voice, "but perhaps we can keep that between us? After what happened before, I don't want anyone to think I'm putting on airs."

"Of course. Your secret's safe with me." April puffed out a breath and shook her head. "Daniel Dempsey. He's brilliant."

"Well, naturally I think so, but I'm hardly impartial."

April laughed, and Lucy suddenly felt very much better.

The good feeling lasted as she passed through inspection and into the Danger Building, where the munitionettes timed in with their punch cards and dispersed to their stations. April and most of the other girls entered an open doorway beneath a sign that read "Filling Shop," but Lucy heard mechanical noises coming through a doorway at the far end of the room, so she decided to head that way. As she passed the Filling Shop, she glimpsed April taking a seat beside the unfriendly girl—Marjorie, April had called her—chatting and smiling as if they were old friends. Maybe April would convince Marjorie to give her another chance. It would certainly make the long shifts more pleasant if they all got along.

The other doorway, above which was painted the words "Finishing Shop," turned out to be a wide, short brick-and-concrete passageway leading into a different building altogether, one noticeably warmer. Entering a vast room about the size of a warehouse, Lucy observed rows of industrial machines, still with the shine of new-ness upon them, and a dozen or so munitionettes and at least as many men and boys turning out copper caps on huge pressing machines. As she approached the first row, a burly, dark-haired man in his mid-forties broke off an intense discussion with a slighter fellow who was wielding a wrench in the guts of the only silent machine in the room. The burly man scowled at the sight of her, which told her with immediate, dismaying certainty that he was the foreman. "I s'pose you're the new girl who fancies herself an operator?" he fairly growled at her.

"I'm Lucy Dempsey, sir," she replied, offering a courteous nod. "I've been assigned to finish shells. Su-perintendent Carmichael ordered me to report to the foreman."

"Aye, that's me." To the man with the wrench, he added, "Keep at it. I'll ask Donovan about those parts." Turning back to Lucy with a glower, he said, "Let me make something clear: This is no place for a girl. Filling shells is one thing, but the Finishing Shop is for skilled work, union labor, and if not for the war I'd have nowt to do with training you."

"Well, naturally." She was too surprised to be intimidated. "If not for the war, I wouldn't be here."

"That's true enough. Don't think you're keeping this job after we thrash the Germans, either. You'll be out, and a soldier returned from the front will get his job back."

"He'll be welcome to it," she said, bewildered. When the war was over, the government wouldn't need munitionettes because it wouldn't need munitions. In the meantime, she needed the wages, and surely the foreman didn't think the jobs should go unfilled because there weren't men enough to fill them. "I understand this job is only temporary. I'm just trying to do my bit, and to earn a wage while my husband is in the service."

The foreman eyed her suspiciously, but apparently she had said the right thing, because his scowl became slightly less fierce. "Don't think you can pass off second-rate work just because you're a novice," he warned. "A badly made English shell can kill our Tommies just as dead as a German bomb. I'll be inspecting your work very carefully, and you'll do over any mistakes until you get it right."

"Thank you, sir." Why did he keep thundering the obvious at her as if he expected an argument? This was her first factory job ever. She had hoped for close supervision, at least in the beginning, but she had been reluctant to ask for it, since the foreman was evidently very busy.

"No need for 'sir.' Save that for the boss. Call me Mr. Vernon." He turned away, gesturing sharply to indicate that she was to follow. "Come on, then. We'll get you started."

He led her past the pressing machines to a more open space at the far end of the building, where munition-ettes worked with a variety of hand tools before rows of large shells set up on their back ends. She expected to be taken through to another chamber containing the sort of machines she had trained on in her course, but instead he halted before the row of eight-inch shells in the far corner of the room, as if he meant to tuck her away out of sight.

"Other girls will bring you the filled shells on a trolley, and you'll help unload them to your station," he said brusquely. "Before you finish the shell, you need to fit the exploder." He selected a hand drill from a rack of tools and demonstrated how to attach it to the tip of the shell and remove the plug with several vigorous turns of the handle. Setting the plug and drill aside, he inserted the nozzle of a long black rubber hose into the shell and tamped down the powder, scraping around the interior sides, presumably to catch every grain. "Where are your gloves?" he asked, eyeing her slender hands.

"I haven't got any."

He grumbled deep in his throat and jerked his thumb, showing off his own gloves, toward a wall of shelves where various caps, aprons, gloves, masks, and other gear were sorted. She hurried over and quickly searched through the gloves for the smallest pair, grabbed a heavy apron for good measure, and hurried back. Mr. Vernon had picked up a metal pitcher with a spout and was stirring the contents with a metal bar, scraping down the sides. "Don't get any on yourself or you'll be badly burned," he advised curtly as he carefully poured a thick liquid into the shell. "You've got to top off the case with molten explosive."

She nodded, feeling the heat of it on her face.

Setting the pitcher aside, he selected a tool that resembled a metal bar with an open, circular cutting tool in the middle. "This is a die stock," he said, fitting the circular part on the head of the shell and grasping the two metal bars like handles. "When you turn it like so"—he paused to demonstrate several firm, clockwise turns—"it cuts uniform threads. Do you know what that means?"

As it happened, since her father-in-law was a carpenter, she did. "Yes, sir—Mr. Vernon."

"Next, use the wheel to clear the screw threads." Taking another tool from the rack, he inserted the shaft into the tip of the shell and turned the wheel clockwise several times with an effort she wasn't sure she could match. Removing the wheel, he inserted a sort of spike into the tip and pounded the end again and again, then withdrew the spike, inserted a rod to measure the depth, and repeated the process until its contents reached the proper level, a number he ordered her to memorize. He then demonstrated how to insert the detonators, narrating the process with warnings and admonitions. Lastly, he stenciled the destructive mark on the shell. "Trolley workers will carry the finished batch away," he added. "You'll help them load. Then you catch your breath, if you can, before the next trolley of shells to finish arrives." He eyed her, frowning. "Are you ready to give it a go?"

There was no other acceptable answer but yes, so she nodded.

For the first two hours Mr. Vernon hovered over her shoulder, observing her every move, correcting and reproving her whenever she fell short of perfection. From the corner of her eye she observed other munitionettes working deftly and assuredly at the same tasks, seeming to complete three shells to her every one. The work was physically demanding, especially turning the wheel and pounding the mallet, and by the time Mr. Vernon trusted her enough to proceed on her own, checking in only every ten minutes, and then every fifteen, her arm and shoulder ached.

Once, when the foreman stepped away, Lucy paused to wipe her brow with her jacket sleeve. "Don't mind Mr. Vernon," another munitionette called to her from the next row. "He doesn't like any of us. You're doing well."

"Thank you," Lucy called back, grateful for the first kind word she'd heard in hours. "Is it normal to feel like your arm is about to fall off?"

"Only on the first day," the other woman replied, grinning. "Maybe the second too."

Lucy was glad for the gloves and the apron, but she would have liked a veil too, or nose plugs. Traces of yellow powder lingered on the tools and her station, and the acrid odor of the molten explosive stung her nostrils and eyes. It was a relief when the bell rang to signal the dinner hour. She quickly finished stenciling a shell, left her gloves and apron on the table, and followed the other munitionettes back into the other building, where the workers were passing through a stone archway into a washroom with several rows of sinks. Chatting and teasing, they lined up to scrub their hands and faces, some vigorously, others indifferently, then passed through a doorway on the opposite wall into the canteen.

Lucy was one of the last to get a turn at a sink, and

she took extra care to wash every yellow speck off her hands; somehow, despite the gloves, powder had gotten on her skin. By the time she entered the canteen, most of the other workers had already collected their food and had claimed seats at one of the many tables for four or six.

"Oh, look, it's Lady Prim," a familiar voice sang out from a table somewhere to her left. Heart sinking, Lucy did not spare Marjorie a glance but walked straight on to the dinner queue. "Why does *she* get the Finishing Shop, I wonder? Why shouldn't she start in the Filling Shop and work her way up like everyone else? Mabel's been here longest."

Cheeks flushed, Lucy ignored Marjorie and the murmurs of agreement her taunting evoked. Tray in hand, she looked around the room for the friendly girl from the Finishing Shop, or the cheerful girl from her interview, but she spotted neither. She found a table where three other workers were nearly finishing eating; they smiled kindly as she seated herself, but they forgot to introduce themselves or ask her name, too busy conversing in hushed, scandalized voices about a lathe operator named Mary who had been sacked that morning after a matchstick had tumbled out of her pocket.

"A matchstick," one of the girls exclaimed. "Why

on earth would she bring a matchstick into the Danger Building?"

"Mary said she forgot it was in her pocket from lighting the fires at home before she left this morning," another replied.

"That doesn't make any sense," the third scoffed. "It would have been in the pocket of her regular clothes. She changed into her uniform in the shifting house like everyone else."

"I'm just telling you what she told the superintendent," the second girl said as they all rose and gathered their trays. "What a sight that was, Mrs. Carmichael swooping in and snatching her up and hauling her off."

"Poor dear," the first girl said as they walked away. "So humiliating, to be sacked in front of everyone! She won't get a leaving certificate either, so she won't be able to find a job somewhere else."

Lucy felt a chill. That disgrace could have been hers, if April hadn't reminded her about her wedding ring.

The afternoon went better than the morning, and at teatime Lucy made sure to stay close to the friendly girl from the Finishing Shop as the crowd passed from the washroom to the canteen. To her relief, when she asked if she might join her and her two companions at their table, they cheerfully agreed. As soon as Lucy introduced herself and learned all their names, the conversation quickly turned to the unfortunate Mary, sacked for a matchstick. "She could have blown up the whole building," one of the girls said, her eyes wide with alarm.

"Not unless she dropped a lit match onto a pile of TNT," said the friendly girl, whose name was Daisy.

"I'm not so sure. That yellow powder drifts everywhere." The third girl held out her hands, the yellow tint of her skin proving her claim. "If someone had stepped on that match with her wooden clog, and scraped it on the floor, and it had sparked—" She pressed her lips together and shook her head, and they all exchanged uneasy looks.

"It could have happened, but it didn't," Daisy said reassuringly.

"Can I look forward to this much excitement every day?" asked Lucy, smiling, hoping to chase away the gloom. They smiled back and assured her that grave mistakes like Mary's almost never happened. Everyone was scrupulously careful. The consequences would be too dire if they were not.

Although she was tired, Lucy finished out her shift well, spirits lifted by the promising new friendships she had made. The next day her muscles were sore, but she had become accustomed to the tasks and worked through the aches, earning a grudging grunt that might have been approval from Mr. Vernon. But at dinner, Marjorie trod on her heel as Lucy carried her tray to her table, causing her to stumble in her wooden clogs and spill her soup. Daisy fetched her another bowl as Lucy cleaned up the mess, so she still had time to eat before she was due back at her station.

The days turned into weeks. Lucy's muscles lost their soreness and she felt her arms growing stronger and leaner. She did her best to avoid Marjorie, but she still endured the occasional ill-timed jostling. More frequent were disparaging remarks about how she had stolen a prime job from Mabel, who, Lucy learned, turned out to be the most popular worker in the Danger Building, a motherly figure to many of the girls who did not get along with their own mothers, or who had moved to London from distant villages and struggled with bouts of homesickness. Mabel and the other long-time workers bore their yellowed skin proudly, evidence of their seniority.

Lucy told herself that invented workplace tiffs were beneath her notice considering the very real dangers all around. In the middle of October, a zeppelin again bombed "a London district," as the papers put it, the censors having forbidden anything more specific; more than three dozen people had been killed and eighty-seven injured. Exhausted from long shifts at the arsenal, Lucy had slept through the entire raid. She was immeasurably grateful to her mother, who kept the boys fed and all of them in clean clothes. On the last Saturday of October, her mother even took Jamie and Simon out to the Dell to see Daniel play for the 17th Middlesex team against Southampton. Lucy could not go because of work, but she hung on every detail of the boys' description of the match the next morning.

"Dad said they expect to get their orders soon," Jamie said, watching her closely for her reaction.

"Just as we've all expected," she said evenly, concealing her dismay. "It's nothing to worry about. Haven't we been fortunate to have seen him so often, even after he enlisted? Most families aren't that lucky."

The boys agreed, but Lucy's mother gave her a sympathetic look, knowing how she really felt.

A week later, Lucy was in the inspection queue, lost in thought, brooding over a recent letter from Daniel in which he said he believed their deployment to France was imminent. Just then her gaze was drawn to a glint at the nape of the neck of a tall, pretty young woman who wore her reddish-brown hair in a braid beneath her cap. She was four people ahead of Lucy, and was next up to approach the overseer. Without thinking, Lucy quickly stepped around the girls in front of her, snatched the hairpin from the taller girl's locks, evoking a cry of surprise. Concealing the hairpin in her fist, Lucy strode back to the shifting house and dropped it into the nearest waste basket. Pausing a moment to settle her nerves, she joined the end of the queue and tried to keep her expression serene despite the curious, astonished glances of the munitionettes who had clearly witnessed everything. The tall girl, hand clasped to the nape of her neck, stood frozen at the head of the queue, her face pale wherever the yellow tint had not touched it. The overseer had to prompt her twice before she responded that she had nothing to declare and moved on into the Danger Building. Right behind her, Mabel held Lucy's gaze for a long moment, offered her a slow nod, and took her turn with the overseer.

Later, Lucy was enjoying dinner with Daisy and her friends when Mabel approached the table, the tall girl trailing after. Everyone respected Mabel, so their conversation abruptly ceased when she halted by Lucy's chair and planted her hands on her hips. "You did a good turn for my Peggy today," she remarked, inclining her head toward the younger woman. "If the overseer had seen that hairpin, my girl would have been sacked, and there would've been no leaving certificate coming to her."

"I'm glad I saw it first," said Lucy, offering Peggy a nod and a smile.

Mabel regarded her knowingly. Behind her, other munitionettes had drawn closer to observe the scene—Marjorie near the front, scowling, April just behind her, absently fingering the cuff of her jacket, her expression hopeful. "If anyone had caught you with it before you tossed it, you would've been the one sacked."

"I'm glad I was quick," Lucy replied.

"I hear you're Daniel Dempsey's wife."

"Did you, now?" Lucy raised her eyebrows at April, who had the decency to look embarrassed.

Mabel paused to cough and clear her throat. "Do you play football as well?"

"Not as well as my husband."

A ripple of laughter rose from the group. "I wouldn't expect that," said Mabel, grinning. "Some of us play now and then after dinner and after tea, in that field near the motor pool. That doesn't leave us much time, of course, not enough for a real match or even a half, but it's a bit of fun in the fresh air. You're welcome to join us anytime, if you like."

A wide-eyed look from Daisy told Lucy this was a great honor indeed. "I'd enjoy that," said Lucy. "Thank you."

"Thank *you*," said Peggy, stepping forward and reaching for Lucy's hand. "I would've been out on my ear if not for you."

Lucy gave her hand a quick squeeze. "Maybe the overseers wouldn't have noticed."

"If not them, *someone* would have noticed," Peggy said, frowning as she glanced over one shoulder and then the other, as if she expected to find a spiteful co-worker or a German spy eavesdropping. "Someone would have reported me."

On her way home that evening, Lucy was fatigued but elated. She had helped a fellow munitionette and had earned Mabel's approval, which surely meant that Marjorie would quit bullying her. She couldn't wait to tell her sons, and Daniel, that she had been invited to join the Thornshire Arsenal football club, even if it was just a few friends having a bit of fun on a makeshift pitch.

But when she arrived home at nine o'clock, her mother met her in the foyer, her expression grave, an envelope in her hand. "Daniel addressed it to the family," she said, holding out the letter, "so Jamie convinced me to let them read it. I apologize if I should have waited, but they were so eager to hear from their father."

"Of course they were," Lucy said, setting down

her bag and taking the envelope. "As you say, Daniel sent it to all of us. It would have been cruel to make them wait."

Daniel had written the letter himself, she reminded herself as she removed it from the envelope. He must be well, safe, uninjured. She mustn't always imagine the worst.

But as she read, her heart plummeted. Though his news wasn't the worst she could have imagined, it was still quite bad indeed.

The 17th Middlesex had received its orders. In less than a fortnight, Daniel would be sailing for France.

8
November–December 1915

April

"I don't understand why Mabel had to invite Lady Prim to play football with us," Marjorie grumbled early one mid-November morning as she and April rode the overcrowded tram to Thornshire.

"Mabel owed her a favor," April reminded her. "Peggy would've been sacked if not for her."

Marjorie rolled her eyes. "I might've seen that hairpin too, if I had been standing as close as she were."

"Maybe, but you weren't and you didn't." Marjorie seemed determined to dislike Lucy, but everyone else thought well of her. Even Mabel didn't begrudge her the job in the Finishing Shop, once word got out that Lucy had undergone weeks of training and was more qualified despite being new. "Lucy risked her own job to save Peggy's. Inviting her to join the club was the least Mabel could do."

"It's all very well that Lady Prim's husband is a footballer," Marjorie went on, her voice shaking as the tram hit a bump that jostled April and Marjorie against each other. They were lucky to have seats at all; most mornings the cars were so packed that they had to stand, and on particularly bad days, they couldn't squeeze aboard at all, but had to wait for a later tram. "But it's not like *she* plays for Tottenham."

"Would you stop calling her that name? What has she ever done to you?"

"Why are you defending her? She's stuck-up."

"No she isn't. She's just shy. If you'd give her a chance, you'd see that." April heaved a sigh, exasperated. "Anyway, even you have to admit she's a great player. It has nothing to do with her husband. Maybe he taught her a few things, but she came by her natural ability herself."

"She's not bad," Marjorie admitted grudgingly. "All I can say is she had better not want to play keeper. That's Mabel's job, and I'm next up."

"You have nothing to worry about. Lucy's a striker." April shook her head. "Honestly, Marjorie. Lucy didn't steal Mabel's job at the arsenal and she's not after anyone's spot on the pitch. You should be glad Mabel's adding more players. If we get enough for two full sides, we can play a proper match, and we'll need two keepers, you and Mabel both."

"That would be grand, if Mabel keeps playing."

"Why wouldn't she? She founded the club." Marjorie only took over in the goal when Mabel needed a rest. Otherwise, which was most of the time, Marjorie played defense.

"Yes, but her cough is getting much worse. Haven't you noticed?" Marjorie shook her head, frowning. "Seems to me she rests a lot more than she used to."

"Maybe, but she's older than we are."

"Yes, but she's hardly *geriatric*." Marjorie rose as the tram slowed to a stop. "Come on, then. Mustn't be late again or we'll both be out of the club, since we'll be sacked."

Nodding, April too rose and grasped the handrail for balance. Her mother's letters made it clear how much April's increased earnings mattered to the family, providing more and better food and new clothes and shoes for her siblings. She couldn't let them down by losing her job. Even transferring out of the Danger Building to an easier position elsewhere at Thornshire would be giving up too much.

As they disembarked the tram and headed toward the arsenal, Marjorie suddenly turned her head, covered her mouth with her mitten, and coughed hoarsely. "Wouldn't you know it? I think I've caught Mabel's cold."

"Something's definitely going around," April agreed as they were swept up in a stream of other workers all heading to Thornshire. Their entrance, Gate Four, was on the far side of the complex, so they took their usual shortcut on the gravel paths that wound through the park in front of Gate One. The park was usually quite pretty, but it was less so now with the flower beds covered in mulch and the shade trees barely holding on to their last dry, brown leaves. April enjoyed walking through the park in any season, and she inhaled deeply, imagining for a moment that she was back in the countryside. London had its delights, and now that she was earning enough to keep back a bit of spending money from the wages she sent home, she occasionally indulged in a visit to a teashop or a confectioner's, or enjoyed a night out at the theatre. Even so, she preferred the green moors, murmuring brooks, deep forests, and rich farmlands of Derbyshire to the odors and noise of the city.

Until she could manage a visit home, which looked unlikely for the duration, the park would have to do.

As they hurried along the gravel path, Marjorie nudged April and nodded to a young man seated on a bench near the center of the park, hands in his pockets, legs stretched out before him and ankles crossed. "Look, there he is again," Marjorie said, scornful. "Lazing about on a park bench while our brothers are fighting in trenches somewhere in France. If this one can't put on a uniform, the least he could do is find a job."

April studied the young man for a moment, not long enough to draw his attention. "Maybe it's his day off."

"Then he has a great many days off," Marjorie retorted. "He's here nearly every morning we are. There's a war on. Everyone who can contribute something in the way of war work ought to do so. In his case, he should enlist. He's a bit scrawny, but he's strong enough to carry a rifle."

"He's not scrawny. He's slender, but he's at least as tall as you." April actually thought he was quite good-looking, although she wouldn't admit that aloud, not after Marjorie disparaged him. He had thick auburn hair so dark it appeared brown from a distance, an oblong face with a straight, narrow nose, dark brown eyes, straight eyebrows often drawn together as if he were concentrating, and a mouth that was neither too narrow nor too full. It tended to quirk upward on the right, which April supposed sufficed for a smile for a serious young man. His suits and coat were not flashy, but they were clearly a better cut than what the workmen who passed him on the way to the arsenal could afford. Curiously, several of those workmen exchanged nods or a few pleasant words with him in passing, something she had noticed on other mornings. Evidently they didn't share Marjorie's disgust for shirkers.

"Maybe he has bad eyes," April suggested as they passed him, lowering her voice so he would not overhear.

"Then where are his glasses?"

"In his pocket? Or maybe he has a heart condition."

"Or maybe he's a coward." As they left the park, Marjorie caught the sleeve of April's coat and brought her to a halt. "Why must you always defend every shirker, or is it only the good-looking ones? Are you a conchie?"

"Of course not," said April, tugging her sleeve free. So Marjorie thought he was good-looking too. "Would a conscientious objector work in munitions? I support our Tommies every bit as much as you do. I'm just not as obvious about it."

"Maybe you should be." Marjorie started walking again, so briskly that April had to run a few steps to catch up. "What good is your silent disapproval? It doesn't get a single shirker to enlist."

"Well, no, but if the government passes conscription—"

"You don't know that they will, and that doesn't let you off the hook in the meantime. You've seen the posters. Getting able-bodied young men to enlist is one of the most important bits of war work we women can do."

"I'd rather fill shells."

"You can do both. I do."

April muffled a sigh and let it go. She didn't want to spend the bright, clear morning arguing, not when they were about to spend the next six hours indoors.

They didn't exchange another word as they approached Gate Four, showed their identification badges to the sentries, entered the shifting house, and changed into their uniforms. Only when they stood in line for inspection did Marjorie turn around, peer at her for a moment, and remark, "You know, in this light, your hair looks a bit ginger."

"Yours too." April wondered why she hadn't noticed before.

"Yellow skin and ginger hair. I s'pose we're fully fledged munitionettes now."

"Canary girls through and through," April agreed. The more experienced workers had told them that changes to their skin and hair were only a matter of time, and not to worry about them. They weren't harmful, and the color would fade soon enough if they quit work or transferred out of the Danger Building. April's skin had taken on a faint yellow tinge, as had Marjorie's, not yet as vivid as Mabel or Peggy or the others who had been munitionettes longer. April had become so accustomed to the canary girls' peculiar coloring that she scarcely noticed it in her friends. She nearly always forgot about the changes to her own appearance unless a passerby on the street gawked, which made her feel both embarrassed and angry, or if a fellow passenger on the tram thanked her for her service, which filled her with pride. Some of the girls lamented their diminished beauty, but all agreed that any fellow who spurned them for a temporary imperfection was beneath their notice.

In addition to the changes to their appearance, they all seemed to acquire the same hoarse cough eventually. Most of the canary girls supposed that it was just a bad cold they kept passing around, working so closely together and often sharing the same hostels. The women who had come to munitions works from the mills disagreed, though, recalling the similar, persistent coughs that girls developed after months at the looms, breathing in all those stray fibers. Yet all of the munitionettes believed that they had more to fear from accidents and bombings than anything floating in the air. They didn't often talk about it because it was simply too grim, but the possibility of a deadly explosion, whether set off by a careless worker or a German bomb, was something they had to accept every time they passed through the arsenal gates.

For her part, once she entered the Danger Building, April pushed her worries to the back of her mind and focused on the task at hand. Although the work was monotonous and repetitive, it was less exhausting than being a housemaid and the hours were much better, just as Marjorie had promised. Sometimes April thought wistfully of the walks into the village from Alderlea, and the happy stolen moments browsing the shops or admiring the storefront windows, but mostly she took pride in her contribution to the war effort and delighted in her substantially higher wages.

Filling shells wasn't difficult, and with experience April had improved her quality and speed, earning praise from the overlookers. The munitionettes in their section worked mostly on eight-inch shells, although sometimes they were shifted over to other armaments depending upon need. Each girl had a tin of TNT, a funnel, a mallet, and a smooth wooden rod that looked like it might have been cut from a broom handle. Inserting the funnel into the tip of the empty shell to prevent spillage, a worker would scoop a measure of the yellow powder inside, then tamp it down firmly with the wooden stick—but not too firmly, or it might detonate. They would repeat the process, again and again, until the shell was sufficiently filled, which they measured by marks on the stick. Then they would fix the cap firmly in place and load the shell carefully onto a trolley, to be wheeled off to the Finishing Shop.

They were as tidy and efficient as they could be, but the yellow powder drifted over everything—not massive piles of it, they were not so wasteful as that, but traces here and there and everywhere. It was little wonder their faces and hands turned yellow, but April didn't understand why blondes should turn into gingers, and in such a patchy fashion. Typically the length of the strands changed, with only the roots showing the natural color. The dark-haired girls looked even more peculiar. Brunettes' hair sometimes took on a greenish hue, while girls with very dark hair saw it leached of color until it became almost white, but usually only in the front, where they faced the shells. The workers' caps, which were meant only to keep their hair out of the way, did nothing to prevent the discoloration.

A week before, Lucy, who had the most enviably beautiful, silky black hair, ruefully lamented the light patch appearing above her brow. She had assumed she was going gray due to stress and lack of sleep until Mabel set her straight. "The color will come back, though, won't it?" Lucy asked worriedly as they kicked the football around after dinner. "I don't want Daniel to see me like this."

"I don't blame you," said Marjorie, voice dripping with false sympathy. "You look a bit like a badger."

"Shut up, you," Peggy said fondly, giving her a shove. Most of the other girls laughed as if it was all in good fun, but not Lucy, and not April.

Marjorie's casual cruelty did not escape Mabel's notice. While she didn't call Marjorie out in front of the club, she did move her from defense to midfield, which Marjorie hated. She liked to see the whole field spread out before her without having to turn this way and that or look behind her, and nobody ran more than the midfielders, as April could attest.

"The color won't come back, but the bleached parts will grow out," April reassured Lucy later as they headed back to the Danger Building. "The hair will grow back the proper color."

"Only to be bleached anew," Lucy said mournfully, but she managed a smile. "It's only for the duration, though, right?"

"Right," April said, putting an arm around her shoulders.

As the weeks passed, the white patch in Lucy's hair spread and her skin turned as yellow as April's. Almost all of the girls in the Filling Shop caught Mabel's cough, and several, including April, were also bothered by persistent sore throats and sneezing. Over a fortnight, three players reluctantly quit the football club, complaining of shortness of breath, fatigue, and chest pains. Mabel told them they were welcome back anytime and urged them to visit the infirmary. Later April learned that two of the girls had transferred out of the Danger Building, while the third had left munitions work altogether.

"If they're tired and short of breath, it just means they aren't fit," Marjorie declared one evening as they rode back to their hostel. Her voice was barely audible over the rattling of the tram, and she rested her head on April's shoulder, eyes closed. "They need more exercise, not less."

"Maybe they do need rest," April said. "Sleep helps you with your migraines. Isn't this your second this week?"

"Third, if you count Monday." Marjorie sighed and clasped a hand to her forehead. "It's the weather. Ever since it turned colder, these stupid migraines—" She winced as the tram jolted. "I'll be fine in a couple of hours."

"It got colder than this in Derbyshire, and you never had migraines there."

"Only because Mrs. Wilson wouldn't allow it." A

wan smile appeared on Marjorie's sallow face, which had always been porcelain and roses before. "D'you mind if we don't talk for a while? My head is throbbing, and I feel like I have to think very hard to keep my words in the right order."

"Of course," April replied in a whisper. She stroked her friend's head gently, smoothing her gingery curls away from her forehead until the tram reached their stop.

The next morning, Marjorie felt perfectly fine again. She had slept a solid eight hours and the weather was a good deal warmer and sunnier than it had been the day before, and so, as they raced off to the arsenal, she and April argued good-naturedly about who was right about the cause and the cure for her migraines. The auburn-haired lad was in the park by the front gate again, but on a different bench this time, chatting with an older fellow April recognized as the foreman of the shell casting shop.

"Maybe Mr. Townes will convince that shirker to get a job, if he won't enlist," Marjorie said, raising her voice as they approached.

"Hush," April murmured. "They'll hear you."

"So what if he does?" Marjorie replied in a somewhat quieter voice. "If he understood how girls like us despise shirkers like him, he might do something about it."

"I'm more concerned about offending Mr. Townes." April linked her arm through Marjorie's and propelled her forward, watching the men from the corner of her eye as they passed. Neither the foreman nor the auburn-haired lad took any notice of them.

When they had left the hostel earlier that morning, April and Marjorie had been obliged to wait nearly a quarter hour until a tram with room for them to squeeze aboard had come along, so they were cutting it close as they raced into the shifting house, threw on their uniforms, timed in, and took their stations with only seconds to spare. The foreman worked them at top speed all morning, which told them a big push was in the works over in France. Whenever demand for armaments surged, within a fortnight the newspapers would report some new offensive, an assault on German forces entrenched near a battered French village or a bold attempt to break through a German salient.

At dinner, April, Marjorie, Peggy, and a trolley girl named Louise discussed what might be happening abroad. They were piecing together details from their brothers' and sweethearts' letters from the front when Peggy suddenly set down her fork and grimaced. "Does this taste strange to anyone else?" she asked, eyeing her meal suspiciously. "It tastes like someone sprinkled iron filings in it."

"Maybe it's copper shavings from the fuse cap shop," Louise said with a grin. "A little accidental extra seasoning."

"I taste it too," said April, sampling her mashed turnips thoughtfully. "Something metallic."

Marjorie studied her plate. "I don't think it's the food," she said, pulling a face. "I've been tasting metal for days, whether I'm eating in the canteen or the hostel or that posh teashop April's always dragging me to. It comes and goes. I figured it had something to do with my migraines, but if you have that metal taste in your mouths too—"

They exchanged uneasy looks.

"Do you think that's why they're always telling us to drink more milk?" asked Louise, nodding to the dispensers and pitchers recently installed near the food queue. "I have friends in other buildings, and they say no one constantly nags them to drink milk the way they do in our canteens."

Peggy folded her arms over her chest as if warding off a chill. "That's another thing. Don't you think it's odd that we have to eat separately now?"

As Louise nodded, April and Marjorie exchanged puzzled glances. "Oh, this was before your time," Louise explained. "We used to be allowed to eat with our friends at other canteens, or they could eat here with us, but early this summer, Superintendent Carmichael put a stop to that."

"She said it was to improve efficiency, so we didn't waste time walking from building to building," added Peggy. "That made sense to us, since our breaks are so short as it is, but I heard that some workers complained about canary girls leaving yellow powder everywhere, on the tables and chairs, the cutlery, the doorknobs."

"I heard it was because we're always coughing," said Louise, frowning. "That, and our yellow skin made them lose their appetites."

The other girls gasped at the rudeness of it all. "I hope that's not true," April said. "Some of our footballers work in other buildings, and they treat us the same as anyone else. Although—" She hesitated, thinking.

"Although what?" Marjorie prompted.

"It's probably nothing, but on the trams, other passengers gawk at our skin and hair—you know those looks." April glanced around the table for confirmation, and they all nodded. "Some people thank us for our service, but they all keep their distance."

"That's true," said Marjorie. "They edge away from us as much as anyone can on a crowded tram."

"I thought it was out of consideration or respect for

us as war workers," said April, "but maybe they're afraid it's catching?"

"Something's not right," said Peggy, shaking her head. "You know what I think? That yellow powder is making us sick. Everyone calls my mum's cough a cold, but no one has a cold for weeks and weeks."

"Maybe we should talk to Superintendent Carmichael," said Louise. "She might tell us what's what."

"Doubt it," Marjorie scoffed.

"I'd be afraid to be labeled a troublemaker," said Peggy. "I can't lose this job. Is there anyone we can ask who doesn't work at Thornshire Arsenal?"

"Lucy's brother is a doctor," said April. "Maybe he knows something."

"Wouldn't hurt to ask." When Louise stuck her hand in the air, April followed her line of sight and spotted Lucy seated at a table a few yards away with Daisy and two other Finishing Shop girls. "Lucy! Lucy!" Lucy glanced up, her eyebrows rising as Louise beckoned. "Do you have a minute?"

Lucy nodded, exchanged a few words with her friends, and then she and Daisy came over. "Hello, girls," she said, a bit warily. "What's going on?"

"Lo, Miss Prim grants the peasants an audience," said Marjorie, smirking.

"That's *Lady* Prim to you," said Lucy, without sparing her a glance. "Is this about that header? I promise you it was an accident. I don't think I could repeat it."

"Never explain away a header that leads to a goal," said Louise. "No, this is about something else. Your brother's a doctor?"

"Yes, but not in London. He's taken over our late father's practice in Brookfield. In Surrey," Lucy added, which was useful to April if no one else, for she had never heard of it.

"Could you ask him if we should be worried about working with the yellow powder?" Peggy grimaced and tugged on the end of her braid. "We all can see what it does to our skin and hair, but is there more to it? Things on the inside, things we can't see?"

"I don't like to break a confidence," said Lucy, lowering her voice, "but some of the girls in the Finishing Shop have been complaining about upset stomachs and sore breasts. We all assumed it was just the monthlies."

"Speaking of women's troubles—" Daisy inhaled deeply, grimacing. "I heard from a friend who works at Woolwich that one of their canary girls gave birth to a bright yellow baby."

They all gasped.

"That can't be true," said Marjorie.

"Can't it?" said Daisy, planting a hand on her hip. "How would you know?"

"Something so odd would've been in the papers."

"The same newspapers that tell us, 'A zeppelin visited a London neighborhood last evening,' instead of just coming out with it, that the Germans bombed Covent Garden and left a massive crater in Wellington Street?"

Lucy raised her hands for peace. "I'll call my brother tonight," she promised. "He did warn me not to work with chemicals. He won't be pleased that I didn't heed him, but he'll help us if he can."

They were due back at their stations, so the conversation ended there with no one's curiosity satisfied. Even Marjorie looked uneasy, despite her flippant dismissals. Throughout the afternoon, April glimpsed a crease of worry between her friend's eyebrows whenever she happened to glance her way.

The next morning, Marjorie seemed unusually prickly as they hurried from the hostel to catch their tram. When April timidly asked her if she were suffering another migraine, Marjorie snapped, "I wasn't until you started nagging me, but now I feel one coming on."

Stung, April nevertheless decided to excuse her friend's temper on account of nerves. Weren't they all feeling a bit unsettled after the revelations at dinner the previous day? "Maybe Lucy will have some word from her brother to put our minds at ease," she said.

"It could be just colds and migraines and the month-lies, as you said. We could be making something out of nothing."

"I never said it was *nothing*," said Marjorie, some-what contritely. "Canary girls are definitely feeling ill. The question is why." Then she tossed her head. "Honestly. A canary baby? Sounds like a creature out of an old-fashioned penny dreadful. Did it have a beak and feathers, I wonder?"

"Now that *surely* would have made the papers."

Marjorie rewarded her with a grin.

When they reached the park in front of Gate One, Marjorie suddenly clutched April's arm and halted. "There he is *again*," she said, an edge to her voice, lifting her chin to indicate the bench up ahead where the auburn-haired lad sat alone, hands in his pockets, collar turned up against the December cold. "I have absolutely no patience for shirkers today. Fortunately, I came prepared." Digging into her coat pocket, she withdrew a white feather and held it up, the shaft pinched between her thumb and forefinger. "I've done my bit. Now it's your turn. You're going to give this to him."

April yanked her arm free. "I most certainly am *not*."

"Think of your brother, risking his life in the trenches. What would Henry say if he knew you were willing to let this shirker off easy because you were afraid to hurt his feelings?"

"Leave my brother out of this. He'd say let the poor fellow alone if he isn't brave enough to enlist on his own."

"Sometimes the lads need a little incentive to be brave."

"Put that silly feather away. I told you, I'm not doing it."

"Fine." Marjorie linked her arm firmly through April's. "Just come with me, then, and I'll take care of it."

"Marjorie, no," April protested as her friend steered her toward the unwitting target. "Let's go find Lucy."

"Lady Prim can wait. This can't."

April tried to slow her down, but it was hopeless. Marjorie was purposeful, unrelenting, and the best April could hope for was to get the embarrassment over quickly.

The lad looked their way as they approached, a corner of his mouth turned up in a faint smile. "Good morning," Marjorie said crisply as she brought April to a halt in front of him. "My friend has something to say to you."

"I most certainly do not," April retorted hotly. The young man's eyebrows rose inquisitively as he regarded them both. "You'll have to forgive my friend. She's barking mad."

"If you have something you need to say, you can tell me." He didn't rise to speak with them, but leaned back against the bench, hands still in his pockets. "You both work in the Danger Building, isn't that so?"

"Yes," said April quickly, "and we're going to be late, so we'd better go. Sorry to trouble you. Come on, Marjorie—"

She tried to walk on, but Marjorie planted her feet and held her back. "I have something for you," Marjorie told him sweetly. "A gift, and some advice." She held out the feather. "You should be in uniform."

He studied her for a moment, the smile in the corner of his mouth turning contemptuous. "Let it never be said that I refused a gift from a lady," he said, removing his hands from his pockets as he stood. He held out his right hand to accept the feather, and Marjorie gave it to him, visibly surprised, for no one had ever submitted to her torment so willingly before. Mortified, April looked away, her gaze falling on the wooden prosthetic where his left hand should have been.

She gasped aloud.

The sound drew his attention. "Put it in my buttonhole for me, would you, love?" he asked coolly, holding out the feather.

"I—I'm so sorry," April blurted. "We didn't know. We're sorry."

Marjorie's laughter trilled. "Oh dear. What a dreadful mistake, and what an excellent joke on us! Is that why you keep your hands in your pockets all the time?" She reached for the feather. "Here, I'll take that back. You obviously don't deserve it."

"Does any man?" He held up the feather in front of his face and examined it, front and back. "I think I'll keep this. You clearly don't understand how dangerous this little white feather can be."

"Don't be angry." Marjorie offered him her most disarming smile, but it failed to work its usual magic. "It was an honest mistake."

"Marjorie, let's go," April nearly shouted. "We're going to be late."

"Hey there, you two!" a deep voice bellowed behind them. Instinctively the girls turned and discovered a very large, very angry man storming toward them. "What's that you're on about, handing Mr. Corbyn a bleedin' white feather? He's a veteran, ye daft bints! He works for the boss!"

"I think it's time to go," Marjorie murmured. She seized April's hand and took off running. April quickly outpaced her, and by the time they reached the edge of the park, they had lost themselves in the throng of workers. Only after they passed Gate One and rounded the corner of the complex did they slow to a walk.

"Do you think he'll recognize us if he sees us again?" Marjorie asked, breathless.

"Of course he will! How could he ever forget us?"

"Not the small one. The large, terrifying one."

"I don't know!" Glaring, April lifted her hands and let them fall to her sides, exasperated. "One glance at us and anyone would know we work in the Danger Building."

"But did either of them get a *good* look, d'you think?"

"I don't know," April snapped again. Shaking her head, she strode off toward Gate Four. "You're going to get us sacked, if you haven't already. You heard what the bigger fellow said. Mr. Corbyn works for Mr. Purcell. All he has to do is say one bad word about us, and we'll be out on our ear."

"Why should he do that?"

"Why shouldn't he?"

"It was an honest mistake!"

"It was a mistake, sure enough. I told you that before you did it, but you didn't listen. You never do."

They fell silent as they joined the queue at Gate Four, showed the sentries their identification badges, and moved on to the shifting house. April's jaw ached from clenching it, and she resolutely ignored the contrite sidelong glances Marjorie threw her as they changed into their uniforms.

"How was I supposed to know he works for the boss?" Marjorie murmured in April's ear as they queued up for inspection. "How was I to know he works at all, when we only ever see him sitting around the park?"

"Sitting in a park in a nice suit and coat in front of a munitions factory that employs thousands of people," said April flatly. "You're right. Who could have imagined that he works here, same as us?"

"You don't have to be sarcastic," said Marjorie, subdued. "I said I was sorry, to him and to you."

"You did *not* say it to me," April retorted over her shoulder as she reached the top of the queue.

"Well, now I will. I'm sorry."

"Have anything to declare?" the overlooker inquired.

April shook her head. "No, miss."

"Be sure to drink a full glass of milk with your dinner today." The overlooker waved her through. "Next."

"I truly am sorry," Marjorie said earnestly, catching up to April at the doorway to the Filling Shop. "Will you ever forgive me?"

"If we don't get sacked, I'll consider it."

As they took their stations, side by side as always, and the trolley girls arrived with the first shell casings of the shift, Marjorie smiled, relieved, as if the whole ugly business was not only already forgiven but entirely forgotten.

Perhaps in Marjorie's case it nearly was, but whenever April remembered the look on Mr. Corbyn's face when Marjorie had handed him the feather, she felt sick with remorse. April might forgive Marjorie, but she could not forgive herself.

9
January–March 1916

Helen

"Listen to this, Arthur," said Helen, reading the *Times* over breakfast on the last day of January. "'Elsie Mary Davey, aged seventeen years, who has been missing from her home at Fleet-road, Hampstead, since January tenth, has been found engaged on munition work in a factory at Woolwich. In trying to obtain assistance from the Marylebone magistrate on Monday, the mother—a widow—said the girl was "mad on munitions."' Can you imagine?"

"I certainly can," replied Arthur, his eyes fixed on the financial papers as he raised his teacup to his lips. "Munitions factories offer young women steady work, lucrative wages, and independence—financial and otherwise—that most of them have never known before."

"You sound like a recruiting poster, darling."

"Add to that the canteens providing good square meals twice a shift, the camaraderie, the social and recreational activities, the pride that comes from patriotic duty, and the only real curiosity is why *more* young women don't run off to become munition-ettes."

"Miss Davey left home without informing her family and was missing for three weeks," Helen pointed out. "From the sound of it, her poor mother was frantic. Surely you don't condone that."

"Well, no, not that," he conceded. "That was inconsiderate. But one has to admire the girl's pluck."

"I suppose." Helen silently read the rest of the article, which described Mrs. Davey's great relief upon reuniting at home with her willful daughter. "Miss Davey is seventeen. I thought the minimum age for munitions workers is eighteen."

"It is, officially, but factories have long employed lads as young as twelve and no one bats an eye. Not Thornshire," he quickly added. "Turn that accusing glare upon someone who actually deserves it."

"I'm not glaring at you. I don't glare."

"Perhaps it doesn't feel that way to you, but it certainly resembles a glare on the receiving end."

"Oh, stop. It's too early to endure your teasing." But she smiled, amused. "I suppose young women go into domestic service much younger than seventeen."

"And let's not forget the lads who lie about their age in order to enlist in the military." Sighing, Arthur set down the newspaper, closed his eyes, and rubbed the bridge of his nose as if to pinch off a headache in the bud. "If more young men in their twenties shared the younger boys' zeal, the government wouldn't need to enact conscription."

Helen paused, teacup cradled in her hands, thinking of Mrs. Pankhurst's recent calls for a national scheme to conscript young men into the military and young women into national service. "I don't approve of conscription," she said. "I think it goes against our great English principle of free will. Nor do I like this ugly business of shaming men into enlisting. One can hardly blame a fellow for not wanting to risk his life on a battlefield if he doesn't have an aggressive nature."

"Enlistments are down," Arthur reminded her. "How do you propose the government make up the numbers?"

"I surely don't know." Yet after a moment to consider, she said, "Why not improve the incentives?

Better pay. Increased separation allowances for soldiers' families. Substantial life insurance policies to be paid out to widows and children. The option to volunteer strictly for the home defense. A man reluctant to go abroad may nonetheless be very willing to defend English soil against an invasion."

"Excellent proposals, darling." Arthur wiped his mouth with his serviette and set it on the table. "We should send you to Parliament to talk some sense into those squabbling politicians."

"I tried that as a suffragette and I ended up in prison."

"Right. Let's avoid repeating that, shall we?" Rising, Arthur passed behind her chair, rested his hand on her shoulder, and kissed her on the top of the head. "I'm off to work. What are your plans for the day, aside from solving all the nation's problems?"

"I'm planning to meet some Marylebone friends for luncheon, and then I thought I might visit the British Museum."

"Splendid idea." He paused, his hand warm on her shoulder. "Darling, if there are any other museums you've been meaning to visit, don't put it off much longer. The war costs the government around five million pounds a day, and there's been talk about closing public museums and art galleries for the duration to cut expenses."

"Oh, but they can't," Helen protested. "What a blow to morale that would be!"

"I agree, darling, but what would you suggest shutting down instead? The hospitals, the railways, the post?"

"Of course not." Suddenly inspiration struck. "They could close Alexandra Palace and send everyone home."

"I'm sure there are many who would argue that internment camps are essential to the war effort," he said wryly.

"For prisoners of war, perhaps. Not for civilians who have committed no crimes other than being German in Great Britain." Once Alexandra Palace in North London had been a vast, seven-and-a-half-acre entertainment and recreation venue. In the early weeks of the war, it had been used as temporary housing for refugees from Belgium and the Netherlands, but in recent months it had been converted into an internment camp for around three thousand German, Austrian, and Hungarian men deemed enemy aliens. "If my father were alive today, he might have been interned there, if he had not been deported outright."

"I never would have let that happen."

"Yes, I know, darling, but what of all those poor people who don't have your connections?" Helen shook her head. "Never mind. I don't expect you to fix it. I complain to you because no one else will listen."

"I'm on your side, Helen," he said. "Fear and suspicion have even sensible people imagining spies lurking everywhere. As I see it, our best hope is to end this war as swiftly as possible so that things can go back to the way they were."

She could tell from the way he shifted his feet that he was running late and needed to set out, but he hated to leave her there alone, disconsolate and frustrated. "Off with you, then," she said briskly, squeezing his hand and forcing a smile. "Go do your bit, and your proud little wife will greet you at the door with a kiss when you return."

"Are you sure you'll be all right?"

She assured him she would, and kissed him goodbye.

After breakfast, she took a brisk walk through Hyde Park hoping to improve her mood. She would have cancelled her luncheon date rather than inflict her ill humor on others, but she had met few women in her new neighborhood with whom she felt she had much in common, and she didn't want their invitations to stop coming.

At one o'clock, she met her friends at the luxurious Great Central Hotel on Marylebone Road, which had been requisitioned by the military for use as a convalescent hospital for wounded officers, but still kept its smaller dining room open to the public. Like herself, her three new friends were educated, married to wealthy, accomplished gentlemen, and determined not to idle away their lives as ladies of leisure. They all had been married longer than Helen, and all were mothers. When Helen confided her worries about her own empty arms, they assured her it was only a matter of time until she and Arthur were similarly blessed. Until then, it was simply a matter of try, try again.

At the moment, her friends' children were either in school, with nannies, or old enough to fend for themselves, so all four friends could relax and savor their consommé fermier, eggs with asparagus tips, fillets of salmon, and several excellent cheeses. It was impossible to avoid some talk about the war, as it influenced nearly everything about daily life in London, but since Beatrice had a son in the British Expeditionary Force, they refrained from discussing its more disturbing aspects.

As their soup bowls were cleared, Helen's next-door neighbor, Evelyn, announced in a whisper that she had heard an astonishing tale about the East End charity hospital where her husband was a trustee.

"Do divulge all," said Beatrice, an amused grin playing on her lips. "I love an astonishing tale."

After a sip of water and a dramatic pause, Evelyn said, "The hospital sees a good many patients from the Royal Arsenal at Woolwich and the Brunner Mond munitions factories at Silvertown—accidents, injuries, burns, and such."

Helen's heart dipped at the mention of munitions, but she said, "Go on."

"Occasionally young women who work with the explosive yellow powder show up in the maternity ward."

"Yes, with yellow skin and ginger hair," said Violet, the eldest of the four, a baroness. "I understand they are often called canary girls, but not in any derogatory sense."

"All true, but that's not the astonishing part." Evelyn inhaled deeply, letting the suspense build. Helen braced herself. "Several of these canary girls have given birth to yellow babies."

Her three companions gasped.

"You're teasing us, surely," said Beatrice.

Evelyn shook her head. "I have it straight from my husband, so unless he was misinformed, it's absolutely true."

"Could it be jaundice?" asked Violet, eyebrows drawing together over the bridge of her nose. "That's not uncommon in newborns. My own Cecily was born with jaundice, but the yellowish tint to her skin faded in a matter of days. Exposure to sunlight was the cure."

"It's not jaundice," said Evelyn. "This is a bright yellow, the same hue as the mother's skin. The babies appear to be in perfect health in every other regard, and the color fades within a few weeks, but I imagine it must be quite disturbing while it lasts."

Helen sipped her water to conceal her dismay. Was this condition afflicting Thornshire's canary girls too? Did Arthur know?

"Even if it is only simple jaundice," said Violet, "an increase in cases among so specific a group of mothers should be cause for concern." She turned to Helen. "Has your husband ever mentioned anything about this?"

"No, he hasn't," Helen replied, carefully setting down her glass. "He wouldn't permit any expectant mothers to work in the Danger Buildings, if he knew. He would have them transferred to a less dangerous site—the laundry or the canteen, perhaps—as long as it was safe for them to continue working."

"I'm sure he would," said Violet sincerely. "One would hope all gentlemen in his position would be as scrupulous as he."

After that, the conversation turned to other matters, but Helen was so troubled she scarcely heard a word of it.

Arthur did not return home until nine o'clock, but Helen had held dinner for him, although she herself had no appetite. She greeted him at the door with a kiss, as she had promised earlier that day, but she could not disguise how heavily her thoughts weighed upon her.

"What's the matter, darling?" he asked, cupping her cheek in his hand. "You look pensive."

She saw the strain and weariness in his eyes, and she could not bear to worsen it. "It's nothing," she said, helping him out of his coat and taking his hat.

"Whenever you say something is nothing, I know it's anything but."

Helen sighed, hung up his coat and hat, and took his hand. "It's just something one of my friends said at lunch today." She led him into the dining room and rang the bell. They had barely seated themselves when the cook bustled in with their first course.

"I see." He studied her. "Out with it."

Reluctantly, she told him what Evelyn had said about the canary girls' babies. Arthur's dinner cooled on his plate as he listened, his expression becoming increasingly solemn. When she finished, he sighed, took his fork in hand, but did not taste his food. "I can't tell you whether this story is true or false," he said. "But I promise you, I haven't heard one word about canary babies, and I trust someone would have informed me."

"I would certainly hope so."

"I can't speak for any other arsenal, but at Thornshire,

if a worker is known to be in a delicate condition, she is immediately transferred out of the Danger Building." He paused for a moment. "Of course, as you know, no place on the arsenal grounds is entirely safe. That is an irrefutable fact of the manufacture of explosives."

"I understand that."

"It's clearly stated in the rule book that workers are required to inform their supervisor if they're expecting, but often they say nothing until their condition is too obvious to conceal."

"Why? Because they don't want to be transferred to a job that pays a lower wage, despite the risks?"

"Exactly so." Arthur took a bite of his dinner, then apparently realized that he was ravenous, for he tucked in with earnest. "We rely upon our overlookers and foremen to keep an eye out. Sometimes a concerned friend will quietly inform the superintendent."

Helen mulled that over as he finished his dinner. "Arthur," she asked carefully, "why *is* this explained in the rule book? If you don't believe that TNT is harmful to canary girls and their babies, why are expectant mothers prohibited from working in the Danger Building? You must have made that decision months ago, before the books went to print."

He set down his fork and took a long drink of wine. "My father and brother wrote the rules for all of the

Purcell factories before Thornshire opened. Munitions work includes many tasks and conditions that expectant mothers should avoid, not only TNT exposure. Heavy lifting, long shifts, the potential for accidents—"

"Of course."

"If I had my way, expectant mothers wouldn't be permitted to do any munitions work, but it's not my decision. I have to answer to my father, and he has to answer to the Ministry of Munitions."

Helen managed a wan smile. "I wasn't aware that your father answered to anyone, except, perhaps, the King."

Arthur laughed shortly. After a moment, he reached across the corner of the table for her hand. "I know you're worried about the munitionettes. Would it reassure you to know that in late December, the Ministry of Munitions established a Welfare Department expressly to look out for munitionettes' interests?"

"I'm pleased to hear that," said Helen. "Dare I hope it won't be all talk and no action? What precisely will this department do?"

"Among other things, the committee has advised factory managers to hire women welfare supervisors, responsible matrons whose sole duty is to look out for the well-being of their munitionettes." He shrugged. "Granted, my father isn't too keen on the idea, but he might come around. In the meantime, my assistant secretary—you met him, Oliver Corbyn—"

"Oh, yes. The veteran. The good-looking chap."

"Yes, him," said Arthur, amused. "For the past few months, I've asked him to spend the first hour of his workday at the park in front of the main gate. That's our busiest shift change."

"So he's your spy? He eavesdrops and takes notes?"

"Nothing as sinister as that. His task is to be available to listen to any complaints or concerns the workers might have. He's from a village northeast of the city, he served in the army, and he's an amiable fellow, so naturally the men feel more comfortable talking to him in a casual setting than coming to my office and speaking with me, or even with Tom."

"Oh, yes," teased Helen. "You and your secretary are both so stuffy and intimidating."

"Perhaps not to you, my dear, but consider that no man wants his fellow workers to think he's a telltale. And if the workers' comments and complaints come through Oliver, they remain anonymous. I can learn what the workers are thinking, and they need not fear retaliation if I hear uncomfortable truths."

"And everyone at Thornshire is aware of this arrangement?"

"Through word of mouth, yes. It's strictly unofficial, based entirely upon trust. Over time, the men have learned that if they share their thoughts with Oliver, before long, problems get sorted."

Helen nodded, but a doubt still nagged at her. "You keep saying 'men' interchangeably with 'workers.'"

"I don't mean to. Force of habit. We employ at least as many women as men these days."

"Yet you might have chosen the correct word at that. How certain are you that the young women you employ feel as comfortable as the men do, approaching Oliver in the park and confiding in him?"

Arthur thought for a moment, frowning, and then shrugged. "As you said, he is rather good-looking."

"All the more reason the girls might be shy. They might not feel comfortable approaching a young man in a park if they haven't been properly introduced."

"Maybe not in Oxford or Marylebone, but this is at an arsenal in wartime. The customs are different than ordinary times."

"I doubt they're as different as you think. These are respectable girls, are they not? And this is a public park in front of the arsenal, not on the grounds of their workplace proper." Helen shook her head. "I suspect the munitionettes are completely unaware of this arrangement, and they might not take advantage of it even if they did know."

Arthur ran a hand through his hair, grimacing. "Fair point," he admitted. "All the more reason to convince my father to permit me to hire a welfare supervisor. In the meantime, if the munitionettes would prefer to confide in a woman, they can speak to Superintendent Carmichael."

Helen regarded him, skeptical. "The woman responsible for hiring, placing, and firing them?"

"It's not a perfect system."

"No, I can see that." Helen could also see that Arthur meant well and was doing his best, but she suspected the munitionettes might have many legitimate grievances that he simply never heard about.

February passed and winter faded as March brought steady winds, spring rains, and grim reports of casualties and terrible losses in France and Belgium. In Britain, zeppelin attacks persisted, especially on moonless nights, when the airships were more difficult for ground defenses to spot. Meanwhile, Arthur seemed to become more exhausted by the day, and as far as Helen could tell, nothing new had been done at Thornshire to ensure that the canary girls were being looked after.

Eventually she decided that she would have to investigate where Arthur could not, or would not, himself.

One morning, she waited until he left for work, then changed into a brown wool walking suit, taking care to leave all hairpins and undergarments with metal fastenings and wires behind. Carrying an empty satchel, she made her way by train and tram to Thornshire, arriving at the park in front of the arsenal just as the last dozen workers were hastening through the gates. For one alarming moment she thought she had missed her chance, but then she spotted Oliver Corbyn, hands in his pockets, striding away from her toward Gate One.

"Mr. Corbyn," she called out, hurrying after him. "Mr. Corbyn!"

He halted and turned, but he did not recognize her until she drew closer. "Mrs. Purcell," he said, surprised. "Hello."

"Good morning," she said, smiling, hands on her hips as she caught her breath. "I'm so glad I found you. I'm on an errand, but I don't have an identification badge, and as you can see, my husband isn't here to escort me. I was wondering if you could vouch for me to the sentries?"

His brow furrowed. "Where is Mr. Purcell?"

She waved a hand. "Oh, he went on ahead. You know him. The early bird seizes the day and all that."

Mindful that her nervous babbling might raise his suspicions, she paused and took a quick, steadying breath. "So, what do you say? Can you get me in?"

He studied her warily. "I wouldn't be aiding and abetting any sort of crime, would I?"

"Certainly not. Why would you think so?"

"I understand you have a . . . rather storied past."

Helen trilled a laugh. "Oh, my husband has been telling tales, has he? I assure you, I have no intention of shattering any windows or staging any protests today. I'm confident my husband would fully support my visit."

"If he knew you were here."

"Well, yes." Beseechingly, she added, "Please, Mr. Corbyn. I only want to look around a bit, anonymously, so people won't conceal problems from me. You understand how important that is, don't you?"

"I suppose I do." He hesitated. "I can get you through the front gate, but after that, you're on your own."

"Perfect," she exclaimed, relieved. "I'm in your debt."

"Let's hope I don't get sacked for this and need to call in that debt." He offered her his right arm. "Shall we?"

She tucked her hand in the crook of his elbow and thanked him with a smile. He escorted her to the queue at Gate One, where he showed the sentry his identification badge and introduced her as Mrs. Purcell. The sentry offered her a cordial good morning and waved them through without hesitation.

"That was easier than I thought," she remarked as they cleared the passageway and emerged on the other side of the stone wall. "Thank you so much."

"You're welcome," he said, inclining his head politely, his expression still wary. "Good luck."

They parted company, Oliver heading quickly toward headquarters, Helen walking slowly down the pavement, looking around to get her bearings. Remembering the way to the laundry, she set off with a confident stride, as if she had every right to be there.

When she reached the laundry, she held the door open for a worker pushing a cart loaded with soiled clothing and followed her inside to a vast room where women toiled near vats of hot water billowing steam, the scents of soap and bleach in the air. One stout woman, older than the others and red-faced from the heat, walked about looking over shoulders and issuing commands, which clearly marked her as the supervisor.

Aware that her time on the arsenal grounds might be cut short the moment someone recognized her, Helen quickly approached the laundress in charge. "Good morning," she said pleasantly. "Could you assist me, please? I need a uniform for the Danger Building."

The older woman's eyebrows rose. "*You* need a uniform for the Danger Building?"

"If you would you be so kind."

"Right." The laundress studied her, dubious. "Weren't it in your cubby in the shifting house?"

"I didn't see it there," said Helen, which was not a lie.

"Likely a girl on the night shift misplaced her own and pinched yours. Wouldn't be the first time." She headed deeper into the stifling, steam-clouded room, gesturing over her shoulder for Helen to follow. "Come along, miss. We'll get you sorted."

Soon thereafter, Helen departed, a uniform, cap, and wooden clogs stowed neatly in her satchel. Arthur had omitted the Danger Building from his tour, but she had seen yellow-hued munitionettes entering a particular factory, and after wandering around a bit, she found it. A few workers with the characteristic yellow skin and ginger hair of canary girls were hurrying through the doorway, which told Helen that she had arrived fortuitously in the last minutes of a shift change. With some effort, she might be able to slip in with the stragglers.

Inside the shifting house, Helen changed into the uniform, stowed her own clothing in her satchel in an empty cubby, and joined the queue for inspection.

"New girl?" one of the overlookers inquired, frowning, after asking whether Helen had anything to declare.

"How did you know?" Helen asked, wary.

"No yellow, of course." She gestured to Helen's face and hands, her only visible skin. "It's bad form to be late on the first day."

"I'm very sorry," Helen replied humbly. "It won't happen again." The overlooker harrumphed and waved her on through. Helen paused by the racks of punch cards but quickly moved on again, hoping no one noticed that she had not timed in.

For the next hour, she wandered from the Filling Shop to the Finishing Shop, from the loud, clanging machinery section to the canteen. She lingered on the periphery, listening, occasionally breaking into a conversation to ask questions, moving on with a respectful nod whenever a supervisor peered at her with curiosity or suspicion. Once, the burly, dark-haired foreman of the Finishing Shop, whom she had briefly met on the arsenal grounds during her tour, paused to give her a second look when they crossed paths in the corridor connecting the two buildings, but she quickened her pace to appear as if she were walking with a pair of workers just ahead of her. She even laughed at one of their jokes. When the foreman did not confront her, she took that as a sign that her ruse had worked, but she sensed that her time was running short.

Even if it was, she had learned so much already. None of the munitionettes she spoke to had ever seen a canary baby, but all had heard rumors from workers at other arsenals. They accepted the changes to their skin and hair with resignation and, occasionally, humor, but the list of other symptoms they mentioned left Helen nearly breathless from alarm: chest pains, fatigue, wracking coughs, painful sore throats, migraines, diarrhea, vomiting, and a persistent metallic taste in their mouths.

"How can you bear it?" Helen asked a group of workers in the Filling Shop, forgetting for a moment that she was supposed to be one of them.

"I need the wages," said one canary girl, tall and strikingly pretty despite her yellow skin, with curls that had probably once been lustrous honey-gold peeking out from beneath her broadcloth cap.

"It's not only the wages," said the woman called Mabel, to whom the others deferred. "Britain can't win the war without the shells we build. The lads risk their lives in the trenches. We risk ours in the arsenal."

Helen found herself too overcome to speak as the other brave girls nodded and chimed in agreement.

"I beg your pardon, Mrs. Purcell," a woman spoke briskly behind her. "Might I have a word?"

With a start, Helen glanced over her shoulder and discovered Superintendent Carmichael regarding her sternly, mouth pinched. When Helen turned back around, the canary girls were staring at her, dumbfounded. She offered them a quick, apologetic smile as she rose. "Certainly," she told the superintendent. "Lead the way."

She was not surprised to be led promptly back through inspection to the shifting house. "With respect, Mrs. Purcell, you are not authorized to enter the Danger Building," Superintendent Carmichael said crisply. "Mr. Purcell requests your presence in his office immediately."

Helen smiled brightly as she retrieved her satchel from its cubby. "Oh, I don't wish to trouble him," she said. "Please let him know that I'll see him at home this evening."

"I'm afraid he insists, ma'am."

Helen muffled a sigh. "Give me a moment to wash and change."

The superintendent nodded assent and moved off to stand by the exit. There was no getting past her, unless Helen wanted to knock her down and scramble over her, but after that she would still have to get past the sentries at the gate. No, there was nothing for it but to comply.

She scrubbed herself clean of yellow powder and changed back into her own clothes, leaving the soiled uniform in the laundry bin. She felt like a naughty schoolgirl being marched to the headmaster as Superintendent Carmichael escorted her to Arthur's office. Helen tried to chat along the way, querying the superintendent about working conditions in the Danger Building, but she gave only curt replies, apparently preferring smoldering silence.

The superintendent left Helen in the antechamber to Arthur's office, offering a haughty sniff in farewell. Alone, Helen paced the length of the small room, alternating between chagrin and indignation. When the door to her husband's office opened and Oliver walked out, they both started at the sight of the other. "Well, hello, Mr. Corbyn," said Helen, too loudly and with false cheer. "I haven't seen you in ages! How are you?"

"Fine, thank you," said Oliver, also loudly, for Arthur's benefit.

Then Arthur himself appeared in the doorway. "Helen, darling, would you come in please?" he asked, his voice quiet and oddly formal.

She nodded, threw a quick, commiserating glance to Oliver, and strode into Arthur's office. "Before you scold me—"

He seized her by the shoulders and swiftly looked her over from head to toe. "Are you feeling unwell?" he asked urgently, his voice strained. "Did you handle the yellow powder?"

"No, I'm not a complete fool. I just had a look around. I wouldn't attempt to do munitions work I wasn't properly trained for."

He released her and ran a hand over his jaw. "What were you thinking?" he asked. "We're trying for a baby, and you just—" He gestured, frustrated, grasping for the words. "You just strolled into the Danger Building like a tourist at the British Museum!"

"Yes, I suppose I did. Imagine if I had been a saboteur. You might want to improve your security measures."

"Don't deflect from the subject at hand. Why would you knowingly and recklessly expose yourself to such danger, when you might be with child?"

"Well, I don't believe I am with child," she said, taken aback by his fervor, by the fear and worry in his eyes. "You realize, Arthur, that you're tacitly admitting that the Danger Building is hazardous for expectant mothers."

He gestured impatiently, brushing that aside. "I've always said that."

"I'm not talking about explosions or lifting heavy loads." She studied his face. "You believe that the yellow powder is poisonous, don't you?"

He began to speak, hesitated, and sat down wearily on the edge of his desk. "I suspect it is," he admitted. "After you shared what your friend told you about the newborns with yellow skin, I made inquiries. It's true. At least six babies with bright yellow skin have been born to canary girls in London alone."

Helen shuddered and clasped her arms to her chest. "And you didn't tell me?"

"I wasn't aware that you were planning an unauthorized inspection, so I didn't think it would affect you. I didn't want you to worry."

"I was worried then and I'm more worried now." Leaning against the edge of the desk beside him, she told him what she had learned from the women in the Danger Building—their symptoms, their dedication to the war work, their brave fatalism, their trust in their supervisors, who they believed were looking out for them.

By the end of her report, Arthur's shoulders were slumped, his expression haggard. "Until we know more about trinitrotoluene, we must assume it's a hazardous substance," he said. "I don't believe its effects are merely cosmetic."

"Nor do I."

"Nor, I think, do our workers. Surely this is no secret. Our munitionettes are clever and observant. They understand the dangers and accept them."

Helen remembered what Mabel had said in the Filling Shop. "Yes, I believe that's so. But even if they're entirely willing to risk their lives, more must be done to protect them."

"Agreed. Absolutely."

She laid her hand on top of his. "What do you intend to do?"

"We can't stop using TNT. We must produce shells, or the war is lost. France, Belgium, England—all will be lost." He brooded for a moment in silence. "The girls told you more in an hour than they've told me, or Oliver, in months. It's obvious what to do next. You should become Thornshire Arsenal's welfare supervisor so you may personally look out for the girls' interests."

"*I* should?" said Helen, incredulous. "Someone should, certainly, but I don't have any qualifications."

He smiled wryly. "On the contrary, I think today you proved you do. You're caring, you're clever, you attack problems with a vengeance, and you've already said you wanted to work here."

"That was when I thought I could be your secretary—bringing you tea, organizing your papers, tormenting you—"

"As delightful as that would be"—he interlaced his fingers through hers—"don't you think this other job would be eminently more rewarding?"

She took a moment to consider. "May I have my own office?"

"Of course. You'll need a place to work, somewhere you can confer privately with the munitionettes."

"Can my office be larger than yours, with a better view?"

"No, it cannot. There's nothing larger, and this is an arsenal. There aren't any good views."

She smiled at him, her gaze holding his. "This one, right here, is rather excellent. But what about your father? You said he wasn't keen on hiring welfare supervisors."

"You let me worry about my father." He leaned closer, a faint, tired smile appearing. "So what'll it be? Do you accept?"

"I'll need to see my office before I decide," she teased, and leaned in to kiss him.

10
April–June 1916

Lucy

Lucy cherished Daniel's letters from France, even though he provided frustratingly few details about his specific location and experiences. The first were omitted to satisfy the censors, the second, she suspected, to avoid upsetting her and their sons. He wrote of football matches, the endless rain and mud, and his chums, but almost nothing of the danger and hardships he faced every day. No doubt he intended to spare her worry, but sometimes he only made her imagine the worst.

If his letters were addressed to the family, Lucy's mother let her grandsons read them when they arrived home from school. If the envelopes bore Lucy's name alone, her mother hid them in a kitchen drawer so Jamie and Simon wouldn't be tempted to open them. Lucy would return home around nine o'clock, exhausted from a long day finishing shells, but after she went upstairs to tuck the boys into bed, and returned to the kitchen to find a cup of tea, a scone or a biscuit, and an overseas letter arranged at her place at the table, her fatigue would suddenly disappear. With a grateful look for her mother, she would snatch up the letter and lose herself in her beloved husband's words from far away.

In early January, he had written of the 17th Middlesex's football team's 6–0 victory over the 2nd South Staffords to win the 6th Brigade Final. Five days later, the Footballers' Battalion team played a "Best of Brigade" side and won 3–1. Then followed a fortnight of no letters at all, and since the extraordinary Royal Mail could deliver letters back and forth between soldiers and their families in Britain in about three days, Daniel's silence told Lucy the 17th Middlesex had returned to the front.

When at last another letter arrived in the beginning of February, Daniel sent dreadful news about his friend and fellow Olympian Captain Vivian Woodward, who had been wounded in the right thigh from grenade splinters. His injuries were so serious that he had been sent back to England for treatment, and it was expected that his football days were over. A few days later Lucy read in the papers that Woodward's wounds were not as serious as the battlefield doctors had believed, and that he might indeed take the pitch for Chelsea again after the war. Lucy was greatly relieved for her husband's friend and former teammate, and her heart went out to his wife, who must have suffered terribly when the dreaded telegram arrived.

Yet despite the fortunate outcome, Lucy brooded over the terrible reminder of the risks the footballers confronted every day. What if the shrapnel had struck Daniel instead? What if the injury had been so severe that he could never play football again? He must have resigned himself to that possibility when he enlisted, but Lucy could not imagine how he would endure the rest of his life without football bringing joy, excitement, and the thrill of competition to it.

In the middle of February, Daniel had sent the family a humorous account of two young German soldiers who had crossed no-man's-land unarmed, hoping to be taken prisoner. They had approached the British lines with their hands raised, shouting, "*Kameraden! Kameraden!*" and had surrendered to Private Tim Coleman, a forward with Nottingham Forest. "The Germans were strapping, square-jawed chaps," Daniel had written, "disgruntled officers' servants who had become so frustrated with their maltreatment that they had deserted. As a parting rebuke, they had carried off their former masters' ample supply of cigars, cigarettes, schnapps, and wine, which they offered to us gratefully in exchange for taking them prisoner. We turned the men over to the authorities and had a jolly celebration in our trenches."

Jamie and Simon loved that story and often asked her to read it again, but although Lucy found the anecdote amusing too, she had to wonder about everything Daniel was leaving out of his letters. She understood why he would not want to upset the boys with too much harrowing detail, but why would he not confide in her? When they were growing up together in Brookfield, Daniel had never played at soldiering or expressed any desire to join the military. For all his courage, intelligence, and inherent steadiness, the experience of war must be jarring. It could not be all football and comic enemy deserters and liberated cigars. Why would Daniel not allow her a glimpse inside his real war, so she could offer him all the comfort and strength she could?

She did not want to upset him with complaints, so she lovingly told him that she knew he was protecting her from the truth, but she neither wanted nor needed him to. "Let me share whatever part of your burden

I can," she implored. In his next letter, which he sent at the end of February and addressed to the family, he described a surprise visit from MP Joynson-Hicks, the founder of the 17th Middlesex, who had brought with him a letter from King George, which expressed His Majesty's best wishes to the battalion. Lucy, the boys, and her mother delighted in the story, and Lucy was very proud that the King had honored Daniel and his comrades so splendidly. Yet Daniel's letter still left her feeling disappointed, despite the warm assurances of his love and his longing to be near her again, with which he closed every letter.

"He's an Englishman, dear," her mother said when Lucy confessed her ongoing frustration and bewilderment. "He's not going to whinge and complain. He's going to quash his fear, do his duty, and soldier on."

"But I'm his wife, not one of his men. He can confide in me."

"Perhaps it's simply too hard for Daniel to put into words the fear and horror that have become a part of his daily life."

"I could bear the horror," Lucy said. "What I can't bear is this distance. Not the miles, but his— remoteness."

Her mother took her hand and held it, her face full of compassion. "Of course you could bear it. You would bear anything for love. But imagine what it must be like for Daniel, to witness and experience these dreadful things, only to relive them as he describes them to you. Perhaps the kindest, most loving thing you could do is to respect his silence, and trust that he will unburden himself when he comes home."

"But what if he—" She could not finish the sentence. Instead she choked out a laugh. "See how foolish I am. I demand honesty from Daniel, even if it pains him, but I want you to lie to me and tell me you're absolutely certain he'll be coming home."

Her mother smiled sadly. "Could you tell me that you're absolutely certain your brother will come home?"

Lucy inhaled shakily, thinking of Edwin, somewhere in France working in aerial reconnaissance—the interpretation of photographs, not the actual photography, a somewhat safer occupation in that his feet remained firmly on the ground. "No," she admitted. "Nor would you wish me to."

Her mother sighed. "Uncertainty is the hallmark of these perilous times, my dear. We must somehow scrape together enough courage to endure it, every day, because raging against it changes nothing."

Lucy knew her mother was right. Some things, the most important things, were certain: She loved Daniel, and he loved her, and their children were safe, happy, and beloved. She also knew, and felt pangs of guilt for it, that she was not offering Daniel the same honesty she sought from him. He knew she had become a munitionette, of course, and he was tremendously proud of her, but she had not told him of her yellowing skin, her whitening hair, her sore throats and headaches, nor the accompanying fears that her symptoms would only worsen with time. Nor had she shared what George had told her about rising concern among physicians that TNT and other chemicals munitionettes worked with were hazardous to their health. Often a canary girl's symptoms would fade over time if she left munitions work, but sometimes they persisted indefinitely, or even worsened, a troubling and unexpected development. A government study was underway, but George urged Lucy to limit her exposure in the meantime, just in case. She passed this information along to the other Thornshire canary girls, but not to Daniel. Why worry him, she reasoned, when he could do nothing about it? Why unburden herself at his expense?

No doubt Daniel asked himself those same rhetorical questions when writing home about life in the trenches.

And so when Daniel wrote in mid-April to announce that the 17th Middlesex had defeated the 34th Brigade, Royal Field Artillery 11–0 to win the Divisional Cup, Lucy and the boys cheered and sent him a marvelous congratulatory letter in reply, complete with illustrations. They had never doubted the outcome, they declared, and their only regret was that they had not been able to see it for themselves. Privately Lucy and her mother agreed that Daniel's stories of the tournament were as reassuring as they were entertaining, for he could not be enduring too much hardship in too dangerous a setting if the regimental team could play football. For that brief interval, they knew he was safe.

Lucy sent Daniel another letter of her own the next day, a breezy, comical account of her adventures with the Thornshire girls' football club—the whimsically uneven surface of their makeshift pitch, which was barely large enough for their small-sided matches, with a single goal built of discarded wood and no net; the challenges of playing in their Danger Building uniforms instead of a proper kit; the admiring fans and jeering critics they had acquired among the other arsenal workers, men and women alike who watched their practices and shouted advice from the sidelines; how she had emerged as the club's top striker, always the first to be chosen when they made up sides; and how jealous this made Marjorie, the younger woman who had decided, much to Lucy's regret, that they were fierce rivals. The conflict was all one-sided and had been since that first day when Lucy had accidentally knocked off Marjorie's cap in the shifting house, but Lucy had grown steadily more annoyed by Marjorie's derisive comments and nicknames, and the elbows in the ribs in the dinner queue, and the treading on her bare toes in the shifting house. Now, she admitted sheepishly, she got a bit of her own back by placing a beautiful shot in the top right corner, just beyond the lanky girl's long reach, or low and swift on the left, just skimming the grass, forcing Marjorie to dive and miss. And that header into the goal—Marjorie had glowered, red-faced, for an hour after that. Lucy emulated her husband's cool, dignified manner on the pitch and never grinned or gloated after scoring. Although she hadn't intended it, her humility encouraged the other girls to praise her effusively to make up for her diffidence, which infuriated Marjorie all the more.

As Lucy had hoped, Daniel delighted in her football stories. "Just play your game, and eventually your hot-headed keeper will come around," he assured her. "I'm not surprised you've turned out to be an excellent striker. I still recall the first time I saw you kick a football, in the schoolyard. Your talent and mettle were evident even then. Do you remember?"

Of course she did. That might have been the day she had fallen in love with him, although at eight years old she would not have known it for love.

It was a crisp, sunny autumn day, and it must have been after lunch because all the children were outside playing, the boys on their side of the schoolyard, the girls on the other, separated by a wooden slat fence, low enough for all but the youngest children to see over.

Lucy was playing hopscotch with her friends when suddenly a football sailed in front of her face. Startled, she landed two-footed and glanced over her left shoulder to find a group of boys, eleven-year-old Daniel and her brother Edwin among them, approaching the fence on the boys' side.

"Lucy, get the ball," Edwin shouted, gesturing. Lucy looked to her right and saw the football first bounding and then rolling away. "Go on! Hurry!"

"She's busy," her friend Nettie shouted back, fists planted on her hips, "and you didn't ask nicely!"

Edwin scowled. "Get the ball, Lucy."

She glanced down at her feet, her scuffed brown shoes both planted in the same square. "I'm out anyway," she told her friends. She picked up her marker and trudged after the ball.

"We don't have all day," her brother shouted irritably.

Lucy picked up her pace, only to hear Daniel shout, "It's fine, Lucy. Take your time." A small smile came to her face, and knowing Daniel was watching, she broke into a run. She snatched up the football and ran back, determined to show off her speed, but for some reason—later, she never knew why—she halted abruptly when she reached her friends at the hopscotch court.

"Come *on*," Edwin shouted when she didn't move except to pass the ball from one hand to the other. "You can't throw it that far."

"Maybe she's going to keep it," said Nettie gleefully, and their friends giggled.

"That's stupid!" Edwin scoffed, but there was worry in his eyes. "Girls can't play football."

Daniel looked at him, bemused. "Of course girls can play football."

"Well, my sister can't." Edwin gestured, scornful. "Look at her, all skinny arms and legs."

Daniel *was* looking, and his smile made Lucy feel warm all over. "Thanks for getting the ball, Lucy," he called. "Could we please have it back now?"

"Well," she said, pretending to consider, "since you said please." She meant to run it back and hand it to him, but the same sudden impulse that had brought her to a halt before now compelled her to hold the ball with her hands outstretched, release it, and punt it over the fence, over the boys' heads, so they all instinctively turned to watch it soar. Her friends clapped and cheered. Several of the boys chased down the ball and immediately resumed play, but Edwin turned around to glare at her, and Daniel caught her eye and grinned. That look, which sent a warm glow from her chest that spread to the tips of her fingers and toes, was worth every bit of Edwin's anger.

And Daniel wondered if she remembered that day.

In that same letter, he told her he wanted to hear every detail about her football club, and after dinner during her shift the next day, she learned that she would soon have exciting news to share.

No sooner had the players arrived for practice than Mabel called them together. "The girls at Brunner Mond in Silvertown heard that we have a football club," she said as they gathered around her in a half circle. "They've challenged us to a match."

Gasps and exclamations of surprise went up from the group. "But we've never played a proper match," said Louise. "We don't even have a proper team."

"We have fourteen girls, don't we?" said Mabel. "That's eleven on the pitch and three reserves."

"We've never played as a team of eleven before," said Daisy, though her eyes were bright with excitement at the possibility.

"For all we know, they haven't either," said April, hands on her hips. "I think we can trust Mabel to get us sorted." Her words met with a murmur of agreement.

Mabel turned her head aside to cough hoarsely, and when she turned back, her gaze was sharp. "I certainly hope we're all feeling up to it. I wouldn't have it said that Thornshire Arsenal had shown the white feather, so I accepted the challenge on the spot."

"Hear, hear," said Marjorie stoutly, clapping her hands. Several others joined in, and then a few more, until all were applauding with steadily increasing enthusiasm as the girls exchanged glances around the half circle, excited, eager, wary.

"How much time do we have to prepare?" Lucy asked, already mulling over who would be best suited for each position.

"Plenty of time." A smile played in the corners of Mabel's mouth. "The match is a week Sunday."

The murmurs turned apprehensive, the glances alarmed and furtive.

"We can do it," April insisted, looking around the half circle. "Today's only Monday. We have nearly a fortnight."

"We *have* to do it," Marjorie pointed out. "We can't back out now or we'll look like cowards. I for one am looking forward to a proper match, on a proper pitch." She turned to Mabel. "They have one, don't they? Because we certainly don't."

"Yes, they've organized a pitch," said Mabel, her smile broadening. "Stratford United agreed to let us have the Globe for the day." When the girls exclaimed, astonished and delighted, she shrugged again. "And why shouldn't they? Nearly all the Upstart Crows have enlisted, so the club isn't using it much, and the gate will go to the Prince of Wales's National Relief Fund."

Lucy clapped her hands twice for attention and to settle the girls down. "We need to practice. If we're going to play on a professional pitch, we need to look the part."

"How can we look the part if we don't have proper kit?" Peggy asked as they ran out onto the grassy field. "We can't play in our munitionette uniforms."

Everyone but Lucy laughed as they took their favorite positions, adjusting for a full side and deferring to Mabel's judgment. They practiced harder than Lucy had even seen them do, but all the while, her mind churned over the question of what they were going to wear at their first real match.

By the time they hurried back inside to their stations, she had a plan.

She caught Mabel at the entrance to the Filling Shop, hoping to speak to her alone, but Peggy, Marjorie, and a few others lingered. "I think we should ask

Mrs. Purcell for help," Lucy said. "She's often said that if there's anything we need—"

"The boss's wife?" Mabel pulled a face, disgusted. "The great lady who pretended to be one of us, and why? To spy for her husband, no doubt. Now here she comes, every week like clockwork, skulking about, asking us how we're feeling, inviting us to chat in her posh little office, always reminding us to wash our hands, as if we don't already, or urging us to get some fresh air whenever we want to, as if we could and still meet our quotas." Mabel shook her head and continued into the shop. "She's insufferable. I don't have anything to say to her."

"You don't have to," said Lucy, trailing after her. "I'll speak to her on the team's behalf. Remember, she's not only the boss's wife; she's also our welfare supervisor."

"Welfare supervisor," Mabel echoed, as if the words left a bad taste in her mouth. "I know that sort. Wealthy do-gooders meddling where they aren't wanted."

"We're the Thornshire Arsenal football club," Lucy persisted, knowing that whatever Mabel decided, the other girls would go along. "Thornshire Arsenal should sponsor us. They've got government money for programs to improve worker morale. This match certainly qualifies, don't you think?"

"It would help *my* morale," Peggy ventured. "Come on, Mum. You know those Brunner Mond girls will take the pitch perfectly kitted out. We can't show up all mismatched. It would be a disgrace."

"Exactly," said Lucy, throwing Peggy a grateful look. "At the very least, we all need decent shoes and shin-guards."

"In the end no one cares how we look, only how we play." Then Mabel hesitated. "Though you make a fair point about the shoes and shin-guards. The other side will have the advantage if we play in our regular shoes. And no one wants to break a shinbone."

"Might as well go for the whole kit, then," said Marjorie, the last person Lucy ever expected to support any idea of hers. "In for a penny, in for a pound."

"And it's not even our pounds we'll be spending," Lucy reminded Mabel, glancing around to include all the onlookers. "Imagine that: a lovely new kit, entirely free of charge, all for the honor of representing Thornshire Arsenal."

"Please, Mum?" Peggy implored.

Mabel sighed. "Very well, then. If they're going to spend the money, they might as well spend it on us."

Lucy thanked her and hurried to the Finishing Shop seconds short of being late, earning a curmudgeonly scowl from Mr. Vernon. When teatime came around, she raced off to the administration building instead, where she found Mrs. Purcell's office amid a warren of small rooms on the ground floor. The welfare supervisor was disarmingly pleased to have a visitor, and she welcomed Lucy into a small, windowless office, really more of an oversized closet, with barely room for a small desk with a chair on either side, a filing cabinet, and a bookcase loaded with files and forms. On the wall hung a landscape painting of the Surrey countryside, so reminiscent of home that Lucy paused to admire it.

"Lovely scene, isn't it?" said Mrs. Purcell, gesturing to the chair in front of the desk while she seated herself in the one behind it. "I've considered hanging curtains around it and pretending it's a window. What can I do for you today, Mrs. Dempsey?"

Lucy took her seat and told Mrs. Purcell about the challenge from Brunner Mond and the Thornshire club's lack of proper uniforms and gear. To her relief, the welfare supervisor was quite keen on the idea. "I believe we have funds for that," she remarked, leaning forward to rest her arms on her desk. "Let me see what I can do. Any thought to team colors?"

"We'll take whatever we can get, honestly."

"That's not the way to ask for something," Mrs.

Purcell protested, smiling. "Tell me what you want, firmly and confidently."

Lucy hesitated. "We didn't discuss team colors." Then it came to her. "Yellow and black. We're the Thornshire Canaries, after all."

"Player names and numbers on the back of the jerseys?"

"Numbers only. And a variety of sizes. I'm not sure who will be wearing what."

"I'm on it," said Mrs. Purcell. "Is there anything else I can do for you?"

When Lucy declined, they rose and shook hands, and Lucy raced back to work.

A week later, the Thornshire Canaries were practicing after dinner when Mrs. Purcell and a handsome young man with a prosthetic arm arrived, pushing a cart full of large boxes. Abandoning their scrimmage, the players hurried over and discovered a marvelous assortment of yellow jerseys numbered on the back in distinct black printing; short trousers, also black; long, black wool socks; proper football boots; and shin-guards.

"Take what looks to be your size and we'll get sorted in the shifting house after work," Mabel called out above the clamor as the girls dug through the boxes, exclaiming with delight or nodding in satisfaction as they chose items for their kit. "Remember to thank our benefactor."

"It was my pleasure," said Mrs. Purcell, looking embarrassed but pleased as a chorus of gratitude rose from the players.

"Thank you, Mr. Corbyn," April added, and Mrs. Purcell's handsome assistant, expressionless, nodded once in reply. Inexplicably, Marjorie trilled a laugh, but that was Marjorie for you.

The rest of the shift dragged on endlessly as the Thornshire Canaries—fortunately everyone approved of Lucy's impromptu choice—awaited the moment they could race off to the shifting house and try on their uniforms. It took nearly a half hour, but eventually everyone had something that fit well enough, although the men's cuts were rather boxy on them, and a few of the girls expressed some dismay at exposing their knees.

"You'd expose more in a bathing costume," Marjorie remarked, admiring her own uniform and pretty knees.

"That's at the seaside," Daisy countered, "not in the city, with thousands of gawking spectators."

"No one will be looking at our knees," Lucy interjected quickly, before anyone got nervous and decided to quit. "They'll be too busy admiring our brilliant play."

As the week passed, she dared hope that her prediction would come true. Their passes were quick and accurate. April sprinted up and down the pitch as if she had boundless reserves of energy, racing for each loose ball and feeding it up to the forwards. Daisy could steal a ball so deftly her opponents sometimes kept running before they realized it was gone. Marjorie prowled the defending third with a ferocity that would strike fear into the heart of any attacker who dared venture too close. Lucy and Peggy alternated between taking shots on goal and passing in front of the box so the other could put it in. Mabel was a bit slow in the goal, perhaps, but although Marjorie clearly ached to be asked to replace her, no one dared suggest Mabel step aside.

At last, and all too soon, the day of the match arrived. Jamie and Simon were beside themselves with excitement as Lucy's mother ushered them aboard the train to Stratford, while Lucy, her stomach in knots, followed a pace behind carrying her kit in Jamie's knapsack. She was familiar with the Globe, having attended several of Daniel's games there, and she remembered it as being older and smaller than White Hart Lane, but still able to seat eight thousand spectators. The rounded, half-timber façade over brickwork was meant to evoke the old Globe Theatre of Shakespeare's day in London, which of course no one had ever seen except in sketches and paintings, but the resemblance ended there.

Lucy parted with her family at the main gate, then joined the rest of her team in the players' changing room. They were all nervous and excited, with the possible exception of Mabel, who seemed perfectly sanguine, even after they took the pitch to warm up and observed how swift, strong, and skilled their opponents were as they ran through warm-up drills with the grace and power of a choreographed dance.

"They're going to crush us," a Canary muttered as the official blew the whistle and raised a flag to signal that the match was about to begin. Lucy did not know who spoke, but no one contradicted her.

After ninety minutes of play, it did not turn out quite as badly as all that. Lucy estimated the size of the crowd to be about five thousand, far short of capacity but really quite remarkable for a women's match. Lucy supposed most of the spectators were friends, family, and coworkers of the players, with the rest turning out to support the charity. A good portion of the audience had been drawn by curiosity, she suspected, since women's matches were quite a novelty. Perhaps a few—a very few, she hoped— had come to steal a glimpse of their knees.

The Canaries had started out strong, moving the ball well and attempting several shots on goal, but eventually their more experienced opponents wore them down. The Brunner Mond Belles scored after the first seventeen minutes, but Lucy put an equalizing goal in with thirty seconds left in the half. The Canaries were ecstatic in the changing room during the interval, reminding one another that it was an even game now and they could come out ahead in the end, but their hopes were short-lived. The Belles' incredibly swift center forward scored on the first play of the second half, which took the wind out of the Canaries a bit. Twenty minutes later, the Brunner Mond left forward scored following a scramble in the box after a corner kick, admittedly a difficult shot to block. After that, nearly all the action was on the Canaries' side of the pitch, except for one breakaway run late in the game which made their fans leap to their feet, cheering and shouting. Lucy even thought she heard Jamie's and Simon's voices carrying above the din. But the Belles' brilliant keeper leapt high in the air to block Lucy's shot just when she was sure it would go in, and neither she nor any of the Canaries had as good a chance to score after that.

In the end, the Belles held on to win 3–1, but the

Canaries had made a respectable showing for their first time out, and the Belles were so friendly and encouraging as they shook hands afterward that none of them, except possibly Marjorie, felt dispirited over the loss. "You should join the Munitionettes' League," their captain said, addressing her remarks to Mabel, but smiling around the circle to include them all. "It's jolly good fun, and if we can raise a few shillings for the Prince's Fund, so much the better."

"Say yes, Mum," Peggy exclaimed, while the other Canaries either chimed in assent or nodded, beaming, bouncing up on their toes with excitement.

Mabel shrugged. "You hear them," she said, extending a hand to the Belles' captain. "Count us in."

The Belles' captain must have done, for two days later when Lucy reported for her shift, Mabel announced that they would have another match on the following Sunday, this time in East London versus the Hackney Marshes National Projectile Factory Ladies. Determined to improve upon their first appearance, they resolved to train harder, but their dinner and tea breaks did not allow much time for it. Marjorie suggested that they stay after work for an hour or so three times a week to run plays, but very few of the Canaries were willing. Some pleaded exhaustion after their twelve-hour shifts, while others had long commutes or families who needed them at home, and some, like Lucy, had both.

Their brief training sessions already taxed them enough, and not only because all the players who worked in the Danger Building had developed coughs by then, and those who had had coughs for months found theirs worsening. They were worn out even before they took the pitch because their foremen had increased production to a nearly breathless pace, increasing their quotas and urging them to pick up speed, but without sacrificing accuracy or safety, a rather fine needle to thread.

"If the Kaiser's spies want to know when a big push is on the way," Daisy remarked to Lucy, huffing with effort as they loaded a trolley, "they need only look to the frantic pace of the Thornshire munitionettes to know that something's in the works."

By late June, Lucy was often so fatigued at the end of a shift that she plodded, yawning, through washing up, changing out of her uniform, and walking to the station, which meant she had to catch a later train and would not arrive home until after her mother had put Jamie and Simon to bed. Lucy regretted every good-night she missed. She always tiptoed into her sons' bedroom and kissed them softly while they slept, but she missed having them greet her at the door with hugs, and asking about their day. Their stories always brought a smile to her face no matter how exhausted she was.

One night she arrived home to find her mother pacing around the kitchen, compulsively scrubbing the already sparkling counters, her face pale and lips tightly pressed together.

"What's wrong?" asked Lucy, sick at heart, thinking of Daniel and Edwin and everyone else their family knew who was in peril.

Her mother gestured to the table, where a newspaper had been folded in an awkward fashion to emphasize a particular column.

"What is it?" Lucy asked, picking up the paper, scanning the page. It was all war news, all dreadful, but nothing leapt out at her as a particular concern of her mother's.

"What is it?" her mother echoed, striding over and snatching the paper, then remembering she could not read the small print without her glasses, retrieving them from her pocket, trying again. "'Woolwich Worker's Death,'" she read aloud, shooting Lucy a pointed look over the rims of her glasses. "'At an inquest at Woolwich on the body of Gwendoline Darrell, twenty-four, employed in the Royal Arsenal, it was shown that her death was due to acute jaundice caused by poisoning by tri—'" Her voice faltered, but she inhaled deeply and carried on. "'—trinitrotoluene, TNT, with which the girl had been working.' That's the same yellow powder you work with, isn't it?"

Lucy nodded and sank into a chair, resting her elbows on the table and cradling her head in her hands.

"'The coroner said that the workers in explosives wore masks, and he hoped it might be possible in the future to treat the masks with chemicals to counteract the effect of the fumes.' Do you wear masks? Tell me you do."

"We do," Lucy replied quietly, hoping her mother would also lower her voice, then amended, "We haven't always done. Our new welfare supervisor made it policy for all Danger Building girls a few weeks ago."

Her mother's chin trembled and her eyes glistened as she returned her gaze to the newspaper. "'A verdict of Accidental Death was returned.' What was accidental about it? She wasn't struck by a lorry on a blind curve. This was steady poisoning over God knows how many weeks or months!"

"I think they mean accidental in the sense that it wasn't intentional. It wasn't deliberate, it wasn't planned—"

Her mother slapped the newspaper down on the table. "But surely the men in charge knew what might happen. Look at your skin, your hair! You cough constantly. I'm going to have George come to London to examine you."

"You know he can't leave his patients. He's the only doctor for miles anymore."

"Then you shall go to him."

"I can't leave my work either."

"You can, and you must." Her mother sat down adjacent to her and put a hand on her shoulder. "Think of your children. Think of your husband. If you won't quit for your own sake, do it for them."

"It's because of them that I can't quit," Lucy said, letting her hands fall, sitting upright and regarding her mother bleakly. "If every canary girl quit, who would make the shells? Without munitions, how could England hope to win the war? Don't you see? I have to do this to bring Daniel home. If my work can shorten the war by even one day, that's one day Daniel isn't in danger."

She felt tears gathering in her eyes, and before she could blink them away, exhaustion and fear and worry made them well up too fast and they spilled down her cheeks. She folded her arms on top of the table, rested her head upon them, and closed her eyes, pressing her lips together to hold back sobs that might wake the boys.

She felt her mother's gentle hand on her back. "Oh, my dear girl," she murmured soothingly. "I'm so sorry. I shouldn't have railed at you like that."

"It's fine." Lucy tried to laugh, but it sounded rather desperate. "I'm sorry for the wretched tears."

"You have every right and reason." Her mother patted her twice on the shoulder, then pushed back her chair. "You go wash your face and put on your nightgown. I'll make you a cup of tea, and I have some of those shortbread biscuits you like."

Lucy managed a wan smile. "Thank you, Mum." She inhaled shakily. "You know I wouldn't be able to do any of this without you."

Her mother waved that off. "You'd manage well enough," she said over her shoulder, already busy with the kettle.

Lucy doubted that very much. She was just pushing herself through the days, longing for Daniel, finding joy in her children, taking heart from the camaraderie of her fellow munitionettes and her teammates. For months she had tried to ignore her own symptoms and to conceal them from her family, but she could almost hear a clock ticking down the minutes until she too succumbed to the mysterious, terrifying illness that had claimed the poor young woman from Woolwich.

"On Her Their Lives Depend," the posters said of the soldiers and the munitionettes, but it was incomplete. Not only the soldiers' lives, but the outcome of the war, and therefore the future of Great Britain, depended upon the munitionettes' work.

How could Lucy walk away?

11
July–August 1916

April

On the first Sunday of July, the Thornshire Canaries beat the Hackney Marshes National Projectile Factory Ladies on their home ground in East London, 3–2, with Lucy scoring two goals and Peggy the third. A week later, buoyed by high expectations of themselves, they were soundly thrashed, 4–1, by the Associated Equipment Company Ladies from nearby Beckton. Mabel allowed three easy goals in the first half, while Lucy scored the Canaries' only goal of the match. At the interval, a wheezing, coughing Mabel told Marjorie to put on the keeper's jersey, while Louise took over for Marjorie at center back. Marjorie allowed only one goal in the final minutes of the game, when she was worn out from fending off the AEC Ladies' aggressive offense, but Lucy and Peggy were so pinned down that they could barely get off a shot. For April's part, she had never run so hard so long in her life.

As they trudged off the pitch after congratulating their opponents—who, it had to be said, were gracious in victory—Mabel tried to assume sole responsibility for the loss. "I was winded after the first five minutes," she said, as if she couldn't quite believe it herself. "Aging is demoralizing, but I s'pose it's better than the alternative." She nudged Marjorie with her elbow, inadvertently making the lankier girl stumble sidewise. "You hold on to that keeper's jersey. I'm relegating myself to team manager."

"If you think that's best, Mabel," said Marjorie deferentially, but her eyes shone with excitement.

"I do." Mabel sighed wearily as they filed into the changing room. "For me, the role of goalkeeper has been officially declared a dangerous trade."

The response was split between protests that Mabel was the very heart and soul of the team and must never forget it, and derisive snorts and wry chuckles from those who understood the grim humor of her reference. A few weeks before, Mrs. Purcell had informed the Danger Building girls that the government had classified TNT work as a "dangerous trade," which would allow the Home Secretary to impose regulations to protect workers. Mrs. Purcell had already distributed two masks apiece to every Danger Building girl, each a piece of cloth with a pair of ties, one that fastened on the back of the head and the other at the nape of the neck, which covered the nose and mouth and were meant to keep the wearer from inhaling the yellow powder. The masks were deemed as essential as every other part of their uniform and were required to be worn whenever they were in the Danger Building, but many of the girls considered them a nuisance. Out of the welfare supervisor's hearing, they declared that they would take their chances, and they kept their ties slack so the masks barely stayed on, tightening them only when ordered to by an overlooker. Even the girls like April who wore theirs properly learned that the yellow powder could slip in through the narrow spaces between the mask and one's face. Still, April figured that every bit of TNT she kept out of her nose and lungs had to be a good thing.

It seemed likely that more precautionary measures would be coming. Mrs. Purcell visited the Danger Building at least once a week, walking the floors, inquiring after each girl's health and well-being, urging them to come to her with any concerns or complaints. Their teammates who worked in other buildings said that Mrs. Purcell made the rounds of their workplaces too. April appreciated the welfare supervisor's concern, and she, Lucy, Daisy, and a few others believed she meant well, but many of the girls were skeptical of the boss's wife and her intentions. Surely she would report any complaints to her husband, who might retaliate or even sack them—or so they believed, even after time passed and only good came of Mrs. Purcell's interventions.

"Have you forgotten that she's the one who organized our uniforms and gear?" Lucy challenged some of her teammates after a match in mid-July. To everyone's surprise, Mrs. Purcell had attended, and she had come down to the pitch afterward to congratulate them on a hard-fought victory clinched by Peggy's fantastic penalty kick. After Mrs. Purcell walked away, some of the girls had joked that it had likely been her first football match, and she probably hadn't understood a thing. They could only hope she hadn't accidentally cheered for the other side. But although the reminder of Mrs. Purcell's support quieted the mockery, those who had mistrusted her before remained just as skeptical after.

Yet even as Mrs. Purcell warned of hazards and took precautions, Superintendent Carmichael cheerfully urged the canary girls to invite all their friends who were not yet doing their bit in war work to register at their local Labour Exchange and request assignment to Thornshire. It wasn't hard to figure out why. Demand for munitions soared as the war churned on, and production had to increase to keep pace, but canary girls frequently resigned due to poor health—not in droves, but enough that replacements were needed continuously. As for the men, Thornshire held on to their skilled, experienced workers as tightly as they could, but that had become more difficult now that conscription was the law of the land. At first the Military Service Act had decreed that all unmarried men aged eighteen to forty-one could be called up for active service, unless they were widowed with children, physically unfit, or members of a "reserved profession," which apparently included every man working at Thornshire. But a few months after the law went into effect, it was changed to include married men as well, and the government also reserved the right to reexamine men who had been previously declared physically unfit. New posters sprung up among the familiar recruitment adverts to announce the changes in the law, noting that men who sought an exemption should apply to their local tribunals.

For male munitions workers, it was a bit of an inconvenience to spend their day off down at an office applying for a Scheduled Occupation Certificate, but at least they were guaranteed to get one. For men whose status was more questionable, they might bring their employers along to vouch for how indispensable they were to a business that would likely collapse without them. If they argued well enough, a fellow might walk out smiling, certificate in hand, but success was not certain. In her last letter, April's mother had written that the tribunal in Carlisle was quite lenient toward the lads who were needed on their family farms as long as they had the proper forms, but their neighbors, the Collins family, worked a rented farm, and the landowners refused to confirm that the two eldest sons were required laborers. "Both lads were taken into the army, and both were sent to France," April's mother wrote. "They were killed within a fortnight of each other. All for the want of a signature on a paper. Why the landowners refused to sign, no one here knows." If the war dragged on much longer, she concluded pensively, she would fear for April's younger brothers, who would soon be old enough to join Henry in the trenches, God forbid.

April imagined the war to be a ravenous beast whose hunger for young men was never sated. As many soldiers as were sent, more were demanded. Since munitions work spared men from conscription and paid well besides, such jobs were eagerly sought after, and April would have expected each one to be filled. But there were some highly skilled positions that women were not allowed to do, even in wartime, and as men continued to leave Thornshire to answer the call to arms, it became increasingly difficult to replace them.

"Eventually they'll have to let us girls take those jobs," said Marjorie one morning as they rode the tram to work in a rainstorm. "If conscription keeps expanding, and if they stop exempting male munitions workers."

"I hope the war will be well over before that happens," said April, thinking of her younger brothers. When the war started, she had never imagined they'd ever have to go, but now it seemed increasingly likely that they might. "You do understand that if conscription expands, it's because they need to replace the soldiers they started with, which means that a great many lads have been killed or wounded and the war is going very, very badly for us, right?"

"Don't get excited," Marjorie protested as the tram reached their stop. "Of course I understand that. I want victory and peace as much as you do. I want my brothers and all the lads to come home."

"I know you do," said April as they disembarked and raised their umbrellas. "Don't mind me."

"I never do," Marjorie replied, flashing a grin.

"I suppose the good thing about conscription is

that they're taking every eligible man." April gave her friend a sidelong look as they hurried along the pavement. "No young men are left in London except those who are officially exempt from military service. That means the end of the Order of the White Feather. You've been made redundant."

"You're forgetting the conchies," said Marjorie as they entered the park. "So-called conscientious objectors are liars and cowards and belong in a uniform or behind bars. If I have to pluck every last goose in the city to shame them, I shall."

"You're incorrigible," said April. "I'm not having this argument again."

"You brought it up."

So she had. Just then, April spotted Oliver Corbyn on the edge of the park closest to Gate One. He was alone, not surprisingly since no one wanted to linger for a chat in that weather. His prosthetic hand was concealed in his coat pocket while the other held up a black umbrella that provided a very inadequate shelter, as wind-driven rain had soaked his trousers from the knees down.

"You go on ahead," said April, pausing at the gravel path that wound in his direction. "I'll see you in the shifting house."

Marjorie followed her line of sight, saw Oliver, and

groaned, exasperated. "Don't bother. He never talks to you."

"One day he might, and that day could be today."

"Doubt it," Marjorie called over her shoulder as she hurried on her way. "Don't be late."

April steeled herself, gripped her umbrella tightly, and approached Oliver, quickening her pace when she realized he had spotted her, in case he made a run for it. "Hello, Mr. Corbyn," she said, halting before him.

He nodded, once, then glanced at the clock above the main gate. Never before had she met a young man who so obviously wanted her to go away—except for Peter Bell, the boy from the village in Derbyshire, and that too had been on account of Marjorie and her stupid white feathers.

"We should get out of this rain," she said, trying to smile, inclining her head toward the gate. "Shall we go?"

"*You* should go," he said flatly. "I have another thirty minutes."

She was so astonished to hear his voice that she forgot what she had planned to say next. "Right," she said. "Mustn't be late."

He nodded again, looking beyond her to reply to a man who had greeted him in passing.

"Very well, then." She turned away, then halted. "Although—" She could have sworn he stifled a groan as she turned back to face him. "I know you don't want to talk to me, but I just want to say, again, how truly very sorry I am about that whole awful business with the feather."

He regarded her levelly. "You're right."

Her heart leapt. "I am?"

"You're right, I don't want to talk to you."

And plummeted again. "Oh, I see."

"Look, Miss Tipton, just leave it alone, would you? I understand that you're embarrassed, but don't look for forgiveness from me."

"Where should I look for it, then?"

"Try the good men who've been blown to bits because a girl like you gave them a white feather and shamed them into enlisting." He laughed shortly. "Hold on, no, you can't. They're gone. Ask their grieving mothers instead."

She felt as if she had been struck. "Right." She cleared her throat and drew in a shaky breath. "Well said." Stiffly, she turned and walked away, shoulders drawn up nearly to her ears against the unseasonable chill, umbrella trembling.

Marjorie was already pulling on her wooden clogs by the time April joined her in the shifting house, dripping and miserable. Marjorie took one look at her face and shook her head. "I told you he wouldn't talk to you."

"Right again," said April, more curtly than she had intended. As she slipped out of her wet raincoat, she smiled and shrugged to take the sting out of her words, and Marjorie smiled ruefully back.

The canary girls' shift seemed especially grueling that day, but as hard as the foremen drove them, they pushed themselves harder. Since the beginning of July, stories had appeared in the press about fierce fighting along both sides of the river Somme, and the usually vague reports from the front spoke of tens of thousands of casualties. Some of the girls in the Danger Building had received telegrams during their shifts bearing the terrible news that their husbands had been killed or wounded, or were missing in action.

"Why would the War Office deliver the telegrams here, instead of their homes?" April wondered aloud as a young woman from the machinery section was escorted from the canteen, weeping, by Superintendent Carmichael and a cluster of sympathetic friends.

"Better to hear it here surrounded by friends than alone," said Marjorie, watching the women pass. "If anything happens to our brothers, our mums will get the bad news, not us. We won't know until days after."

April imagined her mother standing in the doorway of their cottage, the little ones clinging to her skirts, clutching a telegram to her chest and sinking with despair. April felt sick at heart at the thought, but what could she do except keep filling shells and hope it made a difference?

On a warm, sunny Wednesday morning at the end of July, April and Marjorie again came upon Oliver in the park on their way to work. He was seated on a bench beside the main pathway, two men sitting on either side of him and several others gathered in front, all engrossed in a serious discussion, from the looks on their faces. Marjorie was chatting away about strategy for their upcoming match on Sunday, but April caught enough of the men's conversation in passing to figure out that they were discussing the Footballers' Battalion, which had suffered heavy losses on the Somme. Clapton Orient forward William Jonas had been killed, April overheard, as had Norman Arthur Wood of Chelsea and Stockport County, and more players had been seriously wounded. She braced herself, but to her relief, no one mentioned Daniel Dempsey.

They had already passed the men when a change in their voices told April the group was parting ways. "Marjorie, you go on ahead. I'll—"

"I know, I know." Marjorie gazed heavenward and shook her head. "You'll meet me in the shifting house."

April squeezed her arm in thanks and hurried back to Oliver, who was rising from the bench and regarded her with wary resignation. "Mr. Corbyn," she began, falling in step beside him as he strode toward Gate One. "I wanted to tell you that I truly admire your determination to keep doing your bit despite your—" Voice faltering, she gestured quickly to his prosthetic limb, mostly concealed in his pocket.

"Despite leaving a hand behind in France?" he finished for her.

"That's not how I would have put it," she said, stung. "Be rude if you want. Maybe I deserve it. But I really do admire you."

He halted. "Miss Tipton, I don't want or need your pity. I lost my hand, not my life. I'm much better off than most of my pals, as it turns out." He looked at her keenly for a moment, and something like sympathy softened his expression for a moment. "Better off than you are, I fear."

"It isn't pity." Then his words sank in. "What do you mean, you're better off than me?"

"I think you know." He inhaled deeply, frowning, as if he were weighing his words. "Listen. Whatever Mrs. Purcell tells you to do for safety's sake, do it. She knows you girls don't trust her, and that you mock her when you think she can't hear, but she's very clever, and she genuinely has your best interests in mind." He nodded rather than saying goodbye and continued on his way.

"I trust her," April called after him. "I don't mock her."

Without turning around, Oliver lifted his good hand in a dismissive wave. Of course he didn't believe her. Why should he? He only knew her as Marjorie's meek shadow.

It was time to change that. He might never think well of her, but at the very least, she could show him that she wasn't always marching in lockstep with her bolder, occasionally reckless, and often impetuous friend. Oliver wasn't the only one who could contribute more than people expected.

She needed two weeks to speak with all the Danger Building girls on the day shift, and two weeks more to speak with nearly everyone on the night shift, which was a more difficult task since she had to arrive an hour early or stay an hour late to catch them in the shifting house. By the end of August, she had put together a chart several pages long dividing the canary girls according to work assignment. She listed each worker's age, every symptom they suffered, how long the symptoms lasted, if they seemed to be improving or worsening over time, and what remedies, if anything, made them feel better. Everything was strictly anonymous, especially the section at the end where April included lengthier complaints, comments, and questions that could not fit on the chart. She used a ruler and good paper and her very best handwriting, until she was as satisfied with its appearance as with the valuable information it contained.

One day in late August, she left the hostel early, alone, and arrived at the park before Oliver did. She seated herself in the center of his favorite bench and waited. It occurred to her that he might not be scheduled to work that morning, or that he might see her and veer off to another part of the park, but he rarely missed a day, and she figured curiosity more than anything else would compel him to find out why she was there.

Sure enough, about an hour before her shift would begin, Oliver strolled up, halted right in front of her, and peered at her quizzically. "Something on your mind, Miss Tipton?"

For the first time, she realized that he knew her name. She had never given it to him, and yet he knew it, and had used it at least twice before that she recalled. "You're the one we're supposed to go to with concerns, isn't that right?"

"Yes, unofficially," he said warily. "Do you have a concern, and am I going to regret asking?"

Ignoring the question, she scooted over and gestured to the bench beside her. Muffling a sigh, he sat down and regarded her speculatively. Opening her bag, she withdrew the document, which she had carefully wrapped in brown paper, and held it out to him. When he did not take it, she brandished it, frowning, until he did. "You and Mrs. Purcell both say you want to know what's going on with us canary girls," she said. "Well, the girls aren't going to talk to you here in the park like the men do, they don't know you well enough, and they aren't going to speak with Mrs. Purcell when she comes to the Danger Building, not in front of the other girls, and there's hardly any time to run off to her office during our breaks, unless we skip dinner or tea, and no one wants to do that, or to be seen doing it and be called a telltale."

It had all come out in a breathless rush. Oliver was staring at her, eyebrows raised. "Go on," he said. "I'm listening."

She took a deep breath. "Well, since there are things Mrs. Purcell ought to know, and the girls aren't likely to come to *you*, I went to them. I asked them all the things Mrs. Purcell usually asks, but they don't have to be careful with me, so they said what they *really* think. I wrote everything down—except for their names, because I promised I wouldn't—and it's all there, all organized, their answers."

He looked at the document, then back at her, amazed and disbelieving. "You surveyed all the canary girls?"

"Maybe," she said, uncertain. "I don't know. I just asked questions."

He weighed the document in his hand. "This could be very useful."

"Of course. That was entirely the point." Then she remembered something else. "I wrote things down as they were speaking, and I got their words as close as I could. Some of them didn't hold back. Maybe Mrs. Purcell isn't used to indelicate words or too much criticism. You might want to tell her to brace herself first."

A corner of his mouth quirked upward. "I'll do that. Thanks for the warning."

"And you didn't get this from me," she added, closing her satchel with a snap.

"As you wish." He glanced pointedly around the park, where dozens of workers were passing them on their way to the arsenal, and then returned his gaze to her. "Fortunately, there are no witnesses."

She felt heat rise in her cheeks. "Just don't give the boss's wife my name, all right?"

"She may want to thank you."

"She can thank me by helping us not get sick." Abruptly she stood, clasping the handle of her bag in both hands and holding it in front of her. "One more thing, and this is important. Don't let her use this to sack anyone. None of the canary girls wants to quit. We all need the wages and we're willing to do the work. We just don't want to die like that poor girl at Woolwich."

He nodded and rose, all traces of doubt gone from his expression. "Understood."

"I'm trusting you."

"You *can* trust me."

"Well, you can trust me too," she retorted hotly, then bit her lips together, immediately regretting it. "Good day, Mr. Corbyn."

"Good day, Miss Tipton." He lifted the paper-wrapped document. "And thank you for this."

She nodded in reply, then quickly turned and hurried off as if she were expected somewhere else, although she had plenty of time before her shift and he probably knew it.

Two days passed in which April either did not see Oliver in the park, or she saw him from a distance but did not approach. Why she was shy now when she had not been before, she couldn't say, but a part of her feared that all her hard work had been a foolish waste of time, that her survey was idiotic and thoroughly unhelpful, good for nothing but to give Oliver and Mrs. Purcell a hearty laugh. Who was April to take on that sort of work? She had left school at fifteen to go into service. She read books, but not difficult ones, and only the occasional newspaper, mostly to learn about the war, eager for any word about the Lonsdale Pals. Mrs. Wilson had warned her often enough to remember her place and not to follow Marjorie into trouble, but April somehow always forgot that advice until it was too late.

On the third day, April was startled to find Oliver waiting outside the shifting house when she and Marjorie emerged at half seven o'clock. Marjorie looked from her to him and back, bemused, and murmured, "I'll wait for you at the station, unless you'd like me to chaperone."

"Go on." April nudged her friend along as Oliver approached. "See you there."

Marjorie eyed him speculatively as they passed each other, and he gave her a courteous nod, which, considering everything, was rather kind of him. He halted in front of April and offered her an identical nod, which was disappointing. Didn't she merit something a trifle friendlier? "Miss Tipton."

"Mr. Corbyn." She gestured toward the gate. "My hostel is a long way off, and I'd rather not miss my tram."

"I'll walk with you partway," he said. She nodded and they set off together. "I gave your report to Mrs. Purcell. She's very grateful and she sends you her thanks."

Her heart dipped. "You weren't supposed to tell her—"

"What I mean is, she thanks the anonymous employee for providing her with such valuable information. She called the entire report 'illuminating.'"

"She said that?" April felt warmth filling her chest and a grin spreading over her face. "Even about the rough bits at the end?"

"Well—" He winced slightly. "Those bits she called humbling, but instructive. She appreciated the workers' honest opinions."

"Maybe too honest. I could have softened it up a bit."

"No, no. You did exactly what you should have done." They had reached the gate. Just ahead, the sentries were choosing men at random with a tap on the shoulder and taking them aside to be searched. The women were only peered at closely, on the assumption that their guilt would be written plainly on their faces if they were carrying anything they shouldn't. April and Oliver made it past the sentries unchallenged, and by the time they reached the park, April was still marveling over the revelation that Oliver believed she had acted properly for a change. Until then, he had probably thought her incapable of it.

They both spotted Marjorie at the same time, walking on the far side of the park with a few other girls from their hostel. If April hurried, she could catch up to them. "That's all I had to say, really," said Oliver, indicating her friends with a tilt of his head. "I guess this is where I leave you."

"I guess." April felt strangely disappointed. "Let me know if you—if Mrs. Purcell, I mean—need anything else."

She turned and hurried down the most direct gravel path to join her friends. "What was all that about?" Marjorie asked, glancing back toward Oliver, who was walking alone along the edge of the park closest to the arsenal.

"Nothing," April replied, but of course that wasn't true.

On their way to the arsenal two days later, when April and Marjorie saw Oliver up ahead in the park, Marjorie didn't wait for April to speak before heaving a sigh, shaking her head, and continuing on alone. April hesitated in front of Oliver's bench, and when he glanced up and nearly smiled, she sat down beside him. "I have a problem," she said.

"Yes, I know, I read your survey," he replied, offering a sympathetic grimace. "But Mrs. Purcell is on it. She's trying to do right by you girls."

"Good to know." April nodded, thoughtful. "But that's not the problem I meant."

He raised his eyebrows at her and nodded. "Go on."

"I behaved very badly to a fellow worker." She lowered her eyes to her lap, realized she was wringing her yellowed hands, and promptly stopped, grasping the bench on either side of her instead. "I've tried again and again to apologize, but he won't accept it. He's a very cold, dry, rigid sort of person."

He regarded her in utter disbelief. "Is that right." He withdrew his hands from his pockets and rested the prosthetic deliberately on his left leg. "Sounds like we have something in common."

For a moment she was confused, glancing between his shocked, angry expression and the prosthetic that he so rarely displayed. Then she thought about what she had said, and she felt all the blood drain from her face. "I didn't mean—I wasn't referring to—I wasn't making a sick joke about—" Throat constricting, she swallowed hard and shook her head. "I'm sorry. That's all I meant to say."

She rose, but before she could hurry away, he caught her by the wrist. "Don't run off. I'm sorry. I see now you didn't mean anything by it."

She whirled to face him, but didn't pull her wrist free. "I honestly didn't," she said, her voice low and fierce. "Why do you always have to assume the worst about me?"

He tugged her a bit closer. "Will you please sit down, Miss Tipton?"

She hesitated, then did as he asked. "I do admire you, you know," he said quietly after a long moment in silence. "You never once placed all the blame on your friend for giving me that feather, although you could have done. It was obvious that it was all her idea."

"I share responsibility for what happened. I should have tried harder to stop her."

"Do you think it would have mattered?"

"Maybe? I don't know." April shrugged and shook her head, sighing. "Once she's set a course, it's almost impossible to get her to change direction. She never sees the edge of the cliff straight ahead, even if you stand there pointing at it."

His mouth turned wryly. "I know people like that."

"Here at the arsenal, or—" She hesitated. "In the army?"

"Everywhere."

She shifted on the bench to face him. "Why did you enlist, anyway? If you don't mind me asking. My brother did it for the pay, and because all his friends were going."

"It was a bit of that for me," he replied, his gaze falling on his prosthetic. "King and Country, you know. An Englishman's honor, keeping our word to Belgium and France. My friends and I thought we had out-grown our village and we wanted some excitement and adventure, so we all joined up together. I admit I was nervous, but I didn't want to be left behind while all the lads I grew up with went off to claim battlefield glory. You remember how it was. Everyone thought it would be over by Christmas, and we wanted a taste of it before it was too late."

"I remember."

"I don't regret it, you know," he said, with unexpected intensity, but just as quickly, the fire faded. "Well, I regret this—" He raised his left hand an inch and let it fall back to his lap. "But not that I tried to do my duty and help my friends."

Just then, the warning bell above the main gate clanged.

"You'd better run," Oliver advised even as she bolted to her feet. She murmured a hasty goodbye and set off.

"Miss Tipton," he called after her.

She halted and turned around. "Would you please just call me April?"

"Oh, are we chums now?"

"I guess that's up to you. You're the one who was so angry."

He smiled. "All right, April, chum, when is your next football match?"

"Sunday," she replied, surprised. "Two o'clock at the Globe in Stratford."

"Sunday, two o'clock." He rose and tucked his hands into his pockets. "Maybe I'll come."

April shrugged as if it didn't matter one way or the other. "Maybe I'll look for you."

She turned and darted off before he saw from her hopeful smile and flushed cheeks just how much it did matter.

12
September–October 1916

Helen

In the middle of August, the renowned medical journal *The Lancet* published the results of a rigorous five-month study of the effects of TNT on women munitions workers. Dr. Agnes Livingstone-Learmonth and Dr. Barbara Martin Cunningham, both munitions factory medical officers, had concluded beyond all doubt that TNT poisoned the women who directly handled it, as well as others who worked in the same building. They classified the women's symptoms as either "irritative," such as nasal congestion, sore throats, headaches, chest pains, abdominal pain, nausea, vomiting, constipation, diarrhea, and skin rashes; or "toxic," which included continuous bilious attacks, fainting, swollen feet and hands, fatigue, depression, and blurred vision. The most significant factors influencing how sick a worker became appeared to be the frequency and duration of exposure, as well as the individual's health in general.

Much to her annoyance and indignation, Helen did not learn of the study until nearly a fortnight after it was published. When she finally obtained a copy, she read it diligently, thankful to finally have some answers. She was not at all surprised to find striking similarities between the physicians' analysis and the simpler, vernacular report one of their own canary girls had put together.

In the conclusion of their report, the two physicians—both women, Helen was intrigued to see—had recommended measures factories could and ought to take to lessen the severity of TNT poisoning. They strongly urged improved ventilation to disperse the TNT dust, but they cautioned that respirators and masks, which provided excellent protection against airborne germs, could actually do more harm than good as a barrier against the yellow powder, since warmth and moisture worsened the irritation of the nose, throat, and sinuses. Veils were suggested as a more suitable alternative, and like the rest of a worker's uniform, they should be laundered between wearings. The doctors also encouraged serving plain nourishing food and bland drinks in factory canteens, coating the face with a protective powder, and practicing good "personal cleanliness," something factories could best encourage by constructing appropriate washing facilities on their grounds. They strongly recommended not to employ workers under eighteen or over forty in Danger Buildings, and to rotate workers in and out of other departments every twelve weeks. Ideally, TNT workers would be scheduled on three eight-hour shifts rather than two twelve-hour shifts, and every week, each worker would receive a thorough medical examination.

Some of the doctors' recommendations were already in place at Thornshire, but others, Helen knew, would be difficult to implement and might provoke resistance from the very workers they were meant to help. Thanks to her anonymous statistician, Helen knew that the Danger Building jobs appealed to many munitionettes because the risks merited higher pay. Would the canary girls' wages remain the same during their twelve-week rotation to less hazardous work, or would they be paid the going rate? Would the munitionettes currently assigned to less dangerous factories object to being transferred into the Danger Building while the regular workers rotated out? Would workers welcome a less grueling, eight-hour shift, or would they resent having their hours, and therefore their earnings, cut by a third? And with workers in such short supply, where would they find enough new hires for a proposed third shift?

Helen posed these questions and others to Arthur at the office whenever he agreed to grant her an audience. If days passed and he could not fit her into his busy schedule, she grew impatient with his repeated deferrals and queried him at home instead, over breakfast or dinner or even in bed. In her view, nothing was more important than the health of their workers, because on them, all else depended. She didn't want Arthur's ear because she was his wife and thereby entitled; she wanted it because the welfare supervisor ought to be able to speak to the arsenal manager whenever urgent matters required it, and not just when he had spare time.

Helen was surprised to learn, nearly three weeks after the fact, that the Ministry of Munitions and the Health of Munition Workers Committee had met with managers of factories undertaking TNT work, and as a result, a new section of the ministry had been created to develop and administer revised safety regulations. More astonishing yet, Arthur had not attended the meeting. "Why didn't you tell me?" she protested, striding into his office after ignoring Tom's halfhearted claims that Arthur was not available. "If you were too busy, I gladly would have gone in your place."

"My brother attended," he told her, his eyes on several documents spread out upon his desk. "He represented all of the Purcell Products factories."

"What did he learn?" She leaned forward to rest her hands flat on the desk, trying to catch Arthur's eye. "What are the new regulations? Surely I ought to be kept informed."

"Let me think." Arthur closed his eyes and rubbed his forehead with a pinching motion, his thumb on one temple, his fingers on the other. "Check with Oliver. He should have the report."

"*I* should have the report," Helen said crisply as she left the office to find the assistant secretary, who regarded her mildly when she snapped at him that she needed a turn with the report if anyone expected her to do her job. Oliver produced the report so promptly that she felt rather rotten for taking her anger out on him. "Please forgive my ill temper," she said. "I'm not angry with *you*." He accepted that too with his usual imperturbable decency.

She took the report to the nearest canteen to read over a cup of tea, and soon learned that most of the committee's regulations merely echoed the two doctors' recommendations. A few things stood out, however: Full-time doctors would be appointed to all large factories, while smaller factories would be assigned local physicians on a part-time basis. Women would be permitted to work a maximum of sixty hours per week, which in Helen's opinion still pushed the limits of human endurance. Lastly, munitions factories were urged to cancel all labor on Sundays except for repairs, maintenance, and other work of particular urgency.

That suggestion so astonished Helen that she had to set down the report and ponder it. Women already had Sundays off at Thornshire, but as for the men, roughly half had Sunday off, while the other half took Saturday. But it was inconceivable that all munitions production should cease altogether for an entire day, at every arsenal and factory in Britain. The demand for armaments was simply too great, the consequences of falling behind and failing to keep the armies well supplied too dire. Helen didn't suppose the Germans took Sundays off; how could the Allies afford to? She could not imagine Arthur endorsing such a policy, and his brother and father would never give the idea serious consideration.

But that was the arsenal manager's problem to sort, she told herself irritably as she recorded a few notes in her jotter, finished her tea, and returned to headquarters, where she left the report on Oliver's desk and retreated to her cupboard of an office to plan for implementing the new regulations. She was glad the Ministry of Munitions was taking the problem of TNT poisoning seriously, because in her opinion, it seemed to have a rather fatalistic attitude about other dangers—especially accidental explosions.

Some preventative measures were taken, of course. Workers were forbidden to bring matches or metal objects into the factories. Every building was required to have sufficient firefighting equipment at the ready. Each factory had to employ designated firefighting personnel or to organize volunteer firefighters from among their workers. All munitions factories must maintain a first aid facility with an adequate supply of medicines, bandages, and other items needed to treat serious burns and other injuries. But other than that, the prevailing attitude seemed to be that accidental explosions were tragic but inevitable in munitions work, and it was up to each and every worker to follow the rules, use caution, and report careless coworkers to the foreman for additional safety training. Helen didn't know what she would recommend in addition to all that, but she had a terrible feeling that it would all become tragically obvious in hindsight.

In her windowless office, she could not judge the passing of the hours by the fading daylight, but when the need to stretch her legs coincided with the distant clang of the shift bell, she checked her schedule, saw that she had no more appointments, and decided to head home. Taking her coat and bag in hand, she went upstairs to Arthur's office, rapped on the open door, and peered inside. "It's six o'clock," she said, giving him a start. For a moment she held her breath, shocked by how haggard he looked, the dark circles beneath his piercing green eyes, the general disarray of his wavy brown hair. "Shall we go home?"

"You go on—" he began, but a yawn interrupted him. "I have a report due at the Ministry of Munitions at noon tomorrow. Rather not leave it to the last minute."

Setting her bag and coat on the stand by the door, she went around the desk behind his chair and placed her hands on his shoulders. "Can't Tom or Oliver take care of it?" she asked, massaging his tense muscles, which were alarmingly full of hard knots of strain and worry.

He let out a soft groan, relaxing into her touch. "Tom and Oliver have mountains of their own work to attend to."

"Shall I stay and help you? I could take dictation. You could close those gorgeous eyes—"

"Bloodshot eyes, I think you mean."

"If we work together, we could finish the draft quickly and leave it for the typist to deal with first thing in the morning. The courier would still be able to deliver it to the ministry with time to spare."

"Thank you, darling, but you should go home, have a bite to eat, and get some sleep."

"How shall I sleep if I know you're here, toiling yourself into exhaustion?" She let her hands travel down his back, kneading the muscles, hiding her dismay at all the tension she felt in him. "In the time you've spent arguing, we could have finished two paragraphs, perhaps three."

"Irrefutable logic, as ever." He placed his right hand on her left and gazed wearily up at her. "You are so lovely, darling. If I weren't absolutely knackered—"

"And if I hadn't left the door open, and if Tom or Oliver might not wander in and interrupt us—" She bent down to kiss the top of his head, then smoothed his unruly hair. "It's all right, darling. I'm tired too."

"It's just as well, I suppose," he said, straightening in his chair, rearranging papers on his desk. "This would be a bloody terrible time to bring a child into the world."

Stung, she withdrew her hands to her sides. "What do you mean?"

"What do I mean?" He laughed bleakly and turned to peer up at her again. "Well, it's the end of the world, isn't it? Or at least the end of civilization. Chaos and bloodshed, violence and destruction, slaughter on a scale never before seen or even imagined. I wonder what animal will emerge to become master of the earth when all the men have killed one another?"

For a moment she could only look at him in heartsick silence. "Let's finish the report and get you home," she said gently, stroking his hair away from his brow, wishing she could wipe away the double furrow of worry carved there. Managing a smile, she gave his shoulders a quick pat, then retrieved her jotter and a pen from her bag and settled into a chair on the other side of his desk, determined to help him—against his will, if necessary.

Together they made quick work of the rest of his report. Afterward, Arthur would have found other tasks to complete, but Helen planted his hat firmly on his head, put him into his coat, threw on her own, and linked her arm through his to steer him out of the office, leaving the report on the typist's desk on the way out. The Silver Ghost had been mothballed, or whatever the equivalent was for a motorcar, to save petrol, so they caught the train and were home within the hour. Helen had telephoned ahead, so a hot, nourishing meal was waiting for them in the dining room. Helen chose light, amusing topics for conversation, reminiscing about their days back in Oxford. By the time the dishes were cleared away, Arthur seemed much like his old self again—an exhausted, world-weary version of himself, but still, and always, the man she loved.

That night she held him in her arms as he sank into sleep, stroking his hair, kissing his brow. Eventually she fell asleep too, but she woke several times to find him tossing and turning beside her, muttering unintelligibly. Each time she stroked his back and murmured soothingly until he grew calm and drifted off again.

Two days later, a Sunday, she proposed that he not go into the arsenal but spend the day with her instead. "After breakfast, we can take a restorative walk through Hyde Park," she said, smiling, reaching for his hand across the table. "This afternoon, we can attend the Canaries' match in Stratford."

"The what match?" he inquired absently, his eyes on the newspaper.

"The Thornshire Canaries. The arsenal football club." She squeezed his hand, and eventually he looked her way, offering an apologetic smile for his neglect. "Our side is playing the Workington Ladies from the National Shell Factory."

That got his attention. "Workington, in Cumbria? That's a rather long way to come."

"It's a rather important match. All the proceeds

will benefit the Border Regiments' Prisoners of War Funds." Helen smiled, encouraged. "They're supposed to be quite good. I understand they don't have as many munitionettes' teams in their area since they don't have the concentration of factories we do here, so they have to travel far afield sometimes."

Arthur frowned thoughtfully. "I'm glad to know the Workington Ladies are coming here. I'd rather not have our girls travel so far and arrive exhausted for work Monday morning." His brow furrowed. "Where on earth do our players—the Canaries, you called them?"

"Yes. The Thornshire Canaries." She had told him all this when she organized their uniforms.

"Where do the Canaries play? Certainly not on that miniscule field on the arsenal grounds. I thought all the football pitches had been converted to military use."

"Not all of them. Stratford United has allowed our girls, and a few other local teams, to use the Globe until professional football resumes, which I presume means for the duration."

His eyebrows shot up. "The girls play on a professional pitch?"

"Yes, indeed."

"How marvelous." He smiled and shook his head. "To be honest, I didn't even know girls played football."

"I don't believe most of these girls *did* play, at least not regularly, until men's football was cancelled."

"Well, why shouldn't they play?" Arthur tossed off an amused shrug. "If we can have women munitions workers, why not women footballers?"

"Exactly so." Helen was very much pleased to see him in such good spirits. "You'll come with me, then? It should be an exciting match, and I know it would mean so much to our girls to see you in the stands and know they have your support."

Her heart sank as his smile turned regretful. "It sounds like great fun, darling, but I have important matters to attend to at the arsenal."

"On a Sunday? Are you certain? Can't it wait until tomorrow?"

It couldn't, he explained, because new machinery was being installed, and he and the shop foreman had to supervise the operation to make sure it was done properly. So Helen kissed him goodbye in the foyer when he left, and went on her morning walk alone, and rode to Stratford alone.

But when she arrived at the Globe and searched for a good seat in the stands, she realized that she would not have to watch the match alone, for there was Oliver Corbyn, a few rows back right in the middle, apparently also unaccompanied. She had seen him at two previous games that she recalled, but he had always been with friends, and she and he had only exchanged courteous nods from a distance.

His gaze was fixed intently on the Thornshire Canaries as both teams warmed up on their half of the field, but he rose politely when he saw Helen approaching. "May I join you," she asked, suddenly embarrassed, wondering if she should have left him alone, "or is this seat taken?"

"I was saving it for you," he said, gesturing, a corner of his mouth turning up.

"Liar," she scoffed, seating herself beside him. "So, what are our chances today, do you think?"

"The teams seem to be fairly evenly matched," he said, studying the Workington players as they ran through various exercises and drills. Unlike the Canaries, who wore black short trousers as men did, the Workington Ladies wore hip-length red jerseys and black skirts hemmed just below the knee.

"I would imagine those skirts would be an encumbrance in football," Helen remarked, looking from the team in red to the team in yellow. "Short trousers seem to allow a much greater freedom of movement."

"One would think so, but not all ladies feel comfortable in trousers. Or so I hear," Oliver replied, a bit sheepish. She hid a smile. "Some reporters can be a little unkind about so-called unfeminine apparel and the girls who wear it, but our Canaries are used to trousers, because of their munitions uniforms."

"The press covers these matches?"

"Sometimes. Local papers cover local teams. Big matches might be worth a mention in the more important papers. Most of the reporting is actually quite good. Descriptions of the play and players are exactly what you'd expect from a report about a men's game, and the women are respected as the accomplished athletes they are. Unfortunately, some reporters treat women's football as nothing more than an amusing lark, and write condescendingly about the players' hairstyles and charm instead of their strength and skill. A reader could almost mistake one for a story about a garden party rather than an athletic competition."

"No surprises there, I suppose." Helen scanned the pitch as the officials signaled that the start was near. "And is this considered a big match?"

Oliver shrugged as the whistle blew, his eyes on the center circle as the players in red kicked off. "It isn't the Dick, Kerr Ladies versus the Blyth Spartans, but the Workington Ladies have traveled far, which garners interest, and the Canaries are building a solid reputation in the Munitionettes' League."

"All the more reason for us to support our home team," Helen declared, facing forward again. She recognized some of the Thornshire players even at a distance—Lucy Dempsey, who had come to her about the players' uniforms and gear; Marjorie Tate, prowling in the goal as if she were looking for a fight; Peggy, tall and broad-shouldered, a slender version of her mother, Mabel, who stood on the sidelines; and several others who had spoken to her, briefly or at length, in passing on the arsenal grounds or in a quiet conference in her office. She watched the players moving the ball around the pitch, first yellow with the advantage, then red, and then yellow again. Lucy took a shot on the goal that went wide by mere inches, and Helen and Oliver joined in the groaning lament of the crowd.

"Have you ever played football?" Oliver asked as the ball went out of bounds and a Canary set up for a throw-in.

"Me? Heavens, no. Tennis is my game." Helen watched, holding her breath, as a swift, flaxen-haired Canary stole the ball from a red-shirted girl a head taller than herself, worked it down the field, then passed it off to Peggy, who sent the ball soaring toward the goal—and into the arms of the Workington keeper, who made the flying catch and landed with a roll. "How about you?"

"All the boys in our town played growing up. I played at school, too, even played a bit in the army when we had the chance, when we weren't in the trenches. It's been a while, though." He offered a dry chuckle. "The last time I played, I was in France, and I still had two good hands."

She studied him from the corner of her eye, but he sounded strictly matter-of-fact, without a trace of self-pity. "Oh, so you're a player of international renown, then?" she teased.

To her relief, he smiled. "Hardly. I think you're confusing me with Mrs. Dempsey's husband."

"Oh? Does he play football too?"

Oliver laughed. "A little, now and then." When she peered at him, uncomprehending, he explained that Lucy Dempsey's husband was *the* Daniel Dempsey, Olympic champion and longtime popular center forward of Tottenham Hotspur, now serving with the Footballers' Battalion somewhere along the Somme.

On an impulse, Helen asked Oliver if any of the other players had husbands or sweethearts or other loved ones in the military, and naturally they nearly all did; if Helen had asked the same question of any random group of strangers on any street in London, she would have received the same answer. April, the swift midfielder, had an elder brother in the army; Marjorie three; Peggy was engaged to a private in the West Ham Pals; and on the list went, and those were just the ones Oliver knew about. For some of the women, the soldiers they had kissed farewell on their front steps or a train station would never return from the war.

No wonder the munitionettes worked so tirelessly through the long shifts and longer weeks, Helen realized. Every shell they made hastened the end of the war, speeding the return of their absent loved ones. And for the grieving widows and sisters and mothers, every shell was a blow for vengeance, smoldering and bitter and full of anguish and spite.

She shivered at the thought, and pulled up the collar of her coat to pretend it was the wind that had chilled her and not her own grim thoughts.

The match had not been long underway when Helen's questions about certain plays and penalties revealed how embarrassingly little she knew about the sport. Oliver never failed to answer, patiently and clearly, but she knew that he would hardly tell his boss's wife to be quiet and let him watch in peace. "I hope I'm not being a nuisance," she said apologetically, after he explained why April and other players seemed to run wherever they pleased while others tended to remain in one region or another.

"Not at all," he replied. "I enjoy showing off how clever I am. I rarely get the opportunity."

She laughed aloud, for she knew that wasn't true; if she hadn't seen for herself how much Arthur and Tom depended upon him, Arthur's praise alone would have convinced her. She was glad Oliver was willing to help her learn the subtleties of the sport, but she did wonder why he was such a dedicated fan of the Thornshire Canaries. It had to be something more than pure love of the sport, for there were other matches in and about football-mad London, men's matches, charity and recruiting events with teams from regiments that were still in training. Loyalty to Thornshire Arsenal might have prompted him to attend a match or two, but not every Sunday afternoon; no one was *that* fond of their workplace. The most logical explanation was that he was fond of a particular player, but she could not tell who, for he applauded everyone who deserved it, even those on the other side, if a play was especially brilliant.

The first half ended with Workington ahead at 2–1, but after the interval, April came blazing out of nowhere and scored from twenty-five yards away at a ridiculously shallow angle. The defense must have expected her to pass, for they didn't react until the ball was soaring through the air, leaving the keeper on her own. "Yes!" Oliver shouted, bolting to his feet. "Good show, Canaries!"

"Well done," Helen called, applauding her gloved hands. "Brava! Encore!"

Oliver looked at her, astonished, then burst out laughing. "I don't recall ever hearing that particular cheer at a football match before," he said, taking his seat again.

"Let's see if it works," Helen said, folding her hands in her lap and studying the pitch with great anticipation.

Perhaps it did indeed work, albeit not immediately, for with nearly five minutes left, Lucy scored from within the box, and Marjorie successfully fended off a barrage of shots to hold on to a 3–2 victory. "Shall we congratulate the team?" Helen asked Oliver, rising, as the spectators filed from the stadium.

"You go on," said Oliver, tucking his hands into his coat pockets. "I'll wait, if you'd like me to escort you to the station."

She emphatically declined, having taken up far too much of his afternoon already. He bade her goodbye and left so quickly that she wondered whether she had been mistaken to think that he was fond of one of the players. Why squander a perfectly good opportunity to spend time with the person one most admired? It occurred to her that she might ask Arthur, as he did so often enough, and her joy in the team's victory dimmed.

Even so, she enjoyed recounting the match for Arthur that evening over dinner. Her efforts to entertain him were rewarded when genuine interest showed through his fatigue, and his face lit up with delight when she described April's brilliant, game-winning goal. "Perhaps you'll join me at next week's match," she said tentatively, and smiled when he told her he would certainly try.

But very late that night, she woke abruptly, heart pounding, after Arthur shouted in his sleep and sat upright, breathing heavily, turning this way and that as if he were searching desperately for something lost in the blackout darkness. "Arthur, darling, what is it?" she asked, reaching out to lay a comforting hand on his back.

He flinched at her touch, then took a deep, shuddering breath. "It was—" He hesitated, and she could feel the perspiration on his skin beneath his thin pajama shirt. "I don't remember now. It's all fading away." He lay down again and pulled the covers up, shivering. "It was just a nightmare."

"How dreadful," she murmured, lying on her side next to him, resting her head on his shoulder, placing her hand on his chest. His heart was racing. "Try to sleep, darling. It will all look better in the morning."

He kissed her forehead in reply. She listened as his pulse steadied and his breaths became deeper, more even, and only when she was certain he was all right did she allow herself to drift back to sleep.

The next morning, Helen woke first, and in the dim light of the autumn sunrise that seeped around the edges of the blackout curtains, Arthur slept on, motionless except for the slow rise and fall of his chest. Suddenly it came to her: She would let him sleep, for he needed and deserved it. She would telephone Tom and inform him that Arthur would not be in until the afternoon, and possibly not at all. Arthur might rebuke her afterward, but at least he would be well-rested.

Carefully she slipped out from beneath the covers, pulled on her dressing gown and slippers, switched off the alarm clock, and quietly crept across the floor. She eased open the door without a sound, stepped into the hallway, and was closing it behind her when she heard bedsprings creak and her husband murmuring sleepily, "Helen?"

She sighed softly. "Yes, Arthur?" she said, opening the door again.

He propped himself up on his elbows and blinked at her. "Why didn't you wake me?"

She had one gambit left. "Go back to sleep, darling. You don't have to be up for hours."

"Then why do I smell breakfast?" He reached for his wristwatch on the nightstand beside the bed, peered closely, and threw back the covers. "Dash it all, it's half six. What happened to the alarm clock?"

"We must have forgotten to set it."

Grumbling wearily, Arthur climbed out of bed and began getting ready for the day. Her scheme thwarted, Helen did the same, disappointed and anxious for him. She waited for him to mention the nightmare, but it seemed that he had entirely forgotten it.

They rode to the arsenal together and parted ways at the door to the administration building. She had two appointments that morning, one with a young woman whose father demanded that she transfer out of the Danger Building, the second with a scrappy middle-aged woman who was eager to transfer in, so it was an easy fix to have them trade places. Then she began her rounds, and since it was a Monday, she visited all of the canteens, inspecting them for safety and cleanliness, chatting with the girls, reminding them that her office door was always open if they wished to speak with her in confidence. In the canteen kitchen nearest the fuse cap shop, she was surprised to discover three smartly dressed young women, hair meticulously bobbed and coifed, faces adorned with powder and lipstick, shrieking with laughter as they peeled potatoes and chopped onions. It was one of the oddest scenes she had ever observed at the arsenal.

Puzzled, she took the head cook aside. "What's their story?" she asked in an undertone. "They're positively giddy."

The cook heaved a sigh and planted her fists on her broad hips. "You're looking at the nieces of the Duchess of Wellington," she replied, her voice low. "They're part of that, what's it called, the Week End Relief Scheme. I was expecting them yesterday, but here they are, so I put them to work."

"Of course." Helen should have guessed they weren't regular workers from the way they treated their menial tasks as a smashing joke. More than a year before, Margaret, Lady Moir, the wife of the MP for East Aberdeenshire, and Winifrede, Lady Cowan, who was married to a high-ranking official with the Ministry of Munitions, had organized a scheme in which ladies of the leisure class could contribute to the war effort by taking over for the regular workers on the weekends. The objective was to relieve the munitionettes of the strain of working six or seven days a week while keeping the factories in continuous operation. Superintendent Carmichael could always find an appropriate place for a qualified, willing worker, but thus far she had been reluctant to place Week End Relief ladies in any job requiring actual skill or responsibility. "How can I trust them around explosives or heavy machinery," she had asked Helen earnestly, "when they're only here on a lark?"

Perhaps that was not quite fair, Helen supposed. A great many middle- and upper-class women had signed on to do their bit as soon as the need for women workers became evident, without needing a special program for the privileged to prompt them to get their hands dirty. As for the Week End Relief workers, many surely took their work seriously and sincerely wanted to do their bit. Not so the three young ladies presently enjoying themselves overmuch in the canteen kitchen. "None of them has ever chopped or peeled veg before," the cook told Helen, eyeing the fashionable young women with bewilderment and distaste. "I guess the worst they could do is cut off too much tater with the peel, or stab themselves in the finger."

Helen grimaced. "Let's hope neither of those misfortunes come to pass. Sorry their care fell to you, and on a Monday, when you weren't braced for it. Good luck."

"Thank you, missus. I imagine I'll need it today."

Helen finished her rounds, hoping the relief workers did more good than harm, and that their presence did not worsen the existing class tensions at the arsenal. She had noticed a recent push by the Ministry of Munitions to draw more middle- and upper-class women into munitions work, but as regular hires, not merely weekend relief. Upper-class women were a largely untapped source of labor, certainly, but the ministry seemed to have other motives. Documents it had sent to Thornshire revealed an assumption that better-educated women would learn skilled work more quickly, they would naturally assume leadership roles, and they would readily give up their places after the war when the soldiers returned home and sought civilian jobs. Working-class women, on the other hand, the vast majority of the munitionettes at Thornshire, had worked to support themselves and their families before the war, and during it, and would almost certainly need to work for a living afterward. They had become accustomed to the higher wages and greater respect "men's work" had garnered them, and Helen suspected they would not relinquish their hard-won positions so easily. They had taken on difficult work when their country desperately needed them. More than two years into the war, with no end in sight, was the government already planning to push them aside when peace finally returned to Britain?

At six o'clock that evening, weary from a long day, Helen again went to Arthur's office, helped him finish up some paperwork, and firmly steered him out of the office and home. The next day he insisted that he absolutely must work late, full stop, so she stubbornly waited with him, retrieving some files from her own office, making herself comfortable on the davenport by the window, and reading silently while he completed various forms and studied reports. They didn't get home until midnight, but she had made her point without saying a word: She intended to work as late as he did, so if he wanted her to go home for a good meal and essential rest, he had to go too.

After a few days, she was pleased to see positive results from her scheme. Arthur left work and got to bed earlier, he seemed less hoarse and haggard, and although nightmares woke him two more nights that week, he still managed to get more sleep than before.

Then, around midnight on 26 September, something else jolted them awake, a searing, bright light that pierced the edges of the blackout curtains, followed by the deep rumble of explosives, ominously close. "Stay back," Arthur cautioned, but she followed him to the window, and as he drew back the curtain, she shielded her eyes from the glare. "Air raid. Likely no more than four miles off."

"What is that light?" Helen asked, just as it abruptly extinguished. "Some terrible new bomb?"

"Same bombs, but I believe the zeppelin is using Very lights too."

She flinched at another distant explosion. "Very lights?" she echoed, voice quavering.

"Brilliant white flares. The zeppelin crew drop them to illuminate the ground below to aid in navigation, or release them into the air to create a dazzling, baffling glare that our searchlights can't penetrate." He paused to listen. "They're moving off."

"Are you sure?"

"As sure as one could be." He put his arm around her. "You're shivering. Back to bed."

It was obvious he wanted to keep watch at the window, but she refused to go without him, so they both returned to bed, and somehow they both slept soundly the rest of the night. It wasn't until much later the next day that they learned how terribly devastating the air raid had been. Three zeppelins had approached London through Kent, following a five-mile line from Streatham Common past Brixton Hill to Kennington Park, where they dropped their last bomb less than three miles southeast of their home. Along the way, the Germans had bombed the high road as well as residential streets alongside it, leaving massive craters in the streets and destroying shops, a children's playground, countless trees, and many small brick homes and front gardens belonging to middle-class families. Twenty-two people were killed and at least that many injured. Helen found little comfort in learning that two of the three zeppelins had been brought down by British ground defenses as they retreated, one at Billericay, twenty-four miles east of London, and the other at thirty miles northeast of that, at Little Wigborough, on the coast near the Blackwater Estuary. All on board had been killed, their charred and broken bodies found amid the wreckage.

Less than a week later, on the night of 1 October, Helen and Arthur witnessed an even more dramatic, appalling spectacle in the skies above London. They had stayed quite late at the arsenal while Arthur conferred with his elder brother on the telephone, and were aboard a crowded tramcar about three miles east of home near Blackfriars Bridge when they heard frenzied shouts and cries of alarm from passengers seated on the other side. "Oh! Oh! She's hit!" a man called out, and nearly everyone aboard pushed their way to the windows or craned their necks to scan the sky to the north. High above, looking along the straight shot of New Bridge Street and Farringdon Road, Helen spotted a tangle of searchlights concentrated on a ruddy glow, which, as her eyes adjusted, she realized with horror was a blazing zeppelin. Suddenly the searchlights turned off, one by one, as the airship drifted as if on a parallel course with their tram, a massive ball of red and orange flames, a terrible fallen angel plummeting from the heavens to earth, its lurid glow lighting up the streets and buildings below, tinting even the dark waters of the Thames.

Helen watched the burning airship drift away, utterly riveted, scarcely breathing, her chest about to burst from emotion—terror, triumph, she could not say. When at last the doomed craft vanished from sight, two, perhaps three minutes later, a hoarse shout went up from the passengers, and indeed it seemed as if every voice in London joined in, a swelling roar of relief, exultation, and loathing. Helen wondered where the zeppelin had crashed, and her heart trembled with worry for the citizens below, followed a moment later by a small stir of pity for the crew, who had certainly perished.

"Did you see it?" Arthur asked, his eyes wild as he stared into the darkness on the other side of the window. "Do you know what it portends?"

She looked from her husband's pale, haggard face to the night sky and back. "Victory for the Allies?" she replied, uncertain. "Germany going down in flames?"

"No, no." The look he threw her was impatient, desperate, anguished. "That is the fate of Great Britain if I fail to do my duty."

"That's not what it means," said Helen, frightened for him. "That was an enemy ship on a course to destroy our city, only to be brought down by our defenses instead."

The tram had halted at their stop, and Arthur took her hand so they would not be separated in the crush of departing passengers. "I see something else," he said, his voice close to her ear, his earlier frenzy fading. "If we fail and Germany wins, London will burn."

"Germany will not win," Helen retorted, voice catching in her throat. "The whole war is not upon your shoulders alone. You do realize that, don't you?"

"I do," he replied wearily. "Of course I do."

She studied him for a moment, not sure whether he truly did. Then she took his arm and they made their way home in the darkness of the blackout, unable to see more than a few paces ahead of them, trusting their memory of what was familiar only by daylight.

13
October–December 1916

Lucy

O n the fourth Sunday of October, the Thornshire
Canaries left London on an early train and rode
nearly three hundred miles north to Blyth in southeast
Northumberland for a match against the Blyth Spartan
Ladies Football Club. Privately, Lucy and Daisy agreed
that it was an excessively long way to travel for a football
match, but the Blyth Spartans were developing a reputation as one of the finest women's teams in the United
Kingdom. When they had issued their challenge—or
sent their invitation, depending upon how one chose to
read it—the majority of the Canaries had been eager
to accept. When else might they have the opportunity
to challenge themselves against so skilled a team? How
could they hold their heads up if their fans thought they

had declined out of fear? Each club would receive half the gate to donate to a charity of their choice, and given the Blyth Spartans' popularity, the match would likely draw a sellout crowd and raise a substantial amount of money. That was what finally persuaded Lucy the match was worth the trip, although she would have gone along with the team's decision either way.

She didn't want the boys to spend most of their day on a train, so over their protests, she left them behind with their grandmother, who promised them a day full of fun to make up for it. In the end, Lucy was glad she had spared her sons the ordeal of traveling for hours only to watch their mother's team receive a thorough drubbing from a far superior team at Croft Park before a virtually all-Northumberland crowd thousands strong. Lucy took some consolation in her single goal, midway through the second half, which at least put the Canaries on the board, but the 6–1 loss was humbling after so many victories. After the match, as they congratulated the victors with handshakes all around, Lucy was glad to learn that the Blyth Spartans were perfectly friendly girls, gracious and encouraging in victory, which took a bit of the sting out of the lopsided score. As they made their way back to the train station, even Marjorie, who took every loss as a personal affront, agreed that it had been a revelation to watch such talented women in action.

"I didn't know girls could play like that," confessed Peggy as they boarded the train. "And to think, at least half of them were canary girls, just like us."

"If *they* can play like that, *we* can," Marjorie declared, proud and undaunted. Daisy threw Lucy a doubtful look, but most of the other girls brightened, a few applauded, and someone called out, "Hear, hear!"

That burst of enthusiasm drained them of their last reserves of energy, so they settled into their seats, some nursing minor injuries or sore muscles, others opening the boxed dinners they had packed that morning. The return journey was long enough for them to cover every possible topic of conversation, including the state of the war, recent air raids, soaring costs and shortages of food, and news from their own beloved soldiers far away. Peggy practically glowed as she described a recent letter from her sweetheart, who had sent her a beautiful scarf he had purchased while on leave in Paris.

"My brothers don't send me anything," Marjorie grumbled cheerfully. "All our family's parcels go in the opposite direction."

For a while, their chatter circled around the best things to include in a parcel for their dear Tommies. Fish paste and tins of biscuits were a popular suggestion, along with any canned fruits one could find.

Clean, dry socks were always welcome, as were cigarettes. Several Canaries remembered then that they had
brought their knitting along, and soon at least half the
players, including Lucy, were hard at work on a sock
or washcloth. Their friends looked on, either admiring
their handiwork or silently congratulating themselves
for forgetting their own needles and yarn so they could
just sit back and relax.

Eventually the conversation turned to the new regulations the Ministry of Munitions had imposed at the
arsenal, the upheaval they had caused, and the girls'
general dissatisfaction that no workers had been consulted during the process. The Canaries were about
evenly divided between those who disliked the shorter
shifts and those who were relieved to work fewer hours,
but no one was happy about the reduced wages. "Isn't
that just like a boss?" said Mabel, scowling. "Tell us
we're essential to the war effort, lure us in with good
wages and promises, then cut costs without so much as
a by your leave."

"But they haven't cut our hourly wage, just our
hours," said Lucy. "That means they haven't cut costs
at all. It's actually more expensive to run three shifts
with more workers. They're not trying to save money.
They're trying to reduce our exposure to the yellow
powder."

Mabel turned her head aside, covered her mouth with the handkerchief she always carried, and broke into hoarse, wracking coughs. "All I know is that I take home less each week," she said in a strangled voice when she could speak again.

"Just wait until we shift out of the Danger Buildings," said Peggy ominously. "We'll take home even less, for twelve whole weeks."

A disgruntled murmur went up from the group, and Lucy had to admit that the reduced wages would be a hardship. Food was not scarce, but even household staples were becoming more expensive, seemingly by the day. She could eat her fill at the arsenal canteen two times a day, six days a week, but not so the rest of her family. Jamie and Simon were growing boys and were always hungry, and although Lucy's mother was a frugal shopper and a skilled cook, she found it a challenge to keep them all comfortably fed. In Brookfield, Alice and Eleanor had taken over her garden, and throughout the summer and early fall they had frequently sent boxes of produce, but with winter approaching, fresh fruits and vegetables would soon become scarce. Lucy was not sure what the family would do then, especially on reduced earnings.

"We need to talk to Purcell," Mabel declared. "'On Her Their Lives Depend,' they all say, when they want more girls to sign up. Now's his chance to prove what that means to him."

"He needs to look out for our health while he's at it," said Daisy, holding out her hands, palms down, displaying her lurid yellow skin. "Shells must be made, no argument there, but none of us should die for it."

"The lads risk their lives in the trenches," Mabel reminded them, as she often had before. "We risk ours in the Danger Building."

"Yes, but we should minimize that risk if we can," said Lucy.

"Did you hear about the canary girl from Eley's Cartridge Factory in Edmonton?" asked one of the fullbacks. "Her mother says they took fourteen pints of poisoned blood from her at the military hospital before she died."

"I thought she died because her liver, heart, and kidneys were so badly damaged," said another. "There was an autopsy. It was in the papers just last week."

"You're thinking of that poor girl from Leicester who worked at Standard Engineering," said Louise, shaking her head, her expression grim. "She left behind four children under seven. The inquest ruled it death by misadventure, but I don't know if that means the company will be obliged to provide anything for her family."

"All the more reason we need our weekly pay as it were promised us," said Mabel, looking around the group. "So we can put more aside in case of, what-you-call-it, misadventure."

"We need to have it out with the boss," said Marjorie, raising her voice to be heard. "How much money has the Purcell family made off this war, I wonder? They can send a bit more of it our way, for the risks we take."

Hearty cheers and applause met her words.

"It's settled, then," said Mabel firmly. "First thing tomorrow morning, I'll march right into his office and tell him how it's going to be."

"But how *is* it going to be?" asked Lucy, before they could get too carried away. "Shouldn't you work that bit out first? What is it you're going to ask for?"

"We should go through the union," said Daisy. "That's what it's there for. That's how the men get things done."

Mabel took a moment to mull it over before agreeing to try the union first. Since the Danger Building's representative was Mr. Vernon, Mabel told Daisy that they would speak to him together, since it was Daisy's idea and she worked for him in the Finishing Shop.

The following afternoon, Lucy was at her station inserting a detonator into a shell when Daisy returned from the quick conference Mr. Vernon had grudgingly allowed them. When Lucy caught her eye, her friend frowned and shook her head. Later, at football training, Daisy and Mabel reported that Mr. Vernon flatly refused to help them, for women were not and never would be allowed to join the union. "The union's purpose is to protect workers who've been here all along," he had fairly snarled. "It's not for *you* lot, who come in and work cheap and steal our jobs."

"We tried it your way," Mabel said to Daisy, not unkindly. "Now we go to Purcell directly."

"I wouldn't just burst into his office unless you want to get sacked," said Lucy. "Make an appointment. Show him we understand how business is done."

"April can get that appointment sorted for you," Marjorie declared, grinning mischievously and nudging her friend, who looked caught out. "She and his assistant secretary are great chums."

"Is that why he comes to our games?" exclaimed Peggy. "April, you silly sausage, you never said a word!"

April flushed pink beneath her yellow pallor. "There's nothing to say. He didn't come today, did he?"

"Oh, dearie," crooned Marjorie, feigning sympathy. "Did you have a lovers' tiff?"

"No! We didn't have a tiff. And we're not lovers." April glared at her grinning teammates, folded her arms, and turned her head to the window. "If that's how it's going to be, get the appointment yourselves."

It took some cajoling from them all, and a contrite apology from Marjorie, before April agreed to see what she could do. Two days later, she arrived at the shifting house just ahead of the warning bell with news that a meeting had been scheduled for that evening after their shift—but not with Mr. Purcell. "He can't see us. It's simply impossible," said April, tossing her coat into her cubby and quickly unbuttoning her dress. "But we got the next best thing—a meeting with Mrs. Purcell and Superintendent Carmichael."

Some of the girls groaned, disappointed, but Mabel, coughing, waved them to silence. "We'll convince the wife, she'll convince the husband," she said, scanning the crowd of workers pulling on their uniforms. "Lucy, you're coming too."

Lucy froze in the middle of tucking her mottled hair beneath her cap. "Me? Why?"

"Because Mrs. Purcell likes you, going back to when you asked her to organize our football kit. And the superintendent must like you too, since she started you in the Finishing Shop. You know how to talk to their kind. They'll listen to you."

Lucy busied herself with her cap and clogs to conceal her sudden anxiety. Mabel was assertive and loud;

Lucy was shy. Mabel cared most about wages, while Lucy's greatest concern was health and safety. Mabel was a second mum to all the Danger Building workers, especially the working-class girls, and Lucy was Lady Prim, the footballer's wife. It was either the worst pairing of canary girls the Danger Building could have produced, or the most ingenious. "All right," Lucy said, a faint tremor in her voice. "But I can't stay late. I have to get home to my boys."

The hours passed, given over to monotonous, painstaking work, wretched yellow powder dusting her veil and gloves, and more glares than usual from Mr. Vernon, who surely suspected that the canary girls hadn't abandoned their cause despite the union's refusal to help them. Over lunch and tea, Lucy and Mabel discussed what they should say at the meeting, but there was no time to prepare as thoroughly as Lucy would have liked. She hoped that Mabel's confidence would see them through.

After her shift, Lucy washed carefully and changed into her own clothing, smoothing out the wrinkles as best she could. Then she combed out her hair and twisted it up into a Psyche knot, holding it in place with a small wooden comb Jamie had ingeniously carved and polished for her after he overheard her telling her mother that metal was forbidden. Mabel too had clearly taken care with her own appearance, for she wore a smart dark blue suit and hat and kid gloves, and had pinched some color into her cheeks, which had sunken slightly in the months Lucy had known her.

The other girls wished them good luck as they set off together for the canteen nearest the administration building. As they crossed the threshold, Mabel threw Lucy a sidelong look, eyebrows raised, which told her that Mabel too noticed that this canteen was brighter and cleaner than their own, perhaps due to the absence of yellow powder in the air.

Mrs. Purcell and Superintendent Carmichael were at a table for four near the coal fireplace on the far side of the room. Mrs. Purcell spotted them, brightened, and waved them over. "She's friendly enough *now*," Mabel said under her breath, pressing a fist to her mouth to stifle a cough. The superintendent regarded them with cool disapproval as they approached, her mouth pinched in a thin line.

They had all met before, so they exchanged greetings rather than introductions as they seated themselves, Mrs. Purcell and Superintendent Carmichael on one side of the table, Lucy and Mabel on the other, a pot of tea and four cups between them. Mrs. Purcell began by pouring them each a cup and thanking Mabel and Lucy for coming, almost as if she had requested the meeting rather than the other way around. "Mr. Purcell sends his regrets," she said, her smile turning down a bit as she set down the teapot and offered cream and sugar. "He's so frightfully busy that he hardly has time to catch his breath."

"I know what that feels like," said Mabel levelly.

They wasted no time in idle chat but got straight to it. Mabel began with the issue of wages, and after some back-and-forth, Superintendent Carmichael acknowledged that reducing the workers' hours caused enough financial difficulties without also expecting the Danger Building girls to accept reduced wages. The canary girls had not sought the twelve-week respites, and they ought to be rewarded for willingly accepting Danger Building work when so many others had declined. Mrs. Purcell proposed that the current Danger Building workers would continue to receive their current pay even during their required rotations out. The munitionettes who took their places would be paid Danger Building wages as long as their rotation lasted, but they would return to their regular pay when they returned to their original jobs.

Mabel and Lucy exchanged a look, pleasantly surprised, for they had not expected such reasonable terms. Mabel promptly accepted on behalf of all the Danger Building girls.

Next Lucy thanked the two supervisors for the new safety precautions, which were already showing a reduction in the workers' symptoms. The girls complained less frequently of nose, throat, and eye irritations, and absences related to illness were slowly declining. But Lucy had come prepared with a file of articles her brother George had collected from his colleagues in medicine and government, recent studies and observations about precautions other arsenals had tried, with encouraging results. Mrs. Purcell seemed very interested, and she promised to study them thoroughly and to pass on her recommendations to Mr. Purcell. "We both want—we *all* want—our workers to be safe and healthy," she said emphatically, and Lucy believed her.

Lucy was pleased with how well the meeting had gone, and she was just about to thank the supervisors and bid them goodbye when Mabel folded her hands on top of the table and peered sharply first at Superintendent Carmichael and then at Mrs. Purcell. "There's one more matter, just as important as the rest," she said, not sparing a glance for Lucy, who had no idea what she intended to say next. "We want some assurances we won't all be sacked soon as the war's over."

Superintendent Carmichael removed her glasses, sighed, and rubbed her eyes. "Now you've taken things too far," she said wearily, returning her glasses to the bridge of her nose. "It is not in my power, nor in Mrs. Purcell's, to make you any such promises."

"We're doing our bit for the war effort same as any soldier," Mabel said. "Mucking about with explosives, we risk our health and our lives every day, same as soldiers do."

"Indeed, and as we have established, you are well compensated for that," said the superintendent. "Excellent wages, nourishing meals, subsidized housing, recreational activities—"

"And it could all disappear overnight." Turning to Mrs. Purcell, Mabel added, "We've done everything the government and this arsenal has asked of us. We've proved ourselves to be trustworthy workers, skilled workers. We want assurances that those of us who want to stay on after the war will be allowed to. We won't be sacked with the snap of a finger just because we're women."

Mrs. Purcell nodded, her expression sympathetic and concerned, but the superintendent glared at Mabel and Lucy both, incredulous. "You would put yourselves before our veterans?" she asked querulously. "What do you expect us to tell our brave soldiers returning from the front—that *they* shall be unemployed so that *girls* may hold on to the jobs they were given *for the duration?*"

"Tell the soldiers whatever you like," said Mabel bluntly, sitting back in her chair with a scowl. "What am *I* going to tell my girls?"

"Mrs. Burridge, I respect your position and I would like nothing more than to be able to put your mind at ease," said Mrs. Purcell, cupping her hands around her teacup as if to warm them. "Unfortunately, no one, not even Mr. Purcell, can guarantee anyone a job at Thornshire Arsenal after the war."

Mabel frowned, puzzled. "What, not even the union men? Not even the returning soldiers?"

"Not even them." Mrs. Purcell sighed and folded her hands on the table. "We must assume that the need for munitions will plummet after the war, which I trust will end in victory for the Allies."

Lucy and Mabel both nodded. So did Superintendent Carmichael, but with a wary sidelong glance for Mrs. Purcell.

"You may know that this facility closed after the Panic of 1873." Mrs. Purcell looked around the table for confirmation, and they all nodded in reply. "For about forty years, this entire compound was shuttered, quiet, gathering dust behind locked gates. So you see, unlike other factories that were converted to war production for the duration, Thornshire Arsenal essentially has no pre-war purpose to revert to."

"What about sewing machines?" Mabel asked hoarsely, pausing to clear her throat. "Purcell Products made those here once, before the Panic. Why couldn't they again?"

"Perhaps they could. If not sewing machines, then something else." Mrs. Purcell spread her hands and sighed. "But I can't promise that Thornshire Arsenal will remain open in any fashion after the war. I can only assure you that your jobs are secure as long as the war lasts and the Allies need munitions."

"I see," said Mabel flatly. "Thank you for respecting us enough not to give us false hope."

"I understand that you need to plan for your livelihoods after the war," said Mrs. Purcell. "Any munitionette who decides it is in her best interest to take a job at another arsenal, one that is more likely to remain open in peacetime, shall be free to resign. I will personally see to it that she receives a leaving certificate."

"Mrs. Purcell," exclaimed Superintendent Carmichael. "Perhaps you don't understand the purpose of leaving certificates!"

"On the contrary, I understand perfectly. Their purpose is to limit turnover by discouraging workers from resigning, since no other factory shall be permitted to hire them without the current employer's consent."

"That's how it was explained to me in my training course," said Lucy. She liked Mrs. Purcell, and she didn't appreciate the scolding tone the superintendent used with her.

Mrs. Purcell thanked her with a nod before turning her attention to Mabel. "I know that's not the answer you'd hoped for, Mrs. Burridge, but is it acceptable, given the other concessions we've made?"

Mabel thought for a moment, and then extended her hand. "My girls will be happy enough when I explain to them about the wages, and I don't suppose many of them will be leaving to find jobs elsewhere."

Mrs. Purcell shook Mabel's hand, and then Lucy's, and eventually the superintendent grudgingly shook their hands too.

As Mabel predicted, the other canary girls were very pleased with the arrangements she and Lucy had made on their behalf, and not one decided to take Mrs. Purcell up on the offer of a leaving certificate and seek her fortune elsewhere. "The war might drag on for years yet," Marjorie pointed out, something they had all considered but no one hoped for, not even if it meant keeping their jobs. "Why give up good wages now, when for all we know, Thornshire might stay open somehow? Maybe we'll make sewing machines again, or motorcars—something, anything, that doesn't require yellow powder."

Many of the girls brightened at the idea, smiling and nodding and chiming in assent. Lucy nodded too, hopeful that the girls who wanted to keep their jobs after the war might have that opportunity. As for herself, she wanted nothing more than to return to her old life, her *real* life, minding her sons and keeping a warm, happy, loving home for them and for Daniel. She wanted holidays in Brookfield and cheerful family dinners around the long wooden table in her childhood home. She wanted all the people she loved best in the world to be safe and not too terribly far away. She would miss her new friends and football, but perhaps she could find a way to remain on the team.

But with the war dragging on and on, all harrowing misery on the Western Front and lonely apprehension at home, Lucy knew that production would continue at Thornshire Arsenal for the foreseeable future, perhaps for years—years she would spend without her beloved husband by her side.

Her worry and longing for Daniel stayed with her always, a dull ache in the back of her mind that she could never entirely ignore, even when she focused on work or football or her children. She devoured his letters as if she were starving for words, and she scanned the newspapers for any mention of the 17th Middlesex, which she knew was engaged in the fighting on the Somme, but little more than that.

To her indignation, some reporters remained as unduly critical of footballers as they had at the height of public criticism before the Footballers' Battalion was formed. Without provocation, reporters would drop scathing remarks about how the players were "finally" testing themselves in the Greater Game, reminding their readers, with blithe inaccuracy, that footballers had been reluctant to enlist compared to other sportsmen. But in the nearly two years that had passed since December 1914, the footballers themselves had begun refuting the snide commentary in the same papers that mocked them. Private Tim Coleman, the same Nottingham Forest forward who had accepted the surrender of two disgruntled Germans, called out a reporter who said that footballers had waited until they were "nearly forced to join" before enlisting. "The man who wrote that must be 'up the pole,'" Coleman had written, "as we have been on active service for nearly ten months, and have been in some very hot places, and have also taken our part in the great push." They had all joined up to do their bit and some had given all, he noted, listing the names of numerous players who had been killed or wounded. "The professional footballers have done their bit. I was hoping that this little 'tiff' would have been over for next season, but it still wags on."

More recently, Major Frank Buckley, the center halfback for Bradford City, had returned to England to recover from serious wounds to his arm, shoulder, and chest. Though he wore a sling and some shrapnel remained lodged in his lung, he attended charity football matches and sometimes spoke to the press during the interval, never failing to praise the men of the 17th Middlesex. "Even knowing them as I had before the war," he declared, "I had never realized that they would have devoted themselves to their duties so unflinchingly, or proved themselves such efficient soldiers. I am proud to have been one of the officers in such a battalion."

Major Buckley's words warmed Lucy's heart and gave her hope that critics would finally give the Footballers' Battalion the respect and admiration they deserved, especially considering the dangers and hardships they confronted on the battlefield.

On Monday evening in the last week of November, Lucy returned home at seven o'clock, just in time for a late supper with her mother and her sons, thanks to the shorter shifts. Afterward, she helped the boys with their schoolwork, saw them off to bed, and settled down in her favorite chair with a cup of tea and the newspaper. But the news was not relaxing in the least. While they had slept the previous night, several German airships had attacked the northeast coast of England, dropping bombs on Yorkshire and Durham. Two of the German airships had been brought down in flames by aeroplanes of the Royal Flying Corps and by naval guns, one zeppelin plummeting into the sea just off the coast, the other struggling to escape its pursuers only to split into two flaming masses over the Channel and tumble into the rough waters below.

The next day, Lucy was loading one last shell onto the trolley before heading to the canteen for the midday meal when the bell over the main gate pealed, barely audible above the clattering machines. She and Daisy exchanged a puzzled glance, for according to the clock on the wall, it was not yet noon. As the bell rang on, distant enough that most of the girls apparently did not hear it, Mr. Vernon hurried past, scowling.

"What is it?" Lucy called to him. "Is it a fire?"

"No, no, not a fire," he said over his shoulder, waving her off impatiently. "Carry on, carry on."

So she did, for another ten minutes more until her break. In the canteen, a few other girls mentioned hearing the bell and wondering what it was about, but it was not until later, on their way to their training field, that they learned from one of the lorry drivers that an aeroplane flying at a very high altitude, obscured by light mist, had dropped six bombs on West London near the Victoria railway station and Buckingham Palace, and over Belgravia as far as Brompton Road. Four people had been injured, one woman quite seriously, but there had been no deaths and only minor damage to buildings and streets. Yet the raid struck new terror into their hearts—an attack by a swift aeroplane in broad daylight upon the heart of London! It was unimaginable, and yet it had happened, and now they must fear death from above by day as well as by night.

A little more than a week later, on 9 December, Mabel called the team aside as they were entering the canteen for dinner. Her expression was so grim that Lucy knew at once that something terrible had happened, and cold apprehension settled over her.

"Our match on Sunday with the Barnbow Lasses in Leeds has been cancelled," Mabel said, then drew in a shuddering breath and lowered her voice. "Their captain telephoned me, and really, she said more than she should've. We know we're not supposed to talk about such things. It won't be in the papers. But the truth will come out so you might as well hear it now, but don't carry it any further."

"What is it, Mum?" asked Peggy. "Tell us."

"Two nights ago there was a terrible accident at the Barnbow Munitions Factory."

A gasp went up from the group. "What happened?" asked Marjorie.

"The night shift had just started. A four-and-a-half-inch shell had been set in place on the machine that revolves it so as to screw the fuse in tightly. Suddenly the shell exploded, setting off all the shells around it, and on and on . . ." Mabel grimaced and shook her head.

Lucy was almost afraid to know, but she asked, "Was anyone hurt?"

"Thirty-two women and girls killed, and three men, and many more injured," said Mabel. "The Lasses' captain said the night shift workers carried off the victims, carted away the debris, cleaned the blood off the floor, and got back to work within hours. Can you imagine? The munitionettes volunteered to go back to work in the same room where their fellow workers had died only hours before."

"They died for their country," said Marjorie. "And the girls who went back in—how fearless they are! We should all be so brave."

Murmuring agreement, they all went in for a somber dinner, knowing that it could have been Thornshire instead of Barnbow, that before the war was over it still could be Thornshire *and* Barnbow. And yet they could not unburden their aching hearts to the other canary girls, who were laughing and chatting at the tables all around them. Nor would they be able to confide in their families later at home. For the sake of morale and military secrecy, they would have to carry their secret grief and worry in their hearts for the duration.

Until then, Lucy knew there would be no heart-rending eulogies in the national press for the Barnbow Lasses, only thirty-five obituaries in the local paper with loving descriptions of the lost daughter or sister or parent, all with the same date of death and a vague statement about their passing—"killed by accident," perhaps.

Someday, Lucy hoped, when the world was at peace and the truth could be told, their names would be remembered and etched into stone. Then all Britons would honor the Barnbow Lasses as heroes who had given their lives for their country on the munitions front.

14

December 1916–
February 1917

April

In mid-December, half of the munitionettes in the Danger Building, including April, were transferred to other jobs in the arsenal, scattered among different factories where they were obliged to learn new tasks and make new friends. Only half of the canary girls were put on their scheduled rotation out at a time so that the experienced workers who remained could train those rotating in. April was assigned to a gauging shop, where she sat at a long table with other munitionettes measuring fuses and other shell parts with an assortment of calipers to make sure they met specifications. The fuses that passed inspection were collected and sent on to assembly, but those that failed were scrapped. After a few days on the job, April's overlooker took her aside and remarked that her sharp eye and deft touch made her a natural for the work. "If you want to stay on after your rotation, I'll have a word with Superintendent Carmichael," she offered. "The small drop in wages is well worth it to avoid that yellow powder, or so my other girls say."

April thanked her and said she would consider it. She did prefer the gauging work, and her persistent cough and sore throat seemed to improve with every day she spent away from the yellow powder, but she missed her old friends and the camaraderie of the Filling Shop. She also felt a bit guilty knowing that another girl would have to take her place; it seemed cowardly to dump the burden of risk on someone else. Yet she longed to inhale deeply without feeling as if she were breathing through cheesecloth, and she wished the yellow tint would fade from her skin and for her hair to return to the bright, glossy flaxen locks she had once taken for granted. She wished for an end to the shocked stares and pitying glances from strangers when she was minding her own business in a shop or café. She wished Oliver could have seen her when she was pretty, before she became a canary girl, not that he had ever recoiled from her yellow-and-ginger hues as some lads did.

She and Oliver had been seeing more of each other ever since her shifts had been cut back to eight hours, allowing her more time in the evenings to spend as she pleased. Instead of hurrying to catch the tram back to the hostel after her shift and dropping exhausted into bed so she could do it all again the next day, she would walk with Oliver to the station so they could chat along the way, or they might stop to get a bite to eat, and one night they went to the theatre. As they got to know each other better, April learned that Oliver was kind and clever, with a dry sense of humor that took a bit of getting used to, but was actually quite funny. Marjorie thought Oliver was dull, but of course she would; she craved excitement and glamour, and nothing drew her eye like a lad in uniform. Oliver was equally unimpressed with Marjorie, but he didn't criticize her or air old grievances, which April thought spoke well of his character.

As the festive season approached, a light, feathery blanket of snow covered London, white and pure for a brief, beautiful few hours until it turned ash gray on the roofs and pavements and streets. Due to blackout restrictions, no bright lights illuminated parks and store windows for the third and gloomiest Christmas of the war, and only in their absence did April realize how much the season's merriment depended on their warm, jolly glow. The arsenal would not close for Christmas or Boxing Day, so April could not travel home to Carlisle to spend the holidays with her family. She hadn't made the trip the previous Christmas either, but this year her brother Henry was coming home on leave, and she was terribly disappointed to miss his visit. He had promised to see her in London before he returned to France, which she was looking forward to as a bright spot in what she feared would be a lonely, melancholy season.

But even before her happy reunion with her brother, the holidays turned out to be merrier than she had expected. The girls who shared her hostel decorated the front room with greenery and ribbons, and their landlady prepared an especially delicious dinner on Christmas Eve, after which the girls exchanged small gifts, played games, and sang all their old favorite carols. On Christmas Day, Oliver invited her to go for a walk after work, but along the way he surprised her with a lovely dinner at a Barking restaurant known for its splendid plum pudding. He also surprised her with a gift—a warm, soft cashmere scarf and mittens in her favorite shade of Wedgwood blue. She in turn gave him a necktie, silk, with fine gold and black stripes. "My favorite team's colors," he remarked as he admired it.

"Thornshire Canary colors," she clarified.

He smiled at her, amused. "I believe that's what I said."

That was the first time he kissed her—not there in the restaurant, which would have been mortifying—but later, outside the station as she waited for her tram. Since then they had spent nearly every evening after work together, a couple of stolen hours when they could almost forget about the war, and yellow powder, and the rising cost of food, and everything except each other.

Sometimes April marveled that they had ever become fond of each other, not only because of their contentious beginning, but because they had come from such different places in life. If April had stayed in domestic service, and if Oliver had kept his job in his uncle's shop, they never would have met. And if by some strange chance they had, most people would have considered them unsuited for each other. Maybe some nosey parkers still did. But for young people in London, the war had overturned many customs they had once accepted without question. April and Oliver both worked in munitions at the same arsenal, and somehow that made them more equal. Old-fashioned ideas didn't matter anymore, not to them.

On a Friday evening in the middle of January, they were chatting about the Canaries' upcoming football match when April paused at a street corner and looked up at him, a bit shyly. "May I ask you a personal question?" she asked. "You don't have to answer if you don't want to."

The corner of his mouth turned wryly, and he held up his prosthetic hand. "You want to know how I came by this."

April shook her head. "That wasn't what I was going to ask. What I've been wondering is whether it—if it still hurts." She hesitated. "Since you brought it up, I *am* curious—but I wouldn't have asked."

He was silent for a moment. "It doesn't hurt, not in the way you mean," he eventually said. "The injury from the amputation healed long ago. But sometimes I'll feel a sharp pain or a dull ache, and I know my hand isn't there anymore, but it still hurts, sometimes for hours before it goes away." He shook his head, thrust his hands into his pockets, and lifted his chin to indicate the street ahead, and that they should cross. "You probably think I'm mad. I used to think so."

April matched his pace as they crossed the street. "I don't think you're mad."

"As for how it happened—" He grimaced. "I told you I enlisted with my friends from home. We knew our mums would likely try to stop us, so we lit out for London and joined up with the Fifth London Rifle Brigade. We were mobilized right away and sent out to a camp in Bisley for training. By November fifth, we were on our way to Le Havre, but we barely had time to look around before we were sent into the trenches around Ypres."

"That must have been dreadful."

"It was hell on earth." He fixed his eyes on the pavement straight ahead as they walked along. "No matter what you think you know about the trenches, everything you've heard, and everything you can imagine, is just a shadow of how truly wretched it was."

His voice had taken on a brittle edge. April was about to tell him that he needn't say anything more if he didn't want to, but he inhaled deeply and continued. "There were our trenches, and the German trenches, and no-man's-land in between—a nightmare landscape of barbed wire, wooden barriers, bomb craters, and the corpses of men and horses."

In some places where the 5th London Rifles had been posted, no-man's-land narrowed to only a few hundred yards. There, the British frontline trenches were so close to the enemy that on calm nights Oliver could hear the Germans talking or coughing, or smell their sausages cooking. The Germans also liked to sing, often together, as loudly as they could, patriotic songs to steel their hearts and annoy their enemies. Oliver had been subjected to so many performances of "Deutschland über Alles" that he could almost sing along from memory, not that he ever would. To drown out the Germans, and to show off a bit, he and his pals would sing "God Save the King" at the top of their lungs, as well as all their favorite Tommy songs like "Tipperary" and "Pack Up Your Troubles," but only the jolly ones. They were melancholy and homesick enough without sad, slow songs in a minor key deepening the gloom.

On the first Christmas Eve of the war, Oliver was shivering in his trench as snow drifted down upon the mostly frozen mud, dreaming of a warm fireside and his mother's roast goose with sage dressing. Suddenly he heard music on the air. On the other side of no-man's-land, the Germans were singing "O Tannenbaum" with some of the most splendid harmonies Oliver had heard outside of a church choir. When the German voices fell silent, Oliver looked around at his mates. "What do you say, boys?" he asked. "Shall we treat Fritz to a good old English carol?"

His friends grinned and agreed, so Oliver hummed the pitch and led them in a rousing version of "We Wish You a Merry Christmas." When they finished, they had to laugh at the applause they heard from the German lines. "Well done, Tommy!" someone bellowed from afar in a thick Prussian accent.

They traded carols back and forth for nearly an hour before one of their sentries announced that strange lights were appearing all along the German parapets. "They're bloody Christmas trees, with candles burnin' on 'em," he added a few minutes later, incredulous.

Curious and skeptical, but not wanting to risk their necks for a quick look, Oliver and his mates took turns with the wooden periscopes and confirmed the sentry's wildly unbelievable claim. Then, all at once, a clear, warm tenor voice drifted over the ruined earth, a melody Oliver knew well but with words unfamiliar.

They all paused to listen. "Stille Nacht," one of his pals murmured. "Silent Night."

They fell silent, listening. Oliver felt something loosen in his chest, and then a pang of longing so intense he almost couldn't breathe.

"He's singing bloody well, you know," someone remarked. They all shushed him.

"He's climbing on their parapet," the sentry cried, incredulous. "What the devil is he on about?"

"He's comin' towards us," the lad at the periscope shouted. "Still singing!"

"Is he armed?" Oliver called back. This Fritz either put a lot of faith in the Christmas spirit of peace and goodwill, or he was entirely mad. Either way, Oliver had to give him credit for courage.

"I don't see a weapon. His hands are raised." A pause. "Now he's just standing there in the middle of no-man's-land, singing."

"More Germans are climbing up on their parapets," the sentry called. "They're coming over. Hands up, no rifles."

Sure enough, Oliver heard more German voices joining in with the first, some lower in pitch, some trembling, all singing words that lingered on the verge of his understanding.

"What should we do?" a younger fellow asked, alarmed. "Should we shoot?"

"Don't be a bloody fool," the sergeant bellowed, storming toward them from an adjacent trench. "We can't shoot unarmed men!"

"Do they want to surrender?" Oliver tapped his mate on the shoulder and gestured for a turn at the periscope. It took a moment of peering into the darkness for his eyes to adjust. Between the Germans' Christmas trees and scattered ground fires burning, no-man's-land was lit up just enough for him to glimpse eight to ten German soldiers gathered in a clearing of sorts between the twisted rows of barbed wire. Even as he watched, heart thudding, palms clammy in his gloves, another man joined them, then two more. A commotion some distance away in his own trench alerted him that something was going on farther down the line, but he heard no whistles or rifle fire, so he kept his gaze fixed on the Germans. Soon thereafter, shouts of warning and consternation in English told him that British soldiers had set down their weapons and were trudging out to meet the Germans.

Oliver watched, astonished, as men from both sides, including the 5th London Rifles, including some of his own childhood pals, climbed from the trenches and walked out to meet the enemy in no-man's-land. They shook hands, exchanged names, greeted one another like long-lost school chums—these men who had been trying to kill one another only a few hours before.

Oliver watched only a little while longer before he went out to join them.

"We traded chocolates and cigarettes, and shared photos of our families and sweethearts," Oliver told April. They had nearly reached the station, but their steps had slowed until they finally halted altogether on the side of the pavement, Oliver reminiscing, April hanging on every word. "Many of them spoke rather good English, and some had even lived and worked in Britain before the war. I talked to one chap who used to be the head waiter at the Great Central Hotel in Marylebone. We shook hands, and wished each other a merry Christmas, and soon we were chatting like old friends."

"Goodness," April murmured, her breath emerging faint and white on the cold night air.

"All around me, I saw Tommy and Fritz trading souvenirs and food, a Scotsman in a kilt lighting the cigarette of a German in a *Pickelhaube*, Germans and Englishmen laughing and joking as they swapped helmets and posed for photographs together." Oliver paused and shook his head, lost in the memory. "Then someone—a player from one of the battalion teams, probably—brought out a football, and most of us joined in to play."

"You had a football match in no-man's-land?"

"It was more of a kickaround at first. The ground was cratered and uneven, and neither wide nor long enough for a proper pitch. But soon we fell into a friendly match, Tommy against Fritz, of course—"

"Of course."

"The chaplain from the East Lancashire Regiment was the official. We used our helmets to mark the goals, but we didn't keep score. At least I didn't." Oliver managed a thin smile. "Afterward, we passed around a bottle of rum one of our lieutenants had kindly provided, and I struck up a conversation with a German artilleryman. He said he hated the war, and all he wanted to do was live through it and go home to his wife and daughter. In parting, he said something I'll never forget. 'Tonight we have peace. Tomorrow, you fight for your country, I fight for mine. Good luck.' I wished him luck too. Maybe another hour passed, and then, a few men at a time, we all started drifting reluctantly back to our trenches."

April shook her head, marveling. If she hadn't heard it from Oliver himself, she wouldn't have believed it.

"Afterward, I heard that there were truces all up and down the line," said Oliver. "Some of them lasted for days, until furious officers shut them down. Fraternization is never encouraged, but unofficial truces . . ." He shook his head. "That just isn't done, not at Christmas, not ever."

April imagined not. "How long did your truce last?"

"Until midmorning, Boxing Day." Oliver glanced at the station, then offered April a rueful smile. "You're going to miss your train."

"I'll wait for the next one. What happened on Boxing Day?"

"A German soldier was on their parapet, carrying a bucket—I don't know what for. One of our snipers took him down. Not even a minute passed before the Germans hit us with everything they had. It was the worst barrage I'd ever been through." He inhaled, two deep, sharp breaths. "We just kept our heads down in the trenches and waited for it to end, and I for one was cursing whichever one of our boys took that shot. I didn't expect the truce to end the war, but what I wouldn't have given for one more day of peace." He paused and shook his head. "A few hours later, I had to go up top for a bit. I almost made it back, almost, but my arm was over my head, my hand grasping the ladder as I descended—and that's when I was hit."

"Oh, Oliver, no."

"My friends wrapped up the wound so I didn't bleed to death, but I was unconscious by the time the stretcher bearers arrived and got me back to the field hospital. They tried to save the hand, but it had got infected and had to go."

She reached out to touch his shoulder. "I'm so sorry."

"Yes, bad luck, wasn't it? But not all bad. I lived. I was sent back to England to recover and then I was discharged. I went home, started working in my uncle's shop again, but I couldn't bear the pitying looks and false cheer of people coming in and out, gawping at my limb and shaking their heads and clearly thinking my life was ruined, and that I'd be a burden to my poor parents for the rest of my life."

"But that's nonsense," April protested. "There you were, *working at your job*, and they thought you'd be a burden?"

"They assumed my uncle gave me the job out of pity, and that I wasn't really doing much."

"But you had the same job *before* the war!"

"That's also true."

"It doesn't make any sense!"

"Now you understand why I had to leave. I was angry and bitter, and I wanted to prove that I could still contribute to the war effort even if I couldn't hold a rifle. So I took the job at Thornshire Arsenal, and now I help make the weapons that the Allies need to win the war." He frowned. "Of course, I can't ever forget that our victory means the crushing defeat of the German soldiers I befriended at Christmas, many of whom didn't want to be there either. Then it occurs to me that they all might have been killed by now, and I wonder what the whole point of it was. If we common soldiers had just refused to continue fighting after our truce, could the war have ended in December 1914?"

"Could it have, do you think?"

He paused. "Doubt it. If we hadn't started up again on our own, like that sniper did on our part of the line, our officer would have commanded it, and if we disobeyed orders, they would have shot us themselves."

April shuddered. Oliver saw it, and he took her hand. "Sorry you asked?"

"Never, but I wondered—"

"What?" he prompted, when she didn't continue.

"You said you had to leave the trench. Why? Why would your officers order your battalion over the top when the Germans were bombing you so furiously?"

Oliver hesitated. "It wasn't an order, exactly, and it wasn't all of us. Just me."

She shook her head, uncomprehending.

"One of my pals from home, one of my best pals, had got it in his head to take out one of their big guns. He needed a better angle to take the shot, so he climbed out and crawled forward, but we could still see the soles of his boots hanging over the edge of the parapet when he was hit. We shouted at him to come back, and when he didn't, I knew he was either unconscious or dead. So I climbed up to haul him back in, and the other lads caught him as I handed him down. I was descending back into the trench when I got shot. The shattered rung of the ladder came away in my fist."

April shuddered, imagining it all too vividly. "Was your pal still alive?"

"Thankfully, yes. He'd been struck in the shoulder, but he survived. He healed up and returned to the battalion a few months later. He's still there, last I heard."

"You saved his life," April said in wonder. "Oliver, you're a hero. They should've given you a medal for—"

Her voice failed her as suddenly a brilliant, florid light illuminated Oliver's face and the passersby and the station behind them, for a moment transforming night into day. Before the strange light faded, a terrible, booming roar struck them, an unearthly growl that made everything around them—the ground, the buildings, the bare-limbed trees, everything—tremble ominously.

Instinctively, Oliver pulled her closer, shielding her with his torso as he looked around for the source of the explosion. April gasped and stared at the sky, horrified, as an enormous, lurid fireball rose above them, too distant for them to feel its heat, a churning, chaotic mass of colors—violet, indigo, blue, green, yellow, orange, and scarlet—eddying and swirling like a violent sunset. Terrified, April pressed her face against Oliver's chest, blood pounding in her ears, but when she dared peer back up to the sky and saw the fireball still churning, she realized that it couldn't have been an air raid. There had been only one explosion, not a series of dropped bombs, and there was no sign of a zeppelin or aeroplane above, no frantic sweep of searchlights from the ground.

April and Oliver exchanged a bleak look, as they both realized with sinking dread what must have caused the explosion.

Oliver took her hand again, and together they headed toward the bank of the Thames. "It wasn't Thornshire," he said as they broke into a run. "It's too far away, and in the wrong direction."

April nodded agreement. If it had been Thornshire, the pressure wave would have knocked them off their feet, stunned, as shattered glass and rubble fell all around them.

When they reached the riverbank, they saw a red, fevered glow to the west beneath a dark cloud of churning smoke only two or three miles away, and the harrowing reflection in the Thames of a building, perhaps even a compound, engulfed in flames. They heard the distant wail of fire engines and ambulances, and April smelled traces of ash and acrid chemicals, or she imagined she did.

"Good Lord," Oliver murmured close to her ear. "That's north of the river. Silvertown."

April's heart thudded. The chemical munitions factory in the East End, a compound surrounded by densely populated working-class neighborhoods. "Brunner Mond?"

Accustomed to secrecy, he nodded rather than echo the name as other horrified spectators clustered nearby, some of them exclaiming loudly, others with hands pressed to their mouths and faces pale with shock.

"It's directly opposite the Royal Arsenal at Woolwich," Oliver said, his breath stirring the fine, loose strands of hair that had come loose from her coiled braid. "Those flames—if they're hot enough, if they reach far enough, they could set off Woolwich too."

April felt her chest constricting. How many workers had been killed? How many injured? "Can we do anything to help?" she asked as tears gathered in her eyes. "What can we do?"

He convinced her that the best they could do for now was to stay out of the way and let the emergency crews do their jobs unimpeded. Even if bystanders wanted to be useful, they likely wouldn't be allowed to approach the site. The risk of another explosion was too great, and the blocks around both Brunner Mond and the Royal Arsenal were probably being evacuated at that very moment. April nodded bleakly, and she held tightly to Oliver's hand as he led her away from the river and back to the station. As they worked their way through the crowd, amid the mingled sobs and curses and exclamations, she overheard hot, furious accusations that the Germans surely were to blame, German spies, saboteurs. But as a canary girl, April knew it was far more likely to have been a cruel, terrible accident, just like the one that had claimed the lives of the munitionettes in Barnbow.

"We'll learn more in the days to come," Oliver told her before they parted at the station. "The censors will restrain the press as much as they can, but the government can't pretend this didn't happen, not as it did with Barnbow, not when nearly the whole of London saw it or felt it."

Oliver's words proved true. The next day, the Ministry of Munitions issued a statement to the press reporting that an explosion had occurred "at a munitions factory in the neighbourhood of London," an astonishing understatement, as thousands of eyewitnesses had already confirmed that only a huge, rubble-strewn crater remained where the Brunner Mond chemical works in Silvertown had once stood. "It is feared," the press statement continued, "that the explosion was attended by considerable loss of life and damage to property." The official casualty report stated that sixty-nine had been killed and four hundred injured, but everyone who had seen the devastation declared that this was surely an undercount. Would-be gawpers could not judge for themselves, for the police and the military had closed off the area, and no one was allowed past the guards without a written order from the Ministry of Munitions or the War Office.

In the days that followed, April learned more from word of mouth than from the censored newspapers.

Hundreds of homes and flats had been utterly destroyed within a square mile around the crater, and about two thousand people had been rendered homeless. The massive fireball had been seen at a distance of twenty-five miles, and the explosion had been heard eighty miles away. And despite the widely held belief that German saboteurs were responsible, the Thornshire Canaries heard from the Woolwich football club that it was entirely accidental. A fire had broken out on the top floor of the factory. In the few minutes before the flames reached the explosives and chemicals, the chief chemist had managed to get his workers out, but he himself had perished.

Five tons of TNT had exploded, sending a jet of crimson flame across the river toward Woolwich, igniting a gasometer near the Royal Arsenal. At first, the managers feared that the Royal Arsenal too might be destroyed. Many of the workers panicked and fled, but eventually the blaze across the river had subsided and the danger had passed.

Oliver had been right again when he said that the government would not be able to ignore the accident on the grounds of military secrecy. It was impossible to do so when so many men and women were going about the East End with their heads bandaged and arms in slings, when whole streets were lined with the charred shells of houses, when entire families who hadn't had much to begin with had lost everything. Over time, the victims' pleas for government assistance grew into more widespread public outrage. About a month after the disaster, the Ministry of Munitions issued another statement that "without admitting any liability," it would "pay reasonable claims for damage to property and personal injuries caused by the explosion."

April figured that was the least the ministry could do. It hadn't caused the explosion on purpose, but it was responsible, and it ought to make it right.

For weeks following the accident, it seemed to April that everyone at Thornshire was on edge, following safety precautions to the letter and snapping at coworkers whose carelessness would have earned them only a frown and a rebuke before. Several munitionettes quit, including Louise, the Canaries' best fullback, leaving them with only enough players for a side, with no substitutes. Occasionally they found another girl willing to step in for a match or two, but no one would commit over the long term.

Mabel could no longer play, even though she wanted to. It was wrenching to watch her health visibly declining week by week. She had resisted her rotation out of the Danger Building even after striking the deal with management to keep their wages as they were, but she had grudgingly complied when Superintendent Carmichael decreed that it was rotate out of the Danger Building or out of the arsenal altogether. But although April and the other canary girls had found their symptoms ebbing within a week of leaving the Danger Building, Mabel had shown no such improvement. Privately her teammates speculated that it could be because she was older, or because she had started in munitions before any of them. Whatever the reason, they trusted that she would recover eventually, maybe just at a slower pace. Peggy had already resolved to use every argument she could think of to persuade her mother not to return to the Danger Building after her rotation ended, but she knew it wouldn't be easy.

Football and friendships—and that included Oliver's—sustained April when the news of the war and hardships closer to home steadily worsened. Food costs continued to climb, and ordinary staples like bread, sugar, and potatoes had become scarce. The arsenal canteen did not reduce their services, probably due to Ministry of Munitions regulations, and her hostel increased fees only slightly, so April knew she had it better than most, especially compared to her friends with children to feed.

Then one morning in early February, Oliver was so eager to speak with her that she found him pacing on the edge of the park closest to the train station rather than sitting on a bench near the center or strolling the gravel paths. "Did you hear about the Americans?" he greeted her as Marjorie rolled her eyes and continued on alone to the arsenal.

"No," said April, studying him, curious. His face was lit up with eagerness, and he was smiling broadly rather than only turning up a corner of his mouth. "What happened?"

"They've severed diplomatic relations with Germany."

"What?" Even after hundreds of American citizens had perished in the sinking of the RMS *Lusitania*, the United States had not gone so far. "Are you sure? From the very start the Americans have insisted they're going to stay neutral."

"Absolutely sure. Everything changed after the German chancellor announced that Germany is scrapping its restrictions on submarine warfare. Passenger liners and merchant ships are fair game to them again, regardless of nationality."

April felt a wave of dread. It was already difficult enough for ships carrying food and supplies to reach the British Isles through the German blockade. If German U-boats resumed their attacks on any ship that crossed their path, what would become of the British people? Would any food get through? How many more innocent civilians would die, at sea and in Britain? "What does this mean?" April asked. "Severing diplomatic relations—what does that actually mean for us, for Britain?"

"That isn't entirely clear, not yet," said Oliver, his enthusiasm dimming only a trifle. "Yesterday President Wilson spoke to the American Congress for more than two hours. He said that although the United States doesn't desire any hostile conflict with Germany, if the Germans destroy any American ships, they will find themselves in a state of war."

"So the Americans haven't joined the war on the side of the Allies yet."

"No," Oliver said as they turned and walked toward the arsenal together. "But I do think they've taken one step closer to it."

April nodded, hardly daring to hope. She had never been the sort to look to someone else to come to her rescue, but after two and a half hard years of war, it was profoundly cheering to think that the Americans might soon join them in the fight. The United States was rich in resources, and they had their own scores to settle against Germany. Having the Yanks in it at long last might make all the difference.

15
March–May 1917

Helen

In the weeks following the disaster at Brunner Mond, Helen divided her time between implementing the new safety protocols and reassuring anxious munitionettes. It was a fine line she walked, wanting to comfort and yet determined to be scrupulously honest.

The new safety measures had been designed to mitigate or prevent TNT poisoning, and Helen was relieved to see steady improvements in the health of most of her canary girls. But most was not all. Some workers reported that their symptoms had improved only slightly by the end of their twelve-week rotation out of the Danger Building, and inexplicably, a few felt even worse. Helen could not in good conscience send those canary girls back to their former posts. She endured numerous strained discussions on the subject with Superintendent Carmichael, who lectured her about the blows to discipline and morale that would ensue if they did not abide by the agreement they had struck with the canary girls' representatives. "We cannot appear to favor one worker over another," the superintendent warned.

"Declining to send a clearly unwell worker into a situation that is likely to make her sicker isn't playing favorites," Helen replied. "It's playing it safe." They had a long list of volunteers willing to transfer into the Danger Building to give the canary girls a respite, with the understanding that they would return to their original jobs in twelve weeks and would not be required to volunteer again. Fear of the yellow powder had diminished as fewer workers had become seriously ill. Now what worried the munitionettes most was the perpetual threat of an accidental explosion that could level the entire arsenal. But the new safety protocols did not address that problem. Aside from reminding the workers to follow the safety precautions and touring the factories to reassure herself that they were doing so, there was frustratingly little Helen could do to prevent a devastating accident.

As the war dragged on, the unsettling dread that all her efforts as welfare supervisor might ultimately prove worthless troubled Helen deeply—not enough to wake her in the middle of the night, shaking and breathless, haunted by nightmares as Arthur often was, but enough to make her brood over mistakes and resolve not to repeat them. She had already absorbed the humbling lesson that sometimes, despite her good intentions, she simply failed to understand the realities of working women's lives.

Earlier in the year, when the poisonous effects of TNT were first confirmed, if a worker felt unwell, Helen had sent her home to rest for a few days, until a doctor cleared her to return. Helen had considered this to be a sensible, generous, compassionate approach, best for the worker and best for the arsenal. To her astonishment, workers had simply stopped showing up for their scheduled weekly physicals. Overlookers had observed canary girls who were obviously feeling unwell toiling away until they nearly fainted at their stations, insisting that they felt perfectly fine even as they were being carried to the infirmary. Their behavior utterly bewildered Helen until Lucy Dempsey enlightened her. For many canary girls, Lucy had explained privately, several unpaid days off was a hardship, not a respite, and finding a doctor to clear them to return to work was difficult if not impossible. If they felt unwell, a brief lie-down in the shifting house would usually suffice, and failing that, taking the rest of the day off was often enough to restore them. But three days without wages felt like a punishment for weakness, so they skipped their weekly physicals rather than lie to their doctors about their symptoms, pushing through the pain and misery and hoping no one noticed.

Helen was grateful for Lucy's insight and changed their policies accordingly. Henceforth, workers would be permitted to return to work after a single day's rest, and either their own doctor or arsenal infirmary staff could clear them.

There were some canary girls whom neither Helen nor Superintendent Carmichael could justify returning to the Danger Building, and unfortunately, one of their most skilled and diligent workers was one of them. In February, although Mabel Burridge hadn't worked with the yellow powder in two months, her breathing remained so labored that Helen ordered her to take an entire week off. Upon her return, she seemed fine at first, but in early March, after a routine physical, the arsenal's head physician insisted she take a fortnight's leave. He extended that by another week when she again failed her exam. Eventually the arsenal infirmary cleared Mabel to return to a less dangerous job, but that did not satisfy her. Coughing and wheezing behind her veil, her cheeks gaunt and eyes shadowed, she showed up at Helen's office at least once a week to request a transfer back to the Filling Shop.

Helen could almost admire her dogged persistence if it wasn't so misplaced. "Every job at Thornshire Arsenal is essential war work," she reminded Mabel in late March when she stormed into Helen's office to have it out. "Inspecting detonators is as crucial to the process as filling shells, and you receive exactly the same pay. Why are you so determined to get back into the Danger Building when it's obviously taking a toll on your health?"

"My girls need me," Mabel said, sunken eyes glittering with determination. "No one looks out for them the way I do. They're good girls, hard workers, but sometimes they get distracted, chatting and teasing and such, and they need me to keep them on task."

"I admire your commitment, but that's what the overlookers are for."

"The overlookers can't be everywhere at once, and they don't know the job the way I do."

Helen paused. "No, I don't suppose they do."

"I'm not a boastful woman, Mrs. Purcell, so I'm just stating the facts when I say I've lost count of how many accidents I've prevented at the last moment because I know where and when to keep watch. Even with this cough, I'm more useful to you in the Filling Shop than anywhere else."

Helen didn't doubt it. Mrs. Burridge would surely make an excellent overseer—but that was no solution, since any job in the Danger Building would expose her to the yellow powder. Kindly but firmly, she told Mrs. Burridge that she could return to the Filling Shop when the arsenal's head physician cleared her for it, and not one day sooner.

Mrs. Burridge might have argued the point longer except that she was due back at her station, so she departed grumbling and glowering. Alone again, Helen sank back into her chair to recover her composure before moving on to the next crisis. She reminded herself that Mrs. Burridge's own daughter had thanked her for standing up to her mother. "She can be relentless, I know," Peggy had murmured, glancing over her shoulder for eavesdroppers. "I understand that she's finished in the Danger Building, and that's the way it has to be. She won't listen to me, but she has to listen to you."

Helen wasn't so sure. Although she could offer suggestions, the hiring, firing, and scheduling of workers was actually Superintendent Carmichael's responsibility. Helen suspected Mrs. Burridge had pled her case to the superintendent, and when that failed, she had turned to Helen, whom she perceived as less of a stickler for the rules. There was some truth to that, but

Mrs. Burridge underestimated Helen's determination to protect the munitionettes from harm as much as she possibly could, in circumstances that required them to take extraordinary risks every day.

Helen trusted that her work on behalf of the munitionettes truly benefitted them and was appreciated, but rather than taking pride in her accomplishments, she felt deep humility, both for how little she had understood working-class women's lives before Thornshire, and for how much she had yet to learn. She could not advocate for them effectively if they did not trust her, and trust grew out of mutual respect and regard. Touring each building once a week and attending football matches was a good start, but she could do more. So Helen began taking her tea and dinner in different canteens, hoping the workers would find her cordial and approachable, but not intrusive. She attended the munitionettes' musicales and theatricals, and frequently she joined the Lunchtime Knitters Club to make warm socks and scarves for the soldiers. Sometimes she convinced Arthur to accompany her to a recital or a football training, since he would not have to leave the arsenal grounds to attend, but usually he could not spare the time.

Then in early April came astounding, glorious news: In an address to a joint session of Congress, President

Woodrow Wilson declared that "neutrality is no longer feasible or desirable where the peace of the world is involved." He urged Congress to "formally accept the status of belligerent which has thus been thrust upon it." Three days later, after intense debate, both the Senate and the House passed a war resolution by large majorities.

The United States had declared war on Germany.

Helen fervently hoped this meant that the Americans would soon send desperately needed supplies to Britain, including food, munitions, and raw materials. Arthur expected all of that and troops as well. Helen would be grateful for anything that might relieve Arthur of the great burden of responsibility he carried, but the thought of tens of thousands of fresh troops joining the fight on the side of the Allies filled her with the first true, sustained hope she had felt since the outbreak of war.

But her joy was fleeting.

One evening in mid-April, Helen and Arthur had just sat down to supper after a particularly exhausting day when the housekeeper bustled in to tell Helen that her sister Penelope was on the telephone. Helen hurried to the sitting room to answer, trepidation stirring, for her mother and sisters never telephoned so late in the middle of the week. "Penny, darling," she said breathlessly into the mouthpiece, clutching the candlestick stem in one hand and holding the receiver to her ear with the other. "How are you? Is Mother well?"

"Mother is fine, and so are Daphne and I." Yet Penelope's lovely voice, low and rich, trembled with grief. "But as you guessed, I'm afraid I have dreadful news."

Helen braced herself. "Tell me."

"Did you hear about the *Lapland*?"

"The ship?" asked Helen, bewildered. "I only know what was in the papers this morning. She was carrying Canadian troops to Liverpool when she struck a mine off the coast, but she made it into port. I understand there were minimal injuries."

"And one fatality. Roland—Mr. Aylesworth—"

"What? Oh, Penny, no!" Helen sank into a chair, stunned. "How can this be? Mr. Aylesworth, on a troop transport—"

"He was returning from diplomatic missions to Washington and Ottawa. He was below deck when the ship struck the mine, and some debris—well, he was struck rather badly, you see, and they say it was quick and he never felt any pain, but they *would* say that, wouldn't they—"

"Oh, my dear Penny." Helen inhaled shakily, closing her eyes. "Poor Margaret. How is she bearing up?"

"Bravely, of course. Uncomplaining. You know

Margaret. Her only thought is for the children. Hestia has been told that her papa won't be coming home, but she asks for him anyway. Poor Hugh, he's still a babe in arms, he'll have no memory of his papa, and Roland did dote on him so—"

"I'll come to you at once," said Helen, standing. "Shall I come to you?"

"No, no, that's not necessary. You have Arthur to look after, and your war work." Penelope took a deep, shuddering breath. "Margaret's mother and sisters-in-law are here, and I'm here. Between the five of us, Margaret and the children shall be well looked after."

"But who is looking after you, dearest Penny?"

"I'll be fine. I have to be, for Margaret. I—I do love her so, Helen."

"I know you do, Penny." Helen felt tears gathering. "Are you sure I shouldn't come?"

"Thank you, but not now. Roland's family arrives tomorrow. They want only a small funeral in the family chapel, on account of the war—so many other families are grieving, you understand—"

"I do," Helen assured her. "But if you decide you need me, say the word and I'll be on the next train."

Their hearts heavy, they bade each other loving farewells and disconnected.

A fortnight passed. Helen wrote to Margaret to express their condolences, and she telephoned Penelope every few days to offer whatever loving support she could. Helen had met Mr. Aylesworth only once, but his death stunned her more than she would have expected. Perhaps she had assumed that, as a diplomat rather than an officer, he would never be truly in peril. How foolish her assumption seemed now, and the realization made her fear for her own husband all the more.

On Friday, 20 April 1917, London joyfully celebrated "America Day" in honor of the new alliance between the United States and the Allies, marking the occasion with parades, speeches, and solemn religious observances at St. Paul's Cathedral. Arthur had received tickets to the service, but he could not spare the time away from the arsenal, so he had declined the seats for both of them. Helen tried to conceal her disappointment, as well as her frustration that Arthur had not consulted her before sending their regrets. How inspiring and comforting it would have been to share a moment of hope and optimism with their fellow Britons and their new American allies!

Arthur knew her too well, and he was not fooled by her feigned disinterest. "I should have accepted the tickets. You could have taken your mother or one of your sisters." He frowned regretfully, interlacing his fingers through hers. "I'll make it up to you after the war, darling. I promise."

She spotted her opportunity and seized it. "You don't have to wait until after the war," she said. "You can make it up to me tomorrow. The Thornshire Canaries are playing at Stratford, and the weather is supposed to be glorious. Come with me to the match, and we shall call it even."

"Darling, I can't take the time—"

"Yes, you can, and you should," she interrupted emphatically. "This ceaseless toil is not good for you, and it can't be good for the arsenal to have the head man perpetually exhausted."

"The men in the trenches don't get a day off."

"As a matter of fact, they do!" Helen exclaimed. "It's called *leave*. And even when the troops aren't on leave, they are rotated away from the front occasionally so they may rest, while fresh troops replace them. As Thornshire's welfare supervisor, I strongly recommend that you take leave tomorrow to rest and spend time with your devoted wife, who has been working very hard and deserves a bit of fun."

His lengthy pause told her he was wavering. "I don't believe your authority as welfare supervisor extends to the boss."

"Well, it should." She leaned forward, smiling,

and clasped his hand in both of hers. "What do you say, darling? The war shan't be lost if you spend one Sunday away from the arsenal. Think of the boost to morale when the players see that the boss himself has come to cheer them on."

Somehow, something she said convinced him, and he agreed to go. Delighted, she kissed him deeply and promised he would not regret it.

Helen arranged for a late breakfast the next morning, and, just to be sure, she turned off the alarm clock so Arthur would sleep in. After breakfast, she invited him to accompany her on her daily walk, half afraid that he would suggest something mad like going into the office for a few hours and meeting her at the Globe at the start of the match. It was a lovely, perfect May morning, and although Arthur did not entirely lose his air of haggard distraction as they strolled through Hyde Park, the fresh air and sunshine clearly did him good.

Even on a Sunday, the train to Stratford was crowded with soldiers in khaki and workers, mostly women, traveling between factories and home. Helen and Arthur arrived at the Upstart Crows' stadium with a half hour to spare, and she was pleased to see how impressed he was with the size of the crowd already seated, at least seven thousand. A great many Thornshire workers, men and women alike, called out cheerful greetings to the Purcells as they found seats in the center, two rows back. They settled in and turned their attention to the pitch, where the Thornshire Canaries and the Handley Page Girls were running drills and warming up. The Handley Page Girls, from the Handley Page aircraft manufacturer in Cricklewood, wore charcoal gray pinafores over light blue, collarless blouses, allowing more freedom of movement than most of the skirted uniforms Helen had seen. None of them bore the yellow skin of canary girls, whereas half the Thornshire team did.

Helen was studying the Girls, assessing their skills and strength, when Arthur said, "I assume you know most of our players."

"Oh, yes, all of them," she replied, turning her attention to their own team. "Some better than others, of course." Beginning with Marjorie in the goal, she gave him the name and a brief description of each player, but only when she came to the forwards did she understand why their drills had seemed a bit off. "They have only ten players on the pitch, and no one in reserve," she said, bewildered. Even Mabel was absent. She hadn't played in ages, but even when she was on sick leave, she had attended the matches and coached from the sidelines.

"Who's missing?" Arthur asked, but she wasn't quite sure. A few of the canary girls on the team had become too ill to play, and the roster of substitutes was short and inconsistent. Helen had never known the Canaries not to take the pitch with a full side, and she wasn't sure what would happen if their eleventh player failed to show. Would they play one woman down, a decided disadvantage? Would they be required to forfeit? That would greatly displease the thousands of fans who had bought tickets and expected an exciting match. If they demanded refunds, it would be quite a blow to the charity to whom the gate had been promised.

From a distance, the Canaries seemed increasingly uneasy with their numbers, and with fifteen minutes to go, they gathered in their defending third and appeared to be discussing their options. On several occasions, a few players glanced up into the stands directly at Helen and Arthur before returning to their debate. "They know you're here," Helen murmured. "They're proud, and they don't want to disappoint you. They'd rather lose badly with only ten than not dare to make the attempt."

"I don't think they're looking at me," Arthur said, just as Lucy, April, and Peggy broke away from the group and hurried toward the stands. Were they coming to welcome the boss, or to explain why there would be no match that day?

The three Canaries halted in front of Arthur and Helen. "Good afternoon, Mr. Purcell," said Lucy, but the other two only spared him polite nods before turning appraising looks upon Helen. "Mrs. Purcell."

Arthur returned their greetings heartily, but Helen spoke more warily, bemused by their intense scrutiny.

"You might have noticed we're missing a girl," said Peggy.

Before they could reply, April put her head to one side and said to Helen, "You've watched us all season, practically. How well do you know the game by now?"

"Fairly well, I think," she replied.

"Have you ever played before?"

"Me? Play football?" Helen shook her head. "No, never."

"She's an excellent tennis player, though," said Arthur. "And she takes long, brisk walks every day. She's very fit."

As the three Canaries nodded, studying her, Helen realized where the conversation was heading. "Just a moment," she said, holding up a hand. "Before we get carried away—"

"We're running out of time," Marjorie shouted from

the sideline, her hands cupped around her mouth. "Is she in or out?"

"In, of course," declared Arthur, putting his arm around Helen's shoulders and giving her a hearty squeeze.

"Give us a minute, Marjorie," Peggy called back.

"As you can see, Mrs. Purcell," said Lucy, "we need another player, and we'd be exceedingly grateful if you would step in. It's too bad you haven't played before, but you're clever and we know you've picked up the rules over the past few months."

"Oliver Corbyn says you have an excellent grasp of strategy," said April.

Helen found herself unexpectedly flattered by Oliver's approval, even as she was startled to learn that they had been talking about her. "I know the rules, but nothing about technique," said Helen. "I'm afraid I might do more harm than good."

"Nonsense," protested Arthur. "You're a natural athlete."

"There isn't a lot to remember," said Peggy, with false bravado. "Just remember which goal is ours, and which is theirs, and never put the ball in the wrong goal."

"Never use your hands," April added. "If the ball comes your way, kick it down the field toward a girl in a yellow jersey."

"That's really all you need to know to get started," said Peggy, studying her hopefully. "What do you say?"

It was so absurd, Helen had to laugh. "I don't have a uniform."

They assured her that extra uniforms for substitutes were in the changing room, freshly washed and ready for her to try on, and shoes too. Still uncertain, Helen turned to Arthur. "But darling, the whole purpose of this outing was for us to spend time together."

Arthur raised her hand to his lips and kissed it. "Believe me, the only thing I would enjoy more than watching this match *with* you would be to cheer you on as you play."

What else could Helen do then but take a deep breath and agree? She would rather reveal before thousands of people that she was a dreadful football player than admit to a few acquaintances that she was a coward.

While Peggy and April ran off to share the good news with the rest of the team, Lucy quickly led Helen to the changing room, where she tried on black short trousers, yellow jerseys, and football shoes until she found the best fit for each. Shin-guards, long black socks, and a cap finished the kit, and before she could fully comprehend what a dreadful mistake she was in all likelihood making, she was out on the pitch, heart thudding, stomach lurching, warming up with a bit of running and practicing a few kicks with the side of her foot, not the toe, which felt very odd but she did it anyway.

Peggy, who had taken over as team captain for her mother, told her where to stand for the start and gave her an encouraging grin. "Remember, however bad it gets, it's only ninety minutes, and then you're through it."

That was true enough. Anyone could bear ninety minutes of utter humiliation. Perhaps such a thing built character. At least she and Arthur would have a good laugh about it afterward, and she would have a marvelous story to share with the Marylebone ladies the next time they met for lunch.

Then the whistle blew, striking dread in Helen's heart. The match began, and there was no time to reconsider because the ball was in motion and all the other girls were running and passing and she had to keep up, straining her ears for the instructions the other Canaries called out to her. She sprinted for the ball when it came her way, got rid of it as swiftly as she could, and tried to slow down any opponent who dared approach Marjorie's goal by just generally getting in the way and interfering with her opponent's plans. In that, at least, Helen reckoned an inexperienced player was better than none at all.

At one point, as she caught her breath during a brief respite after the ball went out of bounds, it occurred to her that the Girls had no idea she had never played before. If she employed some of the acting skills she had acquired in school theatricals, it might take them a while to discover that she was the weakest player on the team, and to exploit that fact. But then the game resumed and she had no time to do anything but listen to her teammates, pass to the nearest teammate if the ball happened unluckily to come her way, and avoid scoring for the opposition.

The first half was nearly over, the score 1–0 in favor of the Handley Page Girls, when Helen realized that she was one of the fastest players on the pitch. She had only a novice's understanding of strategy and no footwork skills whatsoever, but she was a swift runner with excellent stamina thanks to years of tennis and brisk walks. She discovered she could almost always outrun her opponent when pursuing a loose ball, and if she got to the ball first, she could pass it to a teammate who actually knew what she was doing. The other Canaries seemed as pleasantly surprised by this discovery as she was.

"I told you she would be good," Helen overheard April tell Marjorie as they headed to the changing room for the interval, to her immeasurable delight.

Before she had fully recovered from the first half, they were back on the pitch for the second. Her legs felt like lead, and she was panting and perspiring as much as she ever had in any tennis match. Then Lucy made a brilliant run from midfield and scored, and only minutes after that, Peggy tapped one in, low and swift, from the top of the box. With only ten minutes left in the game, Helen concentrated on sending the ball in the opposite direction whenever a girl in a dark pinafore brought it anywhere near her. She was exhausted and thirsty and incapable of any stratagem more complex than that.

The whistle blew. A tremendous roar went up from the crowd, and suddenly Helen found herself surrounded by exultant girls in yellow jerseys, embracing her and laughing and running off to embrace other teammates. They had done it, she realized. They had won, 2–1. Somehow she had managed to survive the ninety minutes without looking like a complete fool. A partial fool, certainly, but not a complete fool.

The Canaries met the Handley Page Girls in the center circle to exchange handshakes and congratulations, and as they headed off to the changing room, exhausted and happy, Helen heard someone shout her name. She looked up into the stands to find Arthur standing with Oliver Corbyn, both of them applauding wildly, Arthur beaming proudly and laughing from sheer amazement.

As they changed back into their street clothes, the other Canaries thanked Helen for coming to their aid at the last minute, but she already felt them pulling away from her, becoming more formal, addressing her politely as Mrs. Purcell. After folding her perspiration-soaked uniform neatly, she brought the pile with the shoes on top to Lucy. "I'd be happy to launder it and return it to you at the arsenal," she offered. "It's no trouble."

"Oh, that's not necessary," said Lucy, smiling, as she accepted the pile and returned it to the large duffle bag. "I'll wash yours with mine."

Helen managed a smile and thanked her. It was only then, as her heart sank, that she realized she had hoped Lucy would tell her to keep the kit for the next time they needed her to fill in—better yet, to keep it for good because they wanted her to become a permanent member of the team. Of course that was a wildly ridiculous hope, and she was very glad that she had not spoken it aloud.

Arthur was waiting for her on the sideline in front of the stands, and when she emerged from the changing room, he hurried to meet her. "I'm so proud of you," he declared, kissing her on one cheek and then the other. "You astonish me. After all this time, I still marvel at you."

Her heart, which had felt so heavy only moments before, soared, full of light. It had been months, years even, since she had last seen him so happy. "Every muscle I possess aches," she told him, emphasizing each word. "I thought I was fit. Now I know better."

"Nonsense. I just saw you run for ninety minutes. You're perfectly fit." He offered her his arm, and together they left the stadium en route to the train station. "Do you suppose you'll play with the team again?"

"Oh, I don't know," she said lightly. "I suppose I would, if they ever ask me again."

"I should hate to miss that."

She squeezed his arm. "Then you shall have to attend every game with me just in case, whenever the Canaries play in London."

But the following week the Thornshire Canaries had a full side plus two substitutes, so they did not need her, and the next week they played in Birmingham, and Helen did not attend.

Some of the joy of the game had faded by the end of the month, when a wonderful surprise of an entirely different sort again filled Helen's heart with hope and anticipation. More than a year before, the Speaker of the House had established the Speaker's Conference on Electoral Reform to investigate how to make Parliament more representative of the will of the country. In January 1917, the Speaker's Conference had provided the Prime Minister with a concise nine pages of recommendations, which included conferring "some measure of woman suffrage." Helen had heard promises made and broken so many times through the years that she could not allow her expectations to rise too much, but then, four months after the report, Home Secretary George Cave introduced the Representation of the People Bill into Parliament—and it included provisions for limited women's suffrage to be enacted after the war.

Helen rejoiced, as did all of her suffragette friends, for although the bill proposed giving the vote only to certain women within specific, limited circumstances, it still marked a significant step forward, even though they would have to wait until the war ended for the law to come into effect.

That long-awaited day seemed terribly far off as the war dragged on, resources ran low, and casualties mounted, in both France and Belgium and at home.

16

June–August 1917

Lucy

As the summer passed, it became increasingly evident that the Germans intended to starve the British into surrender before the United States could replenish their stockpiles. Lucy knew the country would rather go hungry than submit to Germany's wicked plan, but she dreaded to imagine how bad it might get before it got better. Lucy's mother cultivated vegetables where Lucy usually grew flowers in the front garden of the Dempsey home, and Lucy's sisters-in-law sent boxes of produce from Brookfield, but the gravest danger, for the Dempseys and all their neighbors, was the scarcity of bread. The Americans sent tons of wheat from the vast grainlands of the central United States, but the Germans targeted the wheat ships with impunity, sending the precious cargo to the bottom of the sea. Rumor had it that Great Britain's wheat stocks had dwindled to a nine-week supply, and fearful whispers about the possibility of famine circulated through neighborhoods and workplaces.

The arsenal canteens still managed to provide the workers with adequate meals, but Lucy had always been far more concerned for her sons than for herself. Like all growing boys, Jamie and Simon were always ravenous, and although they rarely complained, she worried that they might suffer long-term harm from their inadequate diet. Sometimes she thought they might be better off if her mother took them to her home in Brookfield for the duration, but the boys liked their school and would miss their friends, and with Daniel so far away, she could not bear to be parted from her sons too.

Lucy knew her mother thought her grandsons would be safer in Brookfield, although she expressed her opinion only in gentle suggestions that she take them for a visit. After the school term ended, Lucy could not really justify refusing, especially since the boys were eager to go. She consented to a fortnight away, knowing they would have a merry time in the countryside with their cousins, wishing she could accompany them.

They had been gone only a few days one sunny Saturday morning in early July, bright and warm, with a faint haze high in the sky. The Thornshire Canaries were training on the arsenal field when suddenly they heard the low drone of engines overhead. They all stopped where they were, shaded their eyes with their hands, and searched the skies. "What a lot of aeroplanes," Peggy exclaimed, just as Lucy glimpsed them coming into view, more than twenty aircraft in a fan formation, surprisingly low and moving slowly toward the north.

Something about it struck Lucy as dangerously amiss. "Are those German planes?" she asked, turning in place, her gaze fixed on the formation as it passed over the arsenal.

"Don't be ridiculous, Lady Prim," scoffed Marjorie, supremely confident. "They must be our airmen carrying out maneuvers. If they were Germans, we would hear our own guns firing upon them."

"How splendid they are," cried Daisy. "And what a comfort to know that London is protected by such mighty aerial defenses! I wonder if the Handley Page Girls built them?"

Marjorie, Daisy, and a few others were discussing that possibility when a low, dull boom sounded somewhere to the west, followed seconds later by the faint rattling of windows in the nearest buildings.

Suddenly Lucy spied Mrs. Purcell running toward them from the edge of the field, waving her arms for attention. "Take cover!" she shouted. "Take cover!"

Her words were drowned out by another distant explosion, and then the percussive booming of several ground guns fired in rapid succession. Lucy heard shrieks as the players scattered, fleeing the open field for the shelter of the nearest buildings, pressing themselves against the brick or stone and covering their heads with their arms. Terrified, Lucy crouched into a corner where a concrete staircase met a stone foundation, but even as she strained her ears for the drone of aeroplanes and the roar of distant bombs, she wondered fleetingly whether it wasn't useless to seek protection from strong, solid walls when a direct hit on the arsenal could set off a massive explosion fueled by their own shells and yellow powder, reducing everything around her to rubble. She heard women sobbing, men shouting, and two, no, three more distant explosions, more defensive ground fire. For five minutes, ten minutes, the roar of guns and bombs continued. Then, as if the violence had paused for breath, all fell silent.

Lucy remained in place a while longer before she cautiously rose and peered out from her corner. Other workers, pale and shaken or red-faced and angry, were emerging onto the streets and open ground, gazing warily up at the sky, seeking out friends, muttering curses against the Germans or asking one another what had happened, what they knew. Then the bell at the main gate pealed, urging them back to work. Lucy hesitated, wondering how the foremen could be sure the raid was over, but lingering in the yard wasn't likely any safer, so she dusted herself off and made her way back to the Danger Building.

The censors must have decided that it was pointless to attempt to conceal what so many Londoners had observed, for the evening papers were remarkably forthcoming. At about half nine o'clock that morning, twenty-two German aeroplanes in two separate groups had appeared in the skies off the Isle of Thanet and the east coast of Essex. After dropping several bombs in Thanet, the raiders had proceeded in a fan formation toward London on a course roughly parallel to the north bank of the Thames. They had approached London from the northeast, then changed course and crossed over the city from northwest to southeast, dropping seventy-six bombs along the way, with most of the destruction concentrated in the East End. The Central Telegraph Office received a direct hit; temporary structures on the roof were reduced to rubble and sawdust, but the interior of the building was only slightly damaged. Fortunately, no one there was killed, since the War Office had warned them of the coming attack in time for everyone to shelter in the basement. Another bomb had set fire to a house near St. Bartholomew's Hospital, but thankfully the hospital itself, and the great many wounded soldiers among its patients, was unharmed. The most horrifying news was that an infant school had been struck, killing many of the children, all of them only four to seven years of age. In all, fifty-seven people had been killed and 193 wounded.

"Hold on," said Marjorie indignantly as they shared information Sunday afternoon while they warmed up for their football match. "The War Office warned the Central Telegraph Office that the German planes were on the way? Why didn't they warn Thornshire Arsenal?"

"Why didn't they warn *everyone*?" April asked. "If the teachers had known, they would have taken those poor children into the school's basement, and maybe they would have survived."

The other players chimed in, their voices rising, angry and indignant.

"I don't know why we weren't warned," said Lucy, "but I know who might be able to find out." She glanced significantly to the stands, where Mrs. Purcell sat with her husband, holding his hand and smiling, eager for the match to begin. Afterward, when the Purcells came over to congratulate the Canaries on their 3–2 victory, Lucy managed to have a private word with Mrs. Purcell, who looked intrigued by her question and promised to look into it.

A few days later, Mrs. Purcell met Lucy outside the canteen, clad impeccably as always in a lovely suit of apricot silk and a straw hat with an upturned brim. "I have some information," Mrs. Purcell said, falling in step beside Lucy as she headed off to football training, "but you didn't hear this from me."

Lucy smothered a laugh. "Very well." Although Mrs. Purcell outranked her at the arsenal, Lucy was five years older, and sometimes Mrs. Purcell reminded her of her girlfriends back in Brookfield.

"The good news is that the government intends to strengthen London's defense with more aeroplanes and ground guns," said Mrs. Purcell. "The army's needs must be satisfied first, of course, but London is next in the queue. Soon they expect our defenses to be so formidable that the Germans will not dare to make any more of these daylight raids."

"I'd rather they didn't make any raids, day or night."

"You and I both. As for notifying the public when an air raid is imminent, Saturday's attack has apparently not changed anyone's mind at Whitehall. They will continue to issue private warnings to particular departments and buildings, but they have no plans at this time to issue warnings to the general public."

"But why not?" Lucy protested. "Think of the lives they would save!"

"The Home Secretary disagrees. Last week, his office issued four private warnings, but only one attack actually occurred. His concern is that if public warnings were issued, a similar percentage of those would also prove to be unfounded, and eventually the public would disregard all warnings altogether."

Lucy frowned. "Maybe the problem is that our defenders need to improve their average. Get better spotters, or better intelligence, or whatever it is they do."

"That's an excellent point, and I sincerely hope they're working on it. But that's not the only reason for their silence." Mrs. Purcell grimaced. "Someone somewhere has calculated that every false alarm would bring all of our factories to a grinding halt for at least four hours. This, of course, would significantly reduce munitions production. As a result, though lives might be saved in London, it would mean a far greater loss of life at the front than if the armies were fully supplied."

"Oh my goodness." Lucy's heart gave such a thud that she pressed a hand to her chest. The government wanted the unwitting munitionettes to stick to their posts, toiling blithely away as bombs rained down upon them. Were their lives really of so little consequence? "The government is putting the soldiers' lives before ours."

"I suppose they are, but shouldn't they?"

"Before *our* lives, perhaps, we munitionettes," Lucy conceded. "We accepted the possibility of death or injury or illness when we took these jobs. But what about the children, the elderly, those who are true civilians in every sense? Don't they deserve fair warning?"

"Perhaps in their case, it's best to evacuate London altogether."

They had reached the training field, and they paused at the edge where the grass met the gravel. "That's not possible for everyone," said Lucy, with a pang of guilt, for it *was* possible for her. Should she tell her mother to keep the boys in Surrey? Her own loneliness would be a small price to pay for their safety. "Most people have nowhere to go."

"Fair point." Mrs. Purcell's gaze had shifted to the Canaries, who were laughing and calling out to one another as they kicked the ball around. For a moment she looked wistful, but then she turned back to Lucy, smiled briefly, and said, "I'll leave you to it, then."

As she set off toward the administration building, Lucy called, "Why don't you join us out here sometime?"

Mrs. Purcell halted and glanced back at her. "I beg your pardon?"

"Why don't you kick the ball around with us sometime?" Lucy urged. "I'm sure you're terribly busy, but if you can ever spare the time, you'd be welcome."

"Would I?"

"Of course. We haven't forgotten how you answered the call on such short notice when we needed you for that match with Handley Page Girls. We would have asked you again, but we didn't want to impose."

Mrs. Purcell uttered a single laugh. "Oh, well, I don't mind a little imposition now and again."

"In that case, why don't you join us after you get yourself a proper kit?" Lucy gestured to Mrs. Purcell's lovely suit. "It's a very becoming ensemble, but you can't play football in a hobble skirt."

"One can't do much of anything in a hobble skirt, not even one with hidden pleats." Mrs. Purcell mimed kicking a football. Her range of motion was greater than Lucy would have expected, but still not enough for sport. "Thank you for the invitation. It would be lovely. I—I'll let you know."

Lucy gave her a parting nod and hurried off to join her teammates, bemused. Should they have invited Mrs. Purcell to join the team before this? She had seemed so reluctant when they had begged her to complete their side for the Handley Page Girls match. Lucy clearly recalled that she had agreed to play only at her husband's urging. Lucy had not faulted her for that; she would give anything to spend ninety minutes with Daniel, and she could well understand why Mrs. Purcell would rather be in the stands with her husband than on the pitch. Was it possible Lucy had misinterpreted the entire scene? Surprise could have accounted for Mrs. Purcell's hesitation, since their request had come at the very last minute, or nerves, since she had never played before. The more Lucy mulled it over, the more their failure to invite Mrs. Purcell to play again seemed neglectful and unkind, especially considering all that the welfare supervisor did on the munitionettes' behalf.

Perhaps the Canaries could still make it up to her.

Lucy decided to propose inviting Mrs. Purcell to join the team as an alternate, but at their next training, she arrived at the arsenal field to find the other Canaries gathered around April, and even from a distance she could tell they were concerned and upset. As she hurried toward them, Daisy saw her and jogged over to meet her halfway. "It's Marjorie," she said. "She got a telegram from her mum."

Lucy's heart plummeted. "A telegram?"

Daisy nodded bleakly. "Two of her brothers were killed in action. The third is missing."

Lucy pressed her hand to her mouth, heartsick. "Oh no. Poor Marjorie." She drew in a shaky breath. "Where is she?"

"April says she left with Superintendent Carmichael as soon as she read the telegram. That was about an hour ago." Daisy shook her head, helpless, as they hurried to join the others. "We assume she went back to the hostel, and from there, maybe home, to be with her family."

April overheard the last. "I wanted to go with her to the hostel, but the superintendent told me to remain at my post," she said, an edge to her voice. "Marjorie shouldn't be alone right now."

"Was she upset?" asked Lucy.

"No, that's just it. She was like stone. I spoke to her but she didn't say a word." Tears appeared in April's eyes, but she blinked them away. "It was Superintendent Carmichael who told me about her brothers—but not their names, not who were killed and who's only missing. They were all in the Cheshire Regiment together. The last time Marjorie mentioned them, she said they were in Belgium, near Ypres."

Lucy saw from her companions' faces that they all shared the same sympathetic dread, but no one knew what to do or how to help their bereaved friend. Someone rolled a football into the center of the circle and they kicked it around halfheartedly, not saying much, thinking of Marjorie and their own beloved soldiers far away, how they might be the next to receive a telegram bearing the worst news imaginable. It was almost a relief when the break ended and they could return to work, where they might forget their worries in the repetitive, dangerous monotony of the machines and the shells and the yellow powder.

In the shifting house at the end of the day, they all urged April to give Marjorie their love when she saw her back at the hostel. But the next morning, April reported that Marjorie had already left for home by the time April arrived, and she had taken nearly all her things with her.

"She's coming back, isn't she?" asked Peggy.

"I think so," said April, pensive. "After the funerals, maybe? I suppose there will be funerals . . . unless her brothers were buried in Belgium?" She looked around, hoping someone would have the answer, but they all shook their heads, uncertain.

A week passed, and then another. Lucy's mother and her sons returned to Clapham Common, but Marjorie did not return to the arsenal and no one heard from her. April said that she desperately wanted to write to her longtime friend, but she didn't know where to send a letter. She knew only that Marjorie's family lived in Warrington, about sixty miles west of Alderlea.

At last, thought Lucy, a way to help.

She sought out Mrs. Purcell in her office, explained their concerns, and asked if she could provide Marjorie's address. Mrs. Purcell thought for a moment, then leafed through some files, removed a blue form, and copied an address onto a small card. "I admire your wish to help your poor friend," she said, handing the card to Lucy, "but—"

"I know," said Lucy, managing a halfhearted smile. "I didn't get this from you."

She turned to go, and was halfway to the staircase when she remembered something else. Hurrying back, she addressed Mrs. Purcell from the doorway of her office. "As to what we were discussing the other day—would you be interested in joining the football club?"

Mrs. Purcell's eyebrows rose. "Because Miss Tate is absent? I'd be delighted, except I could never play keeper. I would be terrified, and you'd lose every match."

"Oh, no, I didn't mean you'd replace Marjorie. You can play halfback as you did before, if you felt comfortable there. Peggy has been filling in as keeper." Lucy hesitated before adding, "We do hope Marjorie will be back in the goal soon."

"As do I, but do you truly believe she'll return? Superintendent Carmichael filled out the paperwork for a leave of absence, but we haven't heard anything from Miss Tate since she left. Unfortunately, the superintendent can't hold the job for her indefinitely."

Lucy held up the card with the Tate family's address. "Give us a week, time for a letter there and a reply back."

"Let's make it two," said Mrs. Purcell.

April wrote to Marjorie that evening after work and posted her letter the next day. A fortnight passed, but Marjorie did not respond. "I'm worried that Marjorie is going to lose her job," April confided to Lucy on the train to Bristol, where they would face the Chittening Factory Ladies in a match at Avonmouth. "And I'm worried that we're going to lose Marjorie."

Lucy did too, but she suspected that Marjorie would lose something more important than her job and her football club if she did not return to Thornshire.

By the time the match ended in a 2–2 draw, Lucy had concluded that the only way to be sure that Marjorie was all right was to send a delegation to Warrington. She proposed the idea to the team as they rode back to London, and all agreed that she was right. Marjorie's silence had become so worrisome that they would not rest easy until they looked in on her. April should go, as Marjorie's closest friend among the Canaries. Lucy offered to accompany her.

The others exchanged looks of surprise and misgivings. "Are you sure you'd want to?" Peggy ventured. "Marjorie hasn't exactly been kind to you through the years."

"All the more reason I should go," said Lucy. "If I'm there, of all people, she'll have absolutely no doubt that the entire club is very concerned."

Everyone conceded that she made a fair point, so the next day, Lucy spoke to Mrs. Purcell and Superintendent Carmichael, who granted her and April two days off. The following day, Lucy packed a small bag, kissed her sons goodbye, thanked her mother, and set out for the train station. She met April at Euston, and together they boarded the train to Warrington. Some of their fellow passengers did a double take at the sight of their yellow skin; others recoiled or averted their eyes. Two middle-aged gentlemen offered them their seats in the crowded carriage, and an elderly woman seated beside April smiled kindly and thanked them for their service to the war effort. Lucy nodded politely in reply, uncomfortably conspicuous in her yellow skin and mottled hair. She had worn gloves, but she almost wished she had worn a veil as well.

As they traveled northwest, Lucy and April spoke

quietly about what they might expect when they found Marjorie, and what they might say to her, how they might persuade her to return to Thornshire, if that did indeed seem to be for the best. Perhaps her grieving family needed her closer to home. Perhaps Marjorie had already found new war work in Warrington, and she was perfectly content—mourning her brothers, of course, but otherwise fine, simply too busy to write.

April, who knew her best, found this explanation very unlikely. "It's just not like her to go an entire month without a word," she insisted. "Either she's too heartbroken to write, or she's fallen ill from the yellow powder."

"If she's heartbroken, we'll try to comfort her," said Lucy. "If it's TNT poisoning, we can make sure she's getting proper care."

April nodded, looking only slightly less anxious than before.

They disembarked at Warrington Bank Quay, and after asking a ticket agent for directions, they made their way to the Tate family home on foot, Lucy carrying her bag, April a small pasteboard suitcase. They weren't sure if they would need to spend the night, but they had agreed they should come prepared.

They soon discovered that the address on Mrs. Purcell's card belonged to a three-story red-brick building on Sankey Street, part of a row that ran the length of the block. Marjorie's home was two flights up above a confectioner's, between a tailor's shop with a "For Let" sign in the window and another business that had been converted to an army recruitment office. They climbed the stairs, exchanged an encouraging look, and knocked on the door.

A lad of about fourteen opened it, his hair thick and wavy beneath a tweed cap, the same honey-gold color Lucy reckoned that Marjorie's had been before she became a canary girl.

"Hello, you must be Jack," said April warmly. "We're friends of Marjorie's. Is she in?"

"She's through here, in her room." Jack opened the door wider and beckoned them inside. "I know you're her friends, since you've got yellow skin same as her. So you've come all the way from London?"

"Yes, we have," said Lucy, thinking of Jamie, so close to this boy's age. "Have you ever been there?"

"No. I want to see it, and Marjorie said she'd let me visit, but—" He broke off and shrugged, as if he knew it would never happen now, and the reasons were too obvious to mention. As he turned to lead them into the front room, Lucy and April exchanged a look. Had Marjorie already decided not to return to Thornshire?

Just then, a tall woman with dark blonde hair fading

to gray entered the room through another doorway. "Oh, hello," she said, wiping her hands on a dish-towel. She managed a smile, but her eyes were red and puffy. "Have you come to see Marjorie, or were you friends of Frank and Even?"

"We're friends of Marjorie," said Lucy, though with regard to herself, Marjorie might disagree. "Please accept our condolences for your losses. We're so sorry."

Mrs. Tate pressed her lips together and nodded, closing her eyes for a moment as if to hold back tears.

"I'm April Tipton." April then gestured to Lucy. "And this is Lucy Dempsey. We work with Marjorie at Thornshire Arsenal."

Marjorie's mother nodded. "Have you come to fetch her back, then?"

"We've come to offer our condolences, and to see if she's all right," said Lucy. "We weren't sure what her intentions are."

"She hasn't responded to my letters," said April. "We're all quite worried."

Marjorie's mother peered at her. "You're the lass who was in service with her at Alderlea."

April nodded. "Yes, that's right. Is she—do you know if Marjorie's planning to come back to the arsenal?"

"Maybe," said Jack glumly, "if you can get her out of her room first."

"What do you mean?" asked Lucy.

"She shut herself in there after the funeral and hasn't left since, except to do her business out back—"

"That's enough, Jack," said Mrs. Tate, cheeks flushed. "Oh, girls, I don't know what to do. She won't speak to us. She won't join us at the table. I leave plates outside her door and sometimes she picks at the food but more often than not she doesn't."

"Is she ill?" asked Lucy. "Sometimes, canary girls like us—"

"Oh, no, no, it isn't that. She's heartsick, I think, but that's all."

"She doesn't cry, though," said Jack, "least not so we can hear it, not like our mum."

"Jack," his mother admonished quietly, cheeks flushing deeper.

"She hasn't cried at all?" asked April, puzzled. "Not even at her brothers' funeral?"

"No, no, she's strong, our Marjorie." Mrs. Tate took a deep, tremulous breath and squared her shoulders. "But I do think it's well past time she joined the world again. We all have to carry on, don't we? We can't just shut ourselves away. My sons wouldn't want that."

"I'm sure they wouldn't," said Lucy gently.

"Will you girls be so kind as to coax her outside for a

bit?" Mrs. Tate pleaded. "Some fresh air and sunshine would do her a world of good."

Lucy and April exchanged a quick glance. "Leave it to us," said April.

Mrs. Tate led them through the room to a narrow hallway, where she stopped at the first closed door and gave it three quick raps. "Marjorie, dearie?" she called. "Some kind lasses from Thornshire have come to visit. Won't you come out to see them?"

There was no reply, only heavy silence.

Mrs. Tate knocked again. "Dearie, please. They've come such a long way."

"Marjorie, come on out," said April, a trifle sharply. "I didn't sit on a train for hours to talk to a closed door."

Lucy turned to Mrs. Tate. "I think a cup of tea wouldn't go amiss. Would you put the kettle on, please?"

"Oh, of course," said Mrs. Tate, flustered to have forgotten such a simple courtesy. She hurried away, and Jack eyed the visitors speculatively before following after.

April pounded twice on the door with her fist. "Marjorie, the boss said we have to give your wages directly to you."

Lucy gasped and gestured sharply for silence.

"What?" April said in an undertone. "If it gets her to open the door—"

"And when she finds out you lied, she'll slam it in our faces." Resting her hand on the doorknob, Lucy called, "Marjorie, we're coming in." Bracing herself, she turned the knob and eased the door open.

Marjorie was sitting on the end of the bed, legs crossed, gazing out the window. She didn't even turn her head as Lucy led April into the room. "Marjorie?" Lucy greeted her tentatively.

"Lady Prim," Marjorie replied flatly, without turning her head away from the window. "Let me guess. You don't really have my wages."

"Sorry," said April, not sounding at all sorry. "If you want your wages, you'll have to come to Thornshire and collect them yourself."

"Are you coming back?" asked Lucy. "Mrs. Carmichael has been holding your job for you, but she can't for much longer."

"We need you on the pitch too," said April. "Peggy has been filling in for you in the goal, but—"

Marjorie turned to face them. "Peggy? Why Peggy?"

"She volunteered," said Lucy, shrugging. "She's tall and has a long reach. It's not like we have a lot of options."

"That's true enough," said April. "We have so few substitutes, Lucy asked Mrs. Purcell to join the club."

Marjorie stared at her friend in utter disbelief, then

fixed Lucy with a glare. "You can't be serious." Her eyes were raw and red-rimmed, with dark shadows beneath from lack of sleep. "She's fast, fair enough, but she hardly knows the sport."

"She's learning," Lucy defended her. "And Peggy is doing rather well as keeper."

April pulled a face. "Well, that's a matter of opinion."

"At least Peggy is *there*," said Lucy. "She hasn't abandoned the team."

"What's that supposed to mean?" snapped Marjorie. "If you've got something to say, Lady Prim, just say it."

Lucy spread her hands and shrugged. "What is there to say? You lost your brothers, and that is a terrible, tragic thing. My heart goes out to you. What I don't understand . . . ." She let her voice trail off.

"What? What don't you understand?"

"Well, it's not just that you've run off without a word for the team, when we're hoping to qualify for the Munitionettes' Cup. That's fine. After all, in the end, football is just sport."

Marjorie regarded her balefully. "Said the footballer's wife."

"I'm not saying football isn't important. It is. But if you abandon the team, we'll manage without you." Lucy steeled herself, choosing her words carefully, knowing that what she said next might make all the difference. "But the thing is, our soldiers *won't* manage without you. You're the girl behind the man behind the gun, remember? On us their lives depend."

Marjorie barked out a hollow laugh, and a tear trickled down her cheek. "Fat lot of good that did my brothers."

"Your brother who's missing—what if he's been captured?" said April. "The sooner the war ends, the sooner he can come home."

Marjorie frowned at her bleakly, and another tear spilled over, and then another. "If he's still alive," she said, her voice breaking. "If he's not lying dead in a trench in Belgium."

Swiftly, April sat beside her on the bed and embraced her friend, and Marjorie allowed it. "Then take revenge," she said, her voice low and angry. "Make them pay."

"Or you can stay here," said Lucy, "and turn the white feather."

Marjorie tore herself from April's embrace and bolted to her feet. "How dare you? You can't possibly understand how I feel."

"No, I probably can't," said Lucy. "But I'm sure that hiding in your room until the pain goes away isn't the answer. I don't think revenge is either," she added, with a glance for April. "The best we can do is to help our armies win the war as soon as possible so that all the killing can stop and the men we love can come home."

Marjorie's tears were flowing freely now, her breath coming in ragged gasps. "My brothers never will."

"Don't give up hope for your third brother," Lucy implored. "He may yet come home."

"Archie," said Marjorie. "It's Archie who's missing."

As she broke down in aching sobs, April put her arms around her, murmuring soothingly. Lucy stood back at a respectful distance, hands clasped behind her back. She had done her part by infuriating Marjorie so much that her stoic mask had shattered. Now she could begin to grieve, but that didn't mean she would tolerate comforting embraces from her unwilling rival.

After a time, Marjorie took a deep, steadying breath and wiped her eyes. "Mrs. Purcell convinced the superintendent to hold my job for me?"

Lucy nodded, and April said, "Yes, for now. Mrs. Carmichael's patience is wearing thin, though."

"Best not keep her waiting, then. And there's a football tournament, you said?"

"The Munitionettes' Cup," said Lucy. "It won't be held until spring, but we have to win our next few games to qualify for the first round. We're sure we can do it."

"Reasonably sure," April added.

Marjorie's eyebrows rose. "With Peggy in the goal, and Mrs. Purcell on the pitch?"

Lucy spread her hands, resigned. "I won't pretend it'll be easy, but what choice do we have?"

"Obviously you'll have a choice." Marjorie squared her shoulders. "You'll have me."

She waved them out of her room so she could wash and dress and pack her things. Concealing their delight and relief until they had closed the door behind them, Lucy and April made their way to the kitchen, where Mrs. Tate poured tea and offered them some bread and cheese with a bit of pork, apologizing for the meager rations. They ate sparingly, assuring her that they were so well-fed at the arsenal that they weren't very hungry.

Within an hour, the three munitionettes were on their way to Warrington Bank Quay, where they boarded the train to London. They passed the first hour chatting, sharing the news of the arsenal and especially of the Canaries, but after that, Marjorie fell soundly asleep, her head on April's shoulder. Undoubtedly she had slept poorly in the weeks since her brothers had been killed. Lucy hoped with all her heart that somehow Archie's life had been spared, and that his family would soon hear from him, or have word of him. But as April had said, only victory would end the war, stop the slaughter, and let the men come home.

They parted at Euston, Lucy heading toward Clapham Common, April and Marjorie nearly as far in the opposite direction. When Lucy reached her own front gate, her sons startled her by bursting out of the house and racing to meet her. "Mum!" Simon cried, flinging his arms around her waist. "The American soldiers are in London! Did you see them?"

"Why, no," Lucy exclaimed, looking to Jamie for confirmation. "American troops are here? Passing through on their way to France, I assume?"

Jamie nodded, beaming. "They're going to parade from Wellington Barracks past Trafalgar Square through Whitehall and Westminster, and after they pass the American Embassy, they're going to march before Buckingham Palace and the King!"

"May we go, Mum?" Simon begged, seizing her hands and jumping up and down. "Please, Mum? It's going to be so grand, with bands and soldiers and everything!"

"I'm sorry, darlings, but I can't take you," said Lucy, truly regretful, for it was sure to be a jubilant spectacle, and she could use a bit of joy and optimism herself.

"I shall take them," said her mother, who also emerged from the house, though at a more sedate pace than her grandsons. "I already promised them."

"Then it's all settled." Still holding Simon's hand,

Lucy reached for Jamie's and smiled upon them both. "You must promise to remember every detail and tell me all about it afterward."

"We will," said Jamie, and Simon nodded vigorously.

And she in turn would share the wonderful news with Daniel. Help was on the way, and victory must soon follow.

17
September–October 1917

April

For several weeks after Marjorie's return to Thorn-shire, whenever a shift was especially grueling or a foreman particularly demanding, she would fix April with a wry look and deadpan, "I can't believe I let you drag me back here for *this*." But April knew she didn't really mean it. On several occasions, April had overheard Marjorie declare to the other canary girls that she was glad to be back in the Danger Building so she could make more weapons to strike back at the enemy who had killed her beloved brothers. Yet aside from the occasional ironic remark, Marjorie's former lighthearted nonchalance was gone. She had become mirthless and reticent in the Danger Building, steely-eyed and fierce on the pitch. The Canaries won match after match with her in the goal, snatching balls out of the air with flying leaps that defied gravity and ended in hard, rolling landings that made April flinch and look away, appalled by her friend's rash indifference to injury. Marjorie seemed to have no regard for her own safety anymore, and in their work, that attitude could prove fatal. April worried for her.

She was equally worried for Mabel, who had become so infirm that she had been obliged to resign from the arsenal altogether. At first, she had still attended the Canaries' football matches when they played on their home ground, sitting on the sidelines, coughing and wheezing as she cheered them on, but by early September she could no longer manage even that. Peggy frequently updated Mabel's friends about her condition, noting her small improvements and good spirits, but Peggy's bleak eyes belied her hopeful words. Nearly every day, a canary girl would send Peggy home with an encouraging note or a small gift for her mother, which Peggy assured them were always gratefully received. Mabel never wrote back, though, which after Marjorie's silence, April took as a foreboding sign.

There were other curious signs that she had no idea how to interpret. One morning in the middle of September, Lucy arrived at the shifting house looking pensive and bemused. Later, at dinner, April was seated at a table with Marjorie and Peggy across the aisle from Lucy and Daisy when she heard Lucy say, "I witnessed the most curious scene this morning at Clapham Junction station."

Marjorie gave April and Peggy a significant look, and they paused their own conversation to eavesdrop.

"My train was delayed, so I was waiting, one eye on the clock, when I saw two special trains pull in on opposite sides of the same platform," said Lucy, her yellow hands resting on the table around her teacup. "The northward-bound train was packed with German prisoners."

"My goodness," said Daisy, eyes widening.

Lucy nodded. "They must have come directly from the battlefield. They were filthy, disheveled, and unshaven, looking more like a gang of hardened convicts than soldiers. I admit I pitied them."

Marjorie caught April's eye. "Pity for Germans," she mouthed silently, her expression scornful. In reply, April threw her an exasperated look and quietly inched her chair closer to Lucy's.

"The southbound train carried our Tommies," Lucy was saying. "They were neatly shaved, hair trimmed and combed, faces scrubbed and smiling, uniforms in perfect order."

"They must have been new recruits," said Daisy. "Off to the front for the first time."

"Yes, that was my thought too. Only a narrow platform divided the two groups physically, but they could not have been more far apart in condition and spirits. Our boys were eager and jovial, the Germans unkempt and despondent, though neither knew what fate awaited them at the end of their journey."

Daisy leaned forward and rested her arms on the table, hanging on every word. "What did they do when they saw one another? Did they shout and curse? Did they rush off the trains and brawl on the platform?"

"You'd imagine so, wouldn't you, but no. The Germans were under guard, so they *had* to stay in their railcars—"

"Of course."

"But when they saw our soldiers, they smiled and waved from the windows and shouted, '*Kameraden!*' Hearing that, the Tommies called back, 'Good old Jerries!' Then they climbed out of their carriages, crossed the platform, and threw packets of tobacco and chocolate through the windows to the Germans!"

"That's astonishing!" gasped Daisy, wide-eyed.

"That's fraternization," snapped Marjorie, giving Lucy and Daisy a start. "They should be ashamed of themselves."

"Why?" asked Lucy, genuinely puzzled. "There's

no personal hatred between the enlisted men of either side. They're all caught up in a war none of them have done anything to cause, and they fight only because their commanders and their heads of state order them to. It's little wonder that this common unhappy fate would evoke a sense of comradeship among them."

April nodded, thinking of the Christmas truce Oliver had experienced, a bit of peace and goodwill in the midst of war. It had not lasted, nor had it ever been repeated, but for a moment, enemies had become friends. The generals had been apoplectic with fury, but what harm had the brief respite done? Everyone had resumed killing one another all too soon.

"It would be different if Tommy and Fritz were fraternizing on the battlefield," said Peggy, as if she had overheard April's thoughts. "But these Germans can't hurt anyone now. What's the harm in giving them a bit of cheer? Wouldn't you want the same done for our lads if they were prisoners?"

Marjorie hesitated for the barest of moments, but then her expression hardened. "The Germans are the enemy. Have you forgotten what horrible things those prisoners might have done to our lads before they were captured?" She gestured sharply to indicate the whole arsenal. "Have you forgotten why we're here?"

"I know why we're here," said Lucy evenly. "It was a

strange scene. I have mixed feelings about it too. That's why I was unburdening myself to Daisy." She extended her hand, palm up, to indicate her friend on the other side of the table. April felt heat rise in her cheeks at the gentle reminder that Marjorie had interrupted a private conversation.

Marjorie abruptly rose and snatched up her tray. "If you had lost someone you loved in this bloody war, you wouldn't be so eager to make friends with the Hun."

Lucy blanched beneath her yellow pallor, but Marjorie was already striding away and didn't see the effect of her words. "That was uncalled for," said Peggy, and Daisy reached across the table to take Lucy's hand. "She knows your husband is in the thick of it with the Seventeenth Middlesex."

Lucy managed a tight smile. "She's upset. She wasn't thinking of that." Then she too rose and cleared away her dinner tray.

Later, as April, Marjorie, and two other girls from their hostel were passing through Gate Four, April heard someone call her name. When she glanced over her shoulder she saw Oliver jogging toward her. His smile warmed her heart, and she told her companions to go on ahead while she waited for him to catch up.

"I have to get back to the office, so I can only walk you to the park," he said, apologetic.

"That's fine," she said, concealing her disappointment as they turned and passed between the sentries at the gate. "Marjorie had a rough day. I should spend some time with her."

"Are you going out?" He glanced overhead, where the moon had risen, nearly full, in a clear, cloudless sky, without a breeze to stir the cool autumn air. If they were not at war, April would have sighed over the evening's romantic beauty, but conditions were ideal, from the Germans' perspective, for an air raid. London had suffered two attacks earlier that week under similar skies.

"No, we're heading straight back to the hostel," she assured him. She wished he would take her hand as they walked along together, but there were too many other Thornshire workers around, and as he put it, he disliked drawing attention to himself.

"Because people would look at us and think you can do better than a housemaid?" she had challenged him once.

"No," he had replied levelly. "We both know it's far more likely that people would think you can do better than a cripple."

April thought that ridiculous and had told him so. He shrugged, and they never mentioned it again, but April had not forgotten it.

They reached the edge of the park, and to April's surprise, Oliver took her hand and squeezed it. "Get home safe, all right?" he said, bending down to give her a swift kiss on the cheek.

"Careful," she said. "Someone might see you and think we're sweethearts."

He grinned, and her heart warmed to him all over again. "People can think whatever they like. I'll see you at your match tomorrow." With that, he nodded and hurried back to the arsenal.

She watched him for a moment, wondering what was keeping him late at the office. In July, Winston Churchill had been appointed Minister of Munitions, and little more than a week ago, he had announced that the leaving certificates workers so loathed would be abolished on 15 October. Maybe Mr. Purcell needed Oliver to come up with another, less tyrannical scheme to encourage workers to stay. Or maybe they had received word that the armies would be making another push soon, and they were preparing to ramp up production. Or maybe it was something horribly dull, like filing paperwork. As she turned to go, April hoped that whatever it was, Oliver would much rather be sitting at a café with her, or sitting beside her in a darkened theatre, anticipating a moment when they might find themselves alone and share a long, slow, breathtaking kiss.

She gave herself a little shake and hurried after Marjorie and the other girls. She caught up to them just as they were boarding the tram. "We thought you'd run off with your fellow," said Marjorie archly as April dropped into the seat beside her.

"He *is* handsome," said one of the other girls, Ethel, glancing back the way they had come as if hoping for another look at him. "Pity about the arm."

"Don't pity him," said April, smiling sweetly, but with a brittle edge to her voice. "He doesn't like it, and neither do I."

She pretended not to notice the raised eyebrows and significant looks the other girls exchanged. At least her words had the desired effect, for they stopped teasing her. Conversation turned to other matters—arsenal gossip, the next day's football match, and the vexing rumors that their landlady intended to raise the weekly rate for room and board at their hostel. Early in the war, they had paid 12 shillings for a shared room and two meals a day, but now they were paying 16s 6d, and another tenant from the night shift had overheard their landlady say that 17s was coming soon.

"We'll need to ask for a rise in our wages, if it comes to that," said April, gazing out the window to the darkened streets.

"We should have a word with our newest teammate,"

said Marjorie, covering a yawn. "Helen will tell her husband what's what."

"Don't ask for a pay rise only on behalf of the Canaries," protested Ethel. "Ask for all of us."

Marjorie spread her hands, feigning uncertainty. "If there's enough money to go around, sure, but—"

"Hush a moment," April broke in, holding up a hand, gaze fixed on the darkness beyond the window. "Do you hear that?"

"I hear *you*, and I hear the tram," said Ethel, but the tram quieted as it slowed on its approach to their station, and they all fell silent, listening. Somewhere on the street, someone was blowing a whistle—a policeman's whistle. Uneasiness settled over the carriage, and as soon as the tram halted, everyone rushed to disembark. The Thornshire girls were separated in the crush, but they quickly reunited on the pavement and hurried on toward their hostel. They had gone little more than a block when they heard the shrill whistle again, growing louder and louder behind them. Suddenly a policeman passed them in the street on a bicycle, blowing his whistle, wearing white placards on his chest and back bearing an inscription in bold red print: "Police Notice—Take Cover."

April had heard that the government had changed its policy against issuing air raid warnings to the general public, but this was the first time she had witnessed it in action. Heart thudding, she and her companions quickened their pace until they were nearly running, but only tentatively in the blackout, the route illuminated by nothing more than moonlight and daubs of luminescent paint on curbs and obstacles. April and Marjorie pulled ahead of the other two, but they waited at street corners for their friends to catch up. Omnibuses and motorcars increased their speed, hastening their occupants to safety; other pedestrians were darting in all directions, fleeing for shelter; shops and businesses were closing their doors and shuttering their windows. A tense, ominous hush descended upon the street, and as the hostel came into view, April sprinted for the front door, with Marjorie right behind her. The door opened as they approached, and they raced inside past their landlady, who stood with one hand on the doorknob, the other waving them on through to the kitchen. There the door to the coal cellar stood open; April flew down the stairs and squeezed in with the other tenants, pressing close to make room for her friends.

They waited, straining their ears for the all-clear signal, starting when the door flew open and more munitionettes tumbled in, followed last of all by their landlady. For a while silence prevailed, broken only by the occasional murmur of anxious voices. Then, at roughly half eight o'clock, the heavy pounding and roar of bombs and gunfire shook the building and the earth all around. April's heart thudded so intensely, blood pounding in her ears, that she could take no more than quick, shallow breaths. She knew that they were threatened not only by German bombs, but by the falling shrapnel of their own ground guns, which fired fierce, terrible barrages into the skies above London, hoping fortune would speed their shots to their unseen targets. The German aeroplanes flew too high to be seen from the ground, so taking proper aim was impossible. April guessed that the defense forces counted on luck to bring the enemy down, or they hoped to shake the Germans' nerves so badly that they turned around and sped back across the Channel.

"I never imagined I'd say this," Marjorie murmured close to April's ear, as the explosions diminished, an encouraging sign that the raiders were moving off, "but I almost miss the zeppelins."

April agreed. If an attack had to come, better a zeppelin than an aeroplane any day. A zeppelin could be spotted at a distance and tracked as it drifted over London, but swift, high-flying aeroplanes could be anywhere, right above you or miles away, and you would never know until the bombs fell.

An hour passed before the all-clear sounded. Only then did they climb wearily from the coal cellar, dust themselves off, stretch their cramped limbs, and sit down to the supper their landlady had prepared for them, long since grown cold. Soon thereafter, as she settled into bed, April doubted that she would be able to sleep out of fear that another attack might come at any moment, but eventually exhaustion overcame her.

Fortunately, the next day was Sunday, so she was able to sleep in and get a proper rest before she had to rise and attend to the usual tasks of her single day off, rushing to finish before setting out for her football match. Oliver attended, she was glad to see as she searched the stands for him, and so did Mrs. Purcell's husband, as well as dozens of Thornshire munitionettes and thousands of other spectators who missed cheering on their favorite men's teams and were satisfied to watch the ladies, for the duration. After the match, a 4–2 victory for the Canaries that moved them one step closer to qualifying for the Munitionettes' Cup, Oliver took April out to a café for a bite to eat. He escorted her back to the hostel afterward even though it was miles out of his way.

"Lie low tonight," he said after kissing her goodnight at the door, glancing warily up at the brilliant sunset lighting up the darkening sky.

"I intend to lie perfectly snug in my bed," she said, blushing a little at his grin. She had not meant it flirtatiously, but there it was. "The Germans better not trouble us two nights in a row. I need to be well-rested for work tomorrow."

But the Germans did come, only minutes after she had fallen asleep, sending her and Marjorie and the other tenants scrambling for their dressing gowns and slippers and racing downstairs to the coal cellar. This time the assault lasted a full ninety minutes, and the pounding of the ground guns seemed louder than ever before, but the munitionettes tried to doze, closing their eyes and resting their heads on one another's shoulders, jolted awake whenever an explosion struck too near and the building trembled around them. Eventually the all-clear sounded and they were able to return to bed, but April woke the next morning groggy and with a faint headache behind her right eye. All that day, she felt as if she were dragging herself through her shift, and instead of meeting the other Canaries on their training field after lunch and tea, she rested in the shifting house, lying on her back on a bench with her eyes closed. She fervently hoped that dense clouds, or better yet, thunderstorms, would roll in by late afternoon, filling the skies with dangerous winds and lightning, unsettling the German pilots so much that they kept their planes grounded.

But it was not to be. Another beautiful clear, moonlit sky greeted her when she exited the shifting house that evening, and as she rode the tram back to the hostel, she steeled herself for another terrifying night of flinching as bombs slammed into London and the ground guns flung deadly fire back. And so it happened, just as she and her friends were finishing dinner, so that several girls snatched up the last of their bread and tea and carefully brought them along, down into the cellar. The guns sounded fainter that night, and the walls around them trembled less than usual, so they reckoned that the attack must have focused on another part of the city. This eased their anxiety somewhat, though they sympathized with their fellow Londoners who were bearing the brunt of it. To keep their spirits up, they chatted and even joked in the intervals between distant explosions, and eventually they were able to return to bed.

Fortunately, the Germans left them alone for the rest of the night, so in the morning April woke feeling somewhat better rested than usual, though far from refreshed. As she and Marjorie hurried off to work, she overheard other passengers on the tram say that although the previous night's attack had seemed less intense in their area than previous raids, the scale of it had actually been larger than any the Germans had attempted before. Three separate groups of enemy aeroplanes had crossed the Essex coast and approached London roughly fifteen minutes apart, but most of the planes had been driven back by the British guns. The few that slipped past their defenses had dropped five bombs on Shoreditch, but most of the damage had been inflicted on the West End. Victoria railway station had apparently been the raiders' intended target, but it had escaped harm, unlike Grosvenor Road near Buckingham Palace, where numerous houses had been destroyed and many residents had suffered serious cuts from shattered glass. A fourth group of aeroplanes had flown separately over Kent, dropping five or six bombs on the outskirts of town, but all had fallen on marshland. The windows of a few cottages had been smashed, and one man had received cuts to his face from flying shards, but there had been no serious injuries and no deaths. No one aboard the tram seemed to know whether there had been any fatalities in London, but April had little doubt that some unfortunate residents had been killed, for so it had been for every other raid over the past week.

Disembarking the tram, she hurried to the Thornshire park, eager to find Oliver and put her mind at ease that he too had made it through the night unharmed.

But he was not there. It was a perfectly sunny autumn day with only a slight cool mist in the air, exactly the sort of morning when workers were inclined to linger and grouse about problems they hoped Oliver could solve, but she didn't see him anywhere. Heart thudding, she pressed a hand to her stomach, took a steadying breath, and tried to reason her fear away. No one on the tram had mentioned any fatalities in London, and no bombs had struck Oliver's neighborhood as far as she had overheard, so he was almost certainly fine. Likely the same business that had kept him late at work a few evenings ago had obliged him to report to Mr. Purcell's office early today. Yes, that was almost certainly it.

She worried about him all the same, of course, and wished she could invent an excuse to dash over to the administration building just to see for herself that he was all right.

Hours later, she was in the washroom scrubbing her hands and face before tea when she heard the hum of anxious conversation coming through the doorway to the canteen. She quickly toweled off and hurried inside, where she found several girls passing around newspapers, others peering over their friends' shoulders to read, and still more discussing something obviously dreadful in tense or tearful voices. Finding Marjorie and Peggy seated on the same side of their usual table, she hurried over without bothering to collect her tea things first. "What's happened?" she asked, bracing herself. "What's the matter?"

Marjorie glanced up from the newspaper spread open on the table before them. "A munitions accident, somewhere," she said grimly, rotating the paper around to face April. "Sounds bad."

April sank into the chair across from her, eyes fixed on the headline, and as she took in the first words, her hand flew to her mouth to smother a gasp.

MUNITIONS EXPLOSION
MUCH DAMAGE TO A FACTORY
Press Bureau, 1.5 p.m.

The Ministry of Munitions announces that a serious fire and an explosion have occurred at a munitions factory in the North of England.

Much damage has been caused to the factory, but up to the present no deaths have been reported, although injuries have been sustained by a number of workers.

"Oh no," April murmured, reading the brief statement again, quickly skimming the rest of the page for more details, thinking of all the munitionettes from the North of England they had met on the pitch over the past few years. "This can't be all the press knows. Where did it happen? And when? Maybe another newspaper will tell us."

"They all say the same thing," said Marjorie, tapping the words "Press Bureau" with her finger. "It's a formal statement from the Ministry of Munitions, not an interview. It's a wonder the ministry made any announcement at all."

"It must have been a truly terrible accident, like the one at Brunner Mond in January," said Peggy. "Only when a disaster's too big to conceal from the public do they make an announcement like this."

April read the article again and found a slender thread of hope to seize. "No deaths have been reported."

"So they say," Marjorie scoffed.

April glanced from Marjorie to Peggy and saw the same skepticism in both of their faces. "Those poor girls, whoever they are," she murmured, sitting back in her chair, heartsick.

"It'll come out," said Peggy. "It may take months, maybe not until the end of the war, but you can't keep something like this secret forever."

Indeed, rumors began wending their way to Thornshire within a matter of days, rumors that were eventually confirmed by reliable secondhand accounts.

The disaster had occurred at the White Lund Factory in north Lancashire, a 250-acre complex of around 150 closely packed one-story buildings that out of wartime necessity had been swiftly constructed of wood with felt roofs. The shells made there were filled with amatol, a mixture of ammonium nitrate and TNT, which was melted and poured into the shell casings. It was incredibly dangerous labor, and worker deaths happened monthly—men perishing from accidents, women from TNT poisoning.

On 1 October, at about half ten o'clock in the evening, a massive explosion occurred in one of the melt plants, setting off a series of explosions in adjacent buildings that continued through the night until six o'clock the next morning, then sporadically until three o'clock the following afternoon. Terrible fires spread from one structure to another, setting off explosions that began with an ominous, demonical hissing and a leaping blue flame, followed quickly by tremors and reverberations that shattered plate glass and windows for miles around. Loaded shells went off, shrieking into the air and exploding over nearby Lancaster and Morecambe, sending the terrified residents fleeing to the waterfront in their nightclothes. The factory fire brigade was quickly overwhelmed, and firefighters from all over the region were summoned to battle the ferocious blaze, but the last fires were not extinguished until early in the morning of 4 October.

Miraculously, only ten people were killed in the disaster, most of them while fighting the blaze—five firefighters, five munitions workers, all of them men. A great many more workers were injured, some of them seriously, by falling debris, flying shrapnel, burns, and the panic of the crowd. In the towns, local residents were hurt by falling masonry, shattered glass, accidents incurred as they fled for safety, and exposure to the cold. It was believed that the casualties would have been much worse except that most of the workers were in the canteen on their dinner break when the alarm was sounded after the first explosion. In the end, nearly the entire compound was destroyed, except for a few brick buildings along the perimeter.

Even before the ashes cooled, rumors and wild speculation abounded that German agents had sabotaged the factories, or that a zeppelin had bombed it. Eventually the workers and their foremen agreed that the most likely explanation was an unknown worker's carelessness with matches and cigarettes.

"That could've been us," April said to Marjorie one chilly, overcast morning as they made their way from the tram to the arsenal, crossing the park, where the brilliant autumn hues were already beginning to fade and the stiff wind whipped the ends of their scarves and sent dried leaves scuttling over the gravel paths.

"It might yet be us," Marjorie replied, her voice strangely emotionless.

But was it strange, really? After all, munitionettes were expected to brave the potential for disaster every day, to keep a stiff upper lip even as their skin turned yellow and their friends became too ill to work, to remain calm when an accident occurred, and, like the girls from the Barnbow Munitions Factory in Leeds, to help remove the debris, mop up the spilled blood, and get back to work. Unless a factory was utterly destroyed, as seemed to be the case with White Lund, they were required to time in for their next shift and carry on as if nothing had happened, even if their own dear friends had lost their lives only a few paces away from where they worked. The soldiers faced worse every day, and as Mabel used to declare, the lads risked their lives in the trenches, and the munitionettes risked theirs in the arsenal.

Whenever April thought of how close Oliver had come to never returning from the battlefield, she felt lightheaded from relief, so narrowly had she escaped terrible loss. *Her* loss, indeed, she mocked herself whenever the thought crossed her mind. She hadn't known him then. Oliver would have suffered the loss, he and his family, his friends and loved ones. She wasn't even sure what she meant to him, not really, and it was silly and sentimental to think of her own feelings when the times required courage and sacrifice. She knew this, and yet the thought of Oliver being absent from the world was too dreadful to contemplate.

He was not in the park again that morning, but there hadn't been any air raids upon London the night before, so she was merely disappointed, not worried, as she and Marjorie quickly made their way around the compound to Gate Four.

She tried to put Oliver out of her thoughts entirely as she worked alongside Marjorie in the Filling Shop, packing yellow powder into shell casings, refusing to think of what the TNT was doing to her lungs and throat and blood. She would be rotated to less dangerous work soon enough. They all had to do their bit until the war was won.

Later that afternoon, she was working away, keenly focused, when Marjorie spoke her name. Glancing up, she realized the other canary girls around their table had paused in their work to watch the corridor as Superintendent Carmichael, her jaw set in grim resolution, a telegram in her hand, strode past the broad open doorway to the Filling Shop—

And kept going. A collective sigh went up from

the table, but only a few girls promptly resumed their duties. The others exchanged wary glances. Someone in the Danger Building—not anyone in their shop, thank goodness, not any of them—was moments away from receiving devastating news.

They all knew the superintendent would soon escort the unfortunate woman past their doorway, back through inspection to the washroom and the shifting house. No one who received one of those telegrams was allowed to finish her shift, even if she felt up to it. As far as April knew, no one had ever wanted to.

They waited, their eyes fixed on the open doorway. Some held their breath, some murmured prayers. Others counted their blessings that this time, they had been spared.

They waited.

Superintendent Carmichael appeared first, passing the open doorway without glancing into the Filling Shop. Close behind her came Daisy, her arm around the waist of another woman, keeping her upright as she stumbled forward, her eyes bleak and unseeing, her face pale with shock beneath the yellow pallor—

"Lucy," Marjorie murmured, a catch in her throat.

They all watched, helpless, silent with stunned misery, until the three women passed the doorway and disappeared from view.

18
October–December 1917

Helen

Helen learned about Lucy Dempsey's heartbreaking news only after Superintendent Carmichael returned from delivering the dreadful telegram and escorting Lucy to the main gate. "I wish you would have told me first," Helen said, bounding up from her chair and leaving the bemused superintendent staring after her. If Helen caught up with her teammate, she could escort her to her tram station, or even all the way home, rather than leave her alone with her grief. But she was too late. When Helen reached the park in front of the main gate, Lucy was nowhere to be seen.

Frowning in consternation, Helen returned to her tiny office to find the superintendent gone but a memo placed neatly in the center of her desk, the significant details of Lucy's telegram transcribed from memory upon it. On 24 September, Corporal Daniel Dempsey had been wounded on the front lines. Immobilized by his injury, he had been taken prisoner before stretcher bearers could evacuate him to a field hospital.

Dire news indeed, but at least Lucy's husband was alive, or he had been at the time of his capture, which meant that hope remained for his safe return home.

Helen hurried to Arthur's office and paced in his antechamber until he finished a phone call with the Ministry of Munitions. After she explained Lucy's circumstances, he agreed that she could use the Purcell name and contacts to seek more information.

It took a few days, and the promise of a coveted bottle of wine to a surly clerk at the War Office, but eventually Helen learned all that had been recorded about Corporal Dempsey's status. On 24 September, the 17th Middlesex was on the front line north of Givenchy, enduring heavy shelling, which the enemy used as cover for a raid. Obscured by a heavy mist, a small party of Germans slipped into the British trenches, seized munitions, and exchanged fire before they were driven off, carrying off bombs, crates of explosives, and boxes of machine-gun ammunition. Thirteen men of the Footballers' Battalion had been wounded, four of them seriously, and two were missing, including Corporal Dempsey. Witnesses observed that he had taken shrapnel to the leg and, unable to withdraw, had been dragged back to the German lines, presumably for interrogation.

Heartsick for Lucy, Helen hoped that the report would still offer her some measure of comfort. Helen had heard from other wives and sisters of soldiers that bad news, distressing though it could be, was easier to endure than interminable uncertainty.

Superintendent Carmichael had urged Lucy to take a few days off, so it wasn't until the following week that Helen was able to share what she had learned. Lucy absorbed the news stoically, eyes shadowed and cheeks hollow, her yellow skin and patchily bleached dark hair evidence of her own sacrifices for the war effort—and now she might lose her husband too. Disregarding the arsenal's desperate need for workers, Helen offered Lucy more time off, but her fellow Canary shook her head. "I need to occupy myself with useful work," she said quietly. "It's the only thing that distracts my thoughts away from . . . all the dire possibilities."

Helen understood, but just to be sure, she asked, "Are you sure you wouldn't benefit from more time at home with your sons?"

Again Lucy shook her head. "I sent them to Surrey to stay with my mother for the duration." She glanced down at her lap, realized she was wringing her hands, and abruptly stopped, spreading her hands flat on her lap and then balling them into fists. "I've been weighing whether to get them out of the city for months, what with these dreadful air raids showing no signs of easing, but this finally convinced me. I may have lost Daniel, but I won't lose them too—" Her voice choked off.

"You don't know that you've lost your husband, not for certain," said Helen, her voice low and soothing. "He was alive and conscious when his companions last saw him."

"Yes, I know. Believe me, I've been holding on to that hope with all my might." Lucy inhaled shakily. "I suppose everything depends upon how serious his wounds are, and how the Germans treat him."

In parting, Helen promised to tell Lucy immediately if she managed to wring any more details out of the War Office, and Lucy thanked her and returned to work. When Helen saw her at football training later, she seemed as determined on the pitch as ever, her expression stoic, her kicks so forceful that Helen reckoned she was taking out her anger and grief on the ball. Afterward, as Helen headed back to the administration building and the other players returned to their various factories and shops, she glimpsed Lucy and Marjorie walking together. Just as they rounded a corner, she thought she saw Marjorie put her arm around Lucy's shoulders. Helen was so astonished by the unexpected gesture that she halted and stared, but the pair had slipped out of sight, and she couldn't be sure she hadn't imagined it. In her time at Thornshire, Helen had observed Marjorie treating Lucy with respect on the pitch but with kindness nowhere. Perhaps Marjorie's own sorrows had rendered her able, at long last, to empathize with someone else's suffering.

At the end of a long day, Helen tidied her desk, gathered her coat and purse, and went to coax Arthur out of his office so they could go home to a late dinner. She had done her bit for King and Country, and she had provided her munitionettes with the resources they sought and the comfort they needed. If only she could tend to Arthur half as well, she would feel like an adequate wife. But although she plied him with nourishing food and practically forced him to rest, he was perpetually exhausted and overstressed, toiling relentlessly at the arsenal, rising early and staying up late to attend to paperwork at home, waking in the middle of the night tormented by terrible dreams. She felt powerless to comfort him, watching anxiously as the war aged him before her eyes, pleading with him to take better care of himself, succeeding only rarely. She prayed for an end to the war, not only to bring the senseless slaughter to an end, but to spare her husband's life. She was terribly afraid that he might actually work himself to death if she did not fight like mad to prevent it.

But she had learned by now that confessing her worries to Arthur accomplished little. The only scheme that worked was to approach him with fond humor, gentle teasing, and loving requests. When the Thornshire Canaries had a match in Stratford or elsewhere around London, he would take a Sunday afternoon off to watch Helen play. In late summer and early autumn, she had occasionally been able to coax him into accompanying her on her morning walks through Hyde Park, but his interest had plummeted after an air raid on the last night of September, one of several that had struck harrowingly close to home. When they set out for their walk the following morning, they discovered that the Germans had dropped a bomb in the Serpentine, the curved lake that narrowed in the west to become the Long Water of Kensington Gardens. As they strode past, they had been stunned and sickened to see dozens if not hundreds of dead fish floating on the water, killed by the concussion. Arthur uttered a string of sharp, disparaging remarks about the Germans' utter disregard for life, but then he abruptly fell silent, and she had barely been able to pry another word from him for the rest of the walk.

On the few occasions they had visited the park after that, he had steered them away from the Serpentine, and for the past fortnight he had declined to go walking with her altogether. She wanted to blame his refusals on the increasingly cold and rainy autumn weather, and on his urgency to leave for the arsenal, but even when she offered to set out earlier and the weather wasn't all that bad, still he would not join her. In the absence of a more logical explanation, she concluded that the sight of the pale, bloated fish bobbing lifeless on the Serpentine, which they had both long admired for its serene beauty, had profoundly unsettled him, and every glance evoked a memory that made him shudder.

So, as October passed, since Helen could no longer enjoy her husband's company and conversation on her morning walks, she instead used the time to plan her day, and to plan, too, bits of encouraging news to share with him later that evening, anything that might ease the worry lines in his face, if only for a moment.

But with British casualty lists lengthening, the demand for munitions rising, and foodstuffs such as tea, sugar, butter, and bacon becoming scarcer by the day, it was often quite a stretch to grasp hold of anything that qualified as good news. Yet she could nearly always find something. The Thornshire Canaries were enjoying an excellent run and were one victory away from winning a spot in the Munitionettes' Cup tournament. The new TNT safety protocols seemed to be working; canary girls were still falling ill, but less seriously and in lower numbers than before. Soldiers and resources from the United States were steadily bolstering the Allies throughout France and Belgium, which must inevitably shift momentum in their favor. Surely they were closer to the end of the war than the beginning.

Yet there were days when all the news was sorrowful, and there was nothing Helen could do to remedy it.

One morning at the end of October, Helen arrived at the administration building to find Oliver waiting outside her office, his expression grim. "What is it?" she asked, heart sinking, as she led him into her office. "Just tell me, quickly. Get it over with."

"I'm afraid it's bad news," he said—stalling, despite her request. "One of our former employees died yesterday of TNT poisoning. The coroner confirmed it."

Helen closed her eyes and took a steadying breath. "Who?"

"Mabel Burridge."

"Oh no."

"I'm sure you're aware that she's been ill for months."

"Yes, but she always had such a strong will. I suppose I thought she would pull through somehow." Helen paused. "Are you sure? Are you absolutely sure it was Mabel?"

Oliver nodded. "Her daughter Peggy told me on her way in this morning."

"Peggy came to work?" said Helen, incredulous. "But she's entitled to bereavement leave."

"I told her. She knows. She doesn't want it."

Helen shook her head, words failing her. She did not know Mabel well, except as a respected adversary at the negotiating table, but she knew Peggy, and her heart ached for her teammate. "I'll talk to her later," she said. She thanked Oliver, and after he left, she shut the door, removed her coat and hat, and sank into her chair. Folding her arms on top of her desk, she closed her eyes and rested her head on them, tamping down her grief and hopelessness, searching for the proper words of comfort, something that didn't sound clichéd and empty from too much repetition throughout this wretched, terrible war.

When she spoke with Peggy later that afternoon, she was relieved to see that her teammate was bearing up well, all things considered, and that her friends were surrounding her with love and support.

Helen told her privately that Purcell Products would pay for her mother's burial expenses and provide a small life insurance payment to her dependents, two longstanding employee benefits that had predated the war. Peggy gratefully accepted, but when Helen again reminded her about bereavement leave, Peggy refused to take any more than two days for the service and burial. She needed the distraction of work and the wages, she explained, turning her head and clearing her throat, then breaking into a fit of hoarse coughing that sent Helen running to fetch her a cup of water. A harrowing thought came to her as Peggy accepted the cup and sipped between coughs—Would the daughter soon follow the mother into an early grave?

Peggy took Friday and Saturday off, as they had arranged. No one expected to see her at the match on Sunday, but she arrived halfway through their warm-up, her eyes puffy and tired but dry. Her teammates embraced her and offered their condolences, and she managed a smile at their surprise that she had felt up to what was expected to be a grueling match. "I couldn't let the side down, could I?" she said, eyeing the team on the other half of the pitch. "They look like they know what's what. You need me if we're going to make it into the tournament."

"And well we know it," said Lucy, and the other Canaries murmured agreement.

April had sewn black armbands for them all to wear, and as she handed one to Peggy, she said, "It's been decided. We're dedicating this match to your mum."

Peggy's eyes glistened with fresh tears as she slipped the black cloth around her upper arm. "I expect you all to play your best, then," she said, and everyone smiled or applauded or laughed through their tears, remembering Mabel.

It was a hard-fought match, one that left Helen with bruises and scrapes and a fresh blister on the ball of her right foot, but the Thornshire Canaries seized victory, 4–3, with a brilliant goal from Peggy on an assist from Lucy with three minutes left in the match. An impressive defensive effort, if she did say so herself, held off their rivals until the whistle blew.

How fitting it was, Helen thought as her teammates went mad with elation, cheering and embracing and tossing their caps into the air, to honor their club's founder by securing a place in the tournament for the first-ever Munitionettes' Cup.

And how grateful she was that Arthur had been there to witness it, and even now was on his feet in the stands, applauding and beaming. If only that light in his eyes would remain after they left the Globe, and if only his delight in their victory would keep his worries at bay long enough for him to get a proper good night's sleep, without his heavy responsibilities jolting him awake at all hours. But as thankful as she was for these brief respites, they were never enough to fully restore him.

Then, in late November, astonishing news from the Western Front relieved the sinking dread that had settled over Britain, like a fresh wind sweeping away storm clouds. On the morning of 20 November, more than one thousand Allied guns had launched an assault against German defenses and artillery positions, and as tanks had pushed forward, the infantry had begun an advance along a six-mile frontage. By nightfall, the British Army had advanced nearly four miles, taking four thousand German prisoners and capturing or destroying more than one hundred enemy guns.

At long last, the Third Army had broken through the Hindenburg Line.

When the news reached Britain a few days later, London church bells pealed in celebration for the first time since the outbreak of war. It was the most wonderful news Helen could recall in ages, perhaps since the United States had joined the war. Although the work of the arsenal continued and she could not spare a moment to join the crowds rejoicing in the streets, she relished the jolly music of the bells, too long silent, and as fatigued as she was, she could not keep from smiling.

Of course the merriment could not last; she had not expected it to, but neither had she expected their soaring hopes to come crashing down again so soon and so suddenly. On 5 December, Russia, now fully under the control of Lenin and his Bolsheviks, signed a cease-fire agreement with the Central Powers. The Russian foreign ministry had invited its counterparts in Britain, France, and Italy to join in the negotiations for a fuller peace, but the Allies were said to have rejected the overture with furious, stony silence. Ten days later, the Russians and Central Powers agreed to a thirty-day armistice, which would be automatically renewed unless one of the parties notified the other of its intention to resume hostilities. When the armistice went into effect on 17 December, Russia essentially withdrew from the war.

That same week, a cloud of despondency darkened the skies over London. The British advance on the Western Front, which they had celebrated so joyfully scarcely three weeks earlier, had become a retreat as the German counterattack forced their troops back so far that nearly all the ground they had gained was lost. Thousands of Tommies had been killed or wounded, and thousands more taken prisoner. Helen hardly knew what to make of dismaying assertions in the press that the Allies were in a worse position now than they had been at any time since the war began. And yet the British people were urged to steel their nerve and strengthen their morale, for Britain would never go the way of their erstwhile ally Russia, and the only way to reach the peace that awaited them at the end of the war was to go through it.

Helen understood the point of such encouragement, for if the choice was to proceed or to surrender, they really had no choice at all. And yet it was difficult to see how one was meant to take heart when an important ally had bowed out of the conflict, casualty lists relentlessly lengthened, pantries were growing bare, especially in the homes of the poor, and food was increasingly hard to find. Each week, an average of fourteen ships bringing food and raw materials to the British Isles were sunk by enemy submarines. Helen had become accustomed to the sight of long queues winding outside the doors of provision shops, the anxiety plain on the customers' faces as they waited to be served, wondering whether anything would be left by the time their turn came. Demands for compulsory rationing were increasing from all corners of government and commerce, but the Food Controller, Lord Rhondda, opposed such measures, insisting that rationing would be difficult to administer and the heaviest burden would fall upon the shoulders of the poor. In the meantime, he assured the press that food and drink remained plentiful, and all that could be desired for the festive season would be in the shops. Even so, citizens were encouraged to be "sparing" in their observances so the abundance would continue into the New Year.

Helen was skeptical of any government statement that included the words "sparing" and "abundance" in such close proximity, but she decided to call Lord Rhondda's bluff, if a bluff it was. If food rationing would be imposed at the end of the year, as others in the government hinted it would, she would take steps now to ensure that there would be plentiful, nourishing meals in the Thornshire canteens in the future—confirming agreements with their suppliers, stocking up on non-perishable items, reviewing kitchen procedures to reduce waste. Then— because she knew her munitionettes deserved it, and because she doubted the much-lauded plenty extended to most working-class homes, and simply because she could—she organized holiday feasts to be served at dinner and tea in the canteens for Christmas Eve and Christmas Day. On Boxing Day, each worker would take home a generous box of food and drink to share with their families. She didn't tell Arthur until after all the arrangements were made, the bills were paid, and it was too late to cancel, but fortunately, he agreed that it was an excellent way to thank their workers for a job well done in arduous circumstances.

"I'm glad you think so," said Helen, reaching for his hand across the dinner table, mealtimes being one of the few occasions when she had his undivided attention. "In addition to the feast, I've arranged for the arsenal's most overworked employee to go on holiday from Christmas Eve through New Year's Day."

His eyebrows rose. "A paid holiday?"

"Not quite. Special circumstances." She leaned forward and clasped her other hand around the one she already held. "Darling, the employee is you."

He frowned and heaved a sigh. "Helen——"

"Arthur." She held up a hand to forestall argument. "You need time off. It's all been arranged. Tom and Oliver have cleared your calendar, and they'll manage everything in your absence. And before you propose to work so they may go on holiday instead, they decided between themselves that Oliver shall take off Christmas Eve and Tom Christmas Day. They are as resolved as I am that you must take a holiday."

"Darling, if you think Christmas in Warwickshire with my family will be restful——"

"Goodness, no, not that. Oxford, darling. Our house in Oxford. The staff is preparing for our arrival even now. My mother and Daphne will pass the holidays with us there. Penelope, Margaret, and the children shall spend Christmas with Margaret's family and join us later in the week. We'll have a lovely, long-overdue reunion." She hesitated. "If you'd like, we could invite your father and siblings and their families to join us—"

"No, no," he broke in, shaking his head. "That won't be necessary. I'm sure they've already made their own plans by now." He clasped a hand to his brow, rubbed his eyes, and wearily added, "Let's keep this a Stahl family gathering, just to ensure peace of mind."

"Then we're agreed?" she asked, hardly daring to believe it. "You'll take a week off, and we'll spend the holidays in Oxford?"

"Agreed," he said, managing a wan smile. "I'm too exhausted to debate you, which I'm sure you'll interpret as conclusive evidence that I need a rest."

"I do indeed, but even so, I always win our debates in the end."

"Not always."

"Often enough."

He shrugged and nodded, conceding the point. Rising, still holding his hand, she drew closer and bent down to give him a fond, lingering kiss.

He would get all the rest he needed; she would see to it. They would celebrate the fourth Christmas of the war with as much joy and hope and gratitude as they could muster, and on New Year's Eve, they would bid farewell to an age of war and strife, and look forward to a year that might, and surely must, bring victory and peace.

19
December 1917–
February 1918

Lucy

It was the fourth Christmas of the war, and the first Lucy had ever spent without a single member of her family near. Her mother had begged her to join the Evanses in Brookfield, but the exigencies of the war would not allow Thornshire Arsenal to shut down even for the day. It broke Lucy's heart to tell her loved ones, especially Jamie and Simon, that she would not be among them to exchange gifts, sing carols, enjoy a delicious if smaller-than-usual feast of their favorite holiday dishes, and to break open Christmas crackers and don the paper hats and laugh at the silly riddles enclosed.

"But Edwin will be home on leave," her mother protested when it was her turn on the telephone.

"Yes, I know he will. He promised to see me in London on his way to Surrey."

"But did you know that Dieter Brandt has been released from Lofthouse Camp? He's back at the bakery, and even with sugar rationing, his breads and rolls are as delicious as ever."

Lucy had to laugh. "Do you really think I wouldn't come just to see the family, but I'd come for sweets?"

"You shouldn't be alone on Christmas," her mother chided. "Not when I know you worry night and day for your Daniel. Not when you have a loving family an easy train journey away."

"I won't be alone," Lucy assured her, struggling to keep her voice from breaking. Yes, she ached for Daniel—and the thought of returning to their childhood village, where every street and meadow and woodland reminded her of him, of all they had shared, of all she might have lost, pained her beyond reckoning. "I'll be at work, but surrounded by friends."

"That's not a proper Christmas, filling shells at an arsenal."

"No, it isn't, but it's wartime, and we all have to make the best of things."

"I wish you'd resign from that dreadful place,"

her mother said, impassioned. "That horrible yellow powder has stolen your beauty and God forbid it should take your life too. The stories I hear about explosions—"

"Mother, please. Jamie and Simon—"

"Are outside playing in the snow with their cousins. Do you really think I would speak so freely if they could overhear?"

"No, of course you wouldn't." Lucy pressed her lips together and squeezed her eyes shut against tears. "Keep their spirits up, won't you? Don't let them worry too much about their father. Remind them that at least now he's out of the trenches, away from the fighting."

"I'll do my best, dear, but they're clever boys and they know what a prison camp is." Her mother sighed. "I can't bear the thought of you coming home from work to an empty house on Christmas. Why don't I bring the boys up to London on Boxing Day? We'll see you in the evenings, and we'll have all Sunday together, and I can take them back to Brookfield on Monday."

For a moment Lucy hesitated, overwhelmed by longing. But then she reminded herself that the danger was too great, that her loneliness was far less important than their safety. She had sent her children out of London to escape the air raids, but after Mabel died, she had found another reason for them to stay away—not from the city, but from herself, and she prayed she had not acted too late. What terrible contamination might she have inadvertently brought home to her mother and sons throughout the long months she had worked in the Danger Building? She always scrubbed herself thoroughly in the washhouse after removing her soiled uniform at the end of a shift, and she changed back into her own clean clothing afterward, but that vile powder got everywhere and she might have missed some. Or what if she had breathed infinitesimal grains into her lungs, only to exhale them at home, where her mother and sons might have taken them in? The thought that she might have unwittingly poisoned the people she loved best in all the world terrified her—which was why the boys could not come home, nor could she go to them, not as long as she worked at the arsenal. And she had to keep working at the arsenal or they would lose their home, and how could she bear the shame if Daniel returned—*when* Daniel returned—to find that she had failed him in this one essential duty? He must have a home to return to, *this* home, with the cozy study where he worked on blueprints at the architect's desk his father had made for him, where his Olympic gold medals were displayed in two glass cases. She would prepare his favorite meals in the kitchen and he would kick the football around with the boys in the garden, and everything would again be as it once was—happy, peaceful, perfect.

If not, what had all their sacrifices been for?

Although the Winter Solstice had passed, the days were still short and the nights cold and long, so Lucy left for the arsenal before sunrise and returned home after nightfall. Her only glimpse of thin winter sunshine came during her breaks, when she and the other Canaries ate swiftly and hurried out to their frozen practice field for a kickaround, and on Sundays, her only day off. On the rare occasions when she went marketing, she found reassuring pleasure in the unexpectedly ample, enticing displays in storefront windows, an abundance she had not seen since before the war. Nor had proprietors neglected the familiar festive touches of the season. Shops were adorned with holly; poulterers decorated their geese and turkeys with cheerful red ribbons, as did butchers with their cuts of beef and mutton. Lucy's mouth watered at the charming arrangements of apples, oranges, and nuts at the fruiterer's, and although she was not a drinker, she marveled at the profusion of wine, whiskey, and brandy at the grocer's. Everything was very dear, of course, but it seemed that everyone had money to spend, thanks to steady government wages for war work, and the increased allowances paid to soldiers' wives and other dependents. Her own allowance had increased, not quite enough for her to resign from the arsenal, but enough to tempt her, just as the marvelous shop displays tempted her to splurge. Yet she resisted, since she had only herself to feed at home, and because the Food Ministry urged prudence during the festive season. With rumors circulating that food rationing would soon be imposed, Lucy worried that the abundance in the shops was an illusion, holiday feasting before midwinter famine.

At least no one went hungry at Thornshire Arsenal. From Christmas Eve through Boxing Day, the canteens served splendid meals—Irish gammon, cabbage and potatoes, roast goose, plum pudding, among other tantalizing dishes—for dinner as well as tea. A jolly mood prevailed elsewhere too, as munitionettes sang carols while they worked, and friends exchanged small gifts in the shifting house at the end of the day. Lucy had knit soft, warm scarves for her fellow Thornshire Canaries in their team colors, yellow and black, and her friends declared themselves absolutely delighted with them.

At dinner on 26 December, Daisy entertained the Canaries with a secondhand report of a football match that had taken place on Christmas Day at Deepdale Stadium, home ground of the Preston North End. Daisy's cousins had joined more than ten thousand other spectators for a spectacular match between the Dick, Kerr Ladies of Preston and their crosstown rivals, the Coulthards Ladies of the Arundel Coulthard Foundry.

"Ten thousand spectators?" said Marjorie, skeptical.

"Ten thousand and then some," said Daisy. "They raised more than six hundred pounds for the local auxiliary war hospital."

A gasp of astonishment went up from the group. Even Marjorie looked impressed.

"Dick, Kerr commanded the pitch from the first whistle," Daisy continued as her teammates inched their chairs closer, enthralled by her descriptions of astonishing goals, brilliant passing, and wildly cheering fans. In the end, Dick, Kerr had triumphed, 4–0, but the lopsided score misrepresented how exciting the game had been thanks to the masterful skill and intriguing personalities of several of the Dick, Kerr players.

"Their center forward is a gorgeous blonde named Florrie Redford," said Daisy. "They're always putting her photo in the papers."

"I was a gorgeous blonde once," said Marjorie mournfully, tugging at a brittle, gingery curl.

"And will be again," April reassured her. "After the war. Give it time."

"My cousins say their inside left player, Jennie

Harris, is an expert dribbler and very quick on her feet," said Daisy.

"She's no match for our Peggy, I'm sure," said Marjorie, "and our Helen can outrun anyone."

"I don't think you're hearing me," said Daisy, with a warning shake of her head. "My cousins said they've never seen a girls' team like Dick, Kerr before. After the most stubborn critics in England watch them play, they never again argue that girls can't or shouldn't play football."

"Doesn't every team in the Munitionettes' League prove that girls can play football?" asked Lucy indignantly, evoking emphatic nods from her friends.

"Agreed, but the Dick, Kerr Ladies go above and beyond," said Daisy. "Their outside left, Lily Parr, is only fifteen years old, and they say she has a kick like a Division One back."

"Fifteen years old?" echoed Marjorie, incredulous. "Is she even allowed to work in munitions? What do they make at Dick, Kerr, anyway? Tea biscuits?"

That earned her a laugh, but Daisy shook her head. "Munitions, same as us. They used to make locomotives and tramcars, but they converted at the start of the war."

"Do you suppose we'll face the Dick, Kerr Ladies when we play for the Munitionettes' Cup?" asked Lucy.

"Not if the Blyth Spartans knock them out of the running first," said Peggy. Everyone nodded soberly, remembering their own humbling 6–1 defeat all too well. "We'll surely face one of those teams eventually—or both of them, if we make it far enough."

"I don't know about the rest of you," said Marjorie, stretching her arms overhead as if warming up for the goal, "but I intend to make it to the finals."

They all sat for a moment, pondering Daisy's report, and then they quickly rose and cleared away their trays and dishes. Minutes later, they were out on the frozen field, heedless of the cold and the snowflakes drifting lazily on the wind all around them, running and dribbling and taking shots on their makeshift goal. The first round of the tournament wouldn't come until late February, but they must keep their skills sharp. The Dick, Kerr Ladies and the Blyth Spartans surely weren't neglecting their training.

Thus Christmas passed, the loneliest Lucy had ever known, and the New Year began, bleak and bitter cold. In the shops and markets, the abundance of the festive season proved as fleeting as she had feared. After years of asking the British people to practice voluntary rationing, the government had finally imposed official restrictions, but only on sugar. Every household was issued a ration card and was required to register at a local grocer, where they could purchase their allotted share and not an ounce more. Some of Lucy's friends praised the measure, because at last they would be assured of getting their portion regardless of where they found themselves in the queue, while others speculated that this was surely a sign of additional, harsher rationing yet to come. Lucy thought that more rationing might actually be desirable, in service to the common good, especially if it included price fixing. Without government intervention, shopkeepers could charge whatever they liked for scarce products, so the rich paid extra to obtain whatever they wanted while the poor did without. Just as some of Lucy's munitionette friends had never eaten so well until they were provided nourishing meals in the arsenal canteen, some less fortunate Londoners had been unable to afford sugar until rationing put everyone on an equal footing. Even the King and Queen had ration cards, which made it very awkward for anyone else to grouse about the scheme.

In the meantime, meat and poultry were increasingly difficult to find—which made her wonder what necessity she now took for granted would be the next to become unexpectedly rare and precious. Not tea, she fervently hoped. She could hardly drag herself out of bed some mornings without the promise of a reviving cup of tea at breakfast.

She wondered what Daniel was provided to drink in his German prison—tea, ersatz coffee, filthy water—but as soon as the thought came to her she shoved it away, before her breath caught in her throat and tears filled her eyes and she collapsed in grief. She could not bear to think of what he might be suffering. Sometimes it was all she could think about.

If only she had some news of him—another report from the War Office, a letter via the Red Cross, anything to assure her that Daniel lived, and might yet come home to her.

January dragged on, as cheerless as the holidays had been hopeful. Lucy felt weary to her bones, plagued by coughs and headaches, dread and grief. She longed for her children and her husband and springtime and rest. London was rife with rumors that the Germans, determined to terrorize the British and break their will, were preparing their most massive bombardment yet, fleets of dozens of their largest aeroplanes armed with their most destructive bombs. Lucy did not know where the rumors had started or how credible they might be, only that the threat of an impending raid seemed to be in everyone's thoughts. As the nights of the full moon approached, dread infused every conversation. Even in the daytime, traveling between home and work or training on the arsenal field, Lucy found herself adopting the common habit of glancing up at the sky or pausing in mid-conversation to strain her ears for the distant drone of German aircraft.

At the end of her shift on the last Monday of January, Lucy stayed a few minutes late at her station to finish up one last shell before racing to the shifting house to wash and change clothes. She quickly slipped into her coat and tugged on a warm knit cap and scarf and mittens, but she and one other girl from the Filling Shop were still the last to leave. Together they stepped out into a clear, frigid, moonlit night, their breath ghosting white on the air as they hurried to Gate Four, commiserating over their belated departures, which might oblige them to wait for later trains. Then, with exasperatingly poor timing, one of the sentries selected Lucy for a random questioning. If she were a man, it would have been a pat-down search, but a less invasive delay was still a delay.

"Bad luck, Lucy," her friend called from the other side of the gate. "Do you want me to wait?"

"No, go on ahead," she called back. "No sense in both of us missing our trains."

"Sorry, miss," the sentry said gruffly, looking her up and down as if she might have a shell poking out of her pocket.

"Not at all," she said briskly, rubbing her mittened hands together for warmth. "You're just doing your job."

A long moment later, he waved her on through the gate. She hurried through the arsenal park as quickly as she dared, mindful of the dark patches of ice on the gravel paths, but her friend had disappeared into the blackout. Fortunately, she did not have to wait long for the next tram, and it was only half full so she easily found a seat, but by the time she reached Barking station, her usual train had already departed. She had to wait another thirty minutes for the next one, pacing for warmth, ignoring the gnawing hunger in her stomach and the double takes of passersby who had apparently never seen a canary girl before, a rather odd thing in a neighborhood so close to an arsenal. She ignored too the raised eyebrows and furrowed brows of fellow would-be passengers whenever she covered her mouth and bent over in a hoarse, prolonged bout of coughing. Her next rotation out of the Danger Building was only days away, but it could not come too soon. She dared to hope that after the war, her symptoms would vanish and her skin and hair would regain their former loveliness, though she knew not everyone fully recovered.

Suddenly a memory came to her, something she had all but forgotten—her interview at Thornshire Arsenal, when Superintendent Carmichael had remarked that she would have hired Lucy to work in her own office, if only she'd had a vacant post. Would it be worthwhile to reintroduce herself to the superintendent and ask if anything had become available since then? She could afford a small pay cut, especially with the boys away in Surrey. At one time Lucy would have been ashamed to abandon Danger Building work to other, braver girls, but with the onset of winter, she had felt herself sinking, and she was not sure how much more exposure to the yellow powder she could endure. Even walking to the train station from the arsenal winded her, and football training had become a struggle. The winter pause in the Munitionettes' League had come just in time. She could only hope that after rotating out, she would recover her strength in time for the tournament.

She caught herself and laughed aloud, incredulous. She was worried about football, when her very life could be at stake.

It was nearly eight o'clock by the time she boarded her train, famished, exhausted, her toes numb with cold that had crept up from the pavement through the soles of her boots. A kind older gentleman gave her his seat, and she sank into it gratefully, murmuring thanks. Muffling a yawn, she settled in for a long ride, hoping that the rocking of the train wouldn't lull her to sleep and cause her to miss her stop at Victoria station, where she changed trains for Clapham.

She closed her eyes, just for a moment, but they flew open again when she imagined she heard the shrill blast of a policeman's whistle. But it was only the brakes squealing as the train pulled into an underground station. As they slowed and halted at the platform, Lucy took in the dismaying sight of hundreds of people packing the chamber—elderly couples, women with infants in their arms, children—huddled against the walls or sitting on the stairs, most of them wrapped in blankets over their coats. A few policemen and special constables milled about in the limited space between them, keeping order, offering assistance. A distant, dull, barely audible roar confirmed what she had already guessed: The air raid Londoners had dreaded for a week had finally come. And yet she observed no trace of fear on the faces of the sheltering people, just a weary, matter-of-fact acceptance, while many of the children slept peacefully in their parents' arms or on their laps. As her train started up again and the faces dissolved into a blur of motion, she was riveted by how dissimilar the scene was to the terror and fear she observed—and had herself felt—during air raids when she had been caught aboveground, or had sheltered in a simple basement or cellar. No doubt these people considered themselves as safe as one could be under assault in wartime, so far beneath the surface. She hoped they were not mistaken.

As she rode on, the awareness that the city was under attack kept her awake and alert. At every station, in the interval between halting and proceeding, she observed different crowds, but the same weary resignation, even boredom. Very rarely she glimpsed smiles and conversation and laughter, and she marveled at them. No one there or anywhere in Britain, not even the most prescient scholar of international politics and warfare, could have imagined four years ago that they would find themselves where they were now. Had they really become so accustomed to the unimaginable? But what choice did they have? It was keep a stiff upper lip or go mad, carry on or surrender.

At last her train reached Victoria station. She disembarked swiftly, but struggled to make her way through the crowds to the platform where her connection would depart. Finally, after some increasingly frantic weaving and dodging, she made it to the platform and boarded with seconds to spare.

Victoria to Clapham Junction was the shortest leg of her commute, and it was heartening to know that she was nearly home, but she could hear the bombs better now, and a frisson of dread passed through her. She realized, too late, that it might have been safer to wait out the raid at Victoria and continue on after the all-clear had sounded. Instead, when she disembarked at her stop, she found what seemed to be a secure corner between two solid walls and waited for the terrible pounding to cease, knowing that she had as much to fear from British shrapnel falling back to earth as from the German bombs. She was not alone; dozens of other travelers waited for the bombing to cease, apprehension and fatigue as plain on their faces as undoubtedly they were on her own.

At last, not long after eleven o'clock, the cannonade fell silent. Lucy was eager to get home and go to bed, but she lingered in the station with the other passengers, awaiting the all-clear, the official signal from military authorities that the raiders had departed British skies. But the minutes passed, and midnight approached, and still the all-clear had not been sounded. The passengers conferred quietly, impatiently, all of them still listening keenly for the signal that it was safe to step out onto the streets. Had the officials forgotten? Had the ground spotters lost sight of the aircraft and had no idea where they were? Or worse yet, was another wave of enemy aeroplanes already on the way, determined to unleash another barrage upon the unsuspecting citizens, who assumed the danger had passed?

Eventually the crowd began to disperse, as passengers

decided the risk was worth taking and left the station. A few others settled down on benches or on the floor to doze while they awaited the all-clear. Lucy, light-headed from hunger and illness and fatigue, tallied up the hours until she would have to hurry off to the arsenal again. If she did not get to bed soon, she would be in no condition to work the next day, and might be a danger to herself and others.

"Best not go out quite yet, miss," a police officer warned as she approached the exit. "I could find you a blanket and keep watch over you and the other ladies. Get a bit of sleep while you're waiting."

She thanked him, but she had made up her mind. It was not far to go, and she could run if she had to.

The darkened streets were deserted as she strode briskly toward home, her pace quickening as she thought of her own front door, the cold supper she had prepared that morning, her warm, comfortable bed. She had reached the corner of her block when she heard a distant explosion. Heart in her throat, she tucked her bag tightly under her arm and ran the rest of the way, sprinting up her front walk, fumbling with the key in the lock, racing inside, shutting the door firmly behind her, dropping her things, snatching up her dinner on the way as she fled through the kitchen into the cellar.

All the while, the roar of bombs and the incessant thud of guns grew louder and louder.

Alone in the dim cellar, she choked down her dinner, then lay down and tried to make herself comfortable on the pallet of blankets she had left for this purpose. Eventually she dozed off, shivering and alone in the dark, even as the house trembled around her.

She woke at half one o'clock to the all-clear.

It was madness, she thought as she climbed wearily upstairs and, after a cursory wash and brushing of teeth, collapsed into her own bed. She ought to evacuate to Brookfield and wait out the rest of the war with her children and family. She had done her bit. The arsenal would carry on without her just fine, as would the Thornshire Canaries. As for her lost wages, Daniel would forgive her if she lost the house. He would be less able to bear the loss of his wife and his children's mother.

In the morning, she rose at her usual hour, still exhausted, drank a cup of hot tea and hastily ate a thick slice of toast, all without sparing time to sit. Then she raced off to the arsenal, dozing on the train, learning from overheard conversation that forty-seven people had been killed in the previous night's raid, and 169 others had been injured. Many of these were women and children who had taken refuge in a printer's works in Long Acre, near Bow Street.

"Tragic indeed," a gentleman remarked to his companion, "but if one considers the millions of homes and businesses in London, the odds of any one particular building being struck by a bomb are actually quite small. We can all take comfort from that fact."

Perhaps he could, but Lucy couldn't.

A week later, Lucy had just arrived at the training field when Helen greeted her with a halfhearted smile. "Congratulations, Lucy," she said sincerely, shifting the football she carried to her left arm so she could shake Lucy's hand. "I'm happy for you. A bit forlorn for myself, I confess, but happy for women like you. My turn will come."

"I'm sorry, but I have no idea what you're talking about," said Lucy, bewildered. "Why am I to be congratulated?"

"The vote, of course," said Helen. "The Fourth Reform Act passed. Women over thirty who are householders or who are married to a man who owns property are allowed to vote in Parliamentary elections now."

Lucy shook her head, astonished. "I hadn't heard. I follow news of the war and little else these days. I thought election reform wouldn't be enacted until peacetime." Then she paused. "Daniel doesn't own our home outright. We have a mortgage. Does that matter?"

"An excellent question." Helen dropped the ball and passed it to Lucy. "I honestly don't know. I suppose you'll find out when you try to register at the polls. As for me, I have to wait another two and a half years to vote for my MP. It's ludicrous. How will I be more capable then than I am now?"

"Didn't you know?" teased Lucy, passing the ball back to her. "Wisdom descends from above the moment a woman turns thirty."

"Really? Well, I look forward to it." Helen attempted a bit of fancy dribbling, gave up, and passed the ball to Lucy. "At least I can vote in local elections now, since I'm over twenty-one."

"My mother owns property," Lucy mused aloud, juggling the ball back and forth from one knee to the other before lofting it higher and heading it over to Helen. "My father left her the building with our family home and his medical practice when he passed. She'll be tickled to hear she can vote now."

"Property restrictions have been abolished altogether for men," Helen said, frowning thoughtfully. "Virtually all men over twenty-one can vote. If you ask me, that's so they can maintain a male majority in the electorate. After the war, we suffragettes will have a thing or two to say about that."

Lucy nodded, deferring to Helen's expertise on the subject. What would happen to Great Britain, she wondered, if one day women voters outnumbered men? Would there be more justice, equality, and peace? She hoped so. But would the nation never again go to war? Unlikely, she reckoned. Englishwomen would honor their promises to their allies as faithfully as Englishmen did, and they would be equally determined to defend their island from attack. As for starting an unprovoked war, it was unfathomable to her that women would go along with that sort of idiotic brutality, not with the grief and loss of this war haunting their memories.

A fortnight later—a blessedly cloudy night with only a sliver of a moon—Lucy returned home from the arsenal to find a letter from the War Office waiting for her in the post. She had a moment of stricken terror before she remembered that announcements of soldiers' deaths came by telegram, not by letter. Even so, her heart thudded as, still standing in her coat and hat in the foyer, she opened the envelope and withdrew two typed pages. She had barely finished the first lines before her legs became too weak to hold her, and she sank to the floor, breathless, eyes fixed upon the stunning pages.

Daniel had been located. He was alive.

A sob escaped her throat as she read on. Daniel had been wounded before his capture by the Germans—this, she already knew—and although his injuries were very serious, he was being attended to in a prison hospital and was expected to survive. The Red Cross had taken a particular interest in his case after reports appeared in German newspapers of the capture of a renowned footballer and Olympic champion. Such triumphant boasting in the press about a particular prisoner of war treaded close to violating the Geneva Convention of 1864, which established the right to the impartial treatment of combatants. There was no evidence, as yet, that the Germans intended to parade Corporal Dempsey in public as a trophy, but to forestall any such disgraceful and inhumane treatment, the British government was determined to secure his release as soon as possible.

An organization known as the Swiss Medical Mission had brokered an agreement at The Hague between Great Britain and Germany for the exchange of disabled prisoners of war. First, medical officers at internment camps on both sides identified eligible prisoners on the grounds that they were unfit ever again to become combatants. The selected prisoners, an equal number of Britons and Germans, would then be transported to an observation camp, where they would be examined by physicians with the Swiss Medical Mission. According to the nature of a prisoner's physical disability, he would either be sent home or to neutral Switzerland, for internment in surroundings more conducive to healing and rehabilitation until the war's end.

At the time of the letter's writing, Corporal Dempsey had already passed the selection and was en route to an observation camp. Whether he would be sent on to England or to Switzerland had not yet been determined, but his family must rest assured that he would not be returned to the German prison camp.

More details would be forthcoming.

Lucy clutched the letter to her chest, tears streaming down her yellowed cheeks. Daniel lived. He would soon be out of German hands. He might be coming home to her soon, but if not that, she could take great comfort in knowing that he would be safe in Switzerland for the duration, and their family would be reunited after the war.

It was only later, after she had telephoned her mother and Daniel's father with the wonderful news, after she had eaten supper and washed her face and felt much restored, that a nagging worry buried beneath the good news came to the forefront of her thoughts.

She read the letter again.

As certain phrases leapt off the page, her hands trembled until the page shook so much she could scarcely read it. But the implicit warning was clear, as were all the terrible questions it prompted.

Only prisoners unfit ever again to become combatants.

The nature of a prisoner's physical disability.

What did these ominous words mean for Daniel? What had happened to him?

20
February–March 1918

April

The Thornshire Canaries rejoiced in Lucy's happy news, but they declared that even if Daniel returned home within a fortnight, which they all hoped he would, Lucy couldn't resign from the arsenal until after the Munitionettes' Cup. "You can't expect us to carry on without our star center forward," Marjorie teased, smiling.

"I wouldn't dream of it," said Lucy, her face alight with happiness and hope as April had never seen her before.

April had no doubt that Marjorie was entirely sincere in her joy for Lucy, but later, when Marjorie and April were alone, Marjorie confessed that she wished the Swiss Medical Mission could do as much for her brother Archie, who was still missing and unaccounted for.

The most obvious reason for Archie's prolonged absence and silence was too heartbreaking for April to admit aloud. "Maybe the Swiss can't help Archie because the Germans never captured him," she said instead. It was the first hopeful explanation that came to mind. "Maybe he's working with the resistance in occupied France or Belgium. Or maybe he *is* a prisoner, but he's in such fine health that he doesn't qualify for the disabled prisoner exchange."

"Yes, I suppose that could be so," said Marjorie, managing a wan smile.

The Canaries' shared delight in Lucy's relief and happiness must have invigorated them, for in the first round of the tournament, they soundly defeated the Associated Equipment Company Ladies at the AEC home ground in Beckton, 4–1, the same margin by which the Ladies had beaten them in their first meeting, when the Canaries were barely fledglings.

A few days later, April came down to breakfast to find the hostel dining room buzzing with anxious conversation. "Did you hear about the munitionettes in Leeds?" Marjorie greeted her when April joined her and two friends, Ethel and Rose, at their table.

April's stomach gave a lurch. "Another accident?"

"No, not that." Frowning, Marjorie leaned forward, resting her arms on the table around her bowl of porridge. "A few days ago, more than one thousand girls were sacked from a munitions factory. No notice, no nothing, just fare thee well, ladies, goodbye."

"One thousand workers?" exclaimed April. "But why? Has the war ended and they forgot to tell us?"

"The war's not over, more's the pity," said Ethel, "but munitions orders are down all over, what with the Russians pulling out. I never realized how many shells and such we British girls made for them until they stopped wanting 'em."

"Then the munitionettes weren't sacked so that lads who've come home from the war could take over?" asked April.

Marjorie shook her head. "Not from the sound of it. The jobs are just . . . gone."

"Goodness." April sat back in her chair. "What's going to become of those girls? Will they get benefits, at least?"

"They're asking for benefits," said Rose, brooding over her teacup. "Whether they'll get them is an open question."

"Most of these girls worked in textiles before the war," said Marjorie. "A secretary from one of their trade unions told the press that most of them don't want to go back to the clothing trade or the mills, not after enjoying such good wages on munitions work."

"And the ones who are willing to go back can't find jobs," said Rose. "What does this mean for us, I wonder?"

"It means you'd better make sure your work is up to scratch," said Marjorie flatly. "The lazy girls and troublemakers will be the first to go. Smile politely at the foremen and the superintendents, and make sure the boss thinks well of you."

"Easy for you to say," said Ethel, eyeing Marjorie and April enviously. "You play football with the boss's wife. You'll be the last to go."

"I don't intend to go at all," Marjorie retorted, finishing up the last of her porridge. "I'll be at Thornshire until the last shell rolls off the line. Whatever happens to the arsenal after that, I'll hang on as long as I can."

Unsettled, April took her spoon in hand and made herself swallow a few bites of porridge, but her appetite had fled. She wanted the war to end and peace to come, and she certainly wouldn't miss that awful yellow powder, but what would become of her and her friends after the men returned home and the factories reverted to their former purposes? April desperately did not want to return to domestic service, not after knowing better hours, higher wages, greater freedom, and far more respect as a munitionette. As much as she missed the beauty of Derbyshire, the thought of returning contrite and humble to beg Mrs. Wilson for her old job back made her clench her teeth in consternation. Returning to Alderlea wasn't even an option for Marjorie, not after she had fled in the night without giving proper notice, unfairly disgraced by that awful soldier's lies.

Suddenly April realized that she and Marjorie might never work together again. And what about the Thornshire Canaries? How could they have an arsenal football club without an arsenal to sponsor them, or a Munitionettes' League without munitionettes?

The following Sunday, the Canaries played the Handley Page Girls at Cricklewood, claiming a 5–2 victory that advanced them to the third round of the tournament. Afterward, players from both teams mingled as they exited the grounds, and conversation soon turned to the layoffs in Leeds and the rumors that more were pending, not only in the North but throughout Britain. They all adamantly agreed on two points: None of them wanted the war to last a single day longer than necessary, but they had to consider what victory would mean for their own livelihoods. The Handley Page Girls were guardedly optimistic that aircraft manufacturing would continue into peacetime, and even grow, as fascination with flight increased. They were less confident that women would be allowed to do the work, because foremen and bosses would surely prefer to hire returning veterans. "But who among us would begrudge a brave Tommy a job, after all they've been through?" the Handley Page Girls' captain asked, and every one of them chimed in agreement, April as loudly as anyone. This was her own elder brother they were talking about, and lads like Oliver. Of course they should have priority, after all they had done for King and Country.

But the munitionettes had sacrificed also, some with their very lives. Was it too much to hope that in peacetime there would be work and decent wages enough for everyone who wanted them?

In the meantime, it seemed to April that it was much too early to sack munitions workers and plan for peacetime employment, for the war raged on as intensely as ever. Air raids continued, devastating homes of innocent civilians as well as public roads and buildings. Food rationing expanded in London and the Home Counties to include butcher's meat, bacon, butter, and margarine as well as sugar.

Then, after months of negotiations, in early March the Bolsheviks formally established a separate peace with the Central Powers. All of Russia's former commitments to the Allies were now officially defunct, and since the Germans no longer had to battle the Russians in the east, they could concentrate all their forces on the Western Front. Although the Russians were no longer purchasing British munitions, April reckoned that the British military would need every shell and bullet and bomb their canary girls could possibly produce, now and for many months to come.

As the weeks passed, April's suspicions seemed spot on. On 21 March, the Germans launched a massive new offensive that the press declared would be "the greatest and most critical battle of the War," a phrase that struck April as both ominous and hopeful. The Germans apparently had concluded that their only chance of victory was to crush the Allies before the United States was fully able to bring its impressive resources to bear on the battlefield. Now Germany seemed intent on one last, desperate effort to break the British line, driving a wedge between the British and French armies and capturing Amiens, the crucial junction for both Paris and the English Channel.

By all accounts, the fighting was fierce and terrible. The official reports from the War Office to the press were deliberately vague and abrupt, stating only that the enemy was advancing and the Allies retreating. By the end of March, official reports from Germany quoted in the British press claimed that the Germans had taken forty-five thousand prisoners and had captured nearly one thousand guns. But April and the other Thornshire munitionettes could estimate the massive size of the battle by a source not available to the general public—by the surge in production that swiftly followed the launch of the German offensive. Shifts were extended, new workers recruited. The foremen urged them to work ever faster, to surpass their quotas and increase their efficiency, but without sacrificing quality or jeopardizing safety. Often April felt too exhausted to train for football, even knowing that the Munitionettes' Cup was at stake. After two more back-to-back victories, she realized that munitionettes from other factories must have been working at the same relentless pace as at Thornshire, because on the pitch their opponents seemed as fatigued as they were.

"At least the surge keeps us evenly matched," April remarked tiredly to Marjorie as they dragged themselves back to the hostel one Sunday after they had barely eked out a 1–0 win against the Hackney Marshes Ladies.

"There's enough hard work to go around," Marjorie agreed, muffling a yawn with her hand. "Think of it this way. The Ministry of Munitions desperately needs our shells. That means Thornshire Arsenal still needs us. They wouldn't dare sack any of us canary girls now."

Maybe not now, April thought, maybe not today, but maybe only as long as this so-called Kaiser's Battle lasted. At best, the current surge in production likely offered munitionettes only a temporary reprieve, one she would just as soon have over and done, if it meant victory for the Allies.

But even she was caught by surprise at how swiftly the reprieve for women workers ended. She had expected it to endure well into spring, judging by the relentless pace at Thornshire, but in the last few days of March, word came that the Kynoch munitions factory at Stanford-le-Hope in Essex had dismissed eight hundred munitionettes. By the first week of April, hundreds of these displaced workers had made their way to Thornshire, clutching their Labour Exchange papers as they queued up for interviews outside the square, oversized low shed that served as Superintendent Carmichael's headquarters.

"We're taking on as many as we can," Helen confided to the team after a particularly messy football training, spring rains and thawed soil having rendered the arsenal field a sodden, muddy morass. "With any luck, the others will find work at other factories, although they may have to venture farther from home."

As they returned to work, Marjorie lowered her voice for April's ears alone. "That's promising," she remarked. "If Purcell is hiring new workers, he can't be planning to sack the experienced workers like us."

"I suppose not," said April, "unless the plan is to squeeze all the work out of the whole lot of us while they need us, and then cut us loose, all at once, when they're through."

Marjorie heaved a sigh. "You probably have it spot on, of all the rotten luck."

April gave her a sharp sidelong look. "Not that you want the war to drag on another year or two."

"Of course not. Not even another month. You should know better than that."

April did know better, really. They were all under tremendous strain—long hours, arduous shifts, chronic illness, sleep interrupted by air raids, worries for their brave soldiers on the Western Front, and now, fear for their livelihoods. April wanted to take heart, as Marjorie had, from the new hires, but her hopes diminished when she overheard the Finishing Shop foreman, Mr. Vernon, boast to one of his mechanics that the National Federation of Discharged and Demobilised Sailors and Soldiers had sent a deputation to the Ministry of Munitions to protest the veterans' unfair treatment in the munitions factories. It was the worst sort of injustice, Mr. Vernon said, while his mechanic nodded vigorously, that throughout Britain, brave men who had fought and had been wounded were being sacked and their places filled by women and girls. "The Ministry of Munitions will put things right, mark my words," Mr. Vernon declared, but then he noticed April listening and clamped his mouth shut in a scowl, glowering.

She hurried on her way, too astonished to challenge the foreman, not that she would have dared even if she had found the words. Did this so-called unfair treatment of men even exist? Where exactly were able-bodied veterans being sacked and replaced by less experienced, lower-paid girls? Certainly not at Thornshire. From everything she had seen, and everything she had heard from munitionettes at other factories, precisely the opposite was true. Women were being sacked by the hundreds, and if men were not hired to replace them, that was only because the jobs had been made redundant. Everywhere, returning soldiers were demanding their old jobs back, submitting petitions to factory managers and politicians and other prominent figures in a position to help them—but no one, aside from the occasional solitary advocate like Helen, was championing the munitionettes. The labor unions, which barely tolerated women doing "men's work" and had fought aggressively against women's advancement throughout the war, had quite unsurprisingly taken up the soldiers' cause.

To April it seemed that a losing battle loomed on the horizon, and they had not yet finished fighting the war.

"It's not fair," April lamented to Oliver one Saturday evening after work as they walked hand in hand to a favorite café. "I know we weren't in the trenches, but we too have served."

"You're the girls behind the man behind the gun," Oliver remarked, squeezing her hand. When she shot him an accusing look, thinking he was teasing her, he quickly added, "I mean that sincerely. We've been lucky at Thornshire. We've had many illnesses from TNT poisoning but only three deaths, and no explosions. There's a factory in Chilwell, in Nottinghamshire, that has already had seventeen."

"Deaths?"

"Explosions. Three deaths, and it could have been much worse." Oliver shook his head. "If you ask me, any worker, woman or man, who is injured, sickened, or killed on the munitions front should be counted among war casualties."

"The munitions front," April echoed thoughtfully. "Yes, that's what it is, isn't it? We girls *have* served. We *are* serving. We answered our country's call and enlisted in war work. Yet after serving King and Country so faithfully throughout this crisis, we girls are almost certainly going to be discarded and forced back into our old jobs—jobs we left for good reason, most of us—unless we prefer idleness and poverty. I'll say it again—it just isn't fair."

Oliver halted, bringing her to a stop too. "What *is* fair, then?" he asked, regarding her curiously. "A soldier goes through hell, somehow survives, mostly intact, then comes home and wants his old job back, wants his old *life* back. Are you going to tell him to shove off?"

"Of course not," said April, feeling heat rising in her cheeks. "Especially not if it was his job first. It's only that—" She drew in a breath and exhaled sharply, angrily. "It'll be a massive relief to be away from TNT, I'll give you that, but I don't want to go back to domestic service. I don't ever want to be a housemaid again, but if I get sacked, what else is there for me?"

She folded her arms and strode off before he saw the tears of frustration gathering in her eyes.

"April." Oliver quickly caught up to her and put his hand on her shoulder. She halted, but she would not look up at him. "You don't have to go back into service. No one can force you."

She snapped out a laugh. "You only say that because you've never met my mother."

A corner of his mouth turned up. "If she's half as formidable as you—"

"Not half. Twice."

"Then I'll be sure to watch my step," he said solemnly, but she heard the amusement in his voice. He turned her toward him and stooped a bit so she could not avoid meeting his gaze, unless she wanted to stand there with her eyes closed, which would have been ridiculous. "Listen, April. I sympathize with the lads coming home from the war. Obviously." With a tilt of his head, he indicated his prosthetic, entirely concealed from prying eyes by his coat sleeve and pocket. "I was one of those lads."

"I understand why you'd take their part," she said, a bit grudgingly. "I just want you to see that there's this whole other side to it."

"I do see that," he said emphatically. "You want to know what else I think?"

The last of her anger faded away. She was too weary to sustain it, and she wasn't really angry at Oliver anyway. "What's that?"

"I think if you want to keep your job, you should fight for it—and I wouldn't want to be the man who finds himself opposed to you."

21
April–May 1918

Helen

As the *Kaiserschlacht* continued, production at Thornshire Arsenal continued apace, without so much as a pause for Eastertide. Minister of Munitions Winston Churchill had issued an appeal to munitions workers and factory owners to voluntarily waive the holiday in order to keep up with the increased demand for war materiel, and with very few exceptions, munitions factories throughout Britain carried on with their duties. Some arsenals, including all of those belonging to Purcell Products Company, had already planned to forgo the holiday even before Mr. Churchill made his appeal. Helen was immeasurably proud of her munitionettes for their dedication and patriotism, working through their fatigue and illness, confident that every shell and bullet they made hastened the end of the war, which they all desired so fervently.

Helen's only regret was that the Thornshire munitionettes' impressive dedication made it all the more difficult to convince Arthur to take any time off. Despite her best efforts to tend to him, with every week his health visibly declined. He did not even attempt to deny it anymore, but stated frankly that he was willing to sacrifice his health and his very life if need be rather than fail in his duty. Equally stubborn, Helen declared that she would do everything in her power to see that it did not come to that. "Then I am already saved," he told her, smiling through his exhaustion.

Helen was grateful to note that the burgeoning spring alleviated her husband's melancholy, if only by a scant degree, his mood rising with the increasing sunlight and warmth of the lengthening days. To her great joy and relief, after a long absence, he once again found comfort and release in her embrace, moments of intimacy that promised better days to come, of the restoration of their own peace and happiness when the war was over.

She found encouragement elsewhere too—in the Thornshire Canaries' steady progress through rounds of the tournament, and in the more temperate weather and pretty scenery that brightened her morning walks.

That season, the gardens of London were remarkable for a different kind of beauty than in previous years, for the government had strongly urged local gardeners to plant vegetables rather than flowers. For Londoners, it was a time-honored custom to spend a good portion of the Easter holiday planting hundreds of flower bulbs in one's home garden, but now the order of the day was to plant tubers instead, or, better yet, to take a plot or an allotment in the nearest open space and sow an assortment of nutritious vegetables. King George himself had set the example by decreeing that the flower beds surrounding the Queen Victoria Memorial at Buckingham Palace should forgo the traditional blaze of scarlet geraniums in lieu of potatoes, cabbages, parsnips, and carrots, less dazzling but far more essential. So it was in the Royal Parks as well. Two hundred acres of Kew Gardens had been set aside for the cultivation of vegetables, and when Helen walked through Kensington Gardens, the only flower on verdant display was an abundance of wild daffodils, thriving on the enclosed grassy lawns, their sunny yellow blooms swaying in the breeze. The delightful fragrances of spring blossoms and freshly turned soil invigorated her, evoking fond memories of her mother's garden at Banbury Cottage and her own beloved gardens at her home in Oxford. She and Arthur had not visited their estate since Christmas and she missed it terribly, but it seemed unlikely that they would be able to spare time away from the arsenal until the surge in demand for munitions subsided.

That day seemed very far off indeed as the *Kaiserschlacht* continued pounding away at the Allied armies on the Western Front. The need for fresh troops as well as armaments came into stark focus in the middle of April when Royal Assent was given in the House of Lords to the Military Service Act, which deemed every man in the United Kingdom between the ages of eighteen and fifty-one to be "duly enlisted in His Majesty's Regular Forces for general service with the Colours or in the Reserve for the period of the War, and to have been forthwith transferred to the Reserve."

To Helen, it sounded alarmingly as if every young man and a great many who had already reached middle age had been instantly, unwittingly conscripted. "It sounds that way, darling," said Arthur, pausing between mouthfuls of a very late dinner, "because that is in effect what has happened."

"But don't you find it distressing?" said Helen, moving food about on her own plate, untasted. "What about our fine old English principle of a man's right to choose for himself? Are they going to drag portly, gouty gaffers from their families and vocations, thrust a rifle in their arms, and send them off to the front lines, where even young and fit men struggle?"

"I hardly believe that's what will happen," said Arthur wryly. "Your portly, gouty gaffers will likely be pressed into service only to defend England against an invasion, in which case I reckon everyone who *can* fight *shall* turn out to fight the Hun, conscripted or not."

Helen supposed he was right. "Then what does this mean for men your age, practically speaking?"

Arthur heaved a sigh. "For me? Not much. My exemption for essential war work remains valid. However, if I thought I could make a greater contribution elsewhere—"

"What do you mean, elsewhere?"

He shrugged, avoiding her gaze. "Tom could step into my role at the arsenal easily enough. Oliver could take over for him, and with you and Superintendent Carmichael continuing your work—"

"You can't mean to enlist," breathed Helen, shocked. "No. Absolutely not. If you take a leave of absence from Thornshire, it should be to recover your health, not to rush headlong into battle."

He grimaced. "I hadn't considered that. I might not pass the physical exam in my current state."

She reached across the table and seized his hand. "Darling, I don't understand. You're already doing your bit, and it's killing you. Why on earth would you want to enlist and hasten the process?"

He tried to smile. "When you put it that way, it sounds quite mad."

"Arthur," Helen said, her voice trembling. "Please talk to me. Why would you even consider this?"

"I never meant it seriously. It was just an idle thought brought on by the new law." Arthur brought her hand to his lips. "I'm sorry I upset you, darling. Think nothing more of it."

But of course she would. How could she not? She wasn't fooled by the forced lightness in his voice. There was something he wasn't telling her, she was certain of it, and it pained her that he wouldn't confide in her.

Two days later, on Saturday, 20 April, a solemn memorial service was to be held at St. Paul's Cathedral in honor of London's war workers killed or injured while performing their duties. The Bishop of London would preside, Minister of Munitions Winston Churchill would attend, and tickets were in such demand that the organizing chairman claimed the cathedral could be filled five or six times over. Twelve hundred members of the Women's Auxiliary Corps would march from Wellington Barracks to the cathedral accompanied by a band of Scots Guards and a detachment of pipers. During the service, the Grenadier Guards, clad in their scarlet uniforms, would sound the Last Post and Reveille "as a tribute to those who in munition factories and other branches of war work have laid down their lives for their country."

Because munitions workers comprised the greatest number of the honored dead, factory owners were invited to attend so they might pay their respects on behalf of the industry. Since Helen and Arthur were the only Purcells in London, Arthur's father instructed them to attend as official representatives of the family and the company. On the appointed day, Helen finished her work early, but Arthur toiled away until the last possible moment, which meant they left the arsenal late and had to run for the tram, and run again for their train in Barking. They arrived to find the streets around the cathedral packed with sightseers eagerly awaiting the parade, so Arthur clasped Helen's hand firmly as he guided her through the crowd. As they slowly made their way to St. Paul's, Helen realized that many of the people gathering there were not sightseers at all but mourners—parents, siblings, or friends of the deceased. Amid the din of eager conversation, she was certain she heard muffled sounds of weeping.

When at last they reached the cathedral, Arthur pulled her closer and she took his arm, the better to keep her balance in the crush. Ascending the stairs, they passed an older couple dressed in solemn, well-worn black and charcoal gray, the woman clutching a handkerchief and a small bouquet of pink and white flowers, her husband with his jaw set grimly. Suddenly the man reached out and touched Arthur's shoulder. "Beggin' your pardon, sir," he said, removing his hat, "but if you're goin' in, would you be so kind as to do me and me wife a small favor?"

"Certainly, if I can," said Arthur, and Helen nodded.

The older fellow looked to his wife, who stepped forward and tentatively held out the bouquet to Helen. "Would you please leave these flowers on the altar for our Susan?" she asked, her voice choked with tears. "It don't have to be on the altar if that's not proper. Anywhere will do."

"Of course," said Helen.

But when she reached out to accept the bouquet, Arthur touched her arm to forestall her. "I assume you lost a daughter in munitions work?" he asked, his voice low and respectful.

They nodded. "Our oldest girl," the man said, a tremor in his voice, as his wife pressed her lips together to hold back a sob. "'Twas but a fortnight ago."

"Please accept our condolences. I'm truly very sorry for your loss." Arthur glanced to Helen, a question in his eyes, and she nodded in reply. "I think it would be best if you left the flowers for Susan yourselves," he said, retrieving the tickets from his breast pocket and holding them out to the man. "These will get you through the door."

The man regarded him, puzzled. "Don't you want to pay your respects too?"

"We can do that just as well out here." Arthur extended the tickets yet closer.

"Please take them," said Helen. "They really should have been offered to you first."

The couple gratefully accepted, thanked them profusely, and hurried off toward the entrance to the cathedral, tickets in hand. When they disappeared into the crowd, Helen turned to Arthur and kissed his cheek. "That was very decent of you," she said. Her heart overflowed with pride and affection, yet with an undercurrent of sadness mingled in. In his kindness and generosity, he resembled so much the idealistic scholar she had fallen in love with years before. She had not realized until that moment how much she had missed him.

Arthur shrugged, his eyes fixed on the cathedral. "I hope it will comfort them to see their daughter honored. It's a sacrifice she—and they—never should have had to make."

Abruptly he turned, but Helen caught his arm and

hurried along beside him. They made their way down the stairs and back to the street, where they paused and turned to gaze back at the magnificent cathedral as the crowd milled about them. When Arthur closed his eyes and bowed his head, Helen realized that he was paying his respects, just as he had told the older couple he would, and she quickly did the same, silently reciting a prayer she remembered from her father's funeral.

Her thoughts turned to Mabel Burridge, and to the other Thornshire munitionettes who had perished over the winter. Her heart plummeted as she tallied the number of canary girls who were currently on sick leave, and those who remained at their posts, their health clearly failing them despite the increasingly strong preventative measures she imposed. How many more would die or suffer irreparable harm before the end of the war? Thornshire Arsenal was only one small munitions works, and their casualties had been relatively few thus far. Only recently, the Ministry of Munitions had announced that more than one million women were working in munitions industries at present. If Thornshire's sick, injured, and killed were extrapolated to all the munitions works throughout the British Isles, Helen scarcely dared imagine the extent of the suffering. The number might be impossible to calculate. But that did not absolve the government of the responsibility to try to make a full accounting and offer compensation wherever it was needed.

But first they had to win the war.

An air raid shattered their sleep that night, catching Helen and Arthur entirely by surprise since the sky was partly cloudy and the moon would not be full for another week. They fled to the shelter beneath their building, and returned upstairs around one o'clock to climb wearily back into bed. The next morning Helen woke late to discover that Arthur had already breakfasted and had left for the arsenal, to make up the work hours he had missed the previous day. Although she had not expected him to accompany her all the way to Birmingham for the Canaries' match against the Coulthards Ladies, she had hoped he would at least see her off at the station. Instead she ate her breakfast while studying the papers, packed her kit, and set off for the station, alone.

She was glad to meet up with the other Thornshire Canaries when she boarded the train to Birmingham. Lightheaded from fatigue, she dozed in her seat surrounded by her equally weary teammates, and when they arrived, she fortified herself with a strong cup of tea. But it was not enough. During their warm-up, she felt as if her legs were weighed down by sandbags, and from the first whistle, she found herself unable to shake off her lethargy. Nor was she the only Canary thus afflicted. The Coulthards Ladies countered their every attack with a steal, and it was all Helen could do to clear the ball from the defending third to give Marjorie a respite between shots on goal. During the interval, down 2–1, the winded Canaries rested and regrouped, while Marjorie, Peggy, and Lucy strategized for the second half.

"The long train ride wore us out," said Daisy, between gulps of water. "Otherwise they wouldn't be running circles around us."

"The Ladies have traveled nearly as far," Helen reminded her. "Birmingham is halfway between Preston and London, which is why our captains agreed to play here."

"Then it must be because of the yellow powder that we're more winded," said Daisy. "You can tell from their skin that they aren't canary girls. That gives them an advantage."

"Perhaps in your case," said Helen wryly. "What's my excuse?"

Daisy thought for a moment. "Air raids. They don't get air raids in Preston, do they? Of course the Coulthards Ladies are better rested."

"That must be it," said Helen, groaning as she rose

from the bench to loosen up her muscles, just as Marjorie, Peggy, and Lucy called the team together to explain their new scheme for the second half.

It proved to be a simple but effective strategy, a matter of concentrating their defense to shut down the Ladies' exceptional striker and second forward, and sending April up with Lucy and Peggy to break open their defense. In the first five minutes, April drove in a goal after an assist from Lucy to even up the score, but the Ladies dug in and would not allow another. Helen and Marjorie were equally tenacious, so the match ended in a 2–2 draw.

"What does this mean for our place in the tournament?" Helen asked later as they boarded the train for London.

"The Ladies already have one loss, so we'll advance," said Peggy, sinking into her seat with a sigh. "That being said, our first loss will be our last. We'll be out of the tournament."

"That's not our only concern," said Lucy, her voice just loud enough to be heard over the murmurs of worry and frustration. "We barely held our own today, but back in December, the Dick, Kerr Ladies beat the Coulthards Ladies four–nil."

The teammates exchanged uneasy glances. "So you mean to say we should expect Dick, Kerr to be twice as good as Arundel Coulthard?" queried Marjorie, frowning. "Two–all compared to four–nil?"

"I wouldn't state it as a maths problem," Lucy replied, "but we should expect the Dick, Kerr Ladies to be a tough team to beat."

"But we already knew that," said Helen, hoping to reassure her teammates, some of whom looked rather anxious. "Their reputation precedes them."

"We weren't at our best today—except for April, who was marvelous." Peggy paused to smile at her, and as a ripple of applause broke out, April blushed and waved off the praise, embarrassed. "All I mean is, if we had played our best game, we would have won handily."

"I always play my best game," declared Marjorie, and although Helen spied some furtive looks passing between the others, no one contradicted her. "And I say we can take the Dick, Kerr Ladies on any pitch, anytime, and I hope we have the chance to prove it!"

Louder applause broke out, evoking glances— some indulgent, others wearily annoyed—from other passengers, who probably wished they had chosen a different carriage. Not that there had been much choice. The railcars were all packed full, mostly with soldiers coming home on leave or returning from it, mixed among other soldiers in uniforms so crisp and unmarred that they were surely new recruits. Some of Helen's unmarried teammates, especially the younger girls, enjoyed chatting or even flirting with the Tommies, and some exchanged addresses and promises to write, but Helen only smiled, exchanged polite greetings, and thanked them for their brave service. They glanced at her wedding band and turned their friendly attention elsewhere, and that was fine with her. There were certain days, bad days, when she could not glimpse a young man in uniform without the unsettling certainty that she was witnessing a fellow human being in his last, precious hours of life. It was an occasion so moving and terrible that only profound words would suffice, but she had none, so gentle smiles and sincere thanks were all she could offer.

Over the course of the war, Britain's train stations had become public stages for such piteous, heart-rending scenes of grief and parting as soldiers left for training encampments or for the front that Helen had learned to brace herself and avert her gaze. In those last moments before boarding, a soldier's family would gather around him—pale, weeping wives with babies in their arms; older children clutching their mother's skirts, wide-eyed and bewildered; mothers and grandmothers, gray-haired, shawls in disarray, faces clouded over with worry; silver-haired or balding men, stoic and silent except when they cleared their throats or issued final words of advice to their sons. The young men would stand with their packs and rifles, some with their faces stony and jaws set, others grinning with the anticipation of adventure. The latter never failed to astonish Helen. Hadn't all young men learned by now, from the returning wounded and the stories of those who would never return, how utterly hollow and false were the promises of battlefield glory that had enticed young men exactly like themselves back in 1914? If not, the evidence was all around them, for elsewhere in that same station was another platform where anxious crowds awaited the arrival of the ambulance trains, parents and wives desperate to catch a glimpse of their own wounded, broken, beloved boys as they were transferred from the railcars to ambulances and on to convalescent hospitals.

How any soldier came through the war unscathed mystified Helen. It seemed inevitable that all would perish in the end, the death of the body or morbidity of the soul. Nothing mattered anymore but to hasten the end of the war so they could all wake from their enduring nightmare of misery.

But the war dragged on and on.

Yet even so, Helen found moments of grace—the blossoming spring, the sweet cries of a neighbor's newborn, bliss in her beloved husband's arms. She cherished the friendships she had discovered at Thornshire and in Marylebone. Neighbors seemed to look out for one another more than they once had, and even strangers offered a kind word in passing where silence would have sufficed before. They were all in this together, their nods and polite greetings seemed to say, and they would all get through it together. England would endure. London would survive the current crisis as it had other calamities throughout the centuries. They only had to carry on and never surrender.

Nor were they alone in their great struggle. Russia had forsaken them, but they had other allies—and on Saturday, 11 May, all of London celebrated the nation that had most recently joined the fight. A regiment of the United States Army, nearly three thousand strong, were to be reviewed by King George at Buckingham Palace, after which they would march through London on their way to Wellington Barracks to prepare for transport to France, where more than a half a million of their fellow Americans were already deployed. Arthur had already gone to the arsenal when Helen ventured out in the late morning with her Marylebone friends, and as they walked along, they spied the Stars and Stripes flying from the flagstaff of every government department building, institution, and club. Old Glory, an alternative title for the flag Helen had heard some Americans employ, also hung from the windows of innumerable offices and private residences. Hundreds of thousands of spectators thronged the streets carrying smaller copies in their hands or wearing them in their buttonholes, while hawkers with trays of tin versions milled through the throng crying, "Stars and Stripes! Old Glory! One penny each!" Unable to resist, Helen bought one for herself and another to give to Arthur later.

She would have been content to remain among the enthusiastic crowd, but her next-door neighbor, Evelyn, escorted their group to a suite of offices her husband owned in Grosvenor Gardens, not far from the American Embassy. The balcony on the second floor offered a perfect view of the street below, where between half twelve and one o'clock, the three battalions passed, led by bands from the Brigade of Guards. One remarkable feature of the procession was a contingent of veterans of the American Civil War, who carried a banner inscribed "Not for Ourselves, but for Our Country." Most striking of all, however, were the soldiers themselves, tall and slim, strong and fit, youthful but sternly serious. Helen did not glimpse a single face relaxed in a smile. The troops' martial demeanor was most impressive as they strode along, displaying no reaction whatsoever to the earsplitting cheers and frantic waving of flags of the tens of thousands of onlookers on the congested pavements.

"Except for their uniforms and good health, they bear little resemblance to the American soldiers who marched through London last August," remarked Beatrice, echoing Helen's thoughts. "They were a jollier set by far."

"If I recall correctly, those lads were engineers sent over early to prepare for the rest of the army's arrival," said Evelyn. "I presume they've been busy constructing quarters, building roads, laying power and telephone lines and such. These troops are infantry soldiers. Naturally they would be fiercer."

"And now they are crossing over by the thousands every day," said Violet, with great satisfaction. "Trained fighting men, well-rested and ready."

"Trained, but inexperienced," Beatrice noted.

"They'll acquire experience soon enough," the baroness replied.

"They shall indeed," said Helen. God help them.

Little more than a week later, she remembered those proud troops as she sat in her darkened home, her face pressed against Arthur's chest, his arm around her, flinching at the dull roar of German bombs and the incessant thudding of their own guns, wishing with all her might that the Americans had brought with them some means to keep the British sky clear of German aircraft—some marvel of engineering or new weapon or ingenious scheme, she did not care what.

It was a Sunday, and until that dreadful night it had been a lovely spring day blessed with clear skies and gentle breezes. The Thornshire Canaries had no match that afternoon, so Helen had convinced Arthur to enjoy a relaxing day off with her. As it happened, he spent several hours poring over documents at a table on the back terrace while she read a novel in the chaise nearby, but at least they were together and he had not stolen off to the arsenal when her back was turned. Later that evening, a waxing moon shone brightly and stars glimmered in a cloudless sky, with only a slight breeze from the east stirring the tree boughs in the garden. "Ominously lovely," Arthur remarked as they drew the blackout curtains and went to bed.

They woke shortly after eleven o'clock to the harrowing noise of the air raid warning. Bolting out of bed, they threw on some clothes and raced downstairs to the cellar. The servants quickly joined them, taking their usual places on the piles of blankets the housekeeper had placed there for comfort, while Helen and Arthur sat side by side on the bottom stair. For an hour they endured the jarring roar of the ground guns, which at times shook the house so intensely that Helen felt as if she were being torn to pieces.

"Should we be any the worse off without the guns?" asked the cook, indicating the defenses with a wave of her hand. "What with their shrapnel raining down on us and the terrible noise? Might it not be better to sit here in silence, with only the German bombs to affright us?"

"Better? Hardly that," a footman scoffed. "If our ground guns weren't there to ward off the German pilots, we'd have more German planes in our sky and more German bombs dropped on our heads."

"More German planes?" a housemaid exclaimed. "Goodness, don't they crowd our skies enough as it is?"

"It's not fair," Helen blurted, her voice breaking. "We're civilians, not combatants, and how dare the enemy treat us as such? What a cruel and savage new form of warfare this is. No wonder we were entirely unprepared for it, and even now we remain utterly powerless to strike back to defend ourselves!"

"Calm yourself, darling," Arthur murmured, stroking her hair. "It'll be all right."

Suddenly conscious of the servants' stares, Helen muffled a sob, thoroughly ashamed of herself. "Forgive me," she said, taking a steadying breath. "What a ghastly display."

"No harm done, ma'am," said the housekeeper kindly. "You're only saying out loud what we're all feeling."

"Shall I fix us all a nice cup of tea?" asked the cook.

"Thank you, but no," said Helen quickly. "It's not safe."

"Oh, I don't know," said Arthur easily, lifting his arm from her shoulders and rising. "One might risk it. How should a few inches of wooden planks and beams make the cellar any safer than the kitchen, really? I'll fetch the tea."

"No, Arthur—" said Helen, reaching for him, but he was already climbing the stairs, and her fingertips only brushed the cuff of his trousers.

"I'll help you, sir," said the footman, hurrying after him.

The women exchanged bemused looks. "Very well," said Helen, forcing a smile. "Let the men see to it while we take our ease."

The others smiled tentatively in reply as the house trembled from the barrage.

Soon Arthur and the footman returned with the tea tray and a plate of biscuits. They ate and drank, conversing now and then about household matters or inquiring about one another's families, but mostly listening to the bombs and guns and waiting for the storm to pass.

Three hours later, the all-clear sounded, and after carrying the dishes to the kitchen, they all wearily went off to bed. Arthur climbed beneath the covers before Helen was finished undressing, and she thought he had immediately fallen asleep, but when she lay down beside him, she discovered that he was shaking. "Darling?" she murmured, alarmed. "What is it? What's wrong?"

"I'm sorry, darling. I don't want to keep you awake." He threw back the covers and would have risen except she clung to his arm. "I'll sleep in the guest room."

"Don't be ridiculous. You'll stay right here with me." Helen sat up and wrapped her arms around him. "Please, please, tell me what's wrong."

He was silent for a long moment, trembling, perspiration on his brow. "You're right, what you said down below. This sort of warfare is savage and cruel, and it treats civilians as if they were soldiers—and I am just as guilty as any German pilot raining bombs down upon London."

"How can you say such a thing? You have nothing in common with these dreadful raiders."

"How can you be so sure? How do we know that Thornshire Arsenal shells haven't killed innocent German civilians?"

"Well, I—I don't know for certain, but we aren't like that—"

"Aren't we? We don't know. We can't know." Throwing off the covers, he bolted out of bed and paced the room. "You don't know how torn I've been, required to produce the weapons our armies need, wracked by guilt that my creations inflict untold death and suffering upon my fellow man—soldiers, yes, but civilians too, and not just men but women and children and the elderly, and not only Germans but French and Belgians, prisoners in their own occupied territory!"

Helen clutched the bedcovers, her throat constricting with grief and worry. "It's wartime," she choked out. "It's all dreadful and I know it doesn't help to hear this but you're only doing your duty. What choice do you have?"

"I do have a choice," he retorted, his chest heaving with deep, ragged breaths. "As it is now, I build bombs. I take lives indiscriminately without ever risking my own."

Suddenly she understood. "That's why you want to enlist."

"Yes! If I must kill, the only honorable thing to do is to give them a fair shot at me in return." Abruptly he sat down on the edge of the bed and buried his head in his hands. She reached for him, but before she could touch him, he whirled upon her, face haggard, eyes wild with torment. "For years, I've resolved to do my duty to King and Country, as well as to my father. I've committed myself utterly to my work. I'm confronted daily by the demands of the Ministry of Munitions, the constant threat of German bombs or horrific work-place accidents, the alarming reports of rising worker illnesses and death—and the pervasive, haunting fear that if I fail, the war shall be lost, and all that I hold most dear lost with it."

"Oh, my dear Arthur." Tears streaming down her cheeks, Helen laid her hand on his cheek and kissed his brow.

He drew back, his expression bleak and haunted, a muscle working in his jaw. Then suddenly he embraced her, pulling her close, burying his face in her hair. "My dearest love," he said, his voice low and trembling with barely controlled anguish. "Forgive me."

There was nothing to forgive, but that was not what he needed to hear. "Of course. All is forgiven."

"I never wanted this."

"I know. None of us did."

"I can't lose you. I can't lose us."

"You won't," she assured him, with all the love and certainty she could give voice to him, her own dearest Arthur, her beloved. "You never will."

22
June–August 1918

Lucy

In early June, Londoners welcomed reports that the United States 1st Division had finally captured Cantigny, a battle-scarred farming village on a high plateau in the Picardy region of northern France. General Pershing's first victory of the war had flattened a deadly German salient, but at the cost of more than one thousand U.S. casualties. It was a small battle, relatively speaking, but the victory was heartening even so, not only because it liberated more French territory, but because it showed the British, the French, and perhaps even the Americans themselves that the novice United States troops could fight and win. Lucy reckoned that if the Germans were not deeply worried, they were seriously underestimating the forces now arrayed against them.

By mid-June, the most intense fighting centered on the town of Château-Thierry on the Marne, where French explosives experts destroyed bridges and American troops provided covering fire to prevent the Germans from crossing the river. Yet although the German army's advance on Paris had been thwarted, their long guns continued to bombard the city with devastating shells. Lucy feared that if the Allies did not continue to hold off the German advance, Paris would fall, and in time, London might suffer the same fate.

Lucy was grateful that her sons, her mother, and all her Brookfield family remained out of harm's reach—at least, they had so far. She only wished she knew whether the same was true for Daniel. She trusted that he had not been returned to a German prison camp, as the letter from the War Office had promised. Whether he was still being held in a Swiss Medical Mission observation camp, and where that might be, or whether he had been transported to Switzerland or was on his way home to Britain, she had no idea. The War Office had said that more details would be forthcoming, but she had heard nothing from them in ages. What she longed for most was a letter from Daniel himself assuring her he was safe and sound, but such a letter never came.

She checked the post every evening as soon as she arrived home from the arsenal, but day after frustrating day, she heard nothing. The silence was especially difficult to bear on the last Tuesday of June, their thirteenth wedding anniversary. She had clung to a superstitious and foolish hope that surely a letter would come on that day of all days, but still there was no word from him, only aching loneliness.

"No news must be good news," Daisy reminded her the next day as they worked side by side in the Finishing Shop, after Lucy confessed her frustration and disappointment. "If anything had happened to your Daniel, you would have received a telegram."

Daisy was almost certainly right, so Lucy found what comfort she could in her friend's words.

Football proved to be a welcome distraction. Since midsummer, the days had been unusually warm, but Lucy and her teammates took to the pitch as vigorously as ever as the last few rounds of play for the Munitionettes' Cup began. On the first Sunday of July, the Thornshire Canaries met at the Globe early so Lucy and Peggy could explain a few new plays they had devised. They were determined to learn every step before their opponents, the Shell Girls from the National Shell Filling Factory in Chilwell, arrived from Nottinghamshire. A few of their most ardent fans, including Mr. Purcell and Mr. Corbyn, observed from the stands as Lucy and Peggy described the new stratagems, and more spectators trickled in as the Canaries walked through the plays in their street clothes. As soon as every player was confident with her role, they hastened into the changing room, certain their opponents would arrive at any moment and relieved to have preserved the element of surprise.

Lucy sensed a frisson of excitement and nervousness as the players donned their uniforms and gear. They had never faced the Shell Girls before, but although the Chilwell munitions works had been troubled by accidents and explosions as well as TNT poisoning cases through the years, the owner, Lord Chetwynd, was said to be very mindful of his workers' well-being. Out of his own vast wealth he had provided them with fine canteens; bands to play dance music at mealtimes; comfortable shifting houses and rest facilities; and many opportunities for sport and entertainment, including sumptuous baths, a swimming pool, well-appointed changing rooms, and spacious outdoor sports grounds. The Purcells kept the Canaries supplied with fine uniforms, balls, and other equipment, but there was nothing to be done about their small, uneven training field. Lucy could well imagine how fit and prepared the Shell Girls must be, with such superior resources at their disposal.

She expected to be thoroughly awestruck as the Shell Girls took the pitch, but when the Canaries emerged from the changing room for their warm-up kickaround and drills, their opponents were nowhere to be seen. Neither were the Shell Girls' supporters, judging by the overwhelming dominance of yellow-and-black pennants and scarves in the stands, with the few scattered appearances of red-and-white seeming entirely incidental.

"Maybe their train was delayed," said April as they ran laps of their half of the pitch.

They all agreed this was possible. As they took shots on the goal and Marjorie ran and leapt to block them, a lighthearted debate ensued regarding whether they should do the sporting thing and delay the start of the game to allow the Shell Girls time to properly warm up once they finally arrived. Marjorie was adamantly against it. Lucy thought they absolutely must, for the Canaries would appreciate the gesture if their places were reversed. Daisy, ever pragmatic, pointed out that the question would probably be decided by the officials. "Tournament rules might require a forfeit," she pointed out. "Does anyone know?"

No one did.

"There might be another match scheduled for the Globe immediately following ours, in which case we'd have to clear off," Peggy noted. "Then there's the officials. They might not be willing or able to stay late."

There was nothing to do but hope the Shell Girls arrived at the last minute.

As the Canaries moved on to passing drills, Lucy noticed that she and her teammates frequently glanced to the entrance hoping to spot the other team, but the minutes ticked away and still they did not appear. With five minutes to go before the opening whistle, the officials beckoned Peggy over for a conference. The Canaries continued to warm up, observing the sideline discussion from a distance but unable to hear a word. When Peggy jogged back, her teammates gathered around her to hear the verdict. "The officials say the pitch is ours for the next two hours," she reported. "We can accept the Shell Girls' forfeit, advance in the tournament, and call it a day. Or we can wait and start the match when they arrive, but the score will stick even if we don't get a full ninety minutes of play."

"Take the forfeit as a win," someone called out from the back. "Why look a gift horse in the mouth?"

"The rules may allow it, but that doesn't mean it's fair play," Helen protested, looking around for affirmation.

"I say we play them when they get here," declared Marjorie. "I don't care how fancy their sporting fields and changing rooms are. They're just working-class girls same as us, not Division One footballers. We can beat them, and I want the chance to prove it."

A few girls cheered and applauded. Craning her neck, Peggy caught Lucy's eye and raised her eyebrows in a question. Lucy made a few small gestures which she knew Peggy would recognize as the opening moves of their new plays. Peggy nodded, understanding her perfectly, and clapped her hands for attention. "Since we're warmed up and our opponents aren't here to watch, let's run through our new plays properly. If the Shell Girls show up before we finish, grand. We'll play. If they don't, we'll decide what to do next."

The players quickly took their places and ran through the plays until they could execute each one flawlessly. Their performance earned them applause from the few spectators who remained, for the crowd had thinned as time passed and the prospect of an actual match became increasingly unlikely. An hour after the match should have begun, Peggy called the team together in the center of the pitch. The sky had clouded over, the breeze was picking up, and the air smelled of rain. By a show of hands, the players agreed to accept the Shell Girls' forfeit and head home before the storm rolled in.

"I have a very uneasy feeling about this," Helen said as they trooped into the changing room. "A train delay of more than an hour on a Sunday afternoon? Doubtful."

"Maybe the Shell Girls thought we were playing at their field," said Marjorie, her voice muffled as she pulled her jersey over her head.

"If they had, they would have figured it out when neither we nor the officials showed up." Lucy turned to Helen. "Would any of your contacts know?"

"Possibly," said Helen, pensive. "I'll make inquiries."

A sinking dread fell over the room, taking all the pleasure out of their smashing new plays and the easy victory that had brought them one round closer to the Munitionettes' Cup. They left the Globe just as a light rain began to fall, and they parted company at the station as they boarded different trains and trams. Lucy made sure to check the platform display before embarking, but nothing suggested that there had been an accident on the route from Nottinghamshire, or any other delay of more than a few minutes.

At home, Lucy checked the post out of habit, remembering with chagrin that of course there was no post on a Sunday. Lonely and unsettled, she telephoned Brookfield and in turns spoke with her mother, her sons, and her brother George, who lectured her so sternly about her ongoing TNT exposure that she almost wished she hadn't rung. Later, after the brief rain shower passed, she and Gloria met in the garden and knitted together until it was time to prepare dinner. "Looks like we're in for a calm night," Gloria said as they parted, gazing with satisfaction at the gray, overcast skies.

"Let's hope so," Lucy replied. London hadn't endured an air raid in more than a fortnight, and she wasn't sure how much longer their luck would hold out.

The next day when the Canaries gathered on their training field after dinner, Helen arrived a few minutes late, her expression stricken. "I've learned why the Shell Girls missed our match," she said.

"What happened?" asked Lucy, dreading the answer.

Helen looked around the circle as the others drew closer. "You didn't hear this from me," she said, "and please don't spread it around. There were hundreds of witnesses, so it's not likely to stay secret forever, but you know how the Ministry of Munitions likes to keep these things out of the press so word doesn't get back to the Germans—"

"Helen, what happened?" Marjorie broke in sharply. "An accident? Tell us."

Helen nodded and closed her eyes for a moment, pressing her hand to her heart as if to steady it. "On the evening of July first, just as the night shift was beginning, there was an explosion in the mixing house at the National Shell Filling Factory in Chilwell."

A gasp of horror went up from the group—hands pressed to mouths, eyes filling with helpless tears.

"As best they can determine now, the casualties include more than one hundred and thirty killed, a few seriously wounded, and a great many slightly wounded." Helen looked around the circle, her expression warning them to brace themselves. "I'm told—I'm told the carnage was beyond imagining."

Lucy took a steadying breath, lightheaded and sick to her stomach. "I saw something in the papers the other day," she said tremulously, "no more than a line or two, about a Midlands factory explosion. Sixty were feared dead. Is this—"

"The same accident," Helen finished for her, nodding. "Yes. One and the same."

A few of the girls sat down on the grass, staring bleakly; others put their arms around one another for support and comfort. "Do we know if any of the Shell Girls were hurt?" asked Marjorie.

"I wasn't given any names of casualties," said Helen, "and I never saw their team roster."

Lucy knew that even if none of the footballers had been injured or worse, the accident would have been enough to drive all thoughts of the match from their minds. "We should do something for them," she said. "Dedicate our next match to the injured and killed.

Give the survivors all the proceeds from the gate. Something. Anything."

Her friends chimed in agreement, but Helen gave her head the slightest shake. "We cannot mention the Chilwell factory by name or the War Office would strenuously object. I trust that Lord Chetwynd will have relief measures well in hand. That said, I'm sure we could organize a benefit for a general fund for injured and ill munitions workers and their survivors."

"I'd like to help with that," said Lucy, and several others quickly volunteered too. From the long, stricken looks her teammates exchanged, Lucy knew they shared one chilling thought: As thorough as their own safety protocols were, and as scrupulously as everyone followed them, the devastating accident just as easily could have happened at Thornshire.

But April apparently disagreed. "There were seventeen explosions at the National Shell Filling Factory before this one," she said sharply. "Did Lord Chetwynd have those well in hand too?"

"Seventeen?" echoed Marjorie, incredulous. "Who told you that?"

"Someone who would know," April retorted, prompting a chorus of bewildered, heated questions from the others.

Everyone's nerves were fraught, Lucy realized, and

little wonder. "Let's not argue," she pleaded, raising her voice. "If there was negligence, that's for the Ministry of Munitions to sort out."

"Enough! Let's play football," Peggy shouted, tossing one ball and then another into their midst. "If ever I needed an official's whistle . . ."

She left the thought unfinished as the Canaries began to pass the ball around, some still looking very much upset for the munitions workers of Chilwell, others scowling, as if they'd like to have a sharp word with Lord Chetwynd. Whoever was to blame, if anyone was, Lucy hoped her mother would not hear of the terrible accident, or she would be on the telephone at once, pleading with her to leave Thornshire. If Lucy were perfectly honest with herself, she knew she ought to consider it. Her health continued to decline. Munitions factories throughout Britain were dismissing women workers by the hundreds. After nearly three years of munitions work, it was fair to say that she had done her bit. Why should she continue to risk her life, especially with the end of the war drawing ever nearer, and Daniel's homecoming surely not far behind?

As July passed, it truly did seem as if the tide of the war had turned. In the middle of the month, the Allies halted the dreadful *Kaiserschlacht*, after the German army attempted to encircle Reims only to be pushed back from the Marne, delivering Paris from the threat of invasion. On 20 July, London newspapers were exultant with reports that the German commander had ordered a retreat, and in the days that followed, the German armies were forced back to the positions from where they had launched the Kaiser's Spring Offensive months before. Then, at the end of July, word came that after weeks of brutal fighting, the Allied counteroffensive had finally driven the Germans out of the Marne region altogether and continued to pummel the German defensive line.

In Britain, hopes for victory soared, but in early August, the Central Powers dug in and renewed their offensives, stalling the Allied counterattack and inflicting massive casualties. Lucy struggled not to sink into despondency after allowing herself to hope that victory was within reach. After all, military authorities reported to the press that the front had been moved eastward roughly 280 miles, containing the Germans behind a line running along the Aisne and Vesle Rivers. There was good reason to believe the Allies would continue to advance until the Germans were driven out of France and back within their own borders. How long this might take was another question altogether.

One Thursday morning, Lucy was heading out the door in the pink light of early dawn, fortified with a strong cup of tea and running through football plays in her mind, when someone called her name. With a start, she glanced toward the voice and discovered Gloria waving urgently from the other side of the low fence that separated their two front gardens. "Lucy," she called out, holding out an envelope. "Thank goodness I caught you. This got mixed in with our post. I didn't see it until this morning."

Lucy felt her breath catch in her throat. Setting down her bag, she hurried over, took the letter, and glimpsed her own name and the return address of the War Office. Heart thudding, she exchanged a quick, stricken look with her friend and opened the flap. Withdrawing a single page, she read quickly, unable to breathe, her head swimming and heart pounding.

"Lucy," Gloria exclaimed, clutching the top of the fence as if she might leap over it. "Heavens, you've gone quite pale. What is it?"

"I—I need to sit down." Stunned, Lucy returned to her front steps and sank down upon them. Daniel, so close. She heard Gloria call her name, alarmed, but her gaze was fixed on the letter, and she was only dimly aware of her friend bolting away from the fence, through her own front gate, and down the pavement toward Lucy's. He was so close, so close he was almost home.

Suddenly Gloria was sitting beside her, supporting

her with a strong arm around her waist. "Dearie, what is it? What's happened? Oh, I pray it isn't—"

"Daniel's alive and well," Lucy said, voice shaking. "He's in Britain. He's been in Britain a week already."

"Oh my goodness! That's wonderful news!" Gloria embraced her. "But—where is he? When is he coming home?"

"Derbyshire." Lucy checked the letter again to be sure, because it was too good to be true, and she was terrified that she had mistaken it. "In Derbyshire, at an estate called Alderlea." Alderlea. The name was familiar, but she couldn't place it; she had never visited Derbyshire except to attend a few of Daniel's football matches through the years.

"Why would they send him to a hospital so far away?"

"I—I don't know." Her thoughts were spinning like scattered leaves in a windstorm. She took a steadying breath and willed herself to calm. "Perhaps it's not a proper hospital, but a country house converted to a military hospital for the duration. I know of a few in Surrey." She gasped, seized the railing, and pulled herself shakily to her feet. "I must go to him at once."

Grasping the handle of her bag, she unlocked her front door and hurried back inside, Gloria following. "Are you in any condition to travel?" Gloria asked worriedly. "You seem distressed. Unwell."

Lucy almost laughed. She was a canary girl; she was always somewhat unwell. "I'm fine, just a bit . . . stunned." She thought for a moment. "I'll need a few things." She hurried off to her bedroom, dumped the contents of her bag onto the bed, and swiftly began filling it with clothing and other essentials.

Gloria watched her from the doorway, uncertain. "Do you even know where to go?"

"I'll check the maps at the station. I'll ask the ticket agent. How difficult could it be?" Lucy closed the bag and snapped the fastenings shut. She should pack something to eat. She darted past Gloria and off to the kitchen, where she quickly threw together a few sandwiches of cheese and bread, two staples that were not rationed, not yet, and so she kept her pantry well stocked. She wrapped the sandwiches carefully in paper and tucked them into her bag, snapping it shut again afterward.

"Is there anything I can do to help?" Gloria asked, trailing after her to the foyer.

"Thank you, no," said Lucy, pulling on her summer coat. "Wait. Yes. Would you please be a dear and telephone Thornshire Arsenal? Ask to speak to Mrs. Helen Purcell in administration. If you reach her, tell her I won't be in today, possibly not for the rest of the week, and tell her why." Lucy opened the door, and Gloria scurried outside ahead of her. "If you have to leave a message with someone else—" She paused to think as she fit the key in the lock. "Tell them I'll be absent, but say—say only that it's a family emergency." If they sacked her for missing work with no notice, Helen could likely get her her job back—if she wanted it back.

"I'll ring the arsenal right away," Gloria promised, giving her a quick hug. "Safe travels. Give my best to Daniel."

Tears of joy sprang into Lucy's eyes. "I shall," she said, blinking them away. She had not spoken to her beloved Daniel in years. To think that in a matter of hours, she would be able to speak to him, to hear his voice, to clasp his hand in hers, to kiss him, to hold him!

Lucy fairly ran to Clapham Junction, clutching her bag, thoughts in a whirl. The ticket agent, a cheerful auburn-haired girl of about nineteen looking very smart in her navy blue uniform and cap, helped her construct a route as far as the train could carry her—short jaunts from Clapham to Victoria, King's Cross, and St. Pancras, and then a long ride all the way to Sheffield. Lucy purchased the tickets and boarded, and caught all of her connections with time to spare. Her last train was passing through Cricklewood when she realized, too late, that she could have telephoned Alderlea before she set out. She could have asked the nurses to tell Daniel that she was on her way, or perhaps she could have spoken to Daniel himself. She could have rung her mother's home in Brookfield to share the happy news.

It was just as well she had not thought of it. Telephone calls would have delayed her at home, and she would be with Daniel all the sooner this way.

She was too full of anticipation to doze, and she had forgotten to pack anything to read, so instead she gazed out the window at the passing scenery, the green hills and meadows, the quaint villages and farmers' fields, summer gold and ripening like a promise. At noon she ate one of her sandwiches, amusing herself by imagining her sons' delight when they reunited with their father. She wondered how long Daniel would need to stay in hospital, how soon she might bring him home. Her heart sank a little when she realized that as long as she continued working at Thornshire, Daniel might be better off in Brookfield, away from the German bombs, from the yellow powder, from his yellow-skinned, mottle-haired wife.

Suddenly a wave of embarrassment and worry swept over her. In her many letters, she had never mentioned the drastic changes to her appearance since she had become a canary girl. Her mother had said that Lucy's war work had stolen her beauty, a painful truth that Lucy had not been obliged to fully reckon with, what with her husband so far away, and his opinion of her beauty being the only one that mattered. What would Daniel think of her, seeing her like this after years apart? Would he be worried and heartbroken? Would he be repulsed? Tears gathered in her eyes, but she dabbed them with a handkerchief and angled her body toward the window so the other passengers wouldn't see. If any kindhearted soul tried to comfort her, she would lose her composure altogether.

It was midafternoon by the time she disembarked at Sheffield, calmer and resolved. She'd had time to think, and to remember how much Daniel adored her, how he always had, ever since they were children. They had planned to grow old together, and she had never doubted that he would still love her after she became wrinkled and stooped and gray. Why should she fear that he would stop loving her now, all because of a persistent cough and sallow skin and strange hair?

Inquiring at the station, she learned that an omnibus made the round trip to Alderlea three times a day, a service for medical staff and families visiting patients, managed by the War Department but funded entirely by Lord Rylance, the master of the estate. On the long, winding drive through the countryside, Lucy's seatmate, a matronly nurse, shared the heartrending story of the bereaved lord and lady who had devoted themselves to the care and rehabilitation of wounded soldiers after their eldest son and heir, Harrison Rylance, an officer with the Derbyshire Yeomanry, had lost his life at the Battle of Scimitar Hill in Gallipoli.

"We take on some of the most difficult cases," the nurse added proudly. "Amputees, shell shock, head wounds, facial mutilations. Oh, those are heartbreaking, but we do our best for them. Lady Rylance converted her finest sitting room into a workshop and hired the best lady sculptors and painters to make the masks these poor Tommies wear—paper-thin copper to replace their missing features, specially painted to match their skin tones. True works of art, easily as fine as anything from the Third London General Hospital, and they're famous for their excellent masks."

"Is that so?" Lucy replied faintly. "Then a soldier with a simple leg wound, even a very serious one, wouldn't be treated here?"

"Oh, no, not likely," said the nurse, shaking her head. "Not unless he's a Derbyshire lad, and he requested Alderlea in particular, to be close to his family." She paused to peer at Lucy quizzically. "So, what sort of nursing did you do at that arsenal, exactly? From the look of it, you must have worked rather too closely with the canary girls, if you'll forgive me for saying so."

"I'm not a nurse," Lucy said, taken aback. "I'm a

munitions worker. I'm coming to Alderlea to visit my husband."

"Oh?" The nurse's smile faltered. "Oh. I misunderstood. Well, as you'll soon see, Alderlea is a lovely, tranquil spot, the very ideal for rest and rehabilitation." She managed a tight smile, glanced idly about for a moment, then retrieved a small book from her satchel and soon appeared engrossed in it.

Lucy felt sorry for the chagrined woman, who clearly never meant to speak so freely to a patient's wife, but her apprehension for Daniel surged, sweeping away every other emotion.

Before long they approached Alderlea, a breathtakingly beautiful three-story Elizabethan mansion of gray slate and buff sandstone nestled among broad, rolling lawns at the edge of a splendid grove of ancient alder trees, which no doubt had inspired the estate's name. Lucy's heart thudded in expectation mingled with worry as the omnibus drove around the back of the mansion and halted near the rear entrances. Clutching her bag, she disembarked as swiftly as she could, murmuring apologies to the passengers seated in the rows before her, whom she hurried past before they even had time to stand. Once outside, she inhaled deeply the cool, fresh air, comfortingly reminiscent of Brookfield, and followed the signs to patient inquiries. The orderly there offered her directions to Daniel's room, which, she realized as she turned down the hallway, was on the amputees' ward.

She halted, braced herself with a hand against the wall, and reminded herself to breathe. It could be worse. As the nurse had unwittingly warned her, it could have been far, far worse. He was her Daniel. She loved him. He was alive. That was all that mattered.

And she was so desperate to see him she could not wait a moment longer.

She hurried to the nurses' station, where a cherubic trainee checked a schedule and told her Daniel was outside in the western gardens. Lucy thanked her and fled down the stairs and outside.

She spotted him from a distance, knowing every curve and line of his form so well that even seated, with his back to her, she could not have mistaken him for anyone else. Setting her bag on a bench, she approached him at a sedate walk, scarcely able to breathe for the pounding of her heart. He must have heard the muffled crunch of her boots on the gravel path, for he glanced over his shoulder at the sound, and when he could not see who approached, he reached for the wheels on either side of his seat—wheels, he was in a wheelchair—and deftly maneuvered himself around to face her.

They both halted at the same time, each gazing in stunned disbelief at the other.

Her eyes lingered on his face—that wonderful, beloved face—for a long, utterly still moment, but eventually her gaze traveled downward, and her stomach dropped. His right leg was missing below the knee.

When she glanced up, she discovered that Daniel was gazing at her in wonder. "Lucy," he said, his voice as warm and dear as she remembered. "You're here. How—"

But she did not let him finish the thought. With a gasp, she ran to fling her arms around him, weeping for joy, for loss, for the years they would never get back, and for all those that she had once feared they would never have, but now dared hope they would.

23
August–September 1918

April

One Monday evening after work, April and Marjorie relaxed in the dining room of their hostel enjoying a late supper—although enjoying might have been overstating things, since rationing and food scarcity had steadily diminished the quality of their subsidized meals. After a long, exhausting shift, it was difficult to soothe one's gnawing hunger with a bowl of bland fish soup thickened with barley and seasoned with a sprinkling of dried herbs, ersatz coffee made from roasted chicory root and rye, and a wheat roll so hard that they were obliged to chip off pieces with their knives or dunk the roll in coffee to soften it before they could chew it. Yet they ate without complaint, for they were more fortunate than most. An unsavory dinner was easier to bear than hunger pangs, and they could rely on luncheon and tea at the arsenal canteen to fill their stomachs.

Conversation distracted them from the bland food. They still marveled at Lucy's unexpected three-day absence from Thornshire, followed by her sudden re-appearance at the Globe just in time for their Sunday match. Most astonishing of all was Lucy's revelation that her husband had returned to England, and that she had seen him, at Alderlea, of all places. Daniel couldn't be discharged from hospital quite yet, but he should be able to come home by the end of September. Lucy's glow of joy had dimmed when she acknowledged that he would never play football again.

"It's sad, but he's luckier than a lot of wounded veterans," Marjorie pointed out, stirring her soup. "He can be an architect sitting down."

"Marjorie!" April exclaimed.

"I'm not being flippant. All I meant is that he can go back to his pre-war occupation, unlike some." She peered at April, curious. "What about your Oliver? What did he do before getting his hand shot off?"

April sighed, exasperated. "Honestly, Marjorie, how can you be so glib about a soldier's injuries? And don't call him 'my Oliver.' I don't know whether he is."

Marjorie gaped. "Are you mad? Of course he's 'your

Oliver.' You see him nearly every day at the arsenal. He comes to all your matches. You kiss and hold hands—"

"Marjorie—"

"Don't deny it. I've seen you."

"I don't deny it, but—" April searched for the words to explain how she felt. "If he is 'my Oliver,' shouldn't he tell me so?"

Marjorie paused. "You mean he hasn't?"

"No."

"He's never told you he loves you?"

"No, not ever."

Marjorie thought for a moment. "That's a bit odd, fair enough, but maybe he's just shy."

"Or maybe he doesn't love me."

"I really don't think that's it." Marjorie shook her head, brow furrowing. "I think he's 'your Oliver,' if you want him to be. It's obvious to everyone but you."

April didn't want to discuss it anymore, so she took up Marjorie's other question. "Before the war, Oliver worked in his uncle's shop, in the same village where he grew up."

"Is that so?" Marjorie mulled it over. "Well, he could always go back to that, if Thornshire closes."

"Do you think it will?" April leaned forward and lowered her voice. "What have you heard?"

Marjorie leaned forward too, but before she could

reply, their friends Nellie and Eliza, canary girls from Woolwich Arsenal, set their dinner trays on the table, pulled out the two remaining chairs, and sank heavily into them, their expressions disconsolate.

"Hello, girls," said April, looking from one to the other, wary. "How was your day?"

"Perfectly dreadful," said Nellie flatly.

"The worst since Brunner Mond exploded across the river and almost took us down with them," Eliza added.

"Now you have me worried," said Marjorie. "What happened?"

Nellie stirred her fish soup, scowling. "When we clocked out today, the lady superintendent told us—us two and about four dozen other girls—that there won't be no work for us next week."

"Oh no!" said April. "That's awful. I'm so sorry."

"Did they give you a character?" asked Marjorie. "Will they give you a week's pay in place of the week's work, to hold you over until you find something new?"

Nellie and Eliza shook their heads, miserable. "A character, yes," Eliza clarified, "but a week's pay, no, and we don't know where we'll find new jobs now."

"There's always domestic service," said Nellie glumly. "Oh, how I hated cleaning up other people's messes! I swore I'd never do that again."

April knew exactly how she felt. "From what I hear," she ventured nonetheless, "it's better than the mills."

Nellie shook her head. "It couldn't be."

"Trust me, it is," said Eliza vehemently. "I've done both and I know. The pay is better in the mills, but that's the only advantage. All the women of my family have worked in the mills for generations. They're even worse than the Danger Buildings. All the toil and lung ailments, plus it was so loud, we couldn't even sing."

"You sing at Woolwich?" asked April, exchanging puzzled glances with Marjorie. "Do you mean in theatricals?"

"No, while we work," said Eliza. "Don't you? It helps pass the time."

"We don't, at least not on the day shift," said April. Singing seemed unwise for the Filling Shop, what with all that yellow powder in the air despite the vastly improved ventilation system Helen had mandated months before.

"Well, we won't be able to sing together anymore," said Nellie, gulping her ersatz coffee and setting the cup down with a bang. "And we even had our own song, one we made up ourselves. What do you say, Eliza? Should we sing it here, one last time?"

Eliza smiled wistfully and nodded. She rose and

beckoned to the other Woolwich girls, who, April now realized, stood out for their expressions, a tearful mix of anger, resignation, and unhappiness. They met in the center of the room and whispered among themselves for a moment. Then someone hummed a note for pitch, they turned to face their audience, and their voices rose in unison in a lively, merry song.

> *Where are the girls of the arsenal?*
> *Working night and day;*
> *Wearing the roses off their cheeks*
> *For precious little pay.*
> *Some people call us "canaries"*
> *Working for the lads across the sea.*
> *If not for munition lasses,*
> *Where would Britain be?*
> *I ask you*
> *Where would Britain be?*
> *So tell me*
> *Where would Britain be?*

The dining room rang with cheers and applause and calls for an encore. The Woolwich girls obliged, but the second time through, their audience shouted out the line "I ask you," and even louder "So tell me." As applause rose again, and the Woolwich girls took their bows, Marjorie leaned close to April and said, "We have to teach this to our canary girls."

April agreed, laughing, but her mirth quickly faded. If the Woolwich Arsenal was sacking munitionettes, how much longer could Thornshire hold out?

The applause faded, the singers returned to their seats, and conversation resumed, a low hum punctuated with occasional bursts of laughter. April wanted to assure Nellie and Eliza that everything would work out in the end, but all she could offer them was sympathy, which wouldn't pay their bills.

After they finished dinner, Nellie asked Marjorie and April not to divulge the bad news to their landlady, out of concern that she might evict them at the end of the month, if they had not found new war work. "She won't toss you out," said Marjorie confidently. "This may be a munitionettes' hostel, but she wants that rent money, no matter what work you do."

Marjorie left unsaid what they all knew was certain: If Nellie and Eliza couldn't find new jobs, any jobs, the landlady would evict them for unpaid rent instead.

It was only later, as they were getting ready for bed, that April remembered the conversation their Woolwich friends' arrival had interrupted. "Marjorie," she ventured, climbing beneath her covers while Marjorie lingered at the mirror, brushing her gingery curls. "Do you really think Thornshire might close?"

Her friend was silent for a moment, attending to a particularly springy lock. Then she set down her brush with a sigh. "This is what I think," she said, sitting down on the edge of her bed and resting her elbows on her knees. "The war seems to be winding down— and thank God for that—and the demand for shells has been falling for months. I don't know that Thornshire will close altogether, but they won't always make munitions, and that's the work we know."

"We can learn other tasks just as we learned to fill shells. Obviously no one wants to work with TNT one day longer than necessary, but we need work—safe jobs that pay a living wage. Don't they owe us canary girls that much, after all we've done?" April lay back and pulled the comforter up to her chin. "Do you think Helen will tip us off if layoffs are coming?"

"She might," said Marjorie thoughtfully, turning off the lamp. "But first she'll say, 'You didn't hear this from me.'"

April managed a smile.

"But hiring and firing is really the superintendent's responsibility," Marjorie went on. "Helen might not find out we're all about to be sacked until right before Mrs. Carmichael delivers the blow."

"But Mr. Purcell would know before anyone at Thornshire. Wouldn't he tell Helen?"

"Maybe not, if he thought Helen might tell *us*." Springs creaked as Marjorie shifted in bed. "Do you think your Oliver would warn you what's coming?"

April yawned. "If he *were* 'my Oliver,' maybe he would." But she was a lot less certain than Marjorie that he was. They had been seeing each other for months, but Oliver never said a word about their future—his future, yes, his hopes for after the war, but nothing very specific, and nothing that included her in the picture.

Was she just a wartime fling after all?

Early the next morning, April and Marjorie were leaving the dining room after breakfast just as Nellie and Eliza were entering. When Marjorie quietly asked if they had a plan for finding new jobs, they said they intended to call at the nearest Labour Exchange as soon as it opened on Monday, their first day of unemployment, in hopes of getting into the queue before the rush. "If that don't turn up anything," said Nellie, pulling a face, "our next stop might be the BWEA office."

Marjorie grinned. "Please tell me you're not serious."

When Nellie burst out laughing, Eliza and Marjorie joined in, and a bit belatedly, April did too. Only later, as she and Marjorie were hurrying to catch their tram, did she abashedly ask, "What's this BWEA office? An employment agency?"

"No, silly." Marjorie leapt onto the tram as it was pulling away and extended a hand to assist April aboard after her. "It's the British Women's Emigration Association. Surely you've seen their leaflets and posters. They've been around for years, but lately they've been busier than usual, and little wonder."

Her words prompted a vague memory. "Wasn't a lady handing out their leaflets at the arsenal park last week?"

"Last week? She or one of her chums has been there nearly every day since the factories started sacking munitionettes. Not that you'd notice, since you're always in such a rush to see your Oliver."

"He's not my—" The tram hit a bump and April bit her tongue. "What does the BWEA want, anyway?"

"They want to help us, of course." Marjorie rolled her eyes. "They resettle surplus women abroad, mostly in Canada, Australia, and New Zealand, I think."

"Surplus women?" April echoed, clinging tightly to the bar opposite Marjorie, since the tram was packed as usual and they couldn't find seats.

"Their words, not mine. You know what they mean—the vast crowds of unmarried women fated to become a burden to their families and society." Marjorie paused to think. "I suppose there'll be more 'surplus women' around than ever before, since Britain has lost practically a whole generation of young men to this bloody war."

April suppressed a shudder. An entire generation lost—what a terrible thought. Yet it wasn't entirely true. It couldn't be. Some young men would eventually return from the war, and she hoped her brother Henry would be among them. He had been away so long, and had only come home once on leave. In all that time he had reported only a few minor scrapes and bruises, although in his last letter he had mentioned several of his chums falling desperately ill from influenza. April fervently hoped he wouldn't catch it. If his luck would hold out a few months longer, maybe he would survive the war and return to Carlisle none the worse for the experience.

"So these so-called surplus women," April said. "They go abroad to—to do what, exactly? Find husbands?"

"Yes, that, but also to find work." Marjorie shrugged. "The BWEA posters say there are loads of jobs throughout the commonwealth."

April fell silent, thinking. It sounded like a marvelous adventure, to travel across the ocean to a new country, full of opportunities, sparkling with possibilities. But a worry or two nagged at her. Didn't these countries have their own women? What sort of jobs were on offer? If it was all domestic service, she could do that here in England, and still visit her family a few times a year. "Have you thought about emigrating?" she asked Marjorie tentatively, not wanting to seem too interested herself.

"Me? Certainly not. I've been working too hard to defend Britain from the Hun to pack up and leave now. Besides," Marjorie added airily, "I'll never be a surplus woman. Once this war is over and all my Tommy pen pals come home, I'll likely marry one of them, when I'm good and ready."

April grinned, imagining a gang of eager Tommies all showing up at the hostel at the same time with bouquets and proposals, beaming adoringly at Marjorie and scowling at their rivals. "How will you ever choose among them? Most handsome, best prospects—"

"Best kisser," Marjorie added emphatically.

They both burst out laughing, and after that, all they had to do was glance at one another and the mirth would bubble up again, until they had to avoid eye contact and bite their lips together rather than annoy the other passengers. Only when they disembarked did they allow themselves to double over with laughter, wiping away tears. April knew the joke wasn't even that funny, but it felt so good to laugh.

As they approached the arsenal park, April looked around until she spotted a woman holding leaflets, standing on the corner nearest the tram stop and farthest from the arsenal's main gate. April hung back a bit, waiting until Marjorie was busy chatting with other canary girls arriving for their shifts. Then she darted over to take a leaflet from the BWEA woman, a gray-haired matron with spectacles who reminded her of her favorite schoolteacher. Folding the leaflet twice, April tucked it into her bag to read later, in private, and hurried to catch up with her friends.

In the shifting house, the Filling Shop, and the canteen, the munitionettes chatted about the latest news of the war and the worrisome rumors of layoffs, but on the training field, the only subject of conversation was football: the Munitionettes' Cup standings, the Canaries' upcoming match, and how to improve as much as they could in a very few days with better drills and clever strategy. Their most recent victory had qualified them for the semifinals, and they had been eager—and more than a little nervous—to learn who their opponents would be. Two days later, Peggy greeted them on the training field fairly bursting with the news that the Blyth Spartans had defeated the Dick, Kerr Ladies 4–2, knocking the celebrated team out of the tournament. The Canaries' next match would pit them against the Spartans, a side that had once defeated them 6–1.

"We're a different team now," Peggy reminded them, panting, as they ran sprints up and down their small training field. "They won't thrash us so horribly this time."

"They won't thrash us at all," Marjorie declared, bolting ahead of her captain to cross the finish line. "We'll do the thrashing this time."

April hoped she was right, but a nervous flutter filled her stomach every time she thought of those swift, strong footballers in their blue-and-white vertically striped, collared jerseys and matched striped caps. They were such kind, admirable girls, gracious in victory and perfectly friendly after a match, but they were fierce and merciless on the pitch. The Thornshire Canaries would have to play better than they ever had just to hold their own. It wouldn't help that the semifinal match would be played at St. James' Park in Newcastle-upon-Tyne, prestigious grounds nearly three hundred miles north of London, but only thirty miles south of Blyth, giving the Spartans an advantage even though St. James' Park wasn't their home pitch. Although some of the Canaries' most faithful supporters and fans had promised to attend, the crowd would no doubt skew as strongly blue-and-white as if the match were at Croft Park.

In the first few days of the week, their trainings went splendidly. Marjorie dazzled in the goal. Peggy's and Lucy's passes were crisp and precise, their attacks powerful and true. Helen ran as if she had a gale at her back, speeding her along the pitch, and she had a steely-eyed look as she swept in to steal the ball that made even April nervous, and April considered her a friend. As for herself, she ran and passed with a swiftness and agility that were unmatched by any of her teammates, if she did say so herself. She only wished her brother could be there to see her play in a semifinal match of a real tournament. Henry had taught her to play football years before, and she knew he would be exceedingly proud of her. As for Oliver, he attended every training that week and seemed impressed with her progress, even if his highest compliment was that she had "done well out there." Oliver was not given to effusive praise—but if his words were few in number, at least she knew he meant every one of them.

On the Thursday before the match, things took a dismal turn. Training was an absolute disaster. Marjorie hurt her wrist, which sent a frisson of panic through the team, even as she assured them, wincing, that she would be fine by Sunday. Every one of Peggy's shots soared over the top of the goal, while Lucy couldn't get anything past Marjorie, despite her wrist injury. Helen—bold, witty, fearless Helen, who had marched with the suffragettes and been jailed for it—had come down with an acute case of nerves. Queasy and pale, she seemed distracted and ran sluggishly—except when she fled to a trash bin to heave her dinner into it. "I'll be fine by Sunday," she said weakly, echoing Marjorie. "I'm fine now." Regardless, Peggy ordered her to sit down and put her head between her knees, and Helen seemed all too grateful to obey.

"Get your heads straight, girls," Peggy chided them kindly as they trooped back to work, discouraged. "Don't let the Spartans intimidate you before we even take the pitch."

Sound advice indeed, April thought, but easier said than done.

Later, back at the hostel, April was sitting cross-legged on her bed mending a torn seam on her football jersey when Marjorie returned from collecting her post. "I've a letter from my mum," she said, her voice distant, her eyes wide and stunned. She shut the door behind her but remained standing, one hand clutching a white envelope, the other pressed flat against her stomach. "It's my brother Archie. They've found him."

April's heart cinched. "And?"

"He's alive." A smile flickered in the corners of Marjorie's mouth, but her eyes were dazed, unfocused. "He's alive, and he's been in France all this time."

She looked so pale that April set her sewing aside, leapt off the bed, and hurried to put an arm around her friend and steer her to her bed, settling her down gingerly upon it. April ran to fetch her a glass of water, which Marjorie sipped, pausing now and then to take a deep, shaky breath.

"What happened?" April asked gently, stroking her friend's back. "You said Archie's in France. I thought he went missing in Belgium."

In reply, Marjorie handed her the letter.

The story it told was so astonishing that April had to read it twice over. Archie had been injured in the same attack that had killed his two brothers, taking minor shrapnel wounds and a severe blow to the head. A Belgian patrol found him days later, wandering alone close to enemy lines. He was unarmed, carrying no gear, wearing only the tatters of a blood-soaked French infantry soldier's uniform and the coat of a French officer. The Belgians took him to a field hospital, where his visible wounds were tended. Medics determined that although he could hear and seemed to understand simple questions in French and English, he could not speak, or write, and he could not remember his name or any detail of his life before he had been taken in by the patrol.

Remnants of insignia on the French officer's coat indicated a particular battalion, so a nurse arranged for a photographer to take Archie's picture and send it to the corps headquarters. Months passed before a response came, and it was disappointing: They were unable to identify the injured soldier, or match up the tattered coat with any missing officer, or even to explain why a man from that battalion would have been where the Belgian patrol had found him. They promised to keep the photograph in case any relevant cases were reported.

By that time, Archie had recovered enough to be evacuated safely. Assuming Archie was French, the chief medical officer had sent him to a convalescent hospital on the outskirts of Tours. In a fifteenth-century chateau hundreds of miles from the front, Archie regained his strength but not his memory. The nurses noticed that he seemed to understand very little of what was said to him, but appeared lost in a fog of melancholy.

The months passed, and still the soldier's voice and memory did not return. As part of his convalescence, he was encouraged to try various handicrafts and trades, and after he displayed considerable aptitude for gardening, he was offered a position on the grounds-keeper's staff. He seemed grateful for the work, for something to do. His physical injuries had healed, but he obviously was in no condition to return to the front, and the staff had no idea where else to send him.

Then, more than a year after he had been found wandering in Belgium, a children's choir from a local convent's orphanage performed for the patients in the chateau's chapel. Archie attended the concert, and he listened impassively as the choir sang several French children's tunes. But when they began a traditional English round, "Come Follow Me," Archie suddenly joined in the song.

After that, the stunned, astonished staff began addressing him in English. In the weeks that followed, his voice and memories came back to him piecemeal. His photograph was given to British military authorities, but there were many missing and unaccounted-for Tommies, and identifying this particular unknown soldier was neither quick nor easy. It was Archie himself who solved the mystery when he remembered his own name, as suddenly and strangely as he had remembered the children's song. One day, another Englishman newly hired on the groundskeeper's staff introduced himself as Archie, and as they shook hands, Archie remarked, "Well, how about that—I'm an Archie too." And then it all came back to him—his name, his family, his home, his childhood— but not the attack that had caused his injury and his brothers' deaths. Indeed, he was unaware that they had died, although he had likely witnessed their deaths. The doctors were obliged to break the news to him, but only after they were confident the shock would not cause a relapse. How he had ended up attired in a French uniform and coat was a mystifying question no one could answer.

"I see your mother expects Archie home by the end of September," said April, returning the letter to her friend. "He'll be back in Warrington within a fortnight. Oh, Marjorie, this is such wonderful news!"

Marjorie turned to her and smiled, tears of joy shining in her eyes. "Yes, can you believe it? I almost can't. It's simply too marvelous!"

They embraced, laughing aloud and bouncing on the edge of the bed, overcome by happiness and relief. For more than a year they had hardly dared believe Archie lived, and now he would be coming home.

The next day, when Marjorie shared her good news with her friends at Thornshire Arsenal, their shared happiness and relief seemed to energize the Canaries, for the blunders of the previous day were forgotten, their usual skill and confidence restored. By their final training on Saturday—a lighter session emphasizing technique over exertion, the better to rest their legs—April reckoned that they were as ready to face the Spartans as it was possible to be.

Match day began early for April and Marjorie, with a quick wash and a hasty breakfast before they hurried off with their bags to catch the tram to the train station. Before long they reached the platform at King's Cross where they met up with the other Canaries, and together they boarded a carriage and settled in for the long ride to Newcastle-upon-Tyne. Oliver was taking the same train, or so he had promised, but April had asked him to ride in a different car so she could sit with her teammates and concentrate on the match ahead.

"Your feelings aren't hurt, are they?" she had asked tentatively the previous evening as they had crossed through the arsenal park after her shift.

"Not at all," he had replied, interlacing his fingers through hers. "If that's what you need to do to play your best, I'd be a poor friend indeed to object."

Stung, April had smiled tightly and thanked him. So that's what she was after all—a friend. Heart heavy, she thought she ought to slip her hand from his grasp, but she didn't want to make a fuss, so she carried on as if nothing were amiss.

It was just as well Oliver was riding in a different carriage, April thought ruefully as the train sped northward. It would have been impossible to conceal her disappointment over so many miles.

Hours later, the Canaries arrived in Newcastle-upon-Tyne to find St. James' Park awash in lovely autumn sunshine, a steady but not too strong breeze stirring the pennants at the top of the stands. The Canaries had discussed their assignments and strategies on the train, so there was little conversation in the changing room as they put on their uniforms and organized their gear. April's heart thudded heavily in her chest as she laced up her shoes. Battling nerves yet again, Helen raced off to the toilet to empty her stomach. Marjorie was cheerful, her eyes alight with anticipation as she pulled her long socks over her shin-guards and tucked her curls beneath her cap. April decided to pretend she felt the same way, and with any luck, the feeling might actually take hold by the time the whistle blew.

But when the Canaries emerged onto the pitch for their warm-up, April's stomach dipped at the sight of the strong, swift women in blue-and-white stripes, running drills and sinking shots into the net with seemingly effortless grace. "Keep your heads," Peggy reminded them as they took their places on their half, and soon, April felt the familiar pre-match routine settling her, until excitement won out and she could finally revel in the moment. How marvelous it was that she, a canary girl, a former housemaid from Carlisle, a girl nobody had ever expected to amount to much, was playing football, a sport she loved, before a crowd of tens of thousands of cheering spectators! If anyone had told her four years before that she would be running up and down Newcastle United's pitch with a massive grin on her face, awaiting the start of a girls' football tournament that would raise thousands of pounds for charity, she never would have believed it. But there she was, taking the center midfielder's position, crouched and poised to run, shifting her weight lightly from one foot to the other awaiting the start.

The whistle shrilled. The Blyth Spartans' brilliant striker, Bella Reay, the eighteen-year-old daughter of a local coal miner, kicked off.

The forty-five minutes that followed sped past in a blur of swift motion, sharp passes, daring runs, and alarming or thrilling shots on the goal depending upon the side, all accompanied by thunderous cheers from the crowd. After the first scoreless twenty minutes, in a brief respite after the ball soared out of bounds and Daisy ran to retrieve it, it occurred to April that the Spartans had improved since their two teams had last faced one another, but so had the Canaries. If anything, the Canaries' dramatic improvement seemed to have caught the Spartans off guard, but they were too skilled and too clever not to overcome their surprise. With ten minutes left in the half, the Spartans' halfback stole the ball from Lucy and sent it up to Reay, who spun and wove her way through the defense to pound a goal into the upper right corner, just beyond Marjorie's outstretched hands. About five minutes later, their right midfielder made a blistering run along the right side, keeping the ball close until she passed up to her forward. Helen flew between them to intercept the ball and sent it off to Daisy, but after a tussle, a defender stole it and fed it to Bella Reay just past midfield. Marjorie prepared to challenge the attack, balancing on the balls of her feet, knees bent, hands spread, but at the last possible moment Reay passed the ball off to her left forward, who was waiting stealthily in the box. Marjorie was still turning around as the Spartans' forward drove the ball into the net behind her.

The Canaries managed to prevent the Spartans from scoring again in the first half, but when the whistle blew, they headed off to the changing room discouraged, winded, and relieved that it hadn't been any worse.

"We have another forty-five minutes to make our mark," Peggy reminded them as they massaged tired muscles and gulped water. "We're only down by two. We're not out of this yet."

"That's right," Marjorie declared, clapping her hands. "We can do this, girls. Remember our training. Stay on your man. Stick to the basics. Talk to one another. They can't beat us unless we let them, and I say we don't let them!"

"That's right," someone shouted.

"Think about everyone who ever told you girls can't play football," Peggy said, looking around at the circle of tired, hopeful faces. "Imagine them sitting out there right now, all smug and superior, watching us play— and prove them wrong!"

"Hear, hear," cried April, and as everyone cheered and applauded, Daisy stuck two fingers in her mouth and let out a piercing whistle. Everyone laughed, and suddenly all was well again, and they were ready to face whatever the second half might bring. Win or lose, they were footballers, and no scowling, whinging, naysaying critic could ever take that away from them.

Smiling as if they were several goals ahead, they checked their shoelaces, adjusted their shin-guards, exchanged proud nods and hand clasps, and followed Peggy back out onto the pitch. They took their places and awaited the official's whistle.

And so the second half began.

Marjorie's and Peggy's inspiring words might have carried them on to victory, but the Blyth Spartans wanted to prove that girls could play football as much as the Canaries did, and in the fullness of ninety minutes, they made the stronger argument. The Spartans attacked fiercely from the kickoff, and nearly made a goal on the opening play, a cross from the right forward to Bella Reay that would have hit the net except for a brilliant flying save from Marjorie. The Canaries rallied and went on the offense, with Lucy in particular making many daring attempts to break into the Spartans' defending third, only to have each attempt thwarted by a halfback line as hard as steel. Ten minutes into the half, the Spartans scored on a penalty, bringing the score to a demoralizing 3–0.

April could feel the game slipping away from them, but she dug in and fought for every loose ball, every steal. Once she sent the ball up to Peggy, who dribbled a few yards before firing a shot that sailed past the Spartan keeper's fingertips only to hit the upright and career away. The Spartans won the battle for the rebound at the top of the box. The ball found the swift feet of Bella Reay, who outran Helen in the race toward the goal. Daisy tried to intervene, but Reay made a deft spin and darted around her to score yet again.

Four–nil.

"Rally, Canaries," Marjorie called from the goal,

clapping her gloved hands, as they returned to their positions for the kickoff. "Let's get on the board."

With only five minutes left in the game, that was about the best they could hope for. April glanced up into the stands and caught Oliver's eye. He nodded and gave her an encouraging smile, applauding, and he shouted something that she couldn't quite make out, but it heartened her even so. They had to score, just one goal to avoid a shutout.

But the Spartans were determined not to let that happen. Despite their best attempts, the Canaries found themselves almost entirely confined to their own half, rarely able to break out. Whenever Peggy or Lucy managed to cross midfield, the Spartans' halfback line not only broke up their attacks but carried the play ahead, allowing their forwards to maintain constant pressure on the Canaries' defense. But Helen and Daisy refused to let them penetrate too deeply, foiling most of the Spartans' attempts on goal. Marjorie took care of the rest.

As the seconds slipped away, the Canaries exchanged grim, determined glances. They all wanted to get one goal on the board before it was over, and they knew Lucy was their best chance. Again and again they fed her the ball, or passed it to Peggy so Lucy could slip past their midfielders and await a long drive that she could turn and pound into the net, but the Spartans figured out their scheme and kept Lucy covered despite every attempt to elude her defenders.

A Spartan attack went wide and out of bounds. Grateful for the breather, April bent over, hands on her knees, and scanned the pitch, searching in vain for some key to unlock the Spartans' defense. Straightening, she saw Marjorie exchanging a few words with Helen as she set up for the goal kick. A frisson of excitement ran through her to see a familiar gleam in Marjorie's eye, a certain set to her jaw that no one but her closest friend would have detected. Something was up, and while Marjorie's schemes off the pitch sometimes went spectacularly awry, as far as football was concerned, April knew to trust her judgment.

Marjorie signaled for the goal kick, and approached the ball so fiercely that everyone jogged back a few paces—but instead of sending the ball deep, Marjorie drove it to the left just before midfield, where Helen was waiting. After a moment of stunned shock, April sprang into action, flanking Helen to clear the way of defenders as she ran swiftly down the side, keeping the ball close.

Suddenly a Spartan midfielder sped in out of nowhere directly in Helen's path. April realized with sinking dismay that she would never get there in time.

But Helen kept dribbling toward the goal, veering neither to the left nor the right, as the midfielder barreled toward her. Seconds before they would have collided, Helen kicked the ball between the Spartan's legs, dodged to the left, and picked up the ball on the other side, behind her confounded opponent. Helen drew back her leg as if she intended to fire a shot straight into the center of the net—but as the Spartan defenders instinctively reacted to block the shot they expected, Helen passed the ball to Lucy, who was darting past her on the right. With the defense momentarily in disarray, Lucy drove the ball into the high right corner.

Four–one.

As their fans leapt to their feet, cheering and applauding and frantically waving their yellow-and-black scarves and pennants, the Canaries went wild with joy, shouting and laughing and embracing as they ran back to their half of the field, everyone wanting to hug Lucy and Helen most of all.

"What was that move, Helen?" Peggy shouted, laughing, as they lined up to resume play, but then she answered her own question. "A perfect nutmeg!"

Even Bella Reay seemed to be enjoying the scene as she lined up the ball at midfield and kicked off to her left forward. Seconds later, time ran out, the whistle blew, and the match went to the Spartans. As for the Canaries, they were out of the competition for the Munitionettes' Cup, but they had played hard for a full ninety minutes, never losing heart, and they had put up a goal on the scoreboard.

They congratulated the victors, waved to their supporters, and trooped off to the changing room, not quite as miserable as April would have expected them to be in defeat. Peggy gathered them together for a moment before sending them off to wash up and change clothes. "My mum would have been proud of each and every one of you," she declared, looking around the circle with shining eyes.

It was all any of them needed to hear.

The excitement of the game was fading by the time April left the changing room, lugging her soiled kit in her bag, wondering when and if she would ever wear it again. She spotted Oliver waiting on the sideline. "I'll catch up," she told her friends, and headed toward him.

He met her halfway, and when she wordlessly held out her bag, he took it, his gaze never leaving her face. "You were marvelous out there," he said, shaking his head in wonder.

"We lost," she reminded him glumly, as disappointment began to sink in.

"It was a moral victory," he said as they turned and

walked side by side to the gate, trailing after her team-mates. "You made them work for every goal, you kept the margin of victory much closer this time."

"I suppose."

"You weren't shut out."

"That's true."

"They'll probably go on to win the entire tourna-ment, so you lost only to the very best."

A smile tugged at the corners of her mouth. "I guess if you have to lose, that's the way to do it."

They walked along in silence as they left St. James' Park and turned down the pavement toward the train station.

"That rule you have about riding in the same car-riage," said Oliver. "That's only on the way to a match, not on the way back afterward, correct?"

"Correct," said April, managing a weary laugh. "You can sit beside me all the way to London if you like."

"I'd like nothing more."

That brought a warm glow to her heart that spread to her cheeks, but she replied, "If you say so."

"I do say so." He gave her a curious sidelong look, followed by a little nudge with his elbow. "You ought to be proud, making it to the semifinals in your first tournament. Better luck next year, eh?"

"I don't know that there will be a next year for us," said April, a sob catching in her throat. "Will there be another Munitionettes' Cup for the Thornshire Canaries if Thornshire Arsenal closes? Will there be a Munitionettes' League at all if there are no more munitionettes?"

Oliver fell silent, studying her with kind sympathy. "I suppose we'll have to wait and see."

"I suppose." Suddenly April halted. "Would you tell me if the arsenal was closing, if I was going to be sacked?"

"I would if I knew for certain," said Oliver. "Right now, all I can say is that it doesn't look promising, but I think you knew that already."

April heaved a sigh. "Of course I did."

"Won't you be relieved to stop working with TNT? That's what you've said—"

"Yes, but that's not the point. I don't want to go back to domestic service." April lifted her hands and let them fall to her sides, frustrated. "But what choice will I have? I'll need to find work, or else I might have to emigrate to New Zealand or Australia as a surplus woman."

Oliver peered at her, bewildered. "What are you talking about?"

"Well, there are these organizations—you've seen the leaflets at the arsenal park, surely—that help surplus women emigrate to other countries where they can find jobs, and—"

"I know *that*. What I don't understand is why you call yourself a surplus woman, of all the wretched phrases, when you already have a fellow right here in Britain who wants to marry you?"

For a moment, April couldn't breathe. "Which fellow do you mean?" she asked, feigning puzzlement, though the tremor in her voice gave her away.

He smiled, his gaze full of love and amusement. "I think you know."

He set down her bag, wrapped her in his embrace, and kissed her until she fairly soared with happiness.

24
October–November 1918

Helen

In early October, the Blyth Spartans faced the Bolckow Vaughan Ladies of Middlesbrough's Bolckow, Vaughan & Co. ironworks in the Munitionettes' Cup Final. The Spartans again had something of a home pitch advantage, since they played frequently at St. James' Park and Middlesbrough lay more than fifty miles to the south. More than fifteen thousand spectators filled the stands for what was expected to be a thrilling match, since the Bolckow Vaughan captain, Winnie McKenna, was considered Bella Reay's equal as a goal-scorer.

But as Helen had learned in her brief career as a footballer, an exciting match did not always mean an abundance of goals.

"A nil–nil stalemate," Marjorie exclaimed, incredulous. "With Bella Reay and Winnie McKenna on the same pitch?"

The Canaries were in the arsenal canteen, some seated, others standing and peering over their teammates' shoulders at a newspaper spread open on the table before them, their attention fixed on a single paragraph tucked amid the sport reports.

"Both fullback lines must have been exceptionally strong," Helen remarked. "It sounds as if the game was still quite exciting."

"If it had been us, we would have put a goal or two on the board," said Marjorie.

"Maybe we'll get another chance next season," said Daisy, hopeful, but the furtive glances the others exchanged suggested that they were less certain there would be another season, for them or any munitionettes' team. Helen braced herself for pointed questions about Thornshire—and muffled a sigh of relief when none came her way.

"So what happens now?" asked Lucy. "Will they share the title?"

No one knew, and they had to wait another week for an announcement that the Munitionettes' Cup Final would be replayed the following Saturday at Ayresome Park in Middlesbrough, not far from the Bolckow

Vaughan ironworks. Daisy proposed that the Canaries attend the match together, since the Danger Building was no longer running weekend shifts and they all had the day off. The outing sounded like great fun, but Helen demurred, not because she wanted to avoid her teammates' questions about the arsenal's future, although she did, but because she had a physician's appointment she simply couldn't put off any longer.

Since the Bolckow Vaughan Ladies would have a clear home pitch advantage in the rematch, Helen reckoned they were favored to win. Fortunately, she was not a gambler, as she learned the following Monday when her friends enthusiastically described the thrilling action for those who had not attended. Finishing one another's sentences in their excitement, they explained how the Spartans' defense had entirely contained Winnie McKenna, whereas Bella Reay had amazed the twenty thousand spectators with dazzling runs and incredible shooting. When the final whistle blew, the Blyth Spartans had won the match, 5–0, to claim the first Munitionettes' Cup.

"I hope it's not the first and only," said April, and the others nodded or chimed in agreement. A few girls sent furtive glances Helen's way, as if they hoped she might enlighten them, but she had nothing to share.

A fortnight after the final, Helen and the Canaries

gathered with other Thornshire Arsenal munitionettes, the Burridge family, and many of their friends at a small church in Poplar to celebrate Peggy's wedding. Earlier that autumn, her fiancé had been given a medical discharge from the army after a terrible bout with pneumonia, but now he was as right as rain, and the long-delayed ceremony could finally take place.

"They thought he'd had the influenza, but it turned out it was only pneumonia," Peggy had explained one day during their tea break as she had handed out the invitations, pretty ivory cards inscribed in a very fine hand. "Can you imagine anyone would ever say *only* pneumonia?"

"In this case, yes," April had replied, admiring her invitation. "I've heard the Spanish Flu is absolutely awful."

"But it's not Spanish at all," Marjorie had said. "The American soldiers brought it over with them from the U.S."

"That's a fine thing to say about our allies," Daisy had teased, nudging her.

"I think you mean, that's a fine thing for our allies to do," Marjorie had retorted, nudging her back.

Everyone had laughed. No one was terribly concerned about this new influenza, wherever it had come from. After four long, difficult years of war, a common illness seemed of little consequence.

On the morning of Peggy's wedding, Helen, Lucy, April, and Marjorie attended the bride in the ladies' lounge, assisting her into her gown, dressing her hair, arranging her veil, chatting and laughing and blinking away tears of joy. After so much loss and sorrow, so many unhappy partings, it was truly wonderful to celebrate a new beginning.

If the bridesmaids had any misgivings—and not all of them did—it was that Peggy had decided to honor their status as proud, loyal munitionettes by having them wear spotlessly clean, well-pressed Danger Building uniforms, complete with trousers, blouses, and jackets, with fresh flowers adorning their caps. Helen had dressed as a munitionette only once before, when she had entered the Danger Building on her reconnaissance mission, and she did not find the ensemble becoming in the least, especially for a formal affair.

"At least we're allowed to wear our own shoes instead of those wooden clogs," mused April as the bridesmaids studied themselves in a full-length mirror, their expressions ranging from amusement to muted dismay.

Helen glanced over her shoulder, and when she saw

Peggy happily engaged in conversation with her aunt, she replied, "Nor did she forbid us to wear metal. We should indeed be thankful for small favors."

"It's Peggy's day," said Lucy. "This makes her happy, and I think we look quite charming."

"It could have been worse," said Marjorie. "Peggy might've asked us to wear our football kit."

Soon thereafter, they took their bouquets in hand and lined up for the procession. "I hope you don't come down with a bad case of nerves like you did in the semifinal," Marjorie teased Helen in a whisper as they waited for the organist to play their cue.

"As it happens, it wasn't nerves," Helen whispered back, but before she was obliged to say anything more, the music reached a crescendo and the ceremony began.

It was a truly lovely, joyful day, and much welcome for it. Yet for every sign that the war was drawing to a close—soldiers returning from the front, dwindling munitions orders—there were other, crushing indications that the Germans meant to drag the fighting out until the last man.

On 10 October, the Irish mail boat *Leinster*, on her way from Kingstown to Holyhead, was torpedoed by a German U-boat twelve miles out to sea. The exact number of passengers on board was uncertain, making the death toll difficult to determine, but it was believed that roughly six hundred passengers and crew had perished, including twenty-one postal workers, while only two hundred souls were saved. All of Britain was outraged by the attack, which many said equaled in atrocity the sinking of the *Lusitania*. Arthur James Balfour, Secretary of State for Foreign Affairs, denounced the attack as "an act of pure barbarism." Of the perpetrators, he declared, "Brutes they were when they began the War, and brutes they remain."

The words chilled Helen as she read them, for the Earl of Balfour did not seem to distinguish between the German sailors who had committed the terrible act, the German military as a whole, and all Germans everywhere. It was another episode in a disturbing trend. Only a few months before, a petition with 1,250,000 signatures calling for the British government to intern every enemy alien without distinction of any kind, and to take drastic steps to eradicate all German influence in British government circles and society, had been delivered with great pomp and ceremony to the Prime Minister's residence at 10 Downing Street. Anti-German sentiment had worried Helen throughout the war, but with outrage flaring in the aftermath of the sinking of the *Leinster*, the safety of her mother and sisters seemed more precarious than it had in years.

Helen often suspected she was more concerned for their safety than they were for their own. Mother was busier than ever, tending to Banbury Cottage and her many volunteer organizations. Daphne had begun her studies at Oxford, amid rumors that female students' qualifications might be formally recognized in the near future. Penelope, ever loyal and loving, remained Margaret's steadfast companion, no longer a paid servant but rather a member of the family. Although her exact role and title were not precisely defined, she had become Margaret's partner in managing the estate and raising the children, who called her Aunt Penny and absolutely adored her. As far as Helen knew, neither Margaret's family nor her late husband's disapproved of the unconventional domestic arrangement, which had clearly brought Margaret and the children much comfort during their bereavement. With so many men lost to the war, households comprised entirely of women and children were not at all unusual, and as a wealthy widow, Margaret had no need to marry again. In fact, she had firmly stated her intention never to do so. Given the circumstances, Penelope confided to Helen, she and Margaret dared to hope that society would not disparage two surplus women who had decided to live peacefully and quietly together, troubling no one.

Helen loathed that wretched phrase—"surplus women," indeed—but she adored her sister and Margaret, and she wished them much joy and contentment together.

Only two days after the attack on the *Leinster*, word broke that the German chancellor had accepted U.S. President Woodrow Wilson's Fourteen Points as a foundation for negotiating peace. "This is significant," said Arthur emphatically as he and Helen pored over the papers at breakfast. "For the Germans even to acknowledge that they'd consider a negotiated truce is a remarkable admission that they're no longer confident of victory."

But all too soon, Helen and Arthur's hopes for an imminent end to the war were dashed when the press reported Supreme Allied Commander Ferdinand Foch's declaration that the Allies would accept nothing short of unconditional surrender. The Germans seemed as if they would never capitulate, regardless of the overtures they made, and Helen was exhausted from having her hopes for peace raised and then dashed over and over again.

And yet, in apparent contradiction, the munitions industry seemed to be wrapping things up. Helen did not know what to make of it. First, following his father's orders, Arthur had reduced work hours at Thornshire

Arsenal across the board. Next he had cancelled most weekend shifts, including Danger Building work. Then, in the third week of October, he summoned Helen, Superintendent Carmichael, Tom, and Oliver to a confidential meeting, arranged at practically the last minute without any explanation of its purpose.

Helen was the first to join her husband in the conference room. "This is all very mysterious," she remarked, taking the seat at his left hand. "You didn't breathe a word this morning."

"I endeavor—with mixed success—to keep arsenal business out of our breakfast conversation."

"Only when it's bad news," she pointed out. He nodded in acknowledgment but said nothing more.

Helen regarded him curiously, eyebrows raised, inviting him to elaborate. When he volunteered nothing, she muffled a sigh and settled back to wait for the others.

When everyone had taken their places at the table, Arthur did not leave them long in suspense. Orders had come down from above that Thornshire Arsenal was to reduce its workforce by a quarter in November, and a quarter more the following month, with additional reductions to be determined later according to the course of the war.

Helen had been expecting an announcement of this

sort, and her heart sank as she thought of the munitionettes, many of whom had become her friends, who were about to be sacked and did not know it. Her only consolation was that Arthur had instructed Tom, and not herself, to consult with the foremen and determine which workers should be let go. Superintendent Carmichael would deliver the bad news. Helen's assignment was to comfort the dismissed munitionettes, explain how they would receive their separation benefits, direct them to various employment resources, and reassure those who remained.

"How am I to reassure them if they ask me whether more layoffs are coming?" asked Helen. "Everyone at the arsenal will wonder. You cannot expect me to lie, knowing that another twenty-five percent will be sacked in December."

Arthur shook his head, brow furrowed. "Of course I wouldn't ask you to lie. They deserve honesty and fair dealing for their years of loyal service to us, and to King and Country."

They deserved all that and more, Helen thought, but she didn't blame Arthur. None of this was his fault.

"I volunteer to help select the munitionettes who ought to be released from their duties first," said Superintendent Carmichael, nodding to Arthur and Tom. "I know the girls' histories thoroughly, and I would be happy to lend my expertise to this regrettable but necessary task."

Perhaps a bit too happy, thought Helen. Surely the superintendent knew that after the last munitionette left, she would have made herself redundant.

In the days that followed, the unlucky workers were selected, and the bad news was delivered to the day shift on the last Friday of October. Helen had deliberately not read the list, knowing she would be tempted to use her influence with Arthur to spare her friends at the expense of workers she knew less well, and that would be both unfair and unprofessional. She lingered in her office after the shift ended, just in case anyone wanted to air her grievances or plead for her job back. If Mabel were there, Helen thought wistfully, she would demand a sit-down at the negotiating table, and she would advocate fiercely for her canary girls. But not even Mabel could have saved their jobs this time. As the need for munitions went, so went the need for munitionettes.

But why must Thornshire make munitions or nothing at all? Surely there would be manufacturing needs in peacetime. They had an ample, skilled workforce. They could retool the various shops. All they needed was a product and a scheme—and a sound argument to put before Arthur's father.

A knock on the open door jolted her from her reverie. "Helen?" asked Lucy from the doorway. "May I have a moment?"

Helen's heart plummeted. Lucy had been let go. "Of course," she said, rising and gesturing to the chair in front of her desk. They sat down together. "I'm so sorry. Even though we all sensed that this was coming—at least, I believe we all did—it must be quite a blow."

"Oh yes," said Lucy, shaking her head sadly. "Those poor girls."

"Oh, you're still with us, then?"

"Yes, for now." Lucy studied her, curious. "Didn't you know?"

Helen shook her head. "It wasn't my task—and thank goodness for that, because I don't think I could have endured it."

A hint of a smile appeared on Lucy's face. "I don't think you're cut out to be a boss, then."

"Certainly not. I'll stick to halfback." Helen interlaced her fingers and rested them on the desk. "What can I do for you, Lucy?"

"Well, about the layoffs . . ." Lucy hesitated. "I'm afraid April was let go."

"Oh no! But she's such a good worker."

"They all are," said Lucy. "Everyone deserves her place here. But some need the wages more than others."

She met Helen's gaze squarely. "I intend to resign, and I want April to be given my place."

Helen studied her, bewildered. "But what about you? What will you do for work?"

"Daniel's coming home soon, and I want to be with him, and with our boys. Our family has been separated too long. Besides, Daniel is eager to get back to work, and he may need my help to do so, especially as he . . . adjusts to his new circumstances." Lucy gave a small shrug. "He's always provided very well for us as an architect, and I'm sure he will again, but April—"

"April has no one else to provide for her."

"No, and indeed she has to provide for others, for her mother and siblings."

Helen admired Lucy's selflessness, but she tried to think of objections others might raise. "April has never worked in the Finishing Shop. She doesn't know your job."

"Not yet, but she's very clever and hardworking, as you know, and I'm certain she can learn. I've already asked Mr. Vernon, and he's agreeable."

Helen smiled. "He didn't grumble and scold and try to talk you out of leaving?"

"He did, actually," said Lucy, laughing, "but after I convinced him that my mind was made up, he said that he'd tolerate April as my replacement, since I endorse her."

"Since Mr. Vernon consents, it should be a simple matter to transfer April to the Finishing Shop. And if Mr. Vernon couldn't persuade you to stay, I know any attempt of mine would be futile." Helen rose and reached across the desk to shake her friend's hand. "Best of luck to you, Lucy. We'll miss you around here."

"Thank you, Helen." Lucy clasped both of her hands around Helen's for a moment, smiling warmly, but then she gave a little start. "I suppose I ought to run after April and give her the good news."

"Yes, please do," Helen urged. She didn't want April to be unhappy a moment longer than necessary.

After Lucy hurried off, Helen began the paperwork to discharge Lucy and transfer April to the Finishing Shop. She felt a twinge of misgiving, knowing that another round of layoffs was coming and that April may have been granted only a temporary reprieve. Still, even if that's all it was, she would earn wages and acquire skills that could help her find work in peacetime, after the arsenal closed.

If Thornshire Arsenal closed. Where was it written that it must retreat to dormancy rather than become something new?

On 28 October, word reached London that Austria had surrendered. It was all so exhilarating that Helen could hear munitions workers shouting and cheering on the arsenal grounds from her windowless office. Soon thereafter, not even the disappointing news that Germany still refused to surrender could demoralize them. Without their staunchest ally by their side, how could the Germans reasonably hope to continue fighting much longer?

Less than a fortnight later, on Sunday, 10 November, Helen and Arthur went down to breakfast together, poured their tea, and opened the papers only to discover the most stunning, glorious news imaginable.

Prince Maximilian of Baden had announced that Kaiser Wilhelm II, having lost the support of his military leaders, had abdicated and had fled into exile to the Netherlands. Two prominent political leaders had each declared themselves in charge of the provisional German government, and while their two factions argued in the Reichstag, their followers marched and fought one another in the streets.

"We're surely coming to the end now," Arthur said, reaching across the table for her hand, his face both haggard and optimistic. Helen hoped with all her heart that it was true. In October, the Allies had signed an armistice with the Ottoman Empire to end the fighting in the Middle East. Only days later, the Austro-Hungarian Empire had signed an armistice with Italy. All that remained was for Germany to bow to the increasingly inevitable.

At last, later that evening, the joyous, long-awaited news came:

The Allies and Germany had agreed to an armistice to be signed early the following morning officially ending the hostilities on land, at sea, and in the air. At the eleventh hour of the eleventh day of the eleventh month, the war would end at last.

The child Helen carried would be born into a world at peace.

She couldn't wait to tell Arthur.

Epilogue
December 26, 1920

Lucy

B oxing Day 1920 proved to be a splendid day for a football match—chilly and brisk, with blue skies and sunshine playing hide-and-seek behind scattered clouds. Jamie and Simon were so excited on the train from London to Liverpool that Lucy and Daniel could hardly get them to sit still. "We wish you were playing today, Mum," Simon said at least twice along the way.

"My football days are over," Lucy would reply, smiling fondly, but the truth was, she wished she were playing too. In the two years since she had left munitions work, her skin had lost its yellow hue and her hair had grown back as dark and silky as before the war, but intermittent stomach ailments and headaches still troubled her, and bouts of coughing wracked her in cold, damp weather, or in smoky rooms, or if she overexerted herself. A kickaround in the garden with the boys was about all she could manage, and as the boys grew, even that was becoming too much. Both boys had clearly inherited their father's athletic skill, especially Jamie, who often said that he wanted to be a footballer and an architect like his father.

Neither of their sons ever said they wished to be a soldier—which Lucy and Daniel privately agreed was a tremendous relief.

Lucy would never forget that moment in the garden at Alderlea in the last months of the war, when she and Daniel had looked upon each other after more than three years apart—three long, hard, painful years that had transformed them both utterly. After the overwhelming joy of their first embrace, Daniel had cleared his throat, and his arms had loosened around her, though he had not entirely let go. "I should wonder," he said thickly, "if you would still want me, broken as I am."

Incredulous, tears trickling down her cheeks, Lucy pulled away just far enough to meet his gaze. "I could ask you the same question," she managed to say, choking on tears and laughter. "How could you still want me, with my horrid yellow skin, mottled hair, and wretched cough?"

"Do you really need to ask?" said Daniel, bewildered. "How could I not want you, having learned what my life is without you?"

They embraced again, and kissed, and promised that each was as beloved as ever to the other. And after that, they never wondered again. All that mattered was that they loved each other and they were together again. That was everything. Daniel would never play football again, and he felt the loss keenly, but within a few months of the Armistice, his architecture career was nearly restored to the heights he had achieved before the war. They were the lucky ones, and well they knew it.

They disembarked at Liverpool. Daniel managed the stairs and the gap rather deftly, aided by his prosthetic leg, his cane, and Simon's sturdy shoulder to lean on. They took a cab to Goodison Park, where Daniel had once led Tottenham Hotspur to several wins against Everton, but where today they and several of the former Thornshire Canaries were reuniting as spectators for a special Boxing Day charity football match between the Dick, Kerr Ladies and the St. Helens Ladies. Tickets had sold out well in advance. Lucy had heard that more than fifty thousand people would be in attendance, and more than ten thousand had been turned away. If the rumors proved true, the match would shatter all records for attendance at a women's football match—but Lucy needed to see only a few particular football fans for her day to be complete.

She glimpsed one of them standing in the queue near the front gate. "Peggy!" she cried out, hurrying ahead of her family to embrace her dear friend, but carefully, because Peggy had a toddler balanced on her hip. The lurid yellow hue had left her skin too, and instead of a long braid, she wore her reddish-brown hair in a stylish, wavy bob. They laughed and teared up a bit and exchanged a few words, with promises to catch up inside the stadium in just a few minutes.

Lucy hurried back to Daniel and the boys, who had taken their places in the queue, which had lengthened behind them and now included April and Oliver. The two former teammates caught sight of one another at the same time, cried out for joy, and broke out of the queue to embrace. Lucy hadn't seen April since she and Oliver had married the previous spring in a lovely ceremony in Carlisle, in the same church where April's parents had wed and she and all her siblings had been baptized. Her brother Henry had walked her down the aisle, looking dashing and proud in his army dress uniform. A year before the wedding, the couple had opened a shop in the town selling books, stationery, toys, and other gifts, and in her most recent letter,

April had described their plans to take over the space next door to add a teashop. She had said nothing of her other work-in-progress; Lucy concealed her surprise and delight at the unmistakable signs that April was expecting. She would wait for her friend to tell her. Perhaps April planned to announce the happy news to the whole team at once, after they were reunited inside.

When the Dempseys found their seats, Lucy was delighted to see many former coworkers awaiting them, some with their husbands and a young child or two. After a flurry of joyful meetings and fond teasing, Lucy took her place with her own family and was delighted to find herself seated beside Helen. Her very active eighteen-month-old son wriggled and laughed and fussed on her lap until Arthur, seated on Helen's other side, swept him up in his arms and walked him around a bit to settle him down. Helen was the Thornshire Canary Lucy saw most often, as Helen and Arthur divided their time between their lovely Marylebone home and their estate in Oxfordshire. Lucy and Helen would meet for lunches or strolls through Hyde Park whenever Helen was in London, and occasionally the Dempseys visited the Purcells at their country house. There was a broad, sweeping lawn where the boys could kick the football around while Daniel and Arthur cheered and coached from the sidelines, and a tennis court where Helen had taught Lucy to play.

Often Helen would pass along news of their former teammate and Lucy's fellow Finishing Shop chum Daisy, who had assumed the role of welfare supervisor at Thornshire Automotive Works as it underwent the transition from munitions work to domestic manufacturing. The retooled Purcell Products factory was a smaller concern than Thornshire Arsenal had been, but it still employed more than two thousand workers, at least a quarter of whom were women, all overseen by Superintendent Carmichael, who apparently intended to remain a permanent fixture at Thornshire whatever incarnation it took.

"Do you ever miss your old job?" Lucy had asked Helen once, soon after her son's first birthday.

"Goodness no," Helen had replied, laughing, shifting her son from one hip to the other. "I have enough to do minding this wee lad, and keeping up with my work for the Women's Party. Someone has to make sure we focus on feminist issues and not anti-German nationalism. We had enough of that during the war."

"Have you considered running for Parliament, now that women are permitted?"

Helen laughed lightly. "My word, wouldn't that be a lark?"

Lucy had noted, with great interest and curiosity, that her friend hadn't said yes, but she hadn't declined, either.

A murmur of excitement passed through the crowd as the players emerged from their separate changing rooms and jogged out onto the pitch. The voices rose to a cheer as thunderous applause rained down upon both teams, but Lucy's gaze was fixed upon the Dick, Kerr Ladies in their narrowly striped black-and-white jerseys, matching caps, and short blue trousers—all but one, who wore a solid blue jersey and gloves—

"There she is," Helen cried out, seizing Lucy's arm. "There's Marjorie!"

The erstwhile Thornshire Canaries rose, applauded wildly, and shouted their former keeper's name. From the goal, where she deftly fended off blistering shots from her new teammates, Marjorie spared her friends one broad, happy grin, and then immediately returned her attention to the pitch, all steely-eyed, canny determination.

A few rows ahead, Peggy turned around and called to her friends, "Do you suppose any of her Tommy pen pals have turned out to watch Marjorie play today?"

Her words met with a wave of laughter.

"She's narrowed it down to three," replied Daisy, climbing into the stands, having arrived just in time with her fiancé, a junior foreman at Thornshire Automotive. "She told me she's having far too much fun to choose between the last of them so soon, and she'll marry when she's good and ready."

"That sounds like Marjorie," said April, shaking her head in fond amusement. Beside her, Oliver nodded, his expression so comically exasperated that April burst out laughing.

Suddenly Lucy felt Simon tug on her coat sleeve. "Mum," he cried, fairly bouncing in his seat as the warm-up ended and the players took their positions. "It's about to begin!"

"I know, darling," she said, exchanging a fond smile with Daniel over their youngest son's head. "Isn't it all wonderful?"

And then the whistle blew.

Author's Note

In the match at Goodison Park on Boxing Day 1920, the Dick, Kerr Ladies defeated the St. Helens Ladies 4–0, with right back Alice Kell completing a hat trick in the second half for an exciting finish. The match raised £3,115 for charity, the equivalent of £148,347.20 (US$195,151.48) in 2022. About 53,000 spectators attended the match, with an estimated 15,000 more fans turned away at the gate for lack of room. The attendance set a record for women's football that was not broken until March 2019, when an audience of 60,739 watched Atlético Madrid host Barcelona at the Wanda Metropolitano.

Even after the soldiers returned from the war and men's football resumed, women's football continued to grow in popularity, with attendance at women's matches averaging 12,000 eager fans. Unfortunately, this alarmed the Football Association, the governing body for football in the UK, responsible for overseeing all aspects of professional and amateur play in its jurisdiction. The FA had tolerated women's football during the war, since men's professional football had essentially gone on hiatus and women's matches usually raised funds for worthy causes. After the war, however, the FA became increasingly concerned that women's football could draw interest away from men's leagues, reducing attendance, and thereby revenues, for Football League matches.

Nearly a year after the record-breaking Boxing Day match, on 5 December 1921, the FA banned women's football from all of its affiliated grounds and forbade its members from serving as referees or linesmen at women's matches. To justify their decision, the FA released a statement declaring that football was "quite unsuitable for females and ought not to be encouraged," citing opinions from doctors who agreed that football posed serious physical risks to women.

Women footballers responded with outrage. "The controlling body of the FA are a hundred years behind the times and their action is purely sex prejudice," declared Jessie "Jean" Boultwood, captain of the Plymouth Ladies. But the women footballers' protests were to no avail. The FA's edict stood, essentially outlawing women's professional football in England. Women could still play at the recreational level on small, non-FA pitches or rugby grounds before reduced crowds, but most women's teams disbanded instead. A few, like the Dick, Kerr Ladies, traveled abroad to play. In 1922, the team embarked on a tour of North America, playing nine men's teams and drawing audiences of up to 10,000 in the United States, where women's football had not yet caught on. The tour did not take the Dick, Kerr Ladies to Canada, as the English FA had instructed Canada's Football Association not to allow the team to play on any of its pitches.

Unfortunately, other nations' football associations began to follow the FA's example by instituting their own bans: Norway in 1931, France in 1932, Brazil in 1941, and West Germany in 1955. "This aggressive sport is essentially alien to the nature of woman," the Deutscher Fußball-Bund declared, according to the *Guardian*. "In the fight for the ball, the feminine grace vanishes, body and soul will inevitably suffer harm . . . The display of the woman's body offends decency and modesty."

But the final whistle had not sounded for women's football quite yet. After England's national men's team won the World Cup in 1966, a movement began to revive women's football in the UK, and in 1969 the Women's Football Association was founded. Yet the FA still refused to lift their decades-old ban on women's professional football. It was only under pressure from UEFA, the Union of European Football Associations, that the FA finally relented, and in 1971 it lifted its restrictions on women playing on FA-affiliated grounds. At long last, after fifty years of exclusion, women footballers could play professionally in the UK.

The munitionettes faced similar challenges as the nation demobilized after the war. Approximately one million women had worked in British munitions factories during World War I, hailing from all regions of the country and drawn from all classes, although the vast majority were working-class women who had held other jobs before taking on war work. For many munitionettes, this was their first time living away from home, earning wages much higher than they had ever earned before, granting them greater social freedom and independence than they had ever known or perhaps had even imagined. Munitionettes became a powerful, visible symbol of the modern woman—confident, strong, patriotic, making her own decisions, spending her own money, and challenging gender roles and assumptions every day.

Munitionettes were essential workers in a time of national crisis, and they firmly believed that they were not merely earning a living, but were directly engaged in the war effort. Many were understandably upset when they were expected to quit their jobs and return to their former occupations or homemaking when the soldiers returned and the factories closed down or transitioned to peacetime manufacturing. On 19 November 1918, only a week after the Armistice, six thousand women munitions workers, mostly from Woolwich Arsenal, marched on Parliament to express to the Prime Minister and the Ministry of Munitions their demand for "immediate guarantees for the future." On 3 December, nearly six hundred newly unemployed munitionettes marched on 10 Downing Street and demanded an audience with Prime Minister Lloyd George, seeking "the immediate withdrawal of their discharges." A small delegation was granted a meeting with officials from the Ministry of Munitions, but the women left unsatisfied, and munitionettes continued to demonstrate in the streets outside the building for hours afterward.

It is impossible to calculate how many hundreds or thousands of munitions workers, women and men alike, were killed, seriously injured, or poisoned as a result of their war work. During 1915 alone, there were nearly 160,000 reported industrial accidents, most of which involved workers between thirteen and eighteen years of age. According to the BBC, 400 cases of toxic jaundice due to TNT poisoning were recorded during the war, and one-quarter of those were fatal. Without question, while the lurid yellow hue eventually faded from the canary girls' skin after the women left TNT work, many continued to suffer serious health problems for the rest of their lives. They were "the Girls Behind the Man Behind the Gun," but one could reasonably ask who had stood behind *them*, and *with* them, in their time of need. Organizations such as the BBC and the Imperial War Museum have done excellent, meaningful work in collecting and preserving the stories of many munitionettes and canary girls so their contributions may be better understood, their significant contributions recognized, and they themselves duly honored.

Canary Girls is a work of fiction inspired by history, as are all of my historical novels. The Blyth Spartans did defeat the Bolckow Vaughan Ladies in 1918 to win the Munitionettes' Cup, but I have altered the timing of the matches and the pairing of sides to better suit my story, and to include fictional teams. Thornshire Arsenal is a fictional munitions works based upon real factories that existed in Great Britain at the time. Other locations in the novel, such as Alderlea and Brookfield, are also fictional, as are most of the characters, with the exception of certain historical figures (including the royal family and various politicians and military officers) and notable football players such as Horace Bailey, Jennie Harris, William Jonas, Lily Parr, Bella Reay, Florrie Redford, Walter Tull, Norman Arthur Wood, and Vivian Woodward. Horace Bailey was a member of England's 1908 and 1912 Olympic teams, but he played primarily for Leicester Fosse and Birmingham City rather than Tottenham Hotspur. He and all historical figures who appear in this novel are used fictitiously and with all due respect intended.

Acknowledgments

I wrote *Canary Girls* at my home in Dane County, Wisconsin, which I respectfully acknowledge as the ancestral homeland of the Ho-Chunk Nation.

I offer my deepest gratitude to Maria Massie, Rachel Kahan, Emily Fisher, Ariana Sinclair, Kaitlin Harri, Laura Cherkas, Francie Crawford, Roland Ottewell, Kyle O'Brien, and Elsie Lyons for their essential contributions to *Canary Girls*. Geraldine Neidenbach, Marty Chiaverini, Michael Chiaverini, and Heather Neidenbach were my first readers, and their comments and questions were invaluable and very much appreciated. My brother, Nic Neidenbach, was an excellent technical consultant, while my sons, Nick and Michael Chiaverini, generously shared their knowledge of Philoctetes and football, respectively.

Many thanks to my former teammates, the fantastic footballers of Just for Kicks and Ignition, for the inspiration and fond memories. I'm grateful to you all.

Thanks also to the staff at the University of Wisconsin–Madison Memorial Library, where I found most of the books that proved essential to my research. Those I found most helpful include:

Braybon, Gail, and Penny Summerfield. *Out of the Cage: Women's Experiences in Two World Wars*. London and New York: Pandora Press, 1987.

Burnett, John, ed. *Useful Toil: Autobiographies of Working People from the 1820s to the 1920s*. London and New York: Routledge, 1994.

Foxwell, Agnes K. *Munition Lasses: Six Months as Principal Overlooker in Danger Buildings*. London and New York: Hodder and Stoughton, 1917.

Hamilton, Peggy, Lady. *Three Years or the Duration: The Memoirs of a Munition Worker, 1914–1918*. London: Owen, 1978.

MacDonagh, Michael. *In London During the Great War: The Diary of a Journalist*. London: Eyre and Spottiswoode, 1935.

Newman, Vivien. *We Also Served: The Forgotten Women of the First World War*. Barnsley, South Yorkshire: Penn & Sword History, 2014.

Riddoch, Andrew, and John Kemp. *When the Whistle Blows: The Story of the Footballers' Battalion in the Great War*. Centennial Edition. Scotts Valley, CA: CreateSpace, 2015.

Roberts, Elizabeth. *A Woman's Place: An Oral History of Working-Class Women, 1890–1940*. Oxford and New York: Basil Blackwell, 1984.

Williams, Jean. *A Game for Rough Girls?: History of Women's Football in Britain*. London: Routledge, 2003.

Woollacott, Angela. *On Her Their Lives Depend: Munitions Workers in the Great War*. Berkeley and Los Angeles: University of California Press, 1994.

Yates, L. K. *The Woman's Part: A Record of Munitions Work.* New York: George R. Doran Company, ca. 1918.

I consulted several excellent online resources while researching and writing *Canary Girls,* including the BBC (bbc.com), the British Newspaper Archive (britishnewspaperarchive.co.uk), the Imperial War Museums (iwm.org.uk), the *Guardian* (theguardian.com), Newspapers.com (newspapers.com), the Library of Congress (loc.gov), and Ancestry (ancestry.com). Although I had been aware of the Christmas Truce for many years prior to writing *Canary Girls,* I was inspired to include the historical event in this novel by the Four Seasons Theatre productions of *All Is Calm: The Christmas Truce of 1914* in 2019 and 2021.

Most of all, I thank my husband, Marty, and my sons, Nick and Michael, for their enduring love, steadfast support, and constant encouragement. *Canary Girls* is my third novel written during the pandemic. I could not have finished this book without you, and the endless supply of hugs, encouragement, laughter, and hope you gave me when I needed them most. I'll forever be grateful for your courage, optimism, resilience, and humor in difficult times. All my love, always.

About the Author

JENNIFER CHIAVERINI is the *New York Times* bestselling author of many acclaimed historical novels and the beloved Elm Creek Quilts series. A graduate of the University of Notre Dame and the University of Chicago, she lives with her husband—and, occasionally, their two college-student sons—in Madison, Wisconsin.

HARPER
LARGE PRINT

We hope you enjoyed reading
our new, comfortable print size and found it
an experience you would like to repeat.

Well – you're in luck!

Harper Large Print offers the finest in
fiction and nonfiction books in this same larger
print size and paperback format. Light and easy to read,
Harper Large Print paperbacks are for the book lovers
who want to see what they are reading without strain.

For a full listing of titles and
new releases to come, please visit our website:
www.hc.com

HARPER LARGE PRINT

SEEING IS BELIEVING!